FRUITS OF A
DISGRACED LEGACY

Published in the United States by Tandem Light Press

950 Herrington Road

Suite C128

Lawrenceville, GA 30044

www.TandemLightPress.com

First printing, February 2014

Library of Congress Cataloging-in-Publication Data:

Harris, Anthony J.

Fruits of a Disgraced Legacy / Anthony Harris

p. cm.

ISBN 978-0-9854437-4-0 (paperback)

2013958370

First Edition

Although some of the stories in this book are based on actual incidents, the characters are all fictitious. Any resemblance to anyone living or dead is strictly coincidental.

10 9 8 7 6 5 4 3 2 1

Printed in the United States of America

Book and cover design by Damonza

FRUITS OF A DISGRACED LEGACY

ANTHONY J. HARRIS

tandem light press

ACKNOWLEDGEMENTS

I wish to thank several individuals for their valuable assistance in completing this book. First, as with my first two books, I want to acknowledge the support of my wife (Smitty) of nearly four decades who constantly reminded me and encouraged me to finish this book. I wish to acknowledge my children, Ashley and Michael, who have always been a remarkable and never-ending source of unconditional love. I must also acknowledge my brothers, James and Harold for being the best brothers in the world and for manifesting the many fine characteristics and values that our mother and father instilled in us. I want to acknowledge and honor the memory of my late father, James Harris, Sr., who inspired several stories in this book. He was one of the "good guys," and he left a lasting impression on all who knew and loved him. Thanks also to my late cousin, the Reverend Maury E. Booth for our many conversations in which he encouraged and inspired me, and most importantly, served as a remarkable role model for how to deal with adversity, physical pain and unabated suffering.

I also wish to thank Bianca Singleton for her editing assistance and Susan Patton, Eric McCaskill, Pat Karas, Rebecca Woodrick, Katie Monroe, Jeff Helton, and Jan Helton for their feedback and suggestions for improving the book. Many thanks to my high school friends from the Rowan High School and Hattiesburg High School Classes of 1971, especially Martha,

Sandra, James, and Odis Ruth, for their unwavering friendship, support, and loyalty. I also wish to acknowledge the decades-long friendship of Lewis Slay, Alvin Cooley, Larry Thomas, and Stan McKee, friends who have been there through the good times and the not-so-good.

Finally, I want to express my deep love and appreciation for my mother, Daisy Harris Wade, who, along with my late father, did a remarkable job in guiding and molding three boys into men. As a warrior in the Civil Rights Movement in Hattiesburg, Mississippi she was the backbone of our family. She was and is a person of deep religious faith, uncompromising commitment to social justice, and selfless devotion to serving others.

INTRODUCTION

The year was 1999. Bill Clinton was in his second term as President of the United States and also the subject of an impeachment trial in the United States Senate. The United States turned over the complete administration of the Panama Canal to the Panamanian government. John F. Kennedy, Jr., son of the thirty-fifth President, and his wife, Carolyn were killed in a plane crash. The Dow Jones Industrial Average closed above the 11,000 mark for the first time in history. The average cost of a gallon of gasoline was a dollar and thirty-three cents. The Denver Broncos beat the Atlanta Falcons to win the Super Bowl. The New York Yankees swept the Atlanta Braves in four games to win the World Series.

The final year of the twentieth century had begun. Y2K fever dominated print and electronic media reports. Doomsday prognosticators predicted a massive and irreparable meltdown of the nation's and the world's technology infrastructure. Some conjecturers even went so far as to predict Armageddon and an apocalyptic end to the entire human race. Twenty-four hour news coverage seemed to shrink the world and made us aware of just how rapidly planet Earth was changing. That same news coverage also served to reassure an anxious public that the world's technology infrastructure and the human race would, indeed, remain intact.

Embedded in those changes were human events that

simultaneously enriched humanity and diminished it. For example, Bluetooth technology, TiVo, and the Blackberry 850 PDA were introduced. Eileen Collins became the first female commander of a U.S. Spacecraft. Amadou Diallo, an unarmed West African immigrant, was killed by four New York City police officers, who shot him nineteen times in the doorway of his Bronx apartment building. Matthew Shepard, a twenty-one-year-old gay college student in Laramie, Wyoming, was brutally beaten, tied to a fence and left for dead. White supremacist John William King was convicted of capital murder in the dragging death of James Byrd, a black man, in Jasper, Texas. The massacre of twelve students and a teacher at Columbine High School in Littleton, Colorado shocked the nation.

Whether we witnessed the enrichment or diminution of our collective humanity, change, as it has been since the beginning of time, remained constant. Yet, despite the constancy of change and the metaphorical shrinking of the world, the more things changed, it seemed, the more they remained the same. Throughout our nation, the winds of change were blowing at gale force strength, renewing, reshaping, and replacing, as needed. However, in some parts of our nation, change was treated as an adversary that needed to be defeated or at least impeded, lest it altered the terrain of the status quo. In such instances, the winds of change blew with the force of a miniature, hand-held, battery-operated fan.

The more things changed the more they remained the same is how many small towns all across the South could be described during and before 1999. The winds of change in those towns were blowing with force that would barely register on the human version of an anemometer. The ambiance, culture, and values of those small Southern towns were virtual replicas of one another and exhibited no discernible distinctions. Like clones of one another, they were umbilically tethered to their bedeviled devotion to Jim Crowism. More likely than not, those towns were racially segregated, predominantly white, and perennially attached to the lowest rung on the economic ladder. Whatever wealth and semblance of a middle class that might have existed were primarily, if not exclusively, under the control and ownership of white residents.

Undergirding and perpetuating that economic and social structure was the presence of sinister cabals masquerading as pillars of the communities. For the most part, members of those cabals were wholly comprised of wealthy white men, who could very accurately be described as ruthless, racist, and unrepentant. Like their ancestors before them, they profited from the *fruits of the disgraceful legacy* of racial segregation, discrimination, and white supremacy. Those fruits—wealth, power, and influence—were derived from an economic system that was based on the purchase and trade of human beings for the sole purpose of creating more wealth for the wealthy, more power for the powerful, and more influence for the influential.

Those publicly pious and privately perverted men also managed to perpetrate their evildoings with the tacit, if not, explicit approval of established social institutions—churches, courts, governments, and the media—all of which were created to provide succor to the powerless and to place limits on the powerful. Those institutions, more often than not, failed to live up to their obligations and responsibilities, and in some cases, intentionally so.

Also like their progenitors, members of those cabals strictly adhered to a distorted, perverse, and self-serving view of Christianity in which they ascribed biblical justification to the existence of racial segregation, racial discrimination, and white supremacy. For no reasons other than the color of their skin and the unearned attendant privileges, they laid claim to what they believed was an inherent and God-given right to be exclusive recipients of God's blessings.

Members of those cabals had an insatiable appetite for wealth, power, and influence. Making money and controlling the lives of others were a blood sport to them. Monthly tallies of body bags, literally and figuratively, were the primary metrics that determined the margin of victory for the winners of that decades-long blood sport. Power was an aphrodisiac. Money was an intoxicant. Influence was a seductress.

You are about to embark upon a journey involving a small group of powerful men and women who were allowed to flourish and prosper for decades in a small town in southeast Mississippi. They were able to do so because their enablers—the public, churches, media, courts, and government—became indifferent toward, oblivious to, or supportive of their illegal, iniquitous, and loathsome actions.

Although this story takes place in the fictitious town of Sharpville, Mississippi, the attitudes, beliefs, and mindsets of people living there are not fictional. The story would be virtually the same in any other town in the South, real or fictitious.

CHAPTER 1

THIS MONTH'S GATHERING of Billy Wayne Sharp and his associates was to be unlike any of the others of the last forty years. Whereas most of their get-togethers were devoted to playing dominoes, drinking, and consummating business deals, this particular meeting on this night involved none of that, except the drinking. Instead, it was a meeting in which the major portion would be devoted exclusively to nostalgia and reminiscing. The decision to depart from the usual routine was done *on* purpose and *for* a purpose—a purpose, however, initially known only by Billy Wayne, as it was his prerogative as convener of the meeting and leader of the clan to permit such rare deviations from the norm of unadulterated revelry.

The truth of the matter is that Billy Wayne's decision to alter the routine of the meeting came about because of a vision that came to him two nights before while he was watching a rerun of an episode of the *Twilight Zone*, the plot of which struck a prophetic and thought-provoking chord with Billy Wayne. The sixty-ish era black and white episode featured the venerable patriarch of an itinerant gypsy family, who was an expert reader of palms, tarot cards, and the stars. The diminutive dark-complexioned, wrinkled-face, chain-smoking gypsy man was accessorized with medium-sized hooped earrings in one ear and a print silk scarf tied around his bald head. The opening scene of the TV classic featured the gypsy man preparing his cards and other paraphernalia in anticipation of the first customer of the night, who turned out to be a perspiring, fidgety, middle-aged man, dressed in an undersized business suit. After accepting a seat on the plastic-covered sofa next to the gypsy man, the fidgety man abruptly announced that he was there on the recommendation of a close friend and recent client of the gypsy man. He had never been to a card reader or fortuneteller before. In fact, he thought gypsy palm readers were money-grabbing, remorseless scam artists, until his friend told him that the gypsy man imparted valuable and sage advice to him, which resulted in a huge burden being lifted from his shoulders. What the hell, he thought. It might work for him too—and God knows that he needs to be relieved of some pretty weighty burdens.

It turns out that the fidgety man held an important position in the local business community and could not afford to have scandal of any sort disrupt his plans to become an even bigger player in statewide business and politics. He was on the fast track to fame, fortune, and power. In a few years, he would be known statewide as an elite power player, and everyone would revere, if not fear him. He desperately wanted to avoid stumbling before he reached the finish line. If he avoided stumbling, he would embark on a life filled with overwhelming pleasures, powers, and prominence. But he needed advice from the gypsy man on how to handle a sensitive situation that had real potential for causing him to stumble, just as he was nearing the finish line.

The fidgety man wanted to know if he should permit his fifteen year-old nephew, who was recently released from reform school, to live with him and his family. The boy's single mother tearfully pleaded on the telephone with her big brother to let the boy live with him for a while until he got back on his feet. He is a good kid, just hung around with the wrong crowd, she told him, and it really wasn't his fault that he robbed that gas station, got caught, and spent the past two years in reform school. He only needs to be around a better caliber of people, people like fidgety man who could place and maintain her precious baby on the path of righteousness and out of the devil's workshop. But fidgety man knows that if the staff at the reform school could not improve his nephew's attitude and behavior, there was no way he could do it. Besides, the last thing he needed during his impending ascension to stardom was someone tagging him as being soft on criminals, as evidenced by having one living under his roof, blood or not. But he loved his sister and hated to turn his back on her in a time of need. Thus, he wanted the counsel of someone with special insight to help him make the right decision.

After accepting a glass of iced tea from the gypsy man and wiping his sweaty brow for the umpteenth time, the fidgety man sat at a metal folding card table across from the gypsy man with his elbows forming a triangle and his chin resting on his clasped hands. The gypsy man understood the fidgety man's predicament and told him that he had made a wise choice in coming to him. This would be the fidgety man's best-ever use of a measly half a C note, especially in light of the fact that he could already see fidgety man in command of the loyalty, respect, and devotion of throngs of admirers and supporters. As the gypsy man turned over the Emperor card, he smiled and told the fidgety man that he should set down rules by which everyone is expected to live and to be the leader he was meant to be. Man is the ruler of his castle and his kingdom—and there is room for only one ruler. The ruler has to rule with somberness, compassion, and most importantly, with authority—authority derived from his inherent and rightful status as the supreme and solitary ruler of his castle and his kingdom. To do anything less is to be less than a man. In that instant, fidgety man stopped fidgeting and mirrored the beaming, toothy smile plastered across the face and maw of gypsy man. With that sage advice and welcomed relief from having just jettisoned a thorny problem from his mind, the now smiling fidgety man stood up to take his leave, exuding extreme confidence and continuing to wear his gypsy man inspired smile. But before allowing his satisfied customer to exit the door, gypsy man took hold of the fidgety man's arm, moved his face close to his ear, and whispered his last bit of advice. The gypsy man's final words were given without any additional recompense.

"It is common for humans to fall prey to temptation and folly without ever fully appreciating the fact that they possess something that separates them from all of God's creatures—free will. They can just as easily avoid temptation and recklessness as they can invite them. They can just as easily be hard-working as idle. They can just as easily build up as tear down. You, my dear man, must endeavor to avoid the harmful temptation and folly born of laziness and slothfulness. You, because of sheer laziness, often seek out and covet the dual life paths of least resistance and complacent familiarity in dealings with your business partners, family, and friends. Such has served you well up to this point in your life. But, my dear man, you are about to move into a different realm, a realm of your own choosing but also one of manifest destiny. This new realm requires a different attitude, a different heart, and a different set of behaviors than those that have brought you to this moment in time. And depending on how you choose to respond to the lure of the two tempting paths that I have warned you about, the remaining years of your life will be accompanied by either unending comfort or incomprehensible peril. You will live either the life of a king or that of a pauper. You will live the life that men would give their eye teeth to own or one that is as useful as an umbrella in a hurricane. You will have people bow to you or they will have you bow to them. Free will. Temptation or resistance. Folly or prudence. The choices are yours. However, in order to take full advantage of the existential choices that are before you and the immeasurable rewards that await you, you must perform a most important act. If you fail to do so, your ability to discern your life and career choices will grow dimmer and more difficult for the duration of time you have remaining on earth. And you will forever remain a fidgety, frustrated, fearful little man, full of potential but falling short of the finish line, forever wondering what could have been. You are wondering now, what is this important act that I have told you to perform. What will it cost you? Is this the hidden string that comes attached to my advice to you? Rest assured, my good man, it will cost you nothing and no strings are now or ever tied to anything I tell you. But here is what you must do to close the deal and seal your fate. You must purge from your soul, the demons that are lying dormant inside you and vigilantly awaiting instructions from the forces that control them. Those demons and their controllers are the dark forces of evil that constantly seek to control your heart, mind, and soul. They never give up. They never tire. They are present in each of us, each and every day of our lives, in and between each rising and each retiring, and between the beginning and infinity. Most dangerous is that they can be easily awakened—by a thought, a feeling, or an action. And once they are aroused, they resist returning to their dormancy. They are at their most resistant when being forced to abandon its control. But there are also angels inside us that resist and battle those demons by forcing them to either remain in their dormant state or forcing them to return to their dormancy once they have been awakened. Listen carefully, my dear man to what I am about to tell you. The act of purging dormant demons is essential for the renewal and rebirth of the spirit and the soul, without which, you will never know peace. Otherwise, your life will be forever controlled by demons, which have an interminable love affair with suffering, despair, and misery. Even with purging, you must beware that demons and their controllers can regroup, refortify, and revisit in the snap of a finger, the bat of an eye, or the tick of a clock," cautioned gypsy man.

"I'm not sure what all that means, but you are scaring the living daylights out of me. I just wanted to find out whether I should let that wayward nephew of mine stay at my house or not. Now you got me confused with all that talk about free will and purging demons. I don't know what I'm supposed to think or do now," said fidgety man.

"Not to worry, my dear man. I could see it in your eyes, even before you said so, that you are confused and wondering how this purging process works. Because everything hinges on your ability to successfully purge those pesky demons, I am about to give you the information you will need to make that happen. There is only one way for you to purge those demons before they are awakened and take control of your life. And that is to honor the angels inside you by acknowledging aloud in the presence of others the morally questionable deeds that you have committed during your lifetime. You see, demons thrive on immorality. Angels thrive on atonement. But ultimately, it is up to you to decide which of the two will guide your life from this point on. Confession or denial. Recklessness or caution. Temptation or self-control. Angels or demons. Free will. The choice is yours, my good man. However, you must remember this. Don't confess those morally questionable deeds to me. No sir. And don't confess them to your family and loved ones. That will destroy the love and trust they presently have for you. Trust me. Learning about your morally questionable deeds from your past will result only in your family not truly loving and trusting you, even though they say they still do. Therefore, you must do so only with people you know well, who will keep your secrets, and who will not judge you," said gypsy man.

With those final words of caution from the oracle gypsy man, a commercial appeared on the television screen and Billy Wayne decided he had seen and heard enough. He turned off the television, kissed his wife goodnight, turned over on his side, and enjoyed the best night of sleep he has had in months.

Following the path of complacent familiarity and acknowledging past deeds resonated strongly for Billy Wayne. He took the warnings from the gypsy oracle as a sign that he, too, should deviate from some of his familiar routines and that he should find a way to acknowledge and speak about some of the morally questionable things that he might have done during his past. After all, what would it hurt, he thought. He would tell such things only to people who already knew about them and thereby avoid any possibility of someone other than his close friends hearing what they already knew. So, he decided that he would change a portion of his routine at the next monthly meeting with his buddies. Further, he would use that same meeting as an opportunity to talk about his past misdoings, thus simultaneously covering both warnings about following too closely and too routinely, the dual paths of least resistance and complacent familiarity in dealings with his business partners, family, and friends. What a stroke of genius and a stroke of good luck, he thought. No point in taking chances that the gypsy could be wrong, he thought.

He also took the warning to avoid some familiar routines as a sign to ask his doctor to consider adjusting the dosage of his anti-depression medication. On doctor's orders, Billy Wayne was supposed to consult with the doctor every six months to determine whether his dosage needed adjusting. Out of sheer stubbornness, he had not done so in twelve months. His depression was diagnosed following the death of a dear friend who died under unexplained circumstances many years ago. Billy Wayne had difficulty sleeping and often awoke in the middle of the night with tears streaming down his face. At one point, he thought he was going insane and would end up at Whitfield State Mental Hospital, but following a diagnosis of chemical imbalance that was treatable with medication, he soon went back to being the normal Billy Wayne Sharp, minus the sleepless nights and uncontrollable night-time crying.

That Billy Wayne would respond so decisively to a television program about astrology and fortune telling was not at all surprising to him. Actually, he was a closeted but ardent devotee of astrology and tarot and had immersed himself in the study of astrology after learning that one of his heroes, a former U. S. President, was also devotee of astrology.

Deviating from the normal routine was not to be the only reason this meeting was destined to be so memorable. In fact, eschewing merry-making for the night would not even come close to being the major reason for this conclave being so extraordinary. Few people in Henderson County and in the city of Sharpville, not even Billy Wayne and his buddies, could have predicted that, by the end of the night, this meeting would become more infamous than last month's revelation that the town's Director of Public Utilities had siphoned off huge chunks of the city's electrical and water supplies and sold them to occupants of a trailer park on the outskirts of town.

CHAPTER 2

O N CUE, THE glossy ten-foot high antique, cherry-colored grandfather clock, conspicuously situated in a distant corner of Billy Wayne Sharp's cavernous conference room mercifully sounded the last of its ten booming, reverberating gongs. On cue again, Sharpville's self-appointed power elite took their usual seats at the shiny, glossy-finished twenty-five-foot long matching oval-shaped cherry-colored conference table to begin their monthly meeting of mirth and merry-making. All seven—Billy Wayne Sharp, Dickey Carter, Jethro Milliken, Joe Lee Roberts, Cletus Sessum, Brock Galloway, and Clifford Morgan—nestled in their plush, ivory, leathered-covered, high back swivel chairs. By birth, they all are white, all men, and all long past their middle years, and by choice, all life-long residents of this college town of 30,000. Through the years, they had distinguished themselves in many ways, the most visible of which were the millions of dollars that they had individually and collectively accrued for themselves. They had done so in their roles as barterers, vendors and procurers of an array of services and commodities—cars, building supplies, construction, funerals, legal advice, financial advice, vice, and sheer influence and power. At various times in their lives they had all been church deacons, civic club presidents, little league coaches, and community chest fund-raisers. They were the quintessential pillars of the community, revered by most and feared by the rest.

They were politically connected to the politically powerful. It did not matter whether it was the local sheriff, the governor, or either U.S. Senator, something as mundane as a phone call from Billy Wayne or one of his associates that call became the most important priority for that politician.

This amalgam of the town's self-styled power elite saw themselves as consummate and self-righteous king-makers and king-breakers. They were unmatched and unrivaled by any individual or groups of individuals in Sharpville, Mississippi for the unofficial but true title of master puppeteers. Accordingly, they saw themselves as anointed by the Creator to act as frontline defenders and guardians of the *Southern way of life*—their way of life. As such, they felt divinely inspired to resist, by any means necessary, the forces of change that might materially alter their exclusive birthrights as sole possessors and brokers of unbridled power in Sharpville, a once racially and still economically segregated burg situated in southeast Mississippi.

The name, lineage, and legacy of Sharpville are directly tied to Billy Wayne's great-great grandfather and Civil War hero, Colonel Thomas Barramore Sharp. Colonel Sharp, in addition to being the namesake of Billy's birthplace, was renowned and revered by many on the Confederate side of the war as a close friend and confidant of General Nathan Bedford Forrest, one of the founders of the Ku Klux Klan. Monuments and statues dedicated to the bravery and sacrifice of confederate soldiers are conspicuously located adjacent to the Henderson County Courthouse. The most prominent amongst the white concrete statues built to pay homage to the legacy and history of the confederacy and its leaders are twenty-five foot high statues of Colonel Sharp and General Forrest.

Despite Colonel Sharp's notoriety and prominence among white Southerners and the legion of devotees of the confederacy and despite his many years as a high ranking military officer, he died a penniless, and nearly-forgotten, former hero. His path to financial ruin started in the middle of the Civil War when he converted all of his monetary assets to confederate money. In doing so, he unquestionably believed that the Confederate States of America would prevail in its war against the United States of America. He further believed that as soon as the United States government surrendered to what he regarded as a superior army and a superior war general in Robert E. Lee, his vast cache of confederate cash would explode in value, making him an instant millionaire. It was a pipe dream built on faulty assumptions about the relative power and perseverance of Union and Confederate soldiers. The Confederacy overestimated its power and perseverance and underestimated that of the United States military. Another faulty assumption of Colonel Sharp was an unwavering belief that slavery and white supremacy would last in perpetuity, thus preserving the bitter fruits of the disgraced legacy of racial segregation for many future generations of Sharps and other similarly devout white supremacists. Of course, history documents the fact that the Confederate States of America lost its war against the United States of America, and as a result, confederate money was about as useful as a rowboat in a tsunami. And with each succeeding generation, the prevalence and power of racial bigotry and white supremacy have, in many respects, diminished, thereby blunting the impact of the disgraced legacy of Colonel Sharp and his compatriots.

History also documents that fact that Colonel Sharp's legacy of white supremacy lived long past his demise. He and others of his ilk, who believed in the confederacy and its currency, passed on to their offsprings and to the offsprings of other votaries of racial discrimination their status as paupers and devout white supremacists. Billy Wayne Sharp put an end to at least one of Colonel Sharp's legacies—poverty. But he indefatigably clung to the Colonel's legacy of devotion to white supremacy.

Although he died a penniless, nearly-forgotten, former hero, Colonel Sharp's spirit and attitude lives on in its many tangible, perverse symbols and manifestations. One of those tangible symbols was a prominently displayed message banner that stretched across Front Street, Sharpville's busiest street and the main thoroughfare that led motorists into the business section of Sharpville. The twenty-five by ten foot white, vinyl banner, which spanned the entire width of Front Street, earned its notoriety from both its gaudy, enormous size and its provocative messages. In large, black, bold, block letters, the four-line banner delivered both a welcome and a warning to all who read it:

WELCOME TO DOWNTOWN SHARPVILLE.

WE HAVE THE BLACKEST DIRT
AND THE WHITEST PEOPLE.

STAY A SPELL.

COLOREDS MUST LEAVE BEFORE SUNDOWN!

For years, the local five and dime store sold postcard replicas of the banner, which only served to further extend and publicize the racial attitudes moral compass of the leadership of the town of Sharpville. Local white residents purchased the postcards and regularly used them in their written communications with friends and family all across the country. Curious travelers sought out the postcards as souvenirs, keepsakes, or as evidence that Sharpville was a town they would love to live in or one they would vow to never set foot in again. A few years after it was hoisted, the banner was ripped down during a violent thunderstorm that also caused major damage to most downtown businesses. A small but influential group of local residents and business owners and politicians convinced the town council the banner was bad karma for the town and even worse for business. The offending sign was never replaced. But by then,

Sharpville, Mississippi had already established itself as a town that people either loved or loathed.

*

Prior to the start of the monthly meeting of Sharpville's septet of self-appointed power brokers, the men spent a fair amount of time shifting their weight in their chairs searching for that perfect symbiosis between body and seat. After all, only God and Billy Wayne knew how long they would be stuck in their seats that evening, and discovering even a slight modicum of seat familiarity and comfort was an absolute must. Over the years, their bodies altered in shape, size, height, weight, and level of fragility. Except for Billy Wayne, they each had gone from tall to less tall, stout to thin, strong skeletal composition to artificial hips and knees, erect posture to slumped shoulders, or adequate muscle mass to nearly atrophied muscles. Such physical changes necessitated a monthly recalibration of the comfort quotient that the current seat yielded. If necessary, they swapped chairs with one of their cohorts until they found the ideal or, at least, a more tolerable chair.

Another absolute must prior to the start of the meeting was for each of the men to indicate their drink requests for the evening by placing a check mark and writing out any specific requests on a specially designed waiter's pad. A catalog of available drinks was listed on the pad: Margarita (frozen or on the rocks), White Russian, Bloody Mary, Martini (stirred, shaken, dry, wet, dirty, apple, or watermelon), Jim Beam, Wild Turkey, Jack Daniels, Beefeater, Gordon's, Tanqueray, Absolut, and Bacardi. The information on the pad also requested their name, number of drinks anticipated, type and ratio of mix, salt or no salt, ice or no ice and size of glass. Billy Wayne's rule was simple when it came to drinking: Order all you want to drink, but drink all you order. Once the liquor requests pads were completed, Billy Wayne collected them, inspected each, noting who ordered what, and took them out to the kitchen for the bartender to begin preparing the first rounds of drinks.

*

Billy Wayne and his associates took unabashed pride in their impeccable four decade-old track record of successfully making and breaking hundreds of elected and appointed officials. They took an equal amount of pride in influencing and ultimately determining the outcome of various and sundry referenda, elections and such, while touting themselves as champions of progress whose only interest was the improvement of the quality of life of all of Sharpville's denizens.

Through the years, Billy Wayne Sharp and his associates came to possess enough unchecked power and influence that there was no major public issue that did not require their blessing and support in order for it to receive favor. Owing to the breadth and depth of their individual collective venality, no one in and around Henderson County and the city of Sharpville was ever elected or appointed to a local or state position, board or agency without their backing and say-so. There were no major arrests, convictions or exonerations within a seventy-five-mile radius of Sharpville without the tacit, if not, explicit approval of Billy Wayne and his buddies. As a group, they ran Sharpville as though they owned it, which they did—but they did so in such a thoroughly clandestine manner that no one, except those who had a need to know, had a clue as to how much they really ran things. They maintained unbounded and justified sangfroid in their surreptitiousness and Teflon armor. They *believed*, without the slightest reservation or doubt, that they would always have plausible deniability in the unlikely event that suspicions or accusations of impropriety were ever directed toward them.

In addition to, and deadly consonant with their well-deserved roles as undisputed and unchallenged kingpins of Sharpville, Mississippi, they also viewed as a lifetime commitment, their many years of overtly and covertly thwarting local efforts to achieve racial equality. Such efforts, for the most part, were driven by an uncompromisingly fanatical resolve to deter, and when necessary, punish what to them was the most objectionable and most detestable of all sins—race-mixing, particularly race-mixing that was sexual or intimate. To their way of thinking, resisting and deterring race-mixing, was in fact, much more than a commitment. Rather, such resistance to and deterrence of race-mixing were part and parcel of a Holy-inspired mission that they believed were given to them by the Almighty Himself. They believed that God created a universe in which the various peoples of the world were commanded by Him to stick with their own kind, to live with their own kind, and most importantly to mix, marry, and multiply *only* with their own kind. To do otherwise was an abomination and an egregious and unforgivable violation of God's divine plan for perpetual racial miscegenation.

Each man seated at the conference table drew his strong allegiance and devotion to the perverse view that Christianity is based on white supremacy from their interpretation of Genesis in the Old Testament. They were introduced to this discredited and debased view of Christianity by a like-minded traveling evangelist who annually rented land from Billy Wayne to host three nights of tent revivals. The Reverend Jacob Thomas, a non-denominational preacher from Forsyth County, Georgia, maintained a fanatical following throughout the South among hard-core, sycophantic, religious zealots who embraced and practiced Thomas' view of race and religion—and he continually recruited new converts to his racist brand of religiosity at his sold-out Holy Roller tent revivals, which, naturally, only whites were allowed to attend.

Impressed with Thomas' theology of racial segregation and his ability to appropriate huge sums of money from worshipers in just three nights, Billy Wayne arranged a meeting with him, his buddies, and Thomas in his motel room to learn more about this alluring view of Christianity. Like sponges, each of them soaked up the twisted, racist, and "Christian-like" views Thomas espoused.

Thomas was a tall, bespectacled, heavy-set man with a rotund mid-section, not unlike that of Billy Wayne. In fact, their physical features were strikingly similar in height, weight and girth. The three-piece, pin-stripe suit he wore was at least two sizes too small, prompting him to frequently tug at the sleeves of the jacket in a fruitless attempt to elongate it into an appropriate length. The forty-eight-year-old Thomas sported a salt and pepper goatee that noticeably clashed with his pale complexion and ink-dark hair, which was perpetually darkened from daily use of Grecian Formula. The tone, volume, rhythm and cadence of his voice were exact replicas of those of famous television evangelists who are adept at delivering long and loud sermons that appeal primarily to the listener's emotions.

"Now, Reverend Thomas, my friends and I are grateful to you for takin' time out of your busy schedule to spend a little speakin' to us 'bout some of the thangs we heard you preachin' 'bout tonight and the other two nights you been here," said Billy Wayne as he nodded his head in the direction of his six friends.

"Well, son, anytime I can spend some extra time spreading the word of our risen savior, I am the one who is grateful. And while I'm at it, Mr. Sharp, and the rest of you, let me say how grateful I am for your generous donations at my meetings. My assistant told me about the checks that y'all put in the collection plate each evening. She told me that y'all seem to be very pious men who showed your faithfulness to the Lord by showing up each night, sitting right there on the front row, and responding most favorably to my words. Your presence and your monetary support are a blessing to me. In return, the Lord will bless you manifold for being his faithful servants. As you know, I don't have a regular congregation or some organization that takes care of my living and traveling expense. So, I depend on the generosity of gentlemen like you and other believers who want to help me spread the word the way the Lord has called on me to spread it," said the Reverend Thomas.

"Well, Reverend Thomas, I have always made a habit of puttin' my money into to thangs I believe in, whether it's the Humane Society, the NRA, March of Dimes, Girl Scouts, or in your case, to the Reverend Jacob Thomas Ministries. And when I say I believe in your ministry, sir, I mean exactly that. I heard how you talked 'bout the proper place in the world for the white man versus the proper place for the niggers. My friends and I have been believin' the same thang for years now 'bout how God intended for the white man to reign supreme in his kingdom, havin' dominion and domination of the descendants of Canaan. That's how we been tryin' to maintain thangs here in Sharpville for goin' near on forty-odd years. We been tryin' our best to be true to God's call on our lives to manifest his commandments to put the white man and the black man in their God-given places. If you don't mind, Reverend Thomas, please, if you would, give us just a little more of that good preachin' you done tonight, respectin' the proper place for white men and niggers. I know you busy and tired and want to get some rest, so you don't have to be too long," said Billy Wayne.

Reverend Thomas proceeded to repeat much of what he said at the tent revival that evening. He reiterated, but in a less dramatic manner, his perverse views on race and Christianity.

The essence of Thomas' message to Billy Wayne and his spellbound buddies was what he called the Thomas Theology of God's Divine Purpose. The Thomas "theology" was as distorted as it was simple and brief: White racial superiority and the correctness of racial segregation were based on Thomas' interpretation of Genesis 9:24-27. *And Noah awoke from his wine, and knew what his younger son had done unto him. And he said, Cursed be Canaan; a servant of servants shall he be unto his brethren. And he said, Blessed be the Lord God of Shem; and Canaan shall be his servant. God shall enlarge Japheth, and he shall dwell in the tents of Shem; and Canaan shall be his servant.*

Thus, in their twisted and self-serving view of that passage, Reverend Thomas, Billy Wayne, and his "followers" believed that because Canaan, who was black and the son of Ham, he and all of his descendants, i.e. black people, were cursed by Noah and commanded by God to spend their entire existence as servants. In other words, the enslavement of Canaan's descendants was, therefore, justified as punishment for sins committed by Canaan. To further bolster their belief in the Thomas Theology of God's Divine Purpose and to provide a convenient reminder that Christianity not only endorses racial segregation and white supremacy but also demands it, Reverend Thomas gave each of the men a special gift. He retrieved from his satchel seven small, white, laminated, wallet-size cards and gave one to each member of his private audience. So that they will not backslide in their racist views of Christianity, the card contained an excerpt from a sermon delivered by a Civil War era, pro-slavery, Presbyterian minister, the Reverend Benjamin Palmer. Reverend Palmer's words ultimately became as important to Billy Wayne's clan as the words to their beloved signature song of the Old South, *Dixie.*

And Reverend Palmer's words were: *The color line is distinctly drawn by Jehovah himself; it is drawn in nature and in history in such a form as to make it a sin and a crime to undertake to obliterate it. Confusion of tongues at Babel shows that race distinctions were probably developed at the same time, and for the same purpose. The duty is plain of conserving and transmitting the system of slavery,*

18

with the freest scope for its natural development and extension. Let us, my brethren, look our duty in the face... My own conviction is, that we should at once lift ourselves, intelligently, to the highest moral ground and proclaim to all the world that we hold this trust from God, and in its occupancy we are prepared to stand or fall as God may appoint.

As the thoroughly contented and holy-ghost filled men exited Reverend Thomas' motel room, Billy Wayne deposited another check into an empty collection plate setting atop the motel's copy of the Gideon Bible. That check brought Billy Wayne's and his buddies' contribution to the Reverend Jacob Thomas Ministries for the week to $75,000, an amount that lent credence to Billy Wayne's earlier statement that he likes to invest his money (and that of his buddies) in causes that he and they believe in.

Largely based on their religious inculcation and indoctrination from the likes of the Reverend Jacob Thomas, Billy Wayne and his associates were zealously driven by an unshakable belief in the inerrancy of racial segregation, the inviolability of white male superiority, and the evil of racial miscegenation. Even more incredulous and twisted is their steadfast belief that Jesus Christ was a white man, and therefore, only white men are true beneficiaries of His grace and favor. In their view of the world, such was the natural order of things, created through divine intervention, for the purpose of establishing the inherent superiority and supremacy of Caucasian men among the various peoples of the world.

*

All told, Billy Wayne and his associates were the quintessential scrofulous, redneck mafia, of south Mississippi. As a group, they possessed many of the same characteristics and tendencies that embody the more well-known *Cosa Nostra Mafioso*. They considered themselves flawlessly stealthy and secretive in their deliberations, planning, and actions, while maintaining unwavering adherence to an explicit and strictly enforced code of silence for themselves and for all of those with whom they had dealings. And most like the *Cosa Nostra Mafioso*, they were unmercifully callous and ruthless. They felt justified—even obligated—to use whatever means necessary to bend people and events to their collective will and to punish anyone who resisted their control. They maintained an extensive and fiercely loyal network of highly secretive and remarkably efficient operatives and enforcers who took corrective action against those who required special convincing to do what Billy Wayne and his associates wanted them to do.

Also, like the more well-known *Mafioso*, Billy Wayne and his buddies were driven by insatiable avarice and were not above or beneath engaging in any type of business activity that would result in hefty enlargements of their personal treasure chests. In fact, despite their claims to be devout, God-fearing Christians, for thrills and money, they engaged, sans remorse, guilt, or punishment, in all manner of illegal, dishonest, and debauched behavior. They owned several illicit but extremely profitable brothels in New Orleans that easily rivaled the famous Bunny and Chicken ranches of Nevada. They were also proprietors of one of the most lucrative illegal gambling operations in the South out of a store front in downtown Biloxi that doubled as a pawnshop and pay-day loan operation. In addition, Billy Wayne and his associates were also majority owners of *Dank Videos*, one of the South's largest distributors of adult movies. Of course, all those businesses were fronted by third parties, designed to mask the true ownership of their morally questionable but profitable enterprises.

In addition to his ownership interests in various morally and legally dubious businesses, Billy Wayne was the silent and sole owner of a chain of eight combination liquor, gas station, and convenient stores, all located in black sections of Sharpville. Publicly, the stores were believed to be owned by C.L. Moody, a diminutive, pudgy, perpetually-grinning, middle-age, bespectacled black man whose relationship to Billy Wayne was that of a true friend, sycophant, gofer, and frequent court jester. In addition to his duties as manager and make believe owner of Billy Wayne's stores, C.L. was also a part-time deputy for the Henderson County Sheriff's Department. In the view of many, however, C.L. was actually a pitiable buffoon and caricature who displayed extreme deference to white people and equally extreme disdain for most black folk, especially poor black folk. To C.L., poor black people were an embarrassment, and in his way of seeing things, they were poor only because they were lazy and lacked initiative and industry.

CHAPTER 3

C.L. MOODY WAS born to Robert and Cleotha Moody and raised in the town of Picayune, Mississippi, a small, rural, segregated burg situated among the piney woods of Pearl River County, approximately sixty miles southeast of Sharpville. He and his three brothers were born and reared on a sharecropper's farm that was owned by Dixie Agricultural Products (DAP), Inc., a farming syndicate headquartered in Greenwood, Mississippi. DAP specialized in growing and selling cotton and sugar cane on the domestic and international markets—and with farms in Mississippi, Alabama, Louisiana, and Arkansas, it was the leading agricultural exporter in the South, with an annual net profit of $350 million. Of course, such profits were principally made possible through the low wages paid to sharecroppers like C.L. Moody's parents and grandparents.

Like their siblings and parents, Robert and Cleotha worked as sharecroppers from the time they were old enough to strap on a cotton picker's croker sack and pick at least 1,600 pounds of cotton a day, the quota they were expected to meet as members of their respective families. As they grew older, fell in love with one another, married, and started their own family, Robert's and Cleotha's quotas were set as high as two thousand pounds per day. With such an enormous quota of cotton to pick and with three growing boys to feed, Robert and Cleotha gradually introduced C.L. and his brothers to the art and science of picking cotton.

C.L., born Cleophus Lamar Moody, was the eldest of Robert's and Cleotha's three sons. By the time he was twelve years old, C.L. easily exceeded the five hundred pounds of cotton he was expected to pick or pull each day. During cotton season, the workday began at sunup and ended at sunset, and the work week started on Monday and ended on Saturday. C.L. preferred picking over pulling cotton because when picking cotton, the cotton was fluffy and loose, thus making it easier to remove it from the boll. When pulling cotton, the cotton was smaller and tighter, which meant that the entire boll had to be removed. C.L. quickly developed a technique for pulling cotton, whereby he would yank cotton from two rows at a time rather than from the customary one row at a time. Thus, he was able to quickly gather enough cotton to meet his quota and some. Meeting his quota so quickly led C.L. to develop a keen business sense and a remarkable entrepreneurial spirit, which earned him and his family extra money. When he reached his quota of five hundred pounds of bagged cotton, he would hire himself out to other families who needed help in reaching their quota. For sharecroppers, failure to meet quota meant reduced income and the attendant reduced ability to keep food on the table and family clothed. No parent wanted to shoulder the burden of telling a hungry child that there was not enough food for everybody, or deciding not to eat anything themselves so that the children would have enough. Thanks to C.L. not many black families on or near the cotton fields that he worked faced such a difficult decision, although his motivation for helping them was not at all altruistic. His savvy business model enabled him to convince those families that with the right financial incentives, he could guarantee that they would meet their quota and thus, remain in the good graces of DAP management and be able to feed their families. For every pound he picked or pulled, he would charge ten cents. On a typical day, C.L. would earn as much as five dollars. By the end of cotton picking season, he would have earned nearly $250 in extra income.

The effects of three miscarriages and the brutal summer heat took their toll on Cleotha. She died of complications brought on by septicemia, which had gone undiagnosed despite the recurring episodes of diarrhea, vomiting, and fatigue. Visiting a doctor meant time away from the fields and the accrual of more debt and more expenses that would have negatively affect her and Robert's ability to keep the children fed and clothed. Her strong sense of self-sacrifice moved her to ignore the progressively worsening symptoms, leading to premature death. Following Cleotha's death, at the age of twenty-eight, Robert made a decision that would have a profound and lasting effect on C.L. and his family. Fed up with the back breaking and low-paying job of sharecropping, coupled with the grief of losing his wife of twelve years, Robert moved to Pittsburgh, Pennsylvania to search for a job in the booming steel mills. His plan was to move his family to Pittsburgh after he had established himself with a good-paying job and a decent home that could accommodate three growing boys and two elderly parents. C.L., his brothers, and grandparents were looking forward to moving north and starting a new life free of the burdens of picking cotton and earning wages that were only slightly better than those "earned" by slaves, which is to say, slightly north of nothing.

On the day that twelve-year-old C.L. Moody and his family were set to make the long-anticipated, two-day long Greyhound bus trip to Pittsburgh, a telegram arrived at C.L.'s home, addressed to Grandmother Moody. After accepting the telegram, C.L. ran inside the house to announce to his grandmother the arrival of a letter from Pittsburgh. She was expecting it after

Robert told her by telephone that she should receive something in writing from him that day or soon afterwards.

"Grandma, a man brought this and told me that it was from Pittsburgh, where Daddy is," announced an excited C.L.

"What man you talkin' 'bout, boy. I don't see no man. What you talkin' bout? What's that you got in yo hand," asked Grandma Moody.

"A white man in a big brown truck just now came and gave me this envelope and told me to give it to you. You was inside. I called for you to come out, but you must didn't hear me, Grandma," said C.L.

"Yep. I see it turnin' the coner up there. That's one of them special delivery trucks. When they come to yo house, boy, and bring somethin', it's gotta be mighty important, or else they just put it in with the other mail they brangs by. It's from yo daddy. Anyhow, the man told you to give it to me, so give it to me," demanded Grandma Moody, who was grinning like a kid on Christmas morning.

For a brief moment, as she reached for the letter, she felt that all of the burdens of her tribulated past—the racial insults, the back-breaking labor in the cotton fields, and the stress of trying to survive with dignity as a black woman in Mississippi— were soon going to evaporate into thin air like steam escaping an angry tea kettle. She was going to experience life outside the South for the first time in her sixty-five years. She would be able to walk the streets, go to the grocery store, or sit on her front porch without worrying that someone would yell a racial epithet at her, or worse, try to harm her because of the color of her skin. What a joy, she thought, after all of those years of enduring racial insults and being treated like a second-class citizen in her own country, to finally find peace and contentment in her remaining years on earth. With tears welling up in her eyes, she considered the opportunities for C.L. and his brothers to finally get a chance to get a good education, have a chance at a decent life, and not have to spend another day in the hot sun, picking cotton. Those had been her prayers—*Lord, you are a mighty God. You turned water into wine and raised a dead man up from the grave. You told ole Pharaoh to let yo people go up out of Egypt land. And Lord, you took five loaves of bread and two fish and fed five thousand. So, ain't no limit to what you can do, Lord. You told us to jest believe in you. To jest knock and the door will be answered. You have blessed me and my family and you kept us through some mighty hard times. You have been there through the tears and through the laughter. Whenever we needed somethin', you was right there to take care of our needs, and you did it all because you gave your blood for our salvation. And Lord, you know it's some mighty mean and hateful people in this town. But you got yo own way of takin' care of a mean and spiteful heart. And as we get ready to leave Mississippi and go up north to a better life, I ask you to look over my boy, Robert. He's a good son, and he's a good daddy. We love him so much and we can't wait to see 'em soon. But, dear Lord, befo he was my son or a daddy to these young-uns, he was yo child. So look after him and keep him safe. And deliver us to him safely, so we can all be together again as a family. We all grateful to you, Lord for hearin' our prayers and I know you hear my prayers. I don't need much for myself, other than some peace of mind as I git closer to that day when you call me to come home. Jest take care of Robert and these boys so they can have a chance at freedom and a chance to live a decent life. In you precious name, I pray. Amen.*

Unable to read, Grandmother Moody handed the envelope back to C.L. and asked him to read the message tucked inside the square-shaped, salmon colored envelope with the words WESTERN UNION—URGENT in large, black, bold letters printed across the front. As C.L. began to excitedly open the envelope, a huge grin registered across his boney face. With so much adrenalin racing through his body, he was unable stand in one place. He skipped around in a circle, hopping from one foot to the other, shouting in a rhythmic monotone, "My daddy done got us a house! My daddy done got us a house! And we be movin' to Pittsburgh! We be movin' to Pittsburgh!"

He repeated the refrain several times, until Grandmother Moody snapped at him.

"Boy, if you don't be yo self still and read what yo daddy got to say, um gonna put my switch on yo black behind, boy. He spose to tell us the address of the house so we can git a cab from the bus depot. Now go on read it boy. Ain't that what he say?"

"Yesum. Um sorry, Granny. Um 'bout to read it now. Okay. Here is what it say: *I regret to inform you that...* C.L.'s excited voice was suddenly replaced by one that began to lose all of its vim and energy as it trailed off to a slow decrescendo and finally muted itself.

Grandmother Moody snapped again.

"Cleophus Lamar Moody, um gonna whup the black off yo hide, if you don't stop jaw-jankin 'round and read the real words that's on that paper."

C.L. continued reading the telegram. But now he was reading in a slow, haltingly, and staccato fashion, unlike the hurried, animated, and excited manner in which he read the first sentence. Each word was pronounced with absolute clarity and at a volume that ensured Grandmother Moody's unmistakable understanding of the words and the meaning of the telegram.

... your son, Robert Moody, was killed last night. Stop. He was brutally attacked by a colored street gang and robbed of a large amount of cash. Stop. He never regained consciousness. Please advise on how to dispose of remains. Reply to the number listed below. With regrets, Benjamin Sullivan, Pittsburgh, Pennsylvania Police Department. Stop.

At that moment, all of the breath in C.L.'s skinny, four-foot tall body just seemed to fail him as though a giant vacuum cleaner had sucked every life sustaining breath from his trembling body. Tears welled up in his eyes and made their way slowly down his deep ebony-hued cheeks and across his trembling lips. The telegram slowly fluttered from his quivering hand and landed on the dusty ground. At the moment it landed, an utterly flummoxed and shocked C.L. turned his gaze and his voice toward the cloudless blue sky.

"Daddy! Daddy! Daddy! What we spose to do now. Lord, tell us what we spose to do now. I don't know what we spose to do now, Lord, Daddy. Y'all hear me? What we spose to do now? My daddy done got beat up by a bunch crazy niggers up in Pittsburgh. It wudn't no white folks that kilt my daddy. No! It was some good for nuthin niggers who just wanted to take what my daddy worked hard for. I hate them niggers," shouted C.L.

Pulling him into her embrace, to console herself as much as to comfort her sobbing grandson, Grandmother Moody tried to calm C.L.

"Now, C.L. the good book don't allow you to hate nobody. Hate is the devil's work. Love is the Lord's work. And we can't be goin' 'round doing the devil's work. You gonna have stop that talk 'bout hatin' somebody, specially people you don't even know and ain't never seen befo," declared Grandmother Moody as she paused to take a deep breath, exhaled slowly, and whispered, *Help me, Jesus.*

"We just gonna have to find a way to git up there to Pittsburg to brang yo daddy back home for a decent Christian burial. I needs you to be strong so we can git through this. Yo granddaddy just ain't strong enough and yo brothers are just too little to be any help to me. So, what um gonna need, boy, is for you to be right in yo head and right in yo heart. The Lord will make a way. He don't put no mo on you than you can handle. Don't you worry none 'bout that. Yo daddy done been took from us, but he is the hands of the Master, right now, C.L. And when the Master wants one of his young uns to come home and be wid him, can't nothin' stop that," said Grandmother Moody.

Grandmother Moody recalled the many times she prayed to the Lord to provide an opportunity for a better life for her son and grandchildren. She recalled that she didn't ask any favors for herself, just for the Lord to provide a way, a better way for her family. Yes, she yearned for peace of mind and contentment for herself in her waning years so that she would be able to know life outside the South, away from the bigotry, hatred, and racism that she had come to know so intimately since she was just a little girl. More poignantly, she remembered her acknowledgements in her prayers that Robert, before he was her son and before he was C.L. and his brothers' father, he was first a child of God. That was the most important message she felt she needed to share with C.L., so that he could try to make some sense out of something that made no sense to him at all.

"C.L., your daddy, he was my son and he was yo daddy, but befo he was any of that, he was God's child. And as Christians that's been washed in the blood, we all gonna want to be where yo daddy's at right now. Ain't no doubt about it, son. We gonna miss him in his physical self. But his spirit ain't never gonna leave us," said Grandmother Moody as she rubbed C.L.'s back.

C.L. raised his head from Grandmother Moody's bosom and lowered his voice to a whisper.

"But granny, why the Lord wanna take away my daddy? He ain't done nothin' bad to nobody. Why didn't the Lord take them no-count niggers that kilt my daddy. They walkin' 'round while my daddy is layin' dead. It ain't fair. It ain't fair. All my daddy wanted was to make thangs better for you and the rest of us. Now he's dead. I don't understand how the Lord could take somebody away that is good as my daddy. It's the bad peoples that ought to die, not the good ones, Granny," sobbed C.L.

Grandmother Moody stroked C.L.'s face and pulled him

into a tighter embrace. She knew that this was a pivotal moment in C.L.'s young, dispirited life. She searched her heart for the right words that would bring comfort to herself and her young grieving grandson.

"The good Lord does everything for a purpose, baby. And right now, we might not know what that purpose is, but we gotta have faith and believe that the good Lord took yo daddy and my son to his heavenly home for a mighty good reason. Man can't always know God's ways. God is God. Man is man. God made man. Man didn't make God. So, we got to be obedient and faithful to the Father and know that he will always take care of his children the way *he* see fit. It might not be the way we want 'em to take care of us, but our way ain't necessarily the Lord's way. Now, you done heard Pastor Ridgeway say a lot of times that the Lord works in mysterious ways. And this is one of them mysterious ways, C.L. Now, you also gotta know that one of these days, um gonna meet my Lord and Savior, my Jehovah, my Creator and Master. Um gittin' on up in age, C.L. Um somewhere 'round eighty-something. So, I ain't got long to be here befo the Lord calls me home to be wid 'em. And when I git there, me and yo daddy gonna sit 'round and rejoice and praise the Lord and sang wid the angels and just worship the Lord all day long," said Grandmother Moody as she became aware of the presence of both a slight smile and a tear track on her face.

From her perch on the top step of her weather-worn, wooden, splintered stoop, she slowly rose and winced from the throbbing pain of arthritis pounding her knees. After fully uprighting herself, she dug her hands deep into the pockets of her flower print duster and retrieved a small gray and white plaid face towel, which she used to wipe the beads of sweat that had accumulated on her furrowed brow. She then gently pulled C.L. to his dusty, bare feet. For a long moment, she lovingly hugged her grieving grandson, and with her face towel, wiped the tears from his face, and then hers. Instinctively, she tried, again, to shift the focus of the conversation.

"Now, son, we gonna ask Pastor Ridgeway to help us git up to Pittsburgh to brang yo daddy back home. And um sho, he gonna do what he can, him along with other members of the church. And I got a little put away myself for my own burial and home going. And we can use some of that to pay for the bus tickets and pay for shippin' his body back home. When we git 'em home, we gonna have the undertaker lay him out in his Sunday suit so all his friends can remember him like he was befo he went to be wid the Master. And that's how we want folks to remember him, son. Dressed in his black Sunday suit, his starched and iron white shirt, and that tie he wo all the time. That long strangy black one with the little shiny sparkles on it," Grandmother Moody said with a slight grin.

Stuck in an emotionally desolate place, filled with anger, hurt, and confusion, C.L. struggled to deal with his feelings. He tried to understand and internalize the words of wisdom and comfort that Grandmother Moody was bravely trying to share with him. In his mind, he knew that the task of retrieving his father's remains was both important and imminent. But his feelings were overwhelming him. The anger, hurt, and confusion melded together into a gigantic emotional tsunami, completely out of control and agonizingly unmanageable, emotional states that would remain with him for years to come.

"But, Granny, I hate them no-count niggers that kilt Daddy. They ain't a bit-o-good, or else they woulda got a job like Daddy did and had money for they own family and not have to take my daddy's money he was gonna use for his family. And then they gotta go and kill 'em on top of that. I just ain't right, Granny. I hate niggers. I hate 'em all. When I grow up, I ain't gonna be no nigger. White folks gonna know me and help me and be my friends, and they ain't gonna hurt me none. It's just niggers I gotta learn to stay away from," announced C.L.

"Now hush, boy. That's jest that hurt and grief talkin'. Now, I want you to stop all dat talkin' 'bout hatin' niggers. That ain't gonna brang yo daddy back. Beside, where you gonna git in life if you go 'round hatin' niggers, like you ain't one yoself. Otherwise you gonna end up thankin' you better than most colored folks. And if you do that, the world ain't gonna be too kind to you, and yo own people ain't gonna have nothin' to do wid ya. And that ain't the way for a colored man to live his life in these parts", Grandmother Moody said in a harsh and forceful tone.

Days later, C.L. and Grandmother Moody made the bus trip to Pittsburgh, not the one they wanted to make, but the one they had to make. They retrieved Robert Moody's body and had it shipped to Picayune for service and burial. The police captured the five men who participated in the murder of twenty-nine-year-old Robert Moody. All five were convicted and sentenced to twenty years at the state penitentiary in Waynesburg, Pennsylvania.

As he grew older, still working in the cotton fields of Picayune and Pearl River County, C.L. dedicated himself to making as much money as he could while intentionally distancing himself from most black people in town. In pursuit of the former, he continued the practice of hiring himself out to fellow cotton pickers who struggled to meet their quota of cotton. He expanded his one-person, money-making enterprise to include local white home owners and business owners, who hired him to rake leaves, clean out gutters, mow lawns, transplant trees, run errands, walk dogs, and any other venture that would add to his growing bank account. In pursuit of the latter—distancing himself from other black people—it was fortuitous for him that the public schools in Picayune desegregated as he was entering high school. As was typical of most Southern towns that reluctantly and unhurriedly ended racially segregated schools following the *Brown* v. *Board of Education* decision in 1954, Picayune's all-black George Washington Carver High School was shuttered, and all students, black and white, were forced to attend the all-white Picayune High School. As a Picayune High School student, who was determined to distance himself from other black students, C.L. was able to expand his circle of friends and acquaintances among the white student body while further reducing and eliminating his nearly non-existent circle of black friends. He took advantage of opportunities to develop friendships with his new-found white friends and to begin embracing an odd sense of racial superiority, the same that his white friends had for other black students at the school. His sharp wit and keen sense of humor garnered him favor with many white students who saw him as happy-go-lucky, non-threatening and comical. C.L. perfectly, and without much prodding, fit the caricature and stereotype of the happy "darkie" who behaved in a self-deprecating manner and showed extreme obsequiousness to whites in general.

The psychological payoff for C.L. was that he felt accepted by white students, who reinforced his diminished view of his black self, and at the same time he welcomed the disdain of black students who grew bold and vocal in their blackness and impatience with C.L.'s intentional immersion into the dominant white culture. Thus continued C.L.s private psychological war with himself over his physical and natural blackness and his public, overt, and frequently successful, attempts to show disdain for blackness by ingratiating himself with every white person he could. The money that he made from his entrepreneurial ventures and the financial networks that he created through his friendships with white people in Picayune and Pearl River County allowed him to move to Sharpville after high school with enough money to start a family and purchase a 3,000 square foot home on seventy-five acres of land.

By the sweat of his brow, and with only a high school education, C.L. Moody successfully raised himself and his family out of poverty, creating a comfortable middle-class existence. He thought that such an enterprising spirit was available to all black people, and those who did not avail themselves of such fruitful opportunities simply opted for poverty over prosperity. Because wealthy white people were C.L.'s chief financial benefactors and social role models, and because they were the only ones who helped him to scale the wall of poverty, he always felt he owed each of them, whether they directly assisted him or not, a never-to-be-fully-paid debt of gratitude. Billy Wayne was pleased with C.L.'s success in overcoming poverty, just as he had done. He could not understand why more poor black people could not do what C.L. had done in throwing off the yoke of poverty. He joined C.L. in his utter loathing of non-enterprising black people, particularly those who lived in poverty.

Billy Wayne truly liked C.L. as he would a benevolent, less intelligent, and less endowed step-brother, and he genuinely enjoyed being around C.L. He was also fond of C.L. because C.L. was frequently good for a sidesplitting laugh with his well-known proclivity for delivering a clever joke, usually ethnic, in a sharp and exaggerated style of Ebonics. Most importantly, however, Billy Wayne enjoyed being around C.L. because C.L. was a constant reminder of his perverse, life-long view that because of the relatively small amount of melanin in his own skin, he possessed natural superiority over C.L. and all other people who had more melanin than he.

Despite warnings from Grandmother Moody, C.L. created and embraced a shameless devotion and deference to everything white and a holier-than-thou hostility toward everything black. In turn, most black people in Sharpville reciprocated in their hostility toward him. No black person in Sharpville regarded him as a friend. And none would ever say anything positive about him. Black people were never invited to social gatherings at his home, and likewise, he was never invited to any at theirs. For the most part, that was an agreeable and mutually satisfactory arrangement for all concerned. The prevailing ethos on both sides was that there is no point in showing love to someone you cannot stand being around.

*

Although C.L. considered himself an honorary member of the white race, most whites did not fully endorse his membership in their group. Many whites, while accepting him in his role as Billy Wayne's friend, flunky, and store manager, never remotely mistook him for someone who naturally possessed the privileges of being white. Without a hint of tact or subtlety he was frequently subjected to the same racial animus and racial epithets some whites directed toward the black race as a whole. Whenever someone would remind C.L. that he had just been insulted by someone's racist remarks, he responded that he did not feel the least bit insulted because "they were just joshing around." One such comment was made directly to him as he was entertaining a group of white men inside one of the convenience stores he managed for Billy Wayne. After delivering the punch line of one of his trademark ethnic jokes, one of the men said, "C.L., you are as funny as a barrel of monkeys. And ain't no monkey funnier than you, boy. And for being so damn funny, I hereby bestow upon you the coveted and well-earned title of CMIC—Chief Monkey in Charge!"

C.L. laughed as loudly and heartily as anyone in the store. When he finally stopped laughing, his predictable but pitiful reply was, "Sho nuf, boss. If you say so, and I appreciate the title. Is that anything like CNIC? Get it? Chief Nigger In Charge. 'Cause 'um that too. Like they say, monkey see, monkey do. And

I'm the monkey that doo-s all the saying and doo-s all the doin' 'round here."

C.L. Moody was blissfully ignorant of the fact that in his role as Billy Wayne's flunky and beneficiary, he was free to devote his life to whomever he wishes. But his efforts to distance himself psychologically, in speech, and in conduct from other black people while seeking to ingratiate himself with whites who despise him as much as they do other black people only add to his reputation as a sellout and an Uncle Tom.

C.L. and Billy Wayne met more than ten years ago at *Car-Splash*, a locally-owned, self-service car wash establishment that consisted of five wash bays and ample space for drying, waxing, and detailing. On most weekends, C.L. worked at the car wash with a special business arrangement with the owner, in which C.L. would be allowed to round-up his own car-washing business from *Car-Splash* customers who did not want to wash their own cars. In return, C.L. agreed to pay the owner ten percent of his earnings. On a typical Saturday afternoon, C.L. could be seen eagerly going from customer to customer at the car wash, asking if they wanted help in washing, drying, vacuuming, or detailing their vehicles. For washing a sedan, he charged five dollars; for drying, three dollars; for vacuuming, two dollars; for waxing, ten dollars, and for detailing, ten dollars. Customers could order a la carte or the entire car cleaning package for thirty dollars. On most weekends, C.L. easily cleared five-hundred dollars. One day, Billy Wayne brought his pickup truck to *Car-Splash* for a much-needed cleaning to remove caked-on mud, road tar, and dead love bugs splattered across the truck's windshield and grill. After observing C.L.'s industry, entrepreneurial spirit, efficiency, Billy Wayne grew interested in this young black man, who was drenched in sweat but kept up a happy-go-lucky demeanor. Billy Wayne ambled over to C.L. and struck up a conversation with him.

"When can I get this truck clean? It's a mess and I'm willin' to pay extra for you to make it look as good as it runs," said Billy Wayne.

"Boss, you next in line," said C.L.

"Ain't some of these other folks ahead of me," asked Billy Wayne.

"Don't worry 'bout that, boss. I can look at you and tell you a business man. A business man is nearly always in a hurry, drivin' here and there and everywhere in between. You gots places to go and thangs to do. And you can't go places and show the people you a big time business man if you ain't got a clean truck to ride in. So, 'um gonna fix you up with a bright, shiny, pick-um-up truck, and have you on yo way quicker than a monkey can jump through a tree. Time is money and money is time, I always say. So, soon as I get through wipin' the water off this car, you be next. By the way, my name is C.L. Moody," C.L. exclaimed with a beaming smile and a firm handshake.

"Well, C.L, 'um Billy Wayne Sharp. And 'um pleased to make yo acquaintance. Listen here, C.L. I've been watchin' you for the past half-hour. You are a pretty smart boy, and you don't mind makin' a little sweat in order to make a little money. I like that in a man, specially a colored man, who don't feed at the trough of the gubment, and is willin' to make money by the sweat of his brow," said Billy Wayne.

C.L. continued to wipe away beads of water from a station wagon that had been transformed into a show-room caliber car, after being delivered to C.L. with several layers of red clay mud covering nearly every inch of it. The owner would be returning later to pick up the vehicle, which was expected, given the sheer volume of cars in the queue.

"Mr. Sharp, suh, you and I is on the same page. I ain't never took no gubment handout, no welfare, no food stamps, and not even no gubment commodity cheese. People who take stuff like that just want to, like you said, feed at the trough where they can get stuff for free and don't have to break a sweat. I been workin' all my life. And I don't cotton to people, specially, my own people, who ain't willin' to put in a honest to goodness day's work for some honest to goodness money," exclaimed C.L. as he continued to move about in quick, hurried motions, never stopping long enough to wipe away the sweat that was pouring down his constantly smiling face.

Like all bigots, C.L. had a tendency to judge an entire group of people based on the behavior of a few. But for C.L., it went far beyond the regular, garden variety bigotry in which many people blithely engage, often with no serious consequences. C.L.'s variety of bigotry involved very serious consequences, mainly for himself. By so doggedly clinging to such a deep-seeded hatred of black people, he was actually engaging in a critical stage of racial identity development—self-hatred, because to hate black people was to actually hate himself. And as much as he hated black people and sought to distance himself from them, in reality—not in his fantasy—he was no better, no different, and no more immune to racial bigotry than any other black person in Sharpville, Mississippi. Although, he never talked about it openly, C.L. genuinely loathed black people primarily because it was a group of black men that killed his father.

"And another thang, and 'um gonna call 'em what they is, I really don't like it when some of the free-loadin', glad-handin' niggers come 'round here wantin' me to give 'em credit for washin' they cars when I know they sorry, no-count asses got money. When they go buy that hooch, they don't ask for no credit. So why the hell they thank 'um gonna give 'em credit for washin' they damn car, the lazy bastards. Hell, I never woulda seen my money if I give 'em credit. And besides, when they do pay, they don't tip worth a damn, the cheap bastards. On a thirty-dollar wash, wax, detail job just this morning, that car was clean enough, inside and out, you could eat a meal on it, and that cheap ass nigger wouldn't tip me but a damn quarter. A goddamn quarter tip for a thirty-dollar job. Can you believe that? Now when folks like you, I mean the decent white folks in town, come 'round for a good car wash, well, y'all tip with a smile and you tip good enough to make me know I done a good job and you 'preciate the job I done, "said C.L. whose facial expression went from dour to elated, as he went from criticizing black customers and praising white ones.

"Cheap and lazy, huh, C.L. I like the way you thank and talk, son. I guess cheap and lazy do go hand in hand together when you thank about it. If you lazy, you probably ain't got a pot to piss in, and if you ain't got a pot to piss in, you more than likely gonna be cheap. Don't hear many coloreds these days talkin' like you talk, C.L.. If mo of 'em thought and talked the way you do, 'um sure yo people would be better off than they are and they wouldn't have to be beholdin' to the gubment for free shit," said Billy Wayne.

"Mr. Billy Wayne, suh, you must be readin' ole C.L.'s mind. They need to git up off they lazy asses and git a damn job. The choice is theys-un. They can live in poverty and cry and complain about segregation and racism all they want. But cryin' and complainin' ain't never put food on my table. Me, myself, I don't cotton to all that talk 'bout racism and race discrimination anyway. As far as 'um concerned, white folks is been good to me, and I don't see no reason to be mad at none of 'em. Colored people ain't done a damn thang to help me git where I am today. It's been the white people that help me git to where 'um at today. Now, them coloreds that got kilt or beat up over that mess, that civil rights mess, well, they brought it on themselves, I say. Don't git me wrong. I don't want to see nobody get killed, but when you been warned to stop stirrin' up shit, and you don't, well all I gotta say is you got to expect the consequences. They brought on theyselves. They need to look at me. I learned a long time ago how to stay in my place, and show proper respect to the people who in power and who got what 'um tryin' to get—mo money, mo money, mo money," said C.L., with a loud laugh and several slaps to his knee.

"C.L., I got plans for you, boy. I want you to come by and see me tomorrow. I thank I can put you to work in my enterprise and you gonna be real good for that enterprise. You got two thangs that I look for in a man. One, you got the right attitude 'bout the white race and the colored race. And two, you believe in makin' money and makin' it the old fashion way, like the commercial say. You earn it. I need somebody to manage some stores of mine and do some errands for me. I needs somebody I can trust like a brother, who ain't gonna try to steal from me or try to thank he is better than me. I thank you fit the bill, C.L. Here is my phone number, call me Monday, and let's talk some mo. I thank you gonna be happy with what 'um gonna offer you. If you take me up on the offer, I thank you can stop washin' cars after today, C.L.," said Billy Wayne as he walked away so that C.L. could start cleaning his car.

Over the next ten years, C.L. earned his place among Billy Wayne's closest friends by gleefully and unhesitatingly doing whatever Billy Wayne asked of him. He put C.L. on his payroll to perform a variety of jobs, including managing Billy Wayne's convenience/liquor store, gasoline stations and running errands. Using his influence with the sheriff, Billy Wayne managed to convince the sheriff to hire C.L. part-time as a deputy sheriff, although C.L. had no law enforcement experience. The official reason for the request/demand was that Billy Wayne thought that hiring C.L. would be helpful for the sheriff in his efforts to placate United States Justice Department, which had initiated an investigation into allegations of racial discrimination in the hiring practices in the Henderson County Sheriff's

Department. The unofficial reason for Billy Wayne wanting C.L. to be hired as a deputy sheriff was to ensure Billy Wayne insider access to information regarding any investigations of his operations that might be planned or executed. As much as C.L. meant to Billy Wayne, personally and professionally, Billy Wayne never allowed him to join the inner sanctum of his white friends, not because he did not trust C.L. He trusted C.L. with his money, his secrets, and regarded him as a close confidant. But being a member of Billy Wayne's inner sanctum was out of the question. The fact that C.L. Moody was born with black skin automatically eliminated any chance of that ever happening.

CHAPTER 4

ONE OF BILLY Wayne's official and legitimate business interests was a hardware superstore that sold every building and construction-related product from electrical gadgets to brick, mortar and lumber. His other legitimate business was Sharpville's only construction company, which was always the lone bidder on every new residential and business development in Sharpville and in other neighboring towns. A very smart, resourceful, and opportunistic businessman, Billy Wayne never went to college, owing to his volunteering for active duty in WWII. After the war, he decided that he would not take advantage of the GI Bill to earn a college degree. He believed that the many life and death experiences he had while serving in Europe and North Africa, more than sufficiently prepared him for life.

Billy Wayne went into the hardware and construction business with his boyhood friend, business partner, and army buddy, Marvin Lee Creel. They spent many hours as friends and army buddies making plans for life after the war. Neither wanted to work for someone else, nor did they want to waste time going to college when they could be earning real money. Their plans were generally pie-in-the-sky types, such as being owners of a world-class amusement park that would rival Disney World and Disney Land. Other plans were more down-to-earth, such as opening a car-wash or a washateria. But they knew down-to-earth businesses would not provide the level of income and status that matched their dreams and egos. So, they pushed each other to dream bigger, take greater risks, and to take on an air of invincibility and confidence that they hoped would impress bankers and other lenders to invest in their dreams and egos. And they did. They blended their down-to-earth plans with the pie-in-the-sky plans and along with the GI Bill and bank loans, they purchased two bankrupt businesses for five percent of their value at an IRS auction. After typical growing pains for a new business, both businesses began to turn a decent profit. But Billy Wayne wanted more than decent, and Marvin Lee was satisfied with decent, which was the source of growing tension between the two longtime friends and nascent business partners. In one of their more recent conversations, Billy Wayne exploded into a diatribe about the weaknesses in Marvin Lee's zest for the big times.

"Marvin Lee, boy, you just don't seem to be willin' to dream big no mo, boy. Looks like you gonna be as pleased as pig in mud with what we done so far with our businesses. But I got to tell, boy, I ain't a damn bit pleased with stoppin' here. Oh, hell naw. I got big dreams and apparently you don't. It's like I want to own the Taj Mahal and you're willin' to settle for a fuckin' Dairy Queen," said a drunken Billy Wayne at one of their business meetings at Shorty's Bar and Saloon.

By the time the meeting commenced, Billy Wayne had already downed several well drinks and half a six-pack of Pabst. Marvin Lee's consumption of libations nearly matched that of Billy Wayne's, minus the well drinks. Marvin Lee was a beer connoisseur and did not have a taste for any other alcoholic beverage. He consumed the other half of the six-pack of Pabst.

"Now, wait just a goddam minute, Billy. Ain't gonna take no shit like that from you. First, you ain't my damn daddy and second, you ain't my damn boss man. I worked just as hard as you to get what we got. And as far as I'm concerned, I intend to enjoy what I done earned. To hell with bustin' my balls just to have a few more thangs than the next fella. Hell, you can't take all that shit with you any way when you dead and gone. Guess what? Despite all the shit you gonna own, when you are six feet under, you just gonna be worm food, just like the poorest son-of-a-bitch in the cemetery. And let me ask you this, Billy Wayne. Ever see a hearse pullin' a fuckin' U-Haul? Hell naw you ain't and guess what, Billy Boy, you ain't gonna never see it. So, if you call it settlin' to want enjoy the fruits of my labor, then god-damit, color my ass s-e-t-t-l-e-d. 'Cause I intend to let my money work for me and be thankful that I got my senses about me to be able to enjoy all them thangs. So, you can run your ass raggedy if you want to, you gonna end up in the intensive care, runnin' 'round tryin' to be all high and mighty. So, heed my word, boy. Take what we got. Enjoy it. Leave some for somebody else. You can't have it all," said Marvin Lee Creel with a pointed index finger an inch from Billy Wayne's crimson-red face.

The argument ended with Billy Wayne storming out of Shorty's. But before he left, he issued an ominous warning to his friend.

"You gonna regret all that shit you just said, boy. Let's just see who's gonna be the last man standin'. You or me? I'm bet-tin' on me," said a red-faced Billy Wayne as he yanked Shorty's door knob so hard that it tumbled to the floor and shattered into about fifteen pieces.

Billy Wayne knew that as long as he was tethered to Marvin Lee as a business partner, he would not be able to realize his ulti-mate dream of being not only a wealthy man, but just as impor-tant, the most notable and feared power and influence broker in the South, without peer or rival.

*

Late one night, while returning home from a business trip to

Jackson, Marvin Lee was in a very good mood as he drove down a quiet, well-maintained, two-lane highway that was not his regular route when traveling between Jackson and Sharpville. He decided to take the less traveled road so that he could enjoy the solitude and avoid the rush of traffic that he would have encountered on the main highway. He was driving his brand new four-door, black C-Class Mercedes Benz—and the quieter highway that he was traveling afforded him the opportunity to better appreciate the amenities that the vehicle offered. Driving on a quiet, uncongested highway rather than on a noisy, jam-packed one seemed like a good idea at the time. Like a proud papa, Marvin Lee gave his Benz exceptional TLC, and treated it with the care and attention befitting a $65,000 automobile. He made sure that it was free of bugs, dirt, bird droppings, tree sap, and road tar, especially when he was on a business trip. He wanted to impress prospective clients and associates with his taste in automobiles and his attention to cleanliness and safety. So, in addition to maintaining a show-room look for the Benz, he made sure that all warranty services and repairs were up to date.

While traveling south on State Highway 27 on that fate-ful evening, with his cruise control set at the legal speed limit of sixty-five, he took a moment to indulge his ego. First, he reminded himself how pleased he was with his purchase of the Benz. Before the purchase of the Benz, he drove a 1966 Ford Station Wagon that tallied 240,000 miles on the odometer before it was sold to a junkyard for parts. In those moments of self-indulgence, he delighted himself with canyon-wide smiles as he deeply inhaled the new-car aroma that emanated from the wood-grain and black leather interior of his luxury vehicle. He noted the lack of road noise and the quiet sound of the Benz's engine. His Ford Station Wagon always announced its arrival two blocks ahead of its destination and seemed to be in regular need of new shock absorbers or a muffler. He dazzled himself even more as he glanced alternately between the dark, curvy, two-lane road and the fancy, aqua blue, instrument panel that was impressively populated with an array of icons that informed him of various and sundry information, from how much air pressure was in his tires to how fast the engine was running. The quietness of his thoughts was accompanied by an overwhelming urge to reflect on his accomplishments. He had finally made it. The sky was his limit. Nobody could run his life anymore. He was driving a fricking Mercedes Benz!!!

His second moment of self-indulgence was accompanied by a smile that reflected self-gratification of having just consummated a deal with a vendor in Jackson that would save his and Billy Wayne's companies tens of thousands of dollars. For a brief moment, he allowed himself to imagine that Billy Wayne would be pleased with him—and all doubts about the fledgling business partnership would disappear like smoke from the end of one Billy Wayne's cigars.

His final act of self-indulgence took the form of pure selfish enjoyment of good music. Adding to his good mood and sanguinity were the smooth, iconic tunes of his favorite singer, Frank Sinatra. Hit songs from *Frank Sinatra's Greatest Hits* album soothingly and relaxingly sounded through the Quadraphonic Bose surround sound speakers that made it sound as though Ole Blue Eyes was sitting right there next to him, behind him, and in front of him, all at the same time. That was the moment when he could appreciate even more all the hard work, sacrifices, and nagging doubts that had characterized his business partnership with his Army buddy and childhood friend, Billy Wayne Sharp. He never imagined he would ever own a luxury car, let alone a Class C Mercedes Benz. And not only was he driving a fancy car and enjoying the intrusion of the new car smell into his nostrils, but he was also being entertained by the greatest crooner of all time. The sounds of Sinatra were like the proverbial cherry on top of a sweet and delicious chocolate sundae. *I Did it My Way, Strangers in the Night* and *It was a Very Good Year* were Marvin Lee's all-time Sinatra favorites. He had memorized every lyric to Sinatra's signature song, *I Did it My Way*, and sang it out loud and off key, at least off the key in which Sinatra was singing. That song, more than any other of his songs, captured not only the prophesy of the present moment for Marvin Lee, but it also summed up his entire life:

And now, the end is near
And so I face the final curtain
My friend, I'll say it clear
I'll state my case, of which I'm certain

I've lived a life that's full
I traveled each and every highway
And more, much more than this
I did it my way

Regrets, I've had a few
But then again, too few to mention
I did what I had to do
And saw it through without exemption

I planned each charted course
Each careful step along the byway
And more, much more than this
I did it my way

Yes, there were times, I'm sure you knew
When I bit off more than I could chew
But through it all, when there was doubt

I ate it up and spit it out
I faced it all and I stood tall
And did it my way

I've loved, I've laughed and cried
I've had my fill, my share of losing
And now, as tears subside
I find it all so amusing to think I did all that

And may I say, not in a shy way
Oh, no, oh, no, not me, I did it my way

For what is a man, what has he got?
If not himself, then he has not
To say the things he truly feels
And not the words of one who kneels

The record shows I took the blows
And did it my way
Yes, it was my way

Lucky for Marvin Lee each of the three songs were in queue in that order, so he did not have to bother fast forwarding or rewinding the tape in order to hear them. When the last of the trio of hits was played, they looped and replayed in the same order for half of the ninety-minute trip to Sharpville.

The Crooner's greatest hits would have played for the entire ninety minutes had something unexpected not happened at the mid-way point in his journey back home. With *I Did it My Way* blaring through the speakers and the lyrics dripping from his lips, he approached a traffic light that was changing from yellow to red. He instinctively placed his right foot above the brake pedal in preparation for a normal stop. In the next moment, his instincts moved him to apply enough normal pressure on the brake pedal to cause the vehicle to come to a gradual and routine stop. But instead of the gradual decrease in speed that he expected when he applied pressure to the brake, the car maintained its cruise-control speed of sixty-five miles per hour. Immediately, panic began to set in. He pumped the brake pedal harder and harder, in rapid succession, desperately trying to activate the Benz's normally reliable hydraulics braking system.

"Oh, my God! Please, Jesus! This is not happening! Please, God. Oh, please God, no. Don't let this happen," shouted Marvin Lee to his Creator.

As he was pleading with God for divine intercession, a series of long forgotten but familiar images from World War II battlefields flashed before him like a graphic three-dimensional movie. He saw wounded, dying, and dead soldiers being transported on stretchers to red-crossed Medics' tents. He saw and smelled smoke coming from the end of Thompson machine guns, which were being rapidly and mercilessly fired into the bodies of enemy combatants—enemy combatants who he now unexpectedly and compassionately saw not as combatants, but as husbands, fathers, brothers, uncles, and grandsons. He saw dark, bellowing smoke gushing from bombed-out apartment buildings. He saw hungry gypsies begging for food. And the very last image that passed before him was an ethereal, floating, pale, outstretched hand that was adorned with his dead mother's silver-plated wedding ring.

He leaned forward slightly in his seat, restrained by the safety-triggered tautness of his seat belt, and continued pumping the brakes faster and faster, applying more and more pressure to the unresponsive braking mechanism. But still no change in speed. He glanced at the speedometer, and it still registered the same sixty-five miles per hour that he had been driving before he started to brake. About fifty yards ahead of him, he could see cars and trucks moving through the intersection, their vulnerable occupants unaware of the impending calamity. He began blaring his car horn in a desperate, dead-man-driving manner to warn drivers that he would not be able to stop. He yelled at them to move, to stop, to turn—anything to make the inevitable avoidable. He knew, viscerally, that his yelling was only an instinctive exercise in futility and nothing more than a natural reaction to what was about to happen. There was no pretense that anyone would hear his desperate warnings, let alone heed them. As he entered the intersection, he swerved to avoid colliding with a gasoline-filled tanker truck. As he did, he closed his eyes, exhaled deeply, leaned back in the seat and focused only on the outstretched ringed hand. The combined effect of the unrestrained speed and the sudden, sharp swerve was final and fierce.

The melodious sounds of the Crooner singing *I Did It My Way* were replaced by the screeching sounds of a fast moving, 1,500 pound metal and glass object colliding with a one ton stationary concrete object that served as an abutment to a bridge that was recently repaired. At that moment, the natural world invoked Newton's Laws of Physics and Einstein's Law of Relativity. The graphic, tragic results were evident—just as Sir Isaac Newton and Dr. Albert Einstein had long predicted. Thirty yards beyond the intersection laid the results of those two laws of nature. *An object at rest tends to remain at rest. A moving object will continue to move until another object causes it to stop. For every action, there is an equal and opposite reaction.* A once fully assembled, completely operational, luxury vehicle was now like scattered pieces of a complex, oversized, jigsaw puzzle. The front seats were no longer in the front of the car. The steering column was no longer in the same location where the assembly worker placed it. The car's eight-cylinder engine rested atop the rear seats. The new car smell was replaced with the smell of burning leather, burning rubber and burning flesh. Marvin Lee Creel, age thirty-seven, died at the scene.

Investigators from the insurance company and the state police initiated an investigation into the car crash and immediately became suspicious of foul play in the crash of Marvin Lee's that was found to have no brake fluid. Not long after the investigation started, it ended, with the official cause of death being trauma to the head caused by a collision with a bridge abutment. No one was ever arrested or indicted in the mysterious crash of Marvin Lee Creel's car, although his family continued to suspect foul play. Billy Wayne secretly carried a life insurance policy on his business partner along with a business insurance policy on both businesses. Following the death of Marvin Lee Creel, Billy Wayne received a windfall in excess of ten million dollars, all free of taxes and attorneys' fees. Adding more value to that ten million dollar windfall profit, the insurance policies contained riders and provisions that paid off all creditors. With no debt and no partner, Billy Wayne poured his newfound wealth into miraculously resuscitating both businesses, which routinely had a combined annual net profit of twenty-five to thirty million dollars. As a business owner, he has received several citations and recognitions from local and state chambers of commerce for his success in not only reviving two struggling and bankrupt businesses, but also for transforming those businesses into shining examples of individual initiative and replicable testaments to the power and promise of the free enterprise system.

From real estate, construction, car dealerships, and funeral services to gambling, brothels and adult videos, Billy Wayne and his associates created and profited from both legitimate and illicit businesses. All of their business activities, particularly those of questionable legitimacy, integrity, and virtue, were set up for the sheer sport and hedonistic enjoyment of them. Considerations regarding the propriety of engaging in such questionable businesses or the fear of being caught never crossed their minds. Local law enforcement heads were in Billy Wayne's clan's collective back pockets and provided whatever protection and cover they commanded to conduct their business.

*

But even more important than any of these sources of motivation for doing what they did, legitimate or otherwise, was their enduring and single-minded Messianic complex born out of a fundamental belief that God made white men smarter than anyone else. The extension of that logic convinced them that white men (at least wealthy ones) were more entitled than anyone else to life's blessings—health, wealth, and wisdom, as proclaimed in the Benjamin Franklin proverb in Poor Richard's Almanac's, regarding the rewards of going to bed early and rising early. To a man, they preached and practiced the time-honored Jim Crow arithmetic belief that *white + male + wealth = power*. In their world, that was the natural order of things, eternally and divinely mandated by the Lord Himself. Given the fact that no one had ever successfully challenged that arithmetic social equation in Sharpville, and the fact that the results of such an equation had always worked to their benefit, as far as Billy Wayne and his associates were concerned, the equation had become an irrefutable, unalterable truth. And of course, ample evidence existed in and around Sharpville, including scores of living and dead bodies that proved to their collective satisfaction that power could only be preserved if they were ruthless and callous enough to cause uncooperative and obstinate people to willingly or unwillingly submit to their will. And in the process, they succeeded in perpetuating their own self-serving interpretation of God's intentions for humankind, which, in their view, was based on the natural superiority of white people and on God's division of the world into permanent and hierarchical racial, social, and economic strata. They gladly and unabashedly espoused their views on race and religion with one another and with anyone else gullible enough to believe that God endorses white supremacy and racial segregation.

*

Billy Wayne was married to Margaret Golightly, a life-long Sharpville resident and an only child. She was adopted by Sherry and Sonny Golightly when Margaret was two years old. Her biological parents were fatally injured in a fiery car crash while on vacation in New Orleans, and she was placed in foster care with Sherry and Sonny. Desperately wanting children and unable to have any, they quickly bonded with little Margaret, and immediately filed for adoption.

Margaret was a natural red-head with the usual assortment of freckles that normally populates the faces of most red-heads. A dimpled chin, unpierced ears, and a wrinkle-free brow framed her thin face, narrow nose, and perfectly aligned pearl white teeth. Her body was thin but proportional. In stocking feet, she stood five feet, three inches tall, and for most of her adult life, her bath scale consistently listed her weight between 125 and 130 pounds.

Margaret and Billy Wayne were joined-at-the-hips sweethearts in high school and never dated anyone else. Unlike her academically challenged boyfriend, Margaret was very studious and made excellent grades throughout high school. She was a member of the marching band and captain of the debate team. In her senior year, she was voted most likely to succeed and most popular. In addition, she was selected by the senior class to deliver the graduation speech, which she carried off flawlessly. Her grades were good enough to receive full-ride scholarship offers from Agnes Scott College, Wesleyan College, and Mississippi College for Women.

She visited all three Southern campuses and was equally

impressed with each of the prestigious women's colleges. In the end, however, she decided to leave Mississippi and venture two states to the east and attend Agnes Scott College located in the Atlanta, Georgia suburb of Decatur. It was a distressing decision for someone who had lived her entire life, literally, inside a three-mile radius of a small, predominantly white Southern town—and symbolically inside a socially and culturally encapsulated bubble. Her little bubble possessed natural properties that repelled any and all progressive thoughts, whether they emanated from the inside or the outside. And now she was about to leave her old familiar town for a new life in a new town with new people, away from the "bubble" and away from the people who knew her, loved her, and supported her. Nevertheless, her heart, mind, and her parents agreed that Agnes Scott College was the best choice, although either of the other two colleges would have been equally acceptable.

After returning from her visit to Agnes Scott College, Margaret was all ready to become a Scottie and experience life outside of Sharpville, Mississippi for the first time. Intellectually, she understood that life in Decatur and Atlanta would be very different than life in Henderson County and Sharpville. She had the normal anxieties and uncertainties that any new college freshman would have: How would she like her roommate? Was she really good enough to compete academically with students from other parts of the country? Would other girls like her? Although serious questions, they were not enough to deter a determined Margaret Golightly from taking the biggest leap of faith she had ever taken in her life. Soon, she would be a college student, the first in her family and one of a just a few from Sharpville High School.

At least that was *her* plan. Billy Wayne Sharp had a different plan. Like the fisherman who was determined not to let the big one get away, Billy Wayne was determined that not only the big one, but the only one, in the form of Margaret Golightly, was not going get away from him.

As she was sitting on her front porch in the green and white metal glider swing and sipping a glass of iced tea late one summer evening, just two days before she was to leave for Decatur, she encountered something totally unexpected that would change her life forever. With the booming, reverberating, and grating sound of a broken muffler announcing his arrival, Billy Wayne pulled up to Margaret's house. The booming sound of the broken muffler and the ear-piercing, metal-on-metal squealing emitted from his brakes competed with one another in a winner take all match of escalating decibel levels. The objective observer would have called it a draw.

He shut off the engine, mercifully bringing to an end the war of competing grating automobile sounds. Pocketing the keys, he hastily ejected himself from his undersized, sky-blue, two-door Ford Comet, ran full speed to Margaret's front porch. With giant sweat beads cascading down his smiling, fat, crimson face, he dropped to one knee in front of a stunned and flummoxed Margaret. He reached out and took her smooth, tiny left hand with both of his huge calloused hands.

"Margaret, I'm fixing to go off to war, and I don't want to wait 'til I get back, if I get back at all to start a life with the only woman I have ever loved. Besides, I'm scared that if you go off to college way over in Georgia, and I go off to war in Europe or wherever they gonna send me, well, you just might forget about me and find a new boyfriend. And that would just break my heart into a million little bitty pieces. So, as far as I'm concerned there ain't but two thangs to do. Marry me, Margaret, and forget going to college," said Billy Wayne as he awkwardly and unsteadily slipped the sterling silver three-quarter carat white diamond halo ring onto her finger.

Before he could complete the obviously rehearsed proposal

speech, she placed a hand over her mouth, gasped, and sob-bingly said, "Yes, Billy Wayne, I will marry you. Yes! Yes! Yes! College can wait. Marrying the only man I ever loved and ever will love can't wait. I can go to college anytime or not all. There's only one man who can make me happy, and Billy Wayne Sharp, that is you, you big knuckle head. Plus, I don't want to rue the day I missed out on this chance to be the woman and wife that I always imagined I would be, Billy Wayne. You might not believe this, but I have been praying and writing in my diary for weeks now that you would ask me to marry you. And the Lord told me if you ask, not to hesitate in saying yes. So, sweetie, I'm ready, whenever you are ready to tie this knot, which I can promise you will never be untied, no matter where you are, no matter what you have to do as a soldier, and no matter what you do when you come back from the war. I'm gonna be right here in Sharpville waiting for you, as your wife, not your girlfriend over in Georgia," said Margaret as she retrieved her ringed hand from Billy Wayne and admired the ring's flawless design and polished glaze.

So, the brightest, the most popular, and the most likely to succeed high school student in the Sharpville High School Class of 1942 abandoned her dreams of becoming a college student, college graduate, and eventually a successful writer, and instead embraced her unexpected but welcomed fate of becoming Mrs. Billy Wayne Sharp. In the ensuing years, she played the role of devoted and subservient spouse of Sharpville's most distin-guished citizen. She had no regrets at all about her decision to forgo her chances of being a college graduate and maybe an acclaimed writer for a big magazine or newspaper. On balance, life treated Margaret Sharp with kindness and fairness. She understood the responsibilities and expectations of being mar-ried to Billy Wayne Sharp, and in her own way, she carried out those responsibilities faultlessly. In doing so, she intentionally chose a low-key approach to being Mrs. Billy Wayne Sharp. She quietly provided generous financial support for her favorite charities—the local community fund drive and the local animal shelter. She did not belong to any social clubs. To keep her writing skills sharp, she anonymously wrote a weekly advice column under the pseudo name and title, *Adeline's Bylines*, for the local newspaper. Unlike her husband, she shunned the limelight, preferring to let her good works speak for themselves.

Better than anyone else, Margaret knew Billy Wayne's foibles and assets. She has seen the compassionate, sensitive, tender Billy Wayne, and she has seen the hopelessly bedeviled Billy Wayne. She has seen him uncontrollably weep after accidently running over a cat crossing an unlit street at night with five kittens in tow. She was there as he wiped tears from his eyes when he first saw the movie, *Fried Green Tomatoes* at the local cinema. As soon as it became available, he purchased the VHS version of the movie and watched it regularly—and just as regularly, he choked up at Ruth's funeral and when Buddy died in the train accident. However, he reveled in the scene in which black customers were forced to take their food out back at the Whistle Stop Café. Margaret has also heard him yell in deep anger at the television when Harry Truman defeated Thomas Dewey for president in 1948. She saw his equally incensed reaction, the same year, when The United States Supreme Court ruled that religious instruction in public schools was unconstitutional. She knew about his bad temper, moodiness, racism, etc. She put up with them but did not patiently entertain or condone them. In Margaret's presence, Billy Wayne exhibited a markedly different personality from the one his close friends and business associates experienced or witnessed. His personality differences were not unlike those of Dr. Jekyll and Mr. Hyde, an evil, dark side, which surfaced when he interacted with friends and business associates and the gentle, compassionate side, which only emerged when he was in the presence of Margaret. In all of their time as boyfriend and girlfriend and as husband and wife, Billy Wayne never raised his voice to her and never directed any of his profanity-laced invectives toward her. When they were together, in public or in private, he treated her like she was *his* queen. He lovingly held her hand in public, took her on date nights, and sent her a fresh flower every week. When they were together, she, indeed, felt like his queen—loved, adored, and honored. Although disappointed that she was unable to bear him an heir, Billy Wayne never wavered in his love for and devotion to his life partner and his darling *Pooky Pie*. She was his refuge and someone who understood him and did not judge him. Whenever he was having a bad day, Margaret had a way of calming Billy Wayne down with a smile, a neck massage, a word of wisdom, or just an unconditional, non-judgmental listening ear. Without her, Billy Wayne undoubtedly would have died of a stroke or heart attack years ago.

There were two pivotal and poignant moments in their lives that illustrated the depth of their devotion to one another. One occurred about twelve years into the marriage when Billy Wayne experienced severe chest pains while getting dressed for church.

"Pooky Pie, I thank I need some Alka-Seltzer. I got this burnin' in my chest. Must be indigestion or heartburn or some-thin' from eatin' that all that rich I-talian food last night. 'Cause it hurts real bad," said Billy Wayne as he lowered himself onto the edge of the bed and laid prostrate on his back.

"Billy Wayne, are you feeling dizzy or nauseous at all, honey," Margaret asked in a tone voice that revealed concern, but not alarm.

"Naw, Pooky, I don't feel sick at my stomach or nothin' like that. The room looks like it spinnin' a little bit, though. I thank if I just had a coupla of them Alka-Seltzers and when they make me belch, I oughta be all right. I don't want you gittin' yoself upset. If you be kind enough to git 'em for me, I thank I'll start feelin' better, and we can go on to church," Billy said as he attempted to raise himself to a sitting position.

Although he was diagnosing his pain as heartburn, neither he nor Margaret was not at all sure that it was not a heart attack.

"Now, Billy Wayne, you don't know that this is heartburn or indigestion. You are not a doctor and you don't play one on television, so stop trying to diagnose what's wrong with you. We gonna get you to the hospital and let the real doctors figure out what's wrong with you, Billy Wayne. It might be heart burn or it might be something more serious. Maybe a few of those loud, smelly, farts of yours might make you feel a little better, too. But just in case you ain't quite ready to cut some cheese or if these Alka-Seltzers don't do the trick, we are going to get you to the hospital. We need to make sure your ticker is ticking the way it should," Margaret said as she dialed the 9-1-1 operator and tried to relax Billy Wayne with a smidgen of humor, although she was scared to death, and she knew Billy Wayne was too.

Margaret's well-intentioned attempt to relax Billy Wayne with a bit of humor failed miserably. The thought of possibly having a heart attack and dying was too much for him. With tears flowing down his face, Billy Wayne stood, hugged Margaret and began sobbing like a baby with colic.

"Pooky, I don't wanna die. I can't. I can't leave you. Not now. I can't go befo' you. Please, God, don't let me die. I can't go first. Lord, I just can't. Pooky, just hold me. Tell me um gonna be all right. I love you so much," cried Billy Wayne.

Margaret spoke to the 9-1-1 operator and simultaneously returned Billy's embrace. The ambulance would arrive in about five minutes, the emergency operator promised.

"Billy Wayne, sweetheart, I'm right here. You are not going to die. You are going to be okay once we get you to the hospital where they can find out what's wrong and fix it," Margaret said with her head pressed against his chest as she prayed aloud.

"Please, Lord, don't take this man away from me. He is my life, my heart, and the love of my life. Just look over him, dear Lord, and keep him. Keep him in your everlasting arms. Heal him. Heal whatever is wrong with him. I know you made the blind man see and the cripple man walk. Noting is too big for you and nothing is impossible when we turn it over to you. And that's what me and Billy Wayne are doing right now, dear Lord. In your name we are both turning him over to you and asking you to just touch him with your healing hand. Whatever is done, it will be your will. You are the Alpha and the Omega. I honor you and humble myself before you in your name. I ask nothing for myself. Just take care of this man, a good God-fearing man, who is not perfect. Only one perfect person ever walked this land, and that is your son Jesus. So, where he and I have fallen short of what you would have us to do and to be and to say, please forgive us, I pray. Where we have upheld your holy name give us the strength and the wisdom to keep doing that. Again, please take care of this man of mine. I need him so much. I pray in your name. Amen," said Margaret.

As it turned out, the chest pains were symptoms of a minor case of Stable Angina, a serious but treatable heart condition. His doctors put him on a regime of Nitroglycerin. In addition, for two months, he received Enhanced External Counterpulsation (EECP) therapy, which helped to improve the flow of oxygen-rich blood to the heart.

The other incident occurred about two years after they were married when Margaret and Billy Wayne met with Margaret's OB/GYN. After trying for months to conceive, Margaret underwent a series of fertility tests to determine why she and Billy Wayne were not successful in combining their egg and sperm to produce a much-desired offspring. Billy Wayne had previously undergone testing with his urologist to determine whether his sperm count could be the reason for them not being able to conceive. As it turned out, his sperm count was not the culprit.

Billy Wayne and Margaret had often talked of having five children. In those hopeful and optimistic moments, they picked out names for each Little Billy Wayne and Little Margaret and imagined teaching them to ride a bike, drive a car, and shoot a gun. They also imagined watching their children's beaming smiles as they opened their toys on Christmas morning. In their imaginings, their sons and daughters married and presented them with a whole slew of happy, healthy, and well-behaved grandchildren. Passing the Sharp gene on to future generations was a high priority for Billy Wayne, even before he proposed to Margaret.

"Good morning, Margaret. And Billy Wayne, I'm glad you came with Margaret today," said a somber Dr. Campanella as he took his seat behind a square shaped oak desk that was a perfect complement to the adjacent pair of book cases stuffed with medical books and journals.

He motioned with his hand to Margaret and Billy Wayne to take the two high-back cushioned chairs directly across from his desk, which were neatly placed in a symmetrically inward position. Margaret lowered herself slowly onto her chair, followed immediately by Billy Wayne onto his.

"Well, Doc, give us the news," Billy Wayne blurted out as he clutched Margaret's hand and repositioned his enormous gluteus maximus close to the edge of the chair.

"Margaret, how do you feel," asked Dr. Campanella.

"Dr. Campanella, I feel just fine. I don't have any complaints. I just want to know why we haven't been able to put one in the oven," answered Margaret with a nervous chuckle.

"Okay, very well, I will get right to it then. First, Margaret, we have established that your inability to conceive is not related to any sperm deficiencies in Billy Wayne. Naturally, we needed to ruled that out because in many, if not most cases, it is the father's infertility that prevents the fertilization process to work. But in your case, Margaret, the tests show that both of your fallopian tubes are blocked, which prevents ovulation, which, in turn, prevents the successful fertilization of the eggs. And when the eggs are not fertilized, as you know, there is no conception," said Dr. Campanella

"Well, can you unblock them," asked Margaret as she leaned forward in her chair.

"Yeah, doc what do we need to do to fix this," asked Billy Wayne after clearing his throat and settling back in his chair.

"Here are three medical options that are normally available in situations like this: Number one. *In vitro* fertilization. But it is not widely used at this time for a variety of reasons including opposition from the Catholic Church and other religious groups and because the medical science and technology are still evolving. Nevertheless, it is an option, and I have used it with patients before. In case you are not familiar with this procedure, let me explain it to you. *In vitro* is a procedure in which we fertilize a number of your eggs with sperm from Billy Wayne in a petri dish in the lab. After a few days, if all goes well, we take the best embryo from the petri dish and inject it into your uterus. If all goes well again, in nine months, you will give birth to a healthy baby. Option number two is surgery, but in cases like yours, surgery will not work. And option number three is a regimen of fertility drugs, but that is not a viable option either because those drugs do not work when both tubes are blocked as yours are," answered Dr. Campanella.

"Wait a minute, doc, in my opinion, you talkin' 'bout do somethin' that goes against nature and against God Almighty when you talk 'bout creatin' life in a frickin' petri dish in a frickin' science lab. Sounds like some Frankenstein shit to me or y'all tryin' to play God," said an angry and disappointed Billy Wayne as he and Margaret thanked the doctor for his time, rose in tandem, and abruptly exited his office, utterly devastated. They soundlessly drove back home, neither knowing exactly what to say or how to say it.

This was not the news Billy Wayne and Margaret were hoping to hear from Dr. Campanella. None of the options they heard from Dr. Campanella offered any hope for them to have children. For religious reasons, they immediately rejected *in vitro* fertilization. The doctor ruled out surgery and drugs as treatment options. They rejected the idea of seeking a second opinion because they were convinced that another doctor would not give them any more hope than Dr. Campanella did—and they did not want to experience that type of angst and anxiety again, ever.

Although they had discussed adoption on several occasions, they both agreed that they were not willing to adopt. They feared that they would not be able to love someone else's flesh and blood as much as they would their own. They convinced themselves that adoption was too risky, given that they were not sure whether they could love an adopted child as much as they could their own. Margaret was thankful that she was adopted as a child, but agreed with Billy Wayne that they should not adopt.

*

That was a critical moment in their marriage. Their hopes and dreams of becoming parents had just been dashed. Margaret, in her sorrow and grief, offered to grant Billy Wayne a divorce so that he could seek out a wife who could give him children.

"Pooky, don't talk like that. I wouldn't let you go for all the gold in Fort Knox. Yes. I'm disappointed that we can't have no young-uns. But, Pooky Pie, living without you for just one day would just about kill me. I married you for better or for worse. And there ain't nothin' under the sun that can ever happen to make me want to divorce you. So, you just get that kinda thankin' out of yo mind and don't ever let me hear you say somethin' like that again. Understand me," said Billy Wayne as he dabbed at his red eyes.

"Billy Wayne, I don't want to ever leave you either. But since I can't give you no kids, maybe you need somebody who can. I love you so much, Billy Wayne. But maybe love alone will not be enough to make you happy. I'm thinking that it will also take some Little Billy Waynes and Little Margarets running around this house to make you truly happy," said Margaret as she wiped away her own tears.

"Margaret Sharp, I am gonna say this for the last time. You are my wife. You will always be my wife. I love you today as much as I loved you the day I got down on my knee and asked your hand in marriage. So, just because we can't have little rugrats runnin' 'round here don't mean I can't stay happy, fat, and be the lucky-as-snake-eyes husband of Margaret Golightly Sharp," said Billy Wayne as they both chuckled.

CHAPTER 5

B ILLY WAYNE WAS born in Sharpville, an only child of poor parents, who barely eked out a living farming fifty acres of fertile land they did not own. Jim Bob and Ella Mae Sharp were sharecroppers on a peanut farm owned by a syndicate headquartered in Ashburn, Georgia. The syndicate also operated a grocery store, gas station, and clothing store on land they owned located adjacent to the land they rented out to the Sharps under a ten-year lease agreement. As in most arrangements between large farming syndicates and poor, uneducated farmers like Jim Bob and Ella Mae, the renters were perpetually in debt to the syndicate from the purchases they made at company-owned gas, grocery, and clothing stores. Instead of cash transactions, the purchases were made on credit, at interest rates that fluctuated between twenty-five and thirty percent. At the end of the planting and harvesting season, the money owed to the syndicate far exceeded the money the Sharps were able to earn from selling peanuts at roadside stands and at the state fair. At least seventy-five percent of the harvested peanuts was shipped to Ashburn for sale by the syndicate, and the rest remained with the Sharps as payment for their work on the farm. From the sale of their own peanuts, the Sharps had to use their paltry profits to pay rent and to provide for the basic necessities, which, of course, forced them to continue their reliance on credit in order to keep their family fed and clothed. As far as the syndicate was concerned, such an arrangement worked well and epitomized the best of the free enterprise system. They earned a profit from the peanuts shipped to them by the Sharps. They earned the monthly rent charges from the Sharps for living on the land. And they earned money from the interest they charged the Sharps for the food, gas, and clothes they purchased from their stores. For the Sharps, however, such an arrangement meant that they were nothing more than indentured servants with few options for escaping their servitude. Actually, they were more like slaves, and the only thing that distinguished them from slaves was the color of their skin. Yet, Jim Bob and Ella Mae held deep hatred and resentment toward all black people, and they passed that hatred on to their only child, Billy Wayne. They succumbed to that seemingly innate human malady in which individuals situated on one of the lowest rung of the socio-economic ladder, in order to elevate their own status, look down upon and resent individuals and groups in similarly situated positions. For their entire lives, the Sharps had been looked down upon by individuals at higher levels of socio-economic status. In return, they sought out others upon who they could look down in a futile attempt to elevate their actual socio-economic status. It did, however, help them to rationalize their own poverty and to justify their hatred toward black people. On trips to town to sale peanuts, Billy Wayne noticed that his clothes and general well-being were no better and in some cases worse off than those of some black residents. As a result, it became easy for Billy Wayne and his parents to identify the scapegoats for their own poverty, the people who were the deserving objects of their racial animus—those people! Those people, with their black skin living as though they thought they were as good as white people. Those people who were making money that his family should be making. Those people who looked so disgusting that they were like roaches that needed to be exterminated before their numbers got out of hand. Billy Wayne's daddy had warned him that black people were like that, and that somebody needed to bring the whole lot of them down a few pegs. He told Billy Wayne that it would be up to him and his generation to pick of the torch of their fore bearers and work to keep the white race pure, black people in their places, and to be prepared for the second coming of the Lord and the second rising of the South.

Growing tired of being poor and growing in his hatred of black people, Billy Wayne made three solemn vows to himself and to his parents. One, he vowed that when he became an adult, he would never work for someone else. He witnessed firsthand how poor people could be manipulated, exploited, and bent to the whim and pleasure of the powerful and the wealthy. He took note of how easily it was done, and vowed that one day he would use those wealthy exploiters and manipulators as role models and examples of how to make others make money for him. He saw the downside and the upside of working for someone else. The downside was that you made money for someone else. The upside was that you made money for someone else. As the son of a poor peanut farmer, he had learned that being the recipient and beneficiary of someone else's labor, was preferable to being the provider of labor to make someone else wealthy. That led to the second vow, to become very wealthy. He reasoned that he had tried poverty and did not like it. Why not give rich an opportunity to make him happy? He knew it would take time to achieve his goal of becoming wealthy, but if being a peanut farmer had taught him anything, it was patience. So, he bided his time, steeled his resolve, and prepared himself for the responsibilities and rewards that are part and parcel of being wealthy.

The third vow was that he would forever make all black people objects of his hatred, ire, and resentment. He never saw the similarities in his family financial predicament and that of his black neighbors. He saw only skin color and not the common economic conditions he shared with poor black people. But Jim Bob Sharp pointed out to Billy Wayne as often as he could that the Good Book said that black people were meant to be servants and slaves, and therefore poor. The fact that he and his family were poor was an anomaly that would be corrected in due time. Besides, whatever black people possessed, they must have stolen, cheated, or lied to get it, which according to Jim Bob Sharp was their nature. You can never trust one of them any farther than you could throw him. Thus, the Sharp family found itself mired in a spiral of poverty due exclusively to the sharecropping arrangements they had with the peanut syndicate in Georgia. Yet, their hatred of black people blinded them to that simple fact and resulted in the illogical conclusion that if it were not for those ignorant, abhorrent, free-loading black people, somehow, their own lot would be better than it was. Billy Wayne internalized those illogical conclusions, which started his journey into the vile world of racial hatred and white supremacy.

Billy Wayne worked tirelessly most of his life to maintain all three vows, beginning in high school and continuing through his military service and early adulthood to the present time. And for most of his life, they were vows that he was quite successful in keeping. In high school, he ran with a gang of boys that drove through black neighborhoods throwing rotten eggs at pedestrians and shouting racial epithets at them. One of the more sickening pastimes for Billy Wayne and his adolescent friends was to intentionally splash water on elderly black men and women waiting at bus stops as they drove on water puddled streets in search of prey.

In the military, Billy Wayne bonded with a group of fellow Southern racists who held nightly discussions on the state of race relations in the military, sports, and in society at large. During one of their late night, alcohol fueled discussions at an off-base country & western bar, they angrily and loudly expressed their outrage over Brooklyn Dodgers President Branch Rickey's decision to sign Jackie Robinson to a major league contract, a decision that prompted them to swear never to watch another major league baseball game that included Jackie Robinson or any other person of color. Billy Wayne and his like-minded racist brethren in the military became choleric in 1948 when President Truman issued an executive order prohibiting racial discrimination in the military. In their off-duty hours, the group frequently attended meetings of The John Birch Society and occasionally a Ku Klux Klan rally in towns where the two notorious racist organizations had a strong and visible presence.

With one-third of his solemn vows to himself and his parents well advanced, he concentrated on the remaining two— becoming wealthy and never working for someone else. It was in the military where Billy Wayne hatched his plans to keep the remaining vows. He and his pal, Marvin Lee Creel, talked endlessly about their plans to start a business when they both got out of the military. Being a married man with financial obligations to his young bride, Billy Wayne had to work a second job as a bouncer at a local country & western honky tonk to earn additional money for his contributions to his and Marvin's plan for becoming wealthy ex-GIs. Their plan was simple, yet promised great wealth. It would all be legitimate, legal, and as easy as taking candy from a baby. They routinely read in the classified section of the *Sharpville Register* notices of unpaid taxes by several businesses, some of which were in bankruptcy and some delinquent because of economic hardships brought on by the war. Their plan was to pay the delinquent taxes on those businesses, thereby becoming sole owners, provided the regular owners could not pay their taxes within thirty days. They were successful in pulling off a perfectly legal maneuver that would eventually pay huge dividends for at least one of them. Billy

Wayne Sharp could divide, multiply, add and subtract as well as anyone. His thoughts turned more sinister as he reasoned that a whole pie was better than half a pie. So, at the age of twenty-five, Billy Wayne was well on his way to keeping the three vows he made to his parents and to himself, in only half the time he originally thought it would take.

CHAPTER 6

BILLY WAYNE, THE most ruthless, arrogant, blusterous and foul-mouthed among the gathered clan, as he had done for forty years, hosted and presided over that month's assemblage of Sharpville's power elite. As was the practice for the last nine months, they met on the top floor of Billy Wayne's recently remodeled eight-story downtown office complex that bore his name—B.W. Sharp Office Complex. The immaculately designed and constructed suite of thirty-two spacious offices lent an air of cosmopolitanism to a once drab and gray downtown area. Standing twice as tall as the next tallest building, B.W. Sharp Office Complex towered above all other edifices in the three-quarter square mile of a small but growing network of downtown office and commercial buildings.

The presence of B.W. Sharp Office Complex was the catalyst for an ambitious downtown revitalization effort that included a number of new and trendy boutiques, sports bars, restaurants, bistros, and coffee houses. The new establishments had great appeal to local residents and to the growing number of college students who had relied on the revitalized downtown nightlife to ensure them of a night or weekend of fun and entertainment. Judging by the increased presence of both groups in and around downtown Sharpville, especially on weekends and evenings, the revitalization plan was working. Business at shops, stores, and boutiques was thriving, waits at restaurants were long, and city sales taxes were booming—all signs of a healthy business climate in downtown Sharpville.

Billy Wayne earned and deserved credit for the success of most of those businesses. The array of flourishing downtown business establishments directly benefitted from Billy Wayne's vast network of investors and state and federal officials. He arranged low-interest loans, grants, and direct investments from individuals and groups with whom he maintained business and social ties. And in case anyone forgot or did not know that he was singularly responsible for the spectacular transformation of downtown Sharpville, attached to the wall in the main entry way of each downtown business was a ten-inch by fifteen-inch wood plaque extolling the magnanimity of Billy Wayne: *Thanks to Mr. Billy Wayne Sharp for his enormous contributions to making this establishment the success that it is. Your patronage is deeply appreciated—The Management.*

The B.W. Sharp Office Complex owed its magnificence and splendor to its world-renowned designer, Helmut Schmidt, the award winning German-born architect who has designed office and commercial buildings on Wall Street in New York, in Les Halles in Paris, and on Regent Street in London. Using overseas business contacts, Billy Wayne arranged a face-to-face meeting with Schmidt while Schmidt was attending a conference in Atlanta, Georgia. Billy sent his private plane to Atlanta to retrieve Schmidt and provide a night of business and pleasure at the Beau Rivage Casino and Hotel in Biloxi. By the end of the evening, Schmidt had earned an advanced payment of $250,000 from Billy Wayne to indulge his ego by agreeing to design the most spectacular edifice in all of Mississippi. Cost was not an obstacle to Billy Wayne in hiring Schmidt to build the office complex. The advance payment of $250,000 was a mere pittance and just a drop in the bucket for Billy Wayne. After all, the money would not come from his own personal business coffers.

It would come from outside sources, so he knew he was play-ing with house money. The B.W. Sharp Office Complex, and its namesake, owed its principal funding to the state and federal officials with whom Billy Wayne had either direct or indirect relationships. Although a vociferous opponent of federal and state spending on pork projects, he often boasted to his friends and business partners about how his generous campaign con-tributions and many political connections in D.C. and Jackson continue to pay hefty dividends.

The B.W. Sharp Office complex was featured in *Architecture Today* as one of the best designed office buildings in the country. The building's spacious, open air design features a food court, a full service bank, a health spa, a cascading water fountain, sound-proof offices, and an A+ rating from the Environmental Protection Agency for its energy efficiency. Prominently dis-played on the eleven alternately colored red, white, and gray paneled walls in the vestibule of the building was a series of eleven, specially commissioned renderings of six of the Civil War battle scenes in which the Confederacy was victorious and five prominent confederate leaders and generals—The First Battle of Bull Run, The Peninsula Campaigns, The Battle of Chancellorville, The Battle of Harper's Ferry, The Battle of Chickamauga, The Battle of Manassas, Robert E. Lee, Jeff Davis, Stonewall Jackson, J.E.B. Stuart, and Nathan B. Forrest. Each painting was hung underneath wall mounted display lights, flanked by a framed confederate flag and a gold plated sign with the name of each of the eleven members of the Confederate States of America-South Carolina, Mississippi, Florida, Alabama, Georgia, Louisiana, Texas, Virginia, Arkansas, Tennessee, North Carolina, Missouri, Kentucky. Although the latter two did not secede from the Union, each is represented by one of the stars on the Confederate flag.

Billy Wayne was not only the convener of these monthly

gatherings, but he also laid claim to the unofficial title of *god-father of the clan*, by virtue of the fact that he considered himself so and because no one ever dared challenge him for the title. He easily intimidated most folks with his six-foot, five-inch, 295-pound bowling-pin shaped frame, booming base voice, and a perpetual look of pain and discomfort, as though he had been weaned, as a child, on lemons. And without trying, he flawlessly came across as tough as a marine drill sergeant, as ornery as a jackass, and as mean as a nest of stirred up hornets. Among this group, he was the undisputed and unchallenged *Alpha Male*— and he feared no competition for the position from his sequacious associates.

*

Nevertheless, the quietude of the moment in Billy Wayne's conference room was disturbed only by the muzak blaring of *Dixie*, which plays on cue at the top of each hour from inside the grandfather clock. The endearing and familiar equanimity brought on by the specially-arranged rendition of *Dixie* was matched only by the stillness and solemnity each of the town's power brokers displayed as they stood at attention with their right hands across their chests while listening and paying homage to that esteemed signature song of the Jim Crow South. After the last note echoed throughout the conference room, they re-took their well-worn leather seats, which over the years had taken the shape of their uniquely flat or fat butts.

On this particular night, Billy Wayne seemed more subdued and not at all like his usually, chatty, effervescent self. Was it his new anti-depressant or was something weighing heavy on his heart? To his associates gathered with him on this unusually cool and breezy fall evening, one of those two conditions was always the likely explanation for Billy Wayne's fluctuation in mood, which seemed to be quite noticeable and pronounced several times a year. Regardless, Billy Wayne continued with the usual order of the meeting by leading the group's preferred prayer, *Psalms 23*. With bowed heads, the others quickly joined Billy Wayne in reciting the well-known prayer, sounding out a peculiar blend of seven different but indistinguishable Southern drawls. And with an accentuated "Amen", which Billy Wayne blurted out ahead of everyone else, so as to further demonstrate his elevated status among these malevolent minions, the others looked up at Billy Wayne for some clue that might explain his lugubriousness this time—medication or heavy heart? The mystery was solved as the naturally deep crimson-faced Billy Wayne rared back in his roomy, custom-fit, fat-ass chair, exposing his basketball-shaped beer belly as it escaped from underneath his undersized faded black Golden Lions Football golf t-shirt. Reaching inside his brown Swaine, Adeney, Brigg leather attaché case, which was never more than a few feet from him at all times, he retrieved an imported Cuban cigar from his Savinelli cigar case, both gifts from Mississippi Senator Tom Lawson. After carefully licking and wetting the entire length of the illegally imported but masterfully blended and crafted cigar, he applied the fire from his Lawson-provided Savinelli lighter to the blunt end of the cigar, bringing a look of pure delight to his otherwise contorted face. After slowly and expertly exhaling several perfectly shaped smoke rings that conveniently masked the sulpher-like smell of his sometimes uncontrollable flatulence, Billy Wayne revealed his plans for the remainder of the meeting.

CHAPTER 7

"BOYS, WE BEEN together for a lotta years. We done everything we could to follow the path of righteousness that the good Lord laid out for each and every one of us here, and we done a pretty damn good job of taking care of our families, our town, and of course, ourselves. But, we're getting old and sometimes we don't remember things just right. Now, mind you, some things we don't want to remember," announced Billy Wayne.

That true but funny remark loosened everybody a bit as they joined Billy Wayne in a bit of hearty laughter, followed quickly by conspicuous somberness that perfectly matched Billy Wayne's sudden shift in moods.

"Billy Wayne, what you wanna talk about the past for? We got things to do *now*, and didn't we talk about some of that stuff a few months ago? And hell, I can't remember half the things we done before I had my tumor took out anyhow," chimed Dickey "DC" Carter, an attorney and owner of the Sharpville's most profitable real estate agency, referring to his near-death experience five years ago when he had a benign golf-ball size tumor removed from the base of his brain. Although the tumor was benign, the surgery to remove the tumor was not without serious complications. Due to his use of the diet treatment drug, fen-phen, which was unknown to his anesthesiologist, his blood pressure plummeted to a dangerously low level, prompting doctors to initiate emergency procedures during surgery. The complications from the removal of the tumor convinced him to give up fen-phen and to take on a weight reduction regimen that involved the daily consumption of semi-healthy food, except the occasional hit from one of the moon pies tucked away in a plain brown paper sack in his bottom desk drawer. The banana and chocolate sweets were regularly ordered from the Moon Pie Store in Chattanooga, Tennessee. He never had fewer than two twelve-count boxes of both the single decker and double decker varieties. His craving for moon pies overwhelmed him at times, especially when he was under stress. Chomping down a few single or double decker chocolate or banana moon pies had the same effect on him that Xanax has on those who prefer medication over moon pies to relieve stress and anxiety.

DC's experience as a surgical patient at the Henderson General Hospital seemed to be taken straight from the headlines of a supermarket tabloid or from the opening segment of an infamously salacious television talk show. DC had a bona fide out-of-body experience while undergoing the routine but delicate procedure to remove the brain tumor. As he lay prostrate, face down on the surgical table's horseshoe headrest, he could see the doctors and nurses bent over him distributing and retrieving scalpels, forceps, scissors, pincers, gauze, and aspirators that came from and returned to the stainless steel surgical instrument table. He transfixed on the bright LED surgical lights that shone on his prone body. After a long minute, he moved his gaze to the six masked humans, who were uniformly attired in either blue or green surgical scrubs. Like others who have had a similar out of body experiences, DC saw a bright light and an amorphous shaped ethereal body with a silver-colored tether pulling him away from consciousness. He wondered whether the blue and green-attired humans were in fact angels and whether the lights were from a natural aura or from man-made illumination. Like other people in his predicament, DC recalled seeing a bright light or floating, brightly lit orb that lured and led him to cross over. Nevertheless, the din of activity taking place in Operating Room three at Henderson General Hospital caused DC to refocus his gaze on the familiar human form stretched out on the operating table. From his elevated position above the operating table, his attention was drawn directly to an exposed bald and bloody spot located between his nape and to the left of the bottom of his head, which encased the tumor. He could actually see the bloody mass of tissue and wondered whether a benign tumor looked any different than a malignant one. He could even see the scar from a wound on the back of his neck that he received as a boy when he tripped and fell backwards on a tent stake at a Boy Scout jamboree.

Without warning, an unexpected and potentially deadly disruption in the delicate operation caught the attention of DC's altered state of consciousness. *CODE BLUE, CODE BLUE, blood pressure dropping, fast!* That led to his attention being drawn more directly to the frenzy of activity taking place below his viewing position. What to make of it, he wondered. Raised voices. Colors being shouted. *Blue, Green, Blue-Green, Green-Blue.* To DC's dissociated and detached mind, body, and spirit, they were just colors of the rainbow and colors in a box of crayons. Beyond those descriptions, he had no idea why those colors were being tossed around so excitedly in the operating room by the blue and green attired humans. Thus, he did not know *Code Blue* from *Code Green* from *Code Red.* At some point, however, he did come to understand that Blue must have been a pretty darn serious color as doctors and nurses stopped operating and started inserting needles into him. With a detached interest that belied the danger of the moment, he listened dispassionately to the brassy announcement by one of the Blue-attired humans. *Oh shit. We're going to lose him if you can't get his pressure back up. Get it up! Now, goddamit! I'm not losing you. Not on my watch, you son-of-a-bitch! Get some epi into him STAT! Open up your IV line—wide open. Give him whatever fluids you've got. Normal saline, albumin—I don't care. But do it fast. Someone get the crash cart in here. Be prepared to do chest compressions. Oh! No, buddy! Not on my watch.*

He saw and heard all of the life and death, back and forth drama while floating above the operating table like a weightless astronaut. It was only after the doctor said, *he's fine* that his floating body returned to his stationary body.

Later, in the recovery room, he shared his out-of-body story with Sara Mae, his decades-long wife and occasional tormenter. Having the patience and tact of a pissed off Africanized queen bee, DC's indelicate consort immediately ordered him to never again mention such foolishness to her, her friends or to any of the other good people of Sharpville. "After all," she asked, "do you want my friends to think that I am married to some kind of stark raving-mad, lunatic? What would people think of me? That's crazy talk, Dickey Carter, and I don't want to ever hear it again. It sounds just like something straight from that sleazy *Jerry Springer Show*, for God's sake. Besides, only the good Lord can take you to the other side—to heaven or hell. And if you keep telling that blaspheming pack of lies about seeing lights and spooks and other such non-sense, Dickey Carter you are just punching your ticket for a one-way trip to the lake of fire. Next thing, you are going to say you were kidnapped by a bunch of space aliens and had your ass hole probed by little pointed head green space men," she warned him. DC secretly wondered whether such an encounter between him and space aliens had occurred for real, or was it just another wet dream.

Such a close call with death accompanied by a hair-raising, almost spiritual out of body experience might have led most morally-challenged people to change their ways. Many people, regardless of their moral compass or spiritual orientation, would have seen such an event as a sign that God or some higher being was trying to tell them something. They would have taken advantage of such a rare spiritual experience and had an honest conversation with God about just what He was trying to tell them. But in DC's world, he and God already had that conversation—many times. In DC's world, God had told him and his friends many times that, in essence, because of their skin color, wealth, and power, they were uniquely and divinely favored, anointed, and consecrated.

DC was married to Sarah Mae McGinnis, who had enough good looks, poise, and symmetrical curves in all the right places to be offered a modeling contract with the Ford Modeling Agency during her senior year of high school. The end of her senior year marked the beginning of DC's second year as a lawyer, fledgling real estate mogul, and president of the Chamber of Commerce. Sarah Mae had caught DC's eye at a beauty pageant at the local high school where DC served as the only male adjudicator of talent, beauty, and poise that helped determined who would represent Henderson County in the Miss Mississippi Pageant. After watching her parade confidently and elegantly across the stage in her black Marilyn one-piece bathing suit and Charleston clear vinyl high heels, DC knew she would become his betroth. Although DC was eleven years older than Sarah Mae, such a disparity in age was not unusual in Henderson County, as women half Sarah Mae's age routinely marry men twice DC's age.

DC proposed to Sarah Mae following a revival meeting at the Main Street Christian Church, where the Reverend Leonidas Wickersham had spiritually stirred something deep inside DC and Sarah Mae. Right there in front of God and the Christian Church portion of white Sharpville, Sarah Mae and DC gave their lives to Christ. Giving their lives to Christ in such a public manner was required under the Christian Church doctrine.

It was not enough to privately profess a belief in Christ. Rather, doctrinal tradition and belief in the Christian Church required professions of faith and expressions of beliefs in Christ as one's personal savior to be consummated ceremoniously, publicly, and in the company of anointed fellow true believers. In turn, the anointed true believers accepted their mandatory role to make sure that the nascent believers would not backslide, or worse, become Catholics, Mormons, or Methodists. For Dickey Carter and Sara Mae McGinnis, everything was in perfect harmony, with God and with one another. With celebrity, wealth, a newly saved soul, and the prettiest woman for miles around as his intended, life for Dickey Carter was like a ride down a giant water slide… fun, stress-free, and refreshing.

With her own newly saved soul, Sarah Mae obligingly turned down the Ford modeling contract offer after DC, not wanting her to get caught up in the glamour, glitz, and bright lights of New York City, asked her to marry him. A marriage offer from a local God-fearing all-American, all-Southern war hero with boat loads of money made the decision to choose matrimony over glamour, glitz, and bright lights only slightly agonizing. Ultimately, she reasoned that becoming Mrs. Dickey Carter was more compelling than being Sara Mae McGinnis, the model, especially in that heathen-infested den of iniquity called New York City. And the shelf life for a pretty young model like Sara Mae McGinnis was no more than five years, tops. And the shelf life for Mrs. Dickey Carter was incalculable. Given such indisputable sets of facts and beliefs, turning down the modeling contract was a classic no-brainer.

DC worshipped the ground on which Sarah Mae walked. No one other than Billy Wayne Sharp held as much sway over him as she did. Sarah Mae knew how to make her husband experience overwhelming joy with a simple wink, a slight smile, or a spontaneous and raucous romp in the hay. Likewise, she could induce excruciating emotional pain with a scowl, a yell, or an unforeseen and crude putdown, "You little spineless, limp dick, wimpy son-of-a-bitch, DC!" Such a Sara Mae-esque, well-timed, venomous tirade was typically uttered whenever Sarah Mae believed that DC's behavior reflected poorly on her as Mrs. Dickey Carter. For example, in her presence, DC would cower and stutter as though he was aping the Cowardly Lion from the *Wizard of Oz* while being the object of one of Billy Wayne's expletive-laden epithets for something as simple as driving too slowly. Insults and praises from his wife and his best friend had become the bitter-sweet nectar of life that had simultaneously elated and depressed Dickey "DC" Carter during the past forty years. Such a paradox was an excellent metaphor for the emotional and psychological duality that characterized much of his life, and contributed to a great extent to his recent diagnosis of early stages of schizophrenia.

DC was a life-long friend of Billy Wayne. They both served in World War Two but in different divisions and in different theaters of operation. Billy Wayne spent the majority of his time in North Africa as a member of the First Infantry Division while DC fought in Europe with the Second Infantry Division. A once confident, stylishly dressed, and physically impressive man had morphed into a docile, frail, slovenly, and sickly old man, conditions and characteristics that have become more noticeable during the past five years when he was secretly taking fen-phen to lose weight. DC, unlike Billy Wayne, resumed his education after the war, cashing in on the New GI Bill and the notoriety that accompanied his Medal of Honor for gallantry. Although the Medal of Honor is often presented posthumously, DC's action on the battlefield merited the rare occurrence of it being presented to someone living. During a fierce firefight with Heer soldiers in the German city of Duehren, DC displayed uncommon valor and courage. Outnumbered by Germany's fiercest fighting force, DC's reconnaissance team was separated from the rest of its unit. They were left with three options: escape, surrender, or fight. In a moment of extreme bravery and desperation that would forever change his life and the lives of his remaining comrades, DC managed to kill half the attacking German soldiers with several well-place hand grenades and expert marksmanship that ended the standoff. The results were mixed. DC lost eight comrades. Seventeen Heers lost their lives, and twelve surrendered.

Following a well-deserved hero's welcome, including the town's first and only parade to honor someone other than Santa Claus or Sharpville High School's homecoming court, DC was left to ponder the four options that lay before him. Option one: leverage the medal and fame to become a career military officer with several perks and possibilities—Stint at the Pentagon. Stint at a US Embassy. Stint at the White House. Option two: run for State Representative and very likely accrue a massive amount of political clout and capital. Option three: go into business with Billy Wayne and become an instant millionaire. Option four: go to law school and accrue massive amounts of political clout and capital and become a millionaire to boot. Sacrificing the chances for an immediate financial windfall offered by options one, two, and three, he decided to attend Henderson State College on the GI Bill. And three years later with B.A. degree in hand, he immediately entered Law School at Ole Miss, where he finished first in his class. With the notoriety born out of his earning the Medal of Honor coupled with ample intellect that clinched his first-place standing in his law school class, DC received hundreds of offers from the most prestigious law firms in Mississippi, Tennessee, and Alabama. Driven by a deeply passionate desire to not disconnect himself from the familiarity and comforts of Sharpville and his already established reputation as a hero and all of the currency that goes with being a bona fide military hero, he rejected all other offers. His decision to stay in Sharpville and to turn down the offers from the more prestigious established law firms was also heavily influenced by the dreams he shared with Billy Wayne—dreams in which the two of them would become the uncontested shakers and movers of Henderson County, Mississippi.

Billy Wayne respected DC's heroism, celebrity, and ambition. However, such respect had caveats. As long as DC's heroism, celebrity, and ambition directly and substantively benefited Billy Wayne and his plans for becoming the preeminent ruler of the fiefdom that he was planning to build in Sharpville and Henderson County, and as long as DC's celebrity and ambition did not result in any diminution in Billy Wayne's power and authority, he would maintain respect for DC. Indeed, he would publicly become his most vocal supporter. Not long after his law firm and real estate practice were established, *Dickey Carter Esq. and Real Estate, Inc.* flourished financially beyond anything he could have earned at another law firm. He was sole owner of a business that netted two-four million dollars annually and was once featured in the state's largest newspaper under the headline: *Local Hero to Local Millionaire,* which generated even more business. To the public and to his family, his business success was due to his intellect, business acumen, and legendary hero status. But despite all he had accomplished as a local hero and local millionaire, his success was not solely his. His success was also Billy Wayne's success. *Dickey Carter, Esq. and Real Estate, Inc.,* with the enormous backing and patronage of Billy Wayne, would become one of many public and legitimate faces of an operation that masked the ignoble activities of some of Sharpville's finest.

CHAPTER 8

WITH HIS INIMITABLE and unique mélange of frown, angst, and smile, Billy Wayne reclaimed the coveted speaker's role from Dickey Carter and continued his monologue. Before speaking, however, he drained his drinking glass of its remaining contents—gin and tonic, no ice, more gin that tonic—and wiped the circles of moisture that had accumulated on the conference table from his frosted, eight-inch tall David Douglas drinking glass. After wiping the moisture with a faded, well-used hankie that he retrieved from a hip pocket, he stood, and with the same hankie, blew his nose, making a sound that mimicked the jangle of a barking sea lion on Pier 39. In the middle of blowing his nose, he paused for an instant to unleash a torrid string of putrid-smelling flatulence that made sounds like a train horn at a railroad crossing.

"Damn! That feels better. I'll try to warn y'all next time, so if you need to get up from the table, you *might* have time. Can't always predict when um gonna let loose one of them Arkansas barking spiders," joked Billy Wayne.

"Billy, you sure as hell ought to feel better. That was loud and stinky. Smells like sheep shit on the hot Rocky Mountains. You need cleaning out, son," chimed in Dickey Carter, in a feeble and futile attempt to wrestle the speaker's role back from Billy Wayne.

"My gin and tonic is the only cleaning out medicine this old boy needs 'cause drinking booze always makes me fart more than piss, unlike the rest of y'all. Speaking of farting and pissing, I better pause for the cause and go and drain the tank and make sure it was just gas that blowed out my ass. Feels kinda funny back there. Let's take a piss break and come back to the table in 'bout ten minutes," replied Billy who pushed the pause button on the meeting as a subtle reminder that he was still in charge of the topics, flow, and length of the night's conversations.

After ten minutes, everyone returned to the conference table and Billy Wayne moved the conversation back to Dickey Carter's original statement, in which he expressed his disagreement with Billy Wayne's plan to bring up deeds from the past. Billy kept recalling what the gypsy man told the fidgety man about purging, renewal and confession. With such a prophetic and powerfully resonating scene from one of his favorite television shows still lingering in his consciousness, Billy Wayne was not about to let the futile protestations Dickey Carter deter him from his Twilight Zone-inspired mission. So, he provided a classic Billy Wayne retort.

"Now see what DC just said is the main thang um talkin' about. If we don't keep thangs straightened out in our minds, some of these sons of bitches who still owe us might figure we just a bunch of harmless old farts who can't remember *shit*. And I know we talked about some of this some time back, but the way I see thangs is that we gettin' older and if we don't start talkin' bout 'em mo often, we gone sho nuf start forgettin' shit... shit we ought not never forget. Plus, you see, I know some of these assholes think that we done forgot about what they owe us cause we ain't bothered to collect. Some of 'em probably think we are a bunch of has-been candy-asses who don't know shine from shinola," bemoaned Billy Wayne.

Billy Wayne paused and stared at his huge calloused hands as though they contained some long-forgotten jewels of wisdom.

He kept replaying in his mind the admonitions directed to the fidgety man by the gypsy man. *Don't confess those morally questionable deeds to me. No sir. And don't confess them to your family and loved ones. That will destroy the love and trust they presently have for you. Trust me. Learning about your morally questionable deeds from your past will result only in your family not truly loving and trusting you, even though they say they still do. Therefore, you must do so only with people you know well, who will keep your secrets, and who will not judge you.* Taking a pull from his half-finished cigar and exhaling with a smirk and a nod, Billy Wayne continued.

"But, like my daddy used to tell me. Sometimes you got to wait a spell, long after plantin' season fo you can start reapin'. He said you gotta wait for *juuust* the right time to start seeing if what you put in the ground start to coming up. You see, some of these assholes who owe us just ain't growed up enough yet to make the harvest worth our time. But, boys, I say that harvest time is drawing near. Cause we gettin' on up in the years and ain't nobody round to carry on what we started. So, we got to give serious considerations bout how we gone collect what' s owed us. And most important, we got to be sure to leave thangs a little bit better than when we started. We owe it to the next generation of proud white Southerners, who God willing, will pass thangs on to the next generation, and hopefully they will make it better than they found it. But fo we start collecting our bountiful harvest, we got to take stock of what we done done *for*, and in some cases, *to* some of these people, so that we could remain true to our calling and the righteous upholding of our way of life, while standing tall and stout for the natural order of thangs, the way the Good Lord meant 'em to be. Y'all know what I'm trying to say to ya," asked Billy Wayne.

Shifting their weight around in their chairs and clicking twice with their knuckles on the top of the shiny mahogany table that they figuratively fancied as the oval-shaped version of King Arthur's Round Table, they each signaled agreement with Billy Wayne's way of seeing things. Cletus contemplated his knuckles, searching for signs of bruising from striking the table with such ferocity.

"The way I see thangs, boys, is that we done done a lotta shit down through the years. Some, cause we had to and some cause, well, it was just the thang to do at the time. Personally, I ain't got no regrets bout nothin' we done. And if it took a little extra mustard to put on a couple of them hot dogs so they'd know we meant bidness, well that's just the way it had to be. I ain't saying I'm sorry, but if people would have just done what they were told to do and mind their own God damn bidness, we could have eased up on the mustard. Like I said, we held up our way of life, specially when it looked like changing times and bleedin-heart shit heads who don't understand the way thangs are done round here tried to come round tryin' to change thangs anyhow. But we stood tall throughout the years and that's somethin' to be damn proud of, boys. And it ain't been so bad neither that we, how shall I put it, improved our standard of living in the process," said Billy Wayne.

"But right now I want us to thank back to the long-ago past and to the recent past, and let's remember some of the stuff we done done and, hell, still do, and all of the times we tried to be true to our calling in doing the right thang for Sharpville. Cause if we start forgettin' shit, fo long, we just gonna become a fucking fading blip on the radar screen of life. So, I wanna get thangs started with recalling a situation that we all oughta remember. Cause it was one of our finest hours and the whole thang pretty much worked out the way it was supposed to. And besides, I always heard my granny say that confessin's good for the soul and when it's done right, quiets the spirit and purges the demons. And we all know 'bout them demons, don't we DC," asked Billy Wayne.

After a long minute, and getting no direct response from DC, Billy Wayne yelled at DC to either wake up himself or go outside and let the cool night air do it for him.

Not daring to invite more rage from Billy Wayne, DC, said, "Ah hell, Billy Wayne. My mind was running through the briar patch huntin for ole brer rabbit." The laughter that ensued seemed to relax everyone a bit and reminded them that whenever DC's mind wandered off, his explanation was always the same—chasing brer rabbit through the briar patch. "But, I heard you, Billy. Them goddamn demons ain't nothing to play with."

Returning to an emotionally calmer place, Billy Wayne continued. "But granny also said you gotta be careful who you confess to. And since we are all amongst friends here, ain't no harm in talkin' bout thangs from the past."

Billy Wayne feigned a smile and wiped sweat from his naturally furrowed brow, even though the temperature in the conference room was sixty-five degrees. Billy Wayne's weight and medication always seemed to make him sweat profusely, even when the inside or outside conditions were anything but hot. Despite the excessive discharge of perspiration and the usual side effects of the Prozac, Billy Wayne remained determined to push forward with his explanation of the first attempt by an African American to enroll at Henderson State University.

CHAPTER 9

"OKAY. NOW, WHO remembers that coon nigger who dat tried to go to school out at State back in '58?" queried Billy Wayne, as though he was giving a pop quiz to a class room full of grade school kids.

"State" was Henderson State University, the local university, founded in 1898 to train white public school teachers. Henderson State's original name was Henderson State Normal College. Through the years its name changed to Henderson State College, then to the current iteration—Henderson State University. Its enrollment has grown from eleven in the first graduating class in 1902 to over 20,000 today, which makes it the largest public university in the state of Mississippi. Although Billy Wayne never attended college, he was exceedingly loyal and supportive of Henderson State. He donated millions of dollars to State, primarily for its athletic programs, and in exchange for those millions were tangible and perpetual honors—the Billy Wayne Sharp Multi-Purpose Arena. This state-of-the-art building featured perfect acoustics, comfortable and unobstructed seating for twenty thousand, a sixty-foot by sixty-foot combination scoreboard, and a jumbo screen. He was on a first name basis with the last four presidents of Henderson State, having served as chair of the search committees for each of their selections. Each president, from the beginning of their tenure until the end, slavishly catered to Billy Wayne's ideas and indulgences, not wanting to jeopardize the financial spigot that Billy Wayne had fashioned and turned on for their benefit. But like all transactions, there was the inherent and inevitable *quid pro quo*, which was Billy Wayne's forte and chief motivation for loaning or donating any amount of money to any one for any cause. He reveled in the ego-gratifying naming of the recreation center in his honor. He also bragged to his close friends that he has not paid to go to an athletic event at State in more than twenty years and wouldn't have to for the next twenty. But his most gratifying privilege for being such a behemoth, loyal, and coveted donor to the University had no visible manifestations whatsoever. Material possessions were important to Billy Wayne, for sure. He appreciated and valued his boats, guns, trucks, planes, and buildings bearing his name, but the possession of power and influence far outranked all of those visible and tangible trappings of material wealth. As someone who never attended college, he was especially mindful of an undeniable and obvious paradox. His influence and power yielded for him the stature and esteem normally afforded only to learned and important men of letters. College presidents, College board members, and elected officials were thrilled to count him as a personal friend. They consulted him on an array of matters, from capital campaigns to lobbying the state legislature or U.S. Congress for earmarks to fund pet projects. Perhaps, the power and influence that he cherished above all others was his ability to decide who would occupy the Office of President of Henderson State University or who would guide its athletic programs. His personal choices for President, Athletic Director, and Head Football Coach prevailed without dissent, as was his choice for the position of Commissioner of Higher Education. Though he could have easily influenced the decision of who would serve as Commissioner of Public Education, he cared very little for public education. In fact, he was convinced that public education had outlived its usefulness in Mississippi. In his view, public education was catering to too many black students, and as a result, white students did not have a place in the public school milieu. In his world, private schools, home schooling, and charter schools were the only answers to Mississippi's horrible record on education.

"That was '59, Billy Wayne," answered Cletus Sessum.

Cletus a tall slim man with thinning silver hair and a matching silver beard, who was owner of Sharpville's largest insurance agency and Billy Wayne's second cousin by marriage. His phony laughter disguised his conflicting feelings of pleasure and angst over the fact that he had just corrected the Mighty Billy Wayne Sharp. Correcting Billy Wayne, whether one-on-one or in the presence of others, carried a penalty that was far worse than any physical punishment.

Cletus Sessum, like everyone else in the room, was born and reared in Sharpville. His Uncle Jedidiah, who was single his entire life, left a thriving insurance business to Cletus, the only living male relative in the Sessum clan. Cletus was married to Billy Wayne's second cousin, Doreen Mulberry, who was once Henderson County's only white mid-wife, a profession she gave up when she married Cletus, her third husband. Cletus was the consummate Renaissance man, which made him standout in Sharpville society like a pumpkin in a watermelon patch, noticeably different but still part of the genus. In addition to his business and insurance acumen, Cletus Sessum was lead actor in the Henderson County Thespians Community Playhouse, reigning champion of the Sharpville Turkey Shoot, a champion bass fisherman, and the proud owner and consumer of a vast and impressive collection of books by such authors as Faulkner, Welty, Yeats, Shakespeare, and Whitman. An erudite and cultured man, Cletus Sessum knew he was intellectually superior to Billy Wayne, but always deferred to Billy Wayne on matters that required a keen intellect and rational thinking. The fact that Cletus was a member of the international high IQ society, Mensa, did not enhance his stature in his or Billy Wayne's eyes. His self-deprecating acts of obsequiousness toward Billy Wayne were genuine and well ensconced in his public and private conduct. His self-effacement was born out of profound respect he held for Billy Wayne along with a well-founded fear of being a recipient of Billy Wayne's legendary capacity to unmercifully upbraid anyone who dared intimate that he was Billy Wayne's intellectual, physical, or verbosity equal. Cletus knew whenever conflict or disagreement arose between him and Billy Wayne, the better part of valor was not only discretion. He knew that the only part of valor that really mattered was the complete surrendering of one's will to Billy Wayne's. Cletus had performed this dance of will and wisdom with Billy Wayne for decades, and never knew a time when he did not. One such time occurred during a search for the next president of the University of Mississippi.

As a learned man, Cletus had a well-cultivated insight in to what intellectual qualities a person should possess as a prerequisite for serving as a college president. Cletus' knowledge of literature, history, art, movies, sports, and medicine was legendary and a testament to his intellect. He served as a well-compensated consultant for a Hollywood producer to write questions and answers for a popular college version of *Jeopardy*, which aired for five years on PBS. In his role of consultant, Cletus spent a good deal of time visiting college campuses throughout the country, including elite, flag-ship, and regionally serving colleges and universities. Those visits, more often than not, allowed him to spend quality time with college presidents, who were anxious to show their support for the PBS program and to showcase their institutions. As a result, Cletus developed a fairly accurate profile of a successful college president. When the State College Board asked Billy Wayne to serve as chair of the search committee for the vacant presidency at the state's only public liberal arts college, Cletus approached Billy Wayne to offer his guidance and insight regarding the qualities that a liberal arts college president should possess. Instead of welcoming the perspectives of someone of Cletus' experience and intellect, Billy Wayne upbraided Cletus as though he had just announced that he had become a life-time member of the NAACP.

"You make me sick, Cletus. No. Not sick. You make me want to rip out your damn tonsils and shove 'em up your sorry ass. You think 'cause of all that book learning, you somehow supposed to be smarter than me. You seem to be forgettin' somethin' you best keep front and center in your brain, boy. You seem to think your shit don't stink, that you somehow holier than the rest of us who didn't see no use to gettin' no college degree," shouted Billy Wayne.

Attempting to blunt the impact of what he knew would be one of Billy Wayne's classic efforts to rip him a new one, Cletus offered a *mea culpa*.

"Billy, I don't think I'm better than nobody, especially you, my friend. I have been around the world and worldly people, and I just want to put that to good use for your benefit. You run in circles that I don't, and I in some that you don't. I just wanted to help you out so that you don't get blind-sided by somebody who might know more than you. But, I didn't mean no harm, Billy," pleaded a thoroughly shaken Cletus Sessum.

Not wanting to let Cletus off the hook too easily, Billy Wayne, like a predatory animal sensing weakness in its prey, went for the kill.

"You got some people fooled with all them damn books you read and TV consulting and genius club bullshit. But boy, that don't mean a damn thang as far as um concerned. You best better know your place in this organization. This organization ain't about books, it is about bucks. And it sure as sin ain't about brain intelligence, it is about common goddamn sense. You see, you got a shit load of the first and diddly squat of the second. So, you just leave the thinking up to me, boy. And remember, your place is exactly where I tell you it is. You are part of this organization 'cause I say so. And anytime you get to thinking that you bigger, badder, and smarter than me, then you can just get the hell a-steppin. Boy, you don't wanna get into no pissin' contest with Big Billy Wayne. Oh hell hah! Any time you do, just remember these words. And this ain't no threat. I guaran-damn tee' you, boy, it's a promise. This organization and this town ain't big enough for two kick-ass, bad-asses. And when you start thinking that you more of a kick-ass, bad-ass than me, when can settle dispute fast and easy. 'Cause I would literally fuck you up, boy. And you know I can do it 'cause I done it before to other ass-holes who thought they were my equal or better than me. And if you have trouble believin' what um tellin' you, just con-jure up the name, Marvin Lee Creel. And he was my best damn friend. We grew up together. I ain't gotta say mo'. So, any ideas you have about who should be president at Ole Miss, just get them out of your head or keep them to yourself. 'Cause Billy Wayne don't want to hear a damn thing you got to say, unless I come to you and ask you tell me what you thinking. Do I make myself clear," angrily asked Billy Wayne as he wiped saliva foam from the corners of his mouth.

A shaking and perspiring Cletus meekly replied, "Yes, Billy. You made yourself clear. I ask for your forgiveness for being so insolent. And I will never again attempt to display any sort of disloyalty toward you or attempt to impugn your intelligence. You have my solemn pledge that I will never ever do that again."

"Now there you go again using fifty dollar words when a five dollar one will do. What that hell you mean by insulin and the other word you just said," Billy Wayne stated with a slight smile.

"Sorry, Billy. I'm a creature of habit sometimes. What I said was that I am sorry for being insolent, which means I am sorry for being disrespectful and rude toward you. And I will never impugn your intelligence. That means that I will never question how smart you are," responded Cletus.

"Hell, boy, shoulda said it that way the first time. Now I know what you was saying. You are forgiven, Cletus. Just make damn good and sure that it don't happen again," replied Billy Wayne, satisfied with himself that he had thoroughly knocked Cletus down a few notches on the self-esteem ladder.

*

Being married to Billy Wayne's second cousin did not exactly create warm familial bonds between Billy Wayne and Cletus, as would normally be the case in many families, especially those who live in the same town. Billy Wayne included Cletus in his clandestine group of money makers and power brokers only because of Cletus' immense wealth and exalted stature in the community as an honorable and upstanding citizen. Warm, fuzzy feelings for Cletus or anyone else, except for his beloved wife, Margaret, by Billy Wayne were nonexistent. While he enjoyed their company, he never regarded these men as his equal. Toleration and tempest more aptly describes his attitude toward each of them.

Exacerbating the tension between Cletus and Billy Wayne was Cletus' wife, Doreen Mulberry. Doreen's family and Billy Wayne's family, at one time, were engaged in a violent multi-generational family feud. The feud at one time was serious enough that some observers, without much exaggeration, compared the Sharp-Mulberry feud to the more well-known blood feud between the Hatfields and McCoys.

It all started right after the Civil War. Owing to the spoils of war as well as for sheer retribution, many Southern plantation and slave owners were forced to relinquish their possessions, including their slaves and their property following Lee's surrender to Grant. As a result, thousands of slaves were granted their freedom, thus bringing about additional hardship for cotton plantation owners who relied on slave labor to pick their cotton and to provide the manual labor that oiled the Southern agricultural machine. In addition, mansions, real estate, and other properties were confiscated by the U. S. Government and given to former slaves or to white Southerners who maintained sympathy if not loyalty toward the U. S. Government during the war. Doreen's family was the beneficiary of the latter. Throughout the civil war, Doreen's great, great grandfather refused to support the confederacy. He was once an infantryman in the U. S. Army and possessed an intense loyalty toward the federal government, its constitution, its military, and its flag. The idea of going to war against the U. S. Government, in his view, was treasonous and an egregious affront to his oath as a soldier to uphold and protect the Constitution of the United States. He not only refused to take up arms against his government, but he also forbade his three sons to participate in waging war against the United States of America. Furthermore, he was willing to express his views to others and made it known to rebel recruiters that neither he nor his sons would be joining the war. He also sent letters to General Ulysses Grant and President Abraham Lincoln, pledging his unqualified support for the Constitution of the United States. Following the war, his loyalty was generously rewarded with a gift of over a thousand acres of land previously owned by a wealthy plantation owner and supporter of the defeated rebel cause. Naturally, such property seizures by the U. S. Government, and the attitude displayed by Doreen's great grandfather, were not popular among rabid rebels, who believed that the federal government was the aggressor in what they termed the War of Northern Aggression. Southerners were convinced that the federal government was out to destroy the

Southern way of life, including its cotton-based and slavery-based economy and generally, to usurp their rights as sovereign states.

The Sharp family was the primary antagonists toward the Mulberry family. Upon his return from the war, Colonel Thomas Barramore Sharp pledged a perpetual pursuit and persecution of Southern traitors and any other Southerners who were northern sympathizers. In Colonel Sharp's world and in the similarly jaundiced attitude toward northern sympathizers held by his legion of supporters, the Mulberry family was at the top of his list of people who had earned the ire and retribution of free-thinking, free-acting, and freedom-loving white patriots of the sovereign South.

For generations, the Sharps and the Mulberrys uninterruptedly carried on a blood feud that frequently claimed scores of lives, young and old, on both sides of the feud. It was not until World War I that the two families agreed to a truce, at least for the duration of the war. After the war, the feud resumed and was interrupted for only the second time, ironically, by ensuing conflicts and wars—World War II, Korean War, Vietnam War, and the Gulf War, all of which claimed the blood and lives of both Sharps and Mulberrys. At the present moment, the feud is dormant but not over. Hard feelings, born of stories of betrayal and courage, true and untrue, passed down through the generations, are still evident, thus explaining the present air of distrust and dislike between Billy Wayne Sharp and Doreen Mulberry.

*

"You right, Cletus. That mean you remember the nigger's name? Cause if you don't, shut your damn mouth," snapped an even redder-faced Billy Wayne in a tone that revealed his infamous touchy side and his persistent need to maintain authority and superiority among a group of people that he considered his friends but whom he considered to be not nearly as smart and important as he was.

Still trying to lead the others down memory lane, a slightly less pissed-off Billy Wayne continued. "Now that Cletus here is our official historian, now I ask you again. Who remembers that nigger's name?"

"His name was Jeremiah Simpson," volunteered Brock Galloway.

"He was one of them uppity niggers from out there in Nigger Town that spent a little time up north with those misguided white liberal pecker heads and thought that gave him the balls to come down here and start stirring up these local niggers with all that talk about integration and civil rights and other such communist bullshit. Billy, I don't know what make niggers think that they got the brains to do anything else but what the good Lord put them here for in the first place… staying in their own fucking place, with their own fucking kind, and using that which the good Lord supplied them graciously and abundantly… the brain of a monkey and the brawn of a jackass. Next thing you know, some pea brain gonna tell us that some nigger gonna be president of these United States one day. Hell, it'll be a cold day in hell fo somthin' like that ever happened," said Brock.

That heart-felt remark triggered red-faced rage and a torrid rant from Billy Wayne.

"If somthin' like that ever happened you can be sure as sin that the end of days is upon us, fellows, and we all might as well be ready to meet our maker," added Billy Wayne.

A delayed chuckle ensued, as if everyone finally got the punch line of a semi-funny joke. Billy Wayne, however, did not intend his remark to be an off-hand display of levity. He was as serious as someone who was about to swear before God to tell the truth, the whole truth, and nothing but the truth. Sensing that laughter was not the expected reaction from Billy Wayne, the group mirrored Billy Wayne's reaction and quickly snapped off the laughter and replaced it with a dour, forlorn look.

"Not only is hell gonna freeze over, but you mark my word… birds gonna start falling out the sky, snow gonna fall in Sharpville in July, and dogs gonna start mating with cats. Since ain't none of such nonsense gonna happen, we can all be assured, for now and for evermore, and hear me when I say this, fellows. There will never be a nigger, colored, Negro, black, Afro American president of the United States of America. Nigger president of the United States of America! The country I fought for and gave blood for? Aw. Hell nah. I know times done changed, but ain't no nigger got more smarts than any white man enough to be president of MY country. And besides, there are mo' of us than them any damn how, so the math alone wouldn't add up to somethin' like that happenin', even if you add in them nigger-loving pecker heads from up north and out west. A Nigger President! A Nigger First Lady! A Nigger in the White House! You damn skippy it ain't gonna never happen. Have to be some retarded pea brain to believe some shit like that would ever happen in the Land of the Brave. Might as well believe that a fat man with rosy cheeks, dressed in a red suit, can go all over the world flying' through the air behind a bunch of stanking ass reindeer. Now let's get back to Cletus, Brock or whoever the hell was talking. I can feel my pressure going up, so we better move on. Cletus, Brock, what was you sayin' befo you said that about a nigger president," said Billy Wayne.

"I was 'bout to say, Billy, that we showed that old boy, Simpson, with his good for nothing sorry ass who the boss is, didn't we Billy Wayne?" volunteered a chuckling Brock Galloway, an emaciatingly thin, short, slightly balding, freck-led-faced man who was the owner of a local car dealership that supplied brand new cars each year to the local college football coaches and a select few football players. Brock was a loyal alumnus of State, contributing thousands of dollars to the school, primarily to the football program. He not only supplied *cars* to players, but also provided jobs for them during the off-season, a brazen act that caught the attention of the NCAA. Feigning ignorance and blind loyalty to his illustrious Alma Mater, Brock was able to convince NCAA investigators that no one at the college knew that he was loaning cars and providing jobs for athletes. Further, he told them that he thought loaning cars was a "nice thing to do for the poorest and most destitute of our community." It did not hurt his and the College's case with the NCAA when he pledged $250,000 to the Henderson State University's general scholarship fund. To his credit, Brock hand delivered a check for $250,000 to the Bursar's Office the same day he made the pledge.

Brock Galloway was a sports legend in Sharpville. He set records in high school and college in the 100 yard-dash—nine point nine seconds and nine point eight seconds, respectively. He set a single-season rushing record of 1,200 yards during his senior year of high school football. And he once scored thirty-five points in a basketball game that his team won fifty to thirty-one. Age and an assortment of ailments have mitigated all semblances of athleticism and fitness that once characterized Brock Galloway. A couple of by-pass surgeries along with being on the losing end of a run-in with his neighbor's pit bull three years ago have left his left leg in constant pain and his gait noticeably slow and weak. Brock is a widower, who has outlived three wives, all of whom were wealthy women and void of any reproductive capacities. That was Brock's biggest disappointment. No children. No heirs. No one to carry on the genes of a fine specimen of a human being, as he liked to style himself.

Brock Galloway's association with Billy Wayne started when he and Billy Wayne co-chaired Sharpville's inaugural community fund drive in 1964. During that drive, which raised funds for the local orphanage, the YMCA, and the public library among others, Brock and Billy Wayne matched each other's donation to the fund in the amount of ten thousand dollars. Each year since that time, they have continued to match each other's donations, which have grown over the years to ten times the original amount.

Except for Billy Wayne, no one in the power group holds stronger views about race relations than Brock Galloway. His views on race relations stem from his father's and grandfather's involvement with such segregationist and conservative groups as the John Birch Society, White Citizens Council, and Dixiecrats. Each of those groups championed conservative causes and fervently fought against equal rights for racial minorities. His father was close personal friends of former Mississippi United States Senators Eastland and Stennis. His grandfather was a close personal friend of former Mississippi United States Senator Theodore Bilbo, renowned for his fierce opposition to federal anti-lynching legislation and his unabashed belief in white supremacy. Inspired by the segregationist legacy of Senator Bilbo, Senator Strom Thurmond of South Carolina, Governor Ross Barnett of Mississippi, Governor Lester Maddox of Georgia, and Governor George Wallace of Alabama, Brock and his older brother, Jesse, lent their money and support to the local Ku Klux Klan chapter. He and Jesse held unwavering views that *all* black people were innately inferior to white people. His only contact with black people, however, was as their boss, either at his car dealership, where black employees were restricted to washing cars and sweeping floors or as boss of his maid, whose family has worked for the Galloway family since before Brock was born. As a high school junior and a member of the Junior League of the White Citizens Council, Brock sent a letter to the Speaker of the U. S. House of Representatives, asking him to introduce legislation that would revive Senator Bilbo's failed amendment to a bill in 1938 that called for the repatriation of all black people to the African country of Liberia. Although, he knew that Speaker McCormick would have no part of something so sinister, he was proud of himself, nevertheless. To distinguish himself as a bona fide white supremacist, Brock submitted the letter to the editor of the *Sharpville Register*, which drew widespread support from local white citizens. Although, as an adult, he participated in numerous Klan rallies and marches, he always avoided direct involvement acts of violence.

In his early twenties, Brock took ownership of a fledgling car dealership, an inheritance from his father. He turned the business into a multi-million dollar enterprise, and eventually caught the attention of Billy Wayne Sharp, who was searching for men with the right blend of wealth, cunning, and conservatism to populate his evolving band of king makers and king breakers. Brock Galloway unequivocally exceeded all three criteria. Brock's and Billy Wayne's relationship grew as they both began financially supporting Henderson State's athletic program, although Brock declined to have any buildings named for himself. That predictable declination was on the strong advice of Billy Wayne, who wanted his to be the only name among the clan to be emblazoned on a building at Henderson State University.

CHAPTER 10

"YEP. THAT COON nigger kept on going out to the college making a goddamn fool outta hisself. The dumb ass jigaboo didn't have the sense God promised the billygoat. And you know, he called hisself puttin' that letter in the paper, trying to make out like he had some smarts, using all of them ten-dollar words. Sure some nigger-loving white man wrote the whole fricking letter cause ain't no normal nigger gone use words that even I couldn't understand. Anyhow, Simpson just kept on showing up at the college like he was some intelligent white boy. But we showed him, didn't we Billy Wayne?", added Joe Lee Roberts, a once tall man who is now five inches shorter due to the effects of osteoporosis.

Owner of the largest CPA firm in Sharpville, Joe Lee Roberts boasts of a growing clientele made up exclusively of businesses and individuals worth at least half a million dollars. He was not an alumnus of Henderson State but lived his entire life in Sharpville. He graduated from Mississippi State University, earning two degrees—a Bachelor's Degree in Accounting and a Master's Degree in Business Administration. His association with Billy Wayne started decades earlier when he and his wife Imogene served as co-teachers in Billy Wayne's Sunday School class at the Sharpville Presbyterian Church. Just as he was fascinated with the white supremacist pastor who introduced him to racist-based religion, Billy Wayne was also impressed with

Joe Lee's command of the Bible and how he frequently cited verses that spoke to the inherent superiority of the white race. Billy Wayne and Joe Lee were especially moved by a Sunday School lesson based on C.R. Dickey's article entitled, *The Bible and Segregation*. In that article, Mr. Dickey offers his interpretation of scripture that justifies white supremacy and racial segregation: *We are indebted to The Southern Conservative for an article by the Rev. James P. Dees, Rector of Trinity Episcopal Church, Statesville, North Carolina. In this article titled, "Conspiracy Is Afoot to Destroy the Social and Cultural Life of the South," the Rev. Dees says in part:*

"There is a conspiracy afoot to destroy the South. The members of this conspiracy are of various backgrounds. Their basic aim, knowingly or unknowingly, is to destroy the social and cultural life of the South and the white race by amalgamation of the races. Component elements of this conspiracy to destroy the South are the Communist Party, the NAACP, the United Nations, the National Council of Churches, the leadership in many denominations of the Christian Church, elements of the TV networks, elements of the movie industry, a number of leading magazines with nationwide circulation, elements in the Republican and Democratic Parties, and, to a large extent, the Press…

"Large foundations reportedly are putting large sums of money into the integration program all over the country. Many others are pushing integration: The YMCA, religious liberals, various dubbed dogooders, etc., and many sincere and good ministers of the Gospel. They have succumbed to and been traduced by the integration propaganda of the Communist Party, the NAACP, and various liberal and unorthodox theologians bleating their shibboleths of 'Justice' and 'Freedom.' In the interest of their unnatural religious and social philosophy, they are working to destroy the races that God has created, crying 'oneworld brotherhood' and 'racial equality,' neither of which conceptions have any substantiation whatsoever in the Scripture or in the study of mankind anthropology, psychology, et cetera…

"The Supreme Court has violated, in my opinion… the

Constitution which they have sworn to uphold, and they should be impeached. Strong sentiment is arising all over our nation to restrict the Court, but when you have such a Court as the one we have now, the only practical remedy is to kick them out and put new men in... This conspiracy to effect the submersion of the white race under a Negro society must not prevail. We are forced to take a stand."

The United States needs many more preachers of the Gospel with the insight and courage of Dr. Dees. The Christian ministers who show the most real love and concern for all races are those who tell them God's truth as revealed in the Scriptures. For no race of mankind will fail to be blessed abundantly if it stays within the orbit assigned to it by the will and purpose of the Creator.

But any commingling of races, that leads to close contacts and the possibility of amalgamation, is as evil now in the Christian Era as it was in the days of Noah. Strange as it may seem to the doubter, it was Jesus Himself who looked forward to our generation, then brought us back in a full circle to the ancient time of Noah. Speaking of His return at the end of the age, Jesus said:

"For as it was in the time of Noah [Gen. 6-7], so it will be at the coming of the Son of Man. At that time, before the deluge, men were busy eating and drinking, taking wives or giving them, up to the very day when Noah entered the ark, nor did they realize any danger till the deluge came and swept them all away; so will it be at the coming of the Son of Man." (Matt. 24:37-39, Weymouth Trans.)

Clearly Jesus implies here the similarity of conditions in the latter days to those existing in the days of Noah. Jesus would not have condemned ordinary legitimate marriages, therefore, He must refer to practices which violate Divine law, as, for instance, multiple marriages, Hollywood style. But His comparison to Noah's era indicates a more specific charge, some evil prevalent at that time, which will recur prior to His Return. In that case we may expect to find the covenant race, Christian in name if not in practice, making numerous marriages with other races, a process that defiles and destroys the purity of all *participating races. This sin brought judgment by water in Noah's day and it will bring judgment by fire in the day of Christ's Return. (See II Peter 2:4-5; 3:6-7.)*

Reading that article and discussing it among fellow white supremacists in Sunday School served to fortify Billy Wayne's already unbending belief in racial segregation and white supremacy. Being surrounded by like-minded "Christians" further reinforced his belief that God intended for whites to have dominion and superiority over all other races and that they had a duty to carry out the Lord's intentions. The convergence of their views on the Bible and race further convinced Billy Wayne that Joe Lee Roberts should be invited to join his clan. Without any hesitation, Joe Lee Roberts accepted the invitation. To further bolster his racial segregationist bona fides among his fellow clan members, he frequently reminisces about the good old days at Mississippi State when the only black people on the campus were maids, cooks, and janitors.

While putting his crossed legs atop the conference table, revealing his ankle-length red socks, Joe Lee Roberts took advantage of the opportunity to remind everyone of the role his uncle, D.D. Roberts played in trying to keep Mississippi State free of any semblance of "race mixing."

"Now y'all remember Uncle D.D., my daddy's oldest brother. He got a college degree from Henderson State, Mississippi State, and Ole Miss, an equal opportunity college student, you might say," said Joe Lee as he uncrossed and recrossed his legs atop the table.

"Can't you find another way to put that, Joe Lee," asked Brock Galloway.

"Why? What's the matter with the way I put it, Brock? Don't you understand the words that I am using? Maybe I need to talk like we in primer grade. That way, maybe my vocabulary and your intelligence won't be out of line with one another. 'Cause

I don't want you to get lost with all these highfalutin words we are using here tonight," replied Joe Lee, uncrossing his legs and standing in front of his chair, which went flying backward across the room from a swift shove from Joe Lee's foot.

"Look here, you snatch-lipped son-of-a-bitch. I don't take no shit from yo ass. I'll jump cross this table and slapped the wrinkles off your sorry ass," shouted Brock.

"Anytime you feel frogish, just jump, old man. 'Cause you ain't too old to have the dip shit slapped out of you. And I'm just the one to do it, too," yelled Joe Lee.

"All right! All fuckin' right! Now just wait a goddam minute, both of ya. That's enough of this kinda talk. Ain't nobody gonna slap nobody. First of all, Brock, Joe Lee got too many damn wrinkles for you to slap off. You be here til the cows come home tryin' to smooth out them bad boys. And second of all, Joe Lee, Brock ain't got enough shit left in him for you slap anymo' outta him. With all them damn prunes that boy eats, his bowels is empty as a slop jar at sow-feedin' time," added Billy Wayne.

With that remark, everyone broke into loud laughter, pounding their hands on the table and sounding like braying jackasses. The tension was released, and Billy Wayne directed Joe Lee to finish his remarks about his Uncle D.D.. Roberts.

"Uncle D.D. is a hero among right thinking white people in Mississippi. That we can all agree on. Ain't no disputin' the fact that this man did all he could to keep our white colleges white and to keep the races separated the way the good Lord intended. Remember when Mississippi State was scheduled to play Loyola in the 1963 NCAA Tournament? Our tradition down here, of course, was that white athletes played at white schools and coloreds played at colored schools. Up north, in that din of iniquity, they didn't have no problems in fielding teams with both colored and white boys on 'em. Turned out this team from Loyola in Chicago had four colored boys on their team. We tried everything we could to keep this abomination from takin' place. Governor Ross Barnett filed an injunction against the Bulldog basketball team that said they would not be allowed to partici-pate in the NCAA tournament. Bless his heart. This was just six months after the Governor gave up his brave fight to keep that nigger, Meredith, out of Ole Miss," said Joe Lee as he returned his crisscrossed legs to the table.

"You right, Joe Lee. Ross put up a brave fight up there at Ole Miss and he knew he had the backin' of the whites in Mississippi. But he was up against the forces of the feds, the Kennedys, and them other communist integrationists. When they threatened to federalize our Mississippi National Guard to help protect that nigger, Meredith, that was a bad situation. Those National Guardsmen wudn't no Yankees. They were our Southern white boys. And to put them in a shit-hole of a predicament by forcing them to turn against their own, well, that wudn't right. So, the best thang for Ross and the rest of us was just to give in 'cause we didn't want our boys faced with the agony of obeying the orders of their so-called Commander-in Chief, or remaining faithful to the Southern way of life that they lived and breathed every day," added Billy Wayne.

"Amen, Billy. And getting back to the Mississippi State fiasco, for the previous three years, Mississippi State won the SEC Championship, and we just declined the invitation to play in the tournament because we wudn't gonna let our boys play in a game that had coloreds on the other team. That would have just meant that we were condoning integration, if them boys hadda been allowed to walk out on the same court with them coloreds. Anyhow, as y'all remember, the judge issued the injunction barring the Bulldog basketball team from play-ing against an integrated team, but Coach Babe McCarthy was bound and determined that he was gonna go on and play in the tournament any damn way. The sneaky son-of-a-bitch put them boys on a Trailways bus, and they got away under the cover of darkness befo' the trooper could serve the papers on him. So, when they got to Michigan to play the game, one of the worst moments in the history of Mississippi State University and the sovereign State of Mississippi happened, right there on national TV right there in front of God and the entire rest of the country. This colored boy, the captain, named Harkness from Loyola walked out to center court and shook hands with our captain, Joe Dan Gold. Oh what a sad sight that was, fellows," lamented Joe Lee.

"And them Mississippi State boys got the shit beat out of them by them coloreds," added Billy Wayne.

"And what the hell all that gotta do with yo Uncle D.D., Joe Lee," inquired Brock Galloway.

"Well if you wait just a goddamn minute, Brock, I'm gonna tell you. I shouldn't have to tell you cause you oughta know any ways. But by that time, Uncle D.D. was sitting on the College Board. And he led the charge in trying to persuade the rest of the board to support his resolution calling on Mississippi State to decline the invitation to participate in the 1963 NCAA Tournament and not add its good name and the good name of Mississippi to these communist-inspired and Lucifer-inspired acts of race-mixing. He put up a good fight, but as we know, he came out on the losing end of an eight to three vote. And Uncle D.D. was serious about not wanting his alma mater to be the first white college in Mississippi to play against a team with coloreds on it. He told my daddy and me and some of us who was sittin' there watchin' the game othingg' I know he didn't want to say, but he had to. He said that he was hoping that the Bulldogs would have their last two games of the season. If they had lost those last two games, they wouldn't have won the SEC championship, and then they wouldn't have to face that problem of deciding to go to the tournament or stay home. He was actually quoted in the paper saying just that. And I was damn proud of him when he said othingg' else. He said that the game between that race-mixed team and our white boys at Mississippi State was a great tragedy and because Mississippi State Bulldogs became the first SEC team and the first white Mississippi school to ever play a race-mixed team, he felt that was the beginning of the end of our Southern heritage, our Southern way of life. And you know what, Uncle D.D. was right as rain. It started unraveling from then on, up to the present time. But it wudn't because of strong white men like D.D. Roberts. It wudn't because of men like us sittin' 'round this here table tonight, either. And it wudn't because of the courageous efforts on the part of the Sovereignty Commission, the White Citizens Council, the Klan, and those many statesmen like Governor Ross Barnett, Governor Paul B. Johnson, Governor John Bell Williams and our esteemed U.S. Senators, Eastland and Stennis. Instead it was all them communist up there in D.C., running the U.S. Government and those pin-head integrationists stirring up all that talk 'bout the poor, oppressed, disadvantaged coloreds down here in Mississippi. And we know what bullshit that was. Our coloreds didn't care othing' 'bout that integration talk. They was all satisfied being fat, lazy, and happy. And who could want more than that", said Joe Lee as he repositioned his feet back on the floor from the table.

"The State of Mississippi was beholding and grateful to Uncle D.D., not just for his standing up for our way of life, but for being a champion for higher education in Mississippi. So, when it came time to put a name on the new football stadium at Henderson State, they named it, of course, the D.D. Roberts Stadium. A very powerful way to honor a man who loved his alma mater and who fought hard to keep all that race-mixing out of our state," lamented Joe Lee Roberts.

Like a light switch that suddenly turned bright lights into

dark shadows, the mood in the room turned eerily solemn. Silence replaced jubilance and laughter. Solemnity replaced bliss. The reality of how the Southern way of life was changing was a sore spot for the men sitting around the table. Each knew that the horses were out of the barn, and despite their fervent efforts, those horses were never going to return to the barn.

They each rose slowly from the table in deafening silence. The pushed back their seats and retired to the restrooms, without a single word being uttered. The only sound was a series of loud burps followed by a series of smelly flatulence by Billy Wayne, which oddly did not draw the attention of anyone.

Joe Lee is married to the former Imogene Parsons, eldest offspring of the Reverend Lonnie Parsons. Imogene and her five siblings were all born in Sharpville and have remained there their entire lives. Reverend Lonnie Parsons is pastor emeritus of Sharpville Presbyterian Church, which has the distinction of being the oldest and largest congregation in Henderson County. The church began as a one-room wooden structure on Main Street when Reverend Parsons was just out of seminary. With an initial membership of twenty-five at its founding in 1951, the church now has a membership in excess of six thousand. Imogene's brother, Lonnie, Jr. took over as senior pastor of the church, following his father's retirement. Imogene serves as Lay Leader and Chair of the Board of Trustees—two appointed and very powerful positions, both of which she began serving in 1970. In her capacity as Lay Leader, Board Chair, and as the principal confidant of both the elder and junior Reverend Parsons, she is regarded by most as the indisputable power behind the leadership of the church.

In addition to her role as church leader, Imogene is equally well-known as the long-time president and founder of the Ladies Auxiliary of Sharpville. The Ladies Auxiliary, under her leadership, sponsors Sharpville's official annual Christmas celebration, which includes a parade, tree lighting ceremony, and toys for tots campaign. The Ladies Auxiliary also sponsors city beautification projects, including the planting and care of beautiful blooming flowers (cherry blossoms, cosmos, dahlias, begonias, and alliums) ensconced in large concrete planters stationed along the sidewalks in the town square. The Ladies Auxiliary has made one of its top priorities the maintenance of certain neighborhoods as models of beauty, charm, refinement, and curb appeal. To that end, Imogene and the Ladies Auxiliary initiated a monthly program of recognizing neighborhoods and homeowners who have maintained the appearance of their properties in the most exemplary manner. Of course, the exclusive focus of all their activities was restricted to the white communities and neighborhoods of Sharpville.

As important as those events are to the vibrancy and vitality of white Sharpville, Imogene's pride and joy is the annual Sharpville Debutante Ball, which she convinced members of the Ladies Auxiliary to sponsor beginning in 1967. Since that first ball, all of white Sharpville's elite has made a point of purchasing an admission ticket, sponsoring a debutante, becoming a sustaining donor, or purchasing a full-page ad for the souvenir program booklet. Being associated with the Sharpville Debutante Ball in some meaningful way has become valuable currency that procures and secures one's membership into Sharpville high society. Thus, there is never a shortage of sponsors, patrons, and supporters of the annual black tie/white gown affair, which produces an annual profit of $95,000 for the Ladies Auxiliary. Anyone who is anyone and anyone who considers financially supporting the Ball as an on-ramp to Sharpville high society cheerfully and generously donate to the Ball. As a result, the Debutante Ball has become *the* event to which all white teenage girls and their mothers annually look forward. To be presented to society in such a formal and elaborate fashion is a cherished privilege and a coveted rite of passage that no self-respecting white teenage girl of breeding would dare miss. To be regarded as a teenager whose time had come to publicly debut her style, grace, and elegance was a special recognition that represented, as it did with their parents' financial backing of the Ball, a proxy for acceptance into Sharpville high society. Time and money are not spared in the quest for the perfect dress, perfect shoes, perfect accessories, perfect hair style, and perfect escort.

In some communities, the high school prom is the big social event for teenagers in the spring. Easily, the Debutante Ball trumps the prom for its importance to Sharpville high society, especially for the twenty-five girls who are selected each year for debut. In Sharpville, Mississippi springtime is not only time for mother nature to debut her annual blooming flowers and magnolia trees, but it is also time for the gentry class of Sharpville to debut the style and elegance of its anointed cadre of eligible, privileged and presumably virtuous white teenage girls.

From the first Sharpville Debutante Ball to the most recent, each event has become increasingly more spectacular and popular, attracting girls from all over Henderson County as well as the neighboring counties of Lamar, Perry, Pearl River, Covington, Stone, and Jones. The pageantry, pomp and circumstance of the Debutante Ball are produced with Hollywood-like artistry and extravagance. The 125-piece symphony orchestra, the décor, and the ambience all meld together to create a breath-taking event that gives goose bumps and chills to everyone in attendance.

Scattered about the commodious ballroom, symmetrically placed on the shiny, black and white checkerboard tiled floor, are rows of oval-shaped tables covered with matching, white elegant French Jacquard tablecloth cloths, slightly accented with sparkling iridescent glitter. Upon each table sets a glass vase centerpiece made up white hydrangeas, white roses, and white peonies. Occupying each of the eight chairs at each table are family and friends of debutantes, all of whom have invested a significant amount money, hopes, and time in the emotional and physical support of their debutantes. At their tables, they sip virgin mint juleps from tall stem glasses or sweet tea from short stem ones. The ambience in the room is like that of a slightly subdued and sophisticated crowd patiently awaiting the start of Act III of the opera. There is a noticeable din, but it matches the reverent mood that permeates the ballroom.

The house lights grow dim. Chatter ceases. The sounds of chairs being repositioned underneath tables quickly end. From behind a red, crushed velvet, floor to ceiling curtain, walks Mistress of Ceremony, Imogene Parsons Roberts, highlighted by a bright spotlight that follows her and the teen escort to the podium. The medium height, medium built, and middle aged Mistress of Ceremony and Queen of the Ball is dressed in a modest, ivory, long sleeve floor-length evening dress. She wears a pair of pearl earrings that match the bracelet and the necklace and her salt and pepper hair is styled in a conservative bouffant fashion. The escort dutifully, and as rehearsed, presents Imogene with a white rose, bows to her, and retreats to the staging area behind the curtain. An even quieter hush ensues. The moment that everybody anxiously awaits has finally arrived. Imogene lowers the microphone so that it is in direct line with her mouth.

"Ladies and gentlemen, it is my pleasure to officially welcome you to the Annual Sharpville Debutante Ball. This is the night that we have all been waiting on for many months. This is the night when we debut twenty-five of Sharpville's most precious, most gorgeous, and most morally upstanding young ladies. Your presence here tonight shows just how much the Sharpville community believes in and supports these fine young ladies. In a time when young people in other towns are doing all sorts of immoral things, we are so blessed to live in a community where the moral standards are set high, and our young ladies either meet or exceed those standards. We, the women of the Ladies Auxiliary, like to believe that our fine organization has played a small role in shaping the morals of these young ladies. But we also know that you—parents, grandparents, aunts, and uncles have been the bedrock of moral behavior that has guided these young ladies along the path of wholesomeness and righteousness. And we thank you for being there for your children and for being here tonight as we celebrate them in a very special way. And with no further ado, please permit me to present the 1990 Class of Debutantes of Sharpville, Mississippi," says Imogene Parsons Roberts.

The audience leaps to its feet and gives a rousing standing ovation.

"Please, don't. Please. Please. You are just too kind. Please. Take your seats. You are making blush," pleaded Imogene, repeatedly, with false modesty, for the remaining ninety seconds of the ovation, which ended when she held both hands in the air and waved them at the crowd in a motion that urged them to stop the applauds and take their seats. On cue, as though it has been thoroughly rehearsed, the members of the audience took their seats and cast their eye-popping gaze and undivided attention toward Imogene for the main course, now that the appetizer has been served.

Imogene read the names of each debutante in alphabetical order, giving full name, age, grade, and name of parents. To illustrate visual contrast and to highlight the whiteness of the debutantes' dresses, each girl was escorted by a blushing boy dressed in a black tuxedo accented with a white boutonniere. The symphony orchestra performed its rendition of *Pomp and Circumstance* as the official musical introduction for the Debutantes. Adding to the Southern heritage of the Ball were the dozens of live magnolia trees with authentic Spanish moss draped across their branches lining the red carpet entryway.

After each girl was introduced, the evening continued with a series of waltzes danced with fathers and escorts. The ninety-minute event ended with the specially commissioned orchestral version of *Dixie*, at which time everyone present stood in complete silence and solemnity for the duration of the ten-minute salute to the Ball's theme—*A Tribute To Our Southern Heritage.*

*

Young white girls dressed in their white evening gowns, white gloves, white pumps, authentic pearl necklaces and matching white earrings seamlessly embodied and symbolized the devotion to whiteness and elitism that has come to characterize the heart and spirit of white Sharpville, Mississippi. The nuanced meaning of whiteness in Sharpville as a descriptor of attitude, skin color, status, and behavior were symbolically and symbiotically enmeshed with the stark and unblemished whiteness on display at the Debutante Ball. The whiteness of the skin, of attitudes, of status, and of behaviors was on full display. The white debutantes naturally blended with the whiteness of their dresses, shoes, and accessories in an unconscious and yet powerful display of racial superiority and purity. The not-so subliminal messages of prestige, racial superiority, and purity of whiteness were on full and regaled display for all of white Sharpville to further ensconce itself in its on-going, decades-old practice of white supremacy.

The overwhelming success of the Debutante Ball under Imogene's leadership has elevated her status to the very apex of the social hierarchy among the gentry class in Sharpville. Most white women of the nobility class automatically demure in her presence and willingly defer to her judgment on all matters, whether of little or great consequence and whether debutante related or not. Most women and their families know that any hint of scandal, public indiscretion, or any activity that Imogene perceives as immoral, indecent or disreputable means automatic exclusion from the Debutante Ball and by extension, from Sharpville high society. Only once has she had to invoke her moral turpitude clause in disqualifying someone from participating. Going into the Debutante Ball's sixth year, Imogene sent a letter to the parents of all girls eligible for the ball for the upcoming season. In the letter, Imogene emphasized the moral turpitude clause, to which every girl and her mother had to agree in writing.

The clause read: *At no time is an eligible debutante to engage in any activity that is deemed to be in violation of the moral standards of the Sharpville community. Such activities include, but are not limited to, smoking, skipping school, swearing, dressing in an unlady-like fashion, not attending church on a regular basis, keeping company with any person or persons who is immorally predisposed, or otherwise behaving in a way that brings into the question the moral fitness of a prospective debutante and her ability to represent the values and traditions of Sharpville, Mississippi. In the event that a girl or a close relative (parents and siblings) is found to be in violation of the moral turpitude clause of this document, at any time prior to the Ball, that girl will be immediately barred from participating in all events associated with the Sharpville Debutante Ball. If the violation occurs at any time after the Ball, her name will be permanently expunged from the official Debutante Ball Registry. By signing this letter and returning it to the address at the top, you hereby agree to all terms, written and implied, in this document.*

Given the importance of being selected a debutante, the conventional wisdom was that everyone would unhesitatingly sign the document, and more importantly, no one would have dared do or say anything that would even slightly violate the moral and blue nose standards of Sharpville as reflected in the turpitude clause of the Debutante Ball contract. Yet, apparently an aspiring debutante did just that, straying into the forsaken land of immorality, Sharpville style, and paid the ultimate Debutante

Ball price. Erica Hillmaster, a candidate for debut in the sixth year of the Debutante Ball, was sighted by a member of the Ladies Auxiliary riding in the car with a group of high school football players, one of whom was the star running back for the football team. Erica was seated next to the star running back. A girl riding around Sharpville, un-chaperoned, with a group of boys represented enough of a scandal to call into question her moral fitness to be a debutante. But the fact that the star running back riding in the car was black and was sitting shoulder-to-shoulder with Erica made the situation undeniably untenable. Based on the account of the sighting as reported to her, Imogene sent a *Dear Parent* letter to Mrs. Hillmaster by registered mail, informing her of the observations of the Ladies Auxiliary member and the actions she was taking pursuant to the moral turpitude clause of the Sharpville Debutante Ball contract.

The letter read:

Dear Mrs. Hillmaster,

It pains me to have to write this letter. You have been a loyal supporter of the Annual Sharpville Debutante Ball for more than five years, and two of your girls participated in the Ball several years ago.

You will recall that you and Erica signed a letter that contained a moral turpitude clause, promising that Erica and her close relatives would not engage in any behaviors or activities that the Ladies Auxiliary considered immoral or unbecoming of a Debutante. We included that clause in the Debutant Ball Participant Contract to affirm our commitment to the highest moral standards as embodied by the entire Sharpville community. Unfortunately, Erica has fallen short of those standards, and that is why you and Erica are receiving this letter. Mrs. Hillmaster,

*girls of fine breeding and sound moral training should
understand the impropriety of being the only girl in the
company of a group of boys, doing only God knows what.
Especially disappointing is that Erica failed to understand
the impropriety of being seen in the presence of a colored
boy sitting so close that they actually touched. I am not
suggesting that anything untoward transpired between
her and the colored boy, God forbid. We know you and
Mr. Hillmaster brought your Erica up to stay away
from scandal of that sort. But it just doesn't look right.
And since looks are very important when it comes to the
Sharpville Annual Debutante Ball, I regret to inform
you that your daughter, Erica Hillmaster, will not be
allowed to participate in the Ladies Auxiliary Annual
Debutante Ball next year or any year hence. Your entry
fee of $750 will be refunded to you minus a seventy-five
dollar administrative fee. If you have any questions, please
do not hesitate in contacting me. May God bless you and
your family.*

Sincerely,

Imogene Parsons Lee,

President and Founder of the Sharpville Ladies Auxiliary.

Six months later, Erica and her family moved to Birmingham, Alabama, supposedly to allow Mr. Hillmaster to take over his ailing father's tire sales business.

Her justification for excommunicating the Hillmaster family from Sharpville' hyped high society further burnished her credentials as the supreme alpha female, *nearly* in the mold of the supreme alpha male, Billy Wayne Sharp. Word quickly spread that Imogene Roberts was not to be messed with. And from that moment on, no one did. Joe Lee was pleased that Imogene acted with such authority and seriousness in light of Erica's moral failings. He was proud of Imogene's achievements and with the notoriety, power, and accolades that she has garnered along the way. She was the unquestioned queen bee of all white, female Sharpville. Joe Lee could not have been prouder. Nevertheless, he was, at times, irritated with her because she had taken on so many responsibilities outside the home. He secretly yearned for the days when Imogene spent most of her time at home, cooking, cleaning, and being the subservient wife she once was. Publicly, however, he applauded her and wished her continued success in her role as alpha female. He knew that the window had closed long ago on any opportunity to discuss with her his wishes that she return to being a homemaker and Mrs. Joe Lee Roberts.

CHAPTER 11

JOE LEE WAS also a member of the state insurance board, his reward for financially supporting the winner in the governor's race eight years ago, although he could have selected any of the thirty-five vacant seats at the twenty state agencies that came under the purview of the governor. He chose the insurance board because that was the only one at which he had never served, and one of his life goals was to serve on the board of every state agency. Joe Lee Roberts claimed a common lineage with General William Paul Roberts, the youngest General in the Confederacy. Such a connection to Confederacy royalty prompted Joe Lee to create a private collection of Civil War memorabilia, which except for the collection of ships, rivaled the Civil War archives at The National **Civil War** Naval **Museum** at Port Columbus, Georgia.

Picking up on his monologue about Jeremiah Simpson's efforts to desegregate Henderson State University, Billy Wayne continued to retell the story of how he, the President of Henderson State University, and other local officials thwarted every effort by Simpson to become the first black student to enroll in a predominantly white college in Mississippi.

"You damn skippy we did, Joe Lee. But you know President General Nathan Sumrall kept Simpson going in circles. Every time that boy showed up out there, the General... What a fine man the General was. A mighty fine military leader and a mighty good president. He and my daddy and me spent many a night huntin' coon and discussin' famous military battles. Had a steel-trap mind. Knew every major battle that was fought in dubya-dubya one and two. That great man who was like a second daddy to me. Came along at a time when the school and the state needed that kinda firm, tough, no bull-shit leadership. Wish we still had it, know what I mean? And he didn't take shit off nobody. Told me he pulled his gun outta his desk draw one day, put it on top of the desk and told this professor that was complaining about some shit that if he didn't get the fuck outta his office, he was gonna blow a goddamn hole in his candy ass and claim self-defense. I guess you know what that whiny son of a bitch did," said Billy Wayne as he brayed like a donkey and slammed his hand down on the table to indicate his admiration of the actions of President Sumrall.

Billy Wayne admired Sumrall as a man who took charge, took no prisoners, and always commanded respect if not fear from those under him. Billy Wayne was a devotee and huge fan of that type of command and control leadership. He witnessed it in the Army and he observed it in Sumrall, with whom he had formed a nearly life-long bond. Sumrall was disappointed that Billy Wayne did not go to college, but he saw in Billy Wayne a person destined for greatness.

For a quick, distracted moment, Billy Wayne allowed his mind to drift back in time when he and Sumrall went hunting for gray wolves in Idaho. One evening while sitting around a crackling campfire, sipping Southern Comfort, Sumrall heaped unsolicited and unexpected praise on Billy Wayne. Sumrall's words were to Billy Wayne what rain is to a flower—meaningful, life-sustaining, and plentiful.

"Billy Wayne Sharp, let me tell you something you probably already know. You have a great mind and a big heart. You are destined to leave a legacy in Mississippi that will likely be unmatched for years to come. And that is because you are proud to be a Southerner, a Mississippian, and a fearless defender of the Southern way of life. Our state needs more men like you. You are unafraid to speak up and stand up for your people—our people. When the mission calls for guts, you supply it in spades. When the mission calls for creativity, it oozes out of you like sap from a sapling. You are a special gift to all of us who have the privilege of knowing you. But I have to tell you that I have this one regret for you, son. If only you had become a learned man, imbued with the many advantages afforded such men of the academy. Who knows? You might have become president of these great United States of America. But, alas, Billy Wayne, your destiny was cast long before you drew your first breath or uttered your first sound. I am convinced that it was simply not God's will that you attend college and become a man of letters. Instead, God has anointed you with gifts of leadership and a spirit and personality that will instill either fear or respect in all who enter your sphere of influence. And that will not only bene-fit you, but I am confident that the righteous men and women of the South will forever benefit from your courage, determination, and your uncommon ability to mold men and to bend them to your will. I salute you. I bless you. And I have infinite hope that you will make all of Sharpville and the entire state of Mississippi proud to call Billy Wayne Sharp its son," Sumrall said.

As quickly as his mind drifted to that warm campfire long ago at No Regret Peak in Custer County, Idaho and the atten-dant ego-boost that was bestowed on him by his mentor, it came back just as quickly to the conference table, in the B.W. Sharp Office Complex, in Sharpville, Mississippi.

"And out the pure goodness of his heart, the General took on this simple-minded nigger to do odd jobs for him round his house. Heard that buck couldn't follow the simplest damn instructions to save his frickin' life, even though he was thirty-somethin' years old at the time. He was like old Step-n-Fetchit. Had to tell that nigger something real slow, one sentence at a time, over and over again. But it wudn' t his fault he was so damn slow. I think he was one of them imbeciles, born when a brother and a sister have relations. You know they do that shit all the time. But the General felt sorry for the boy's granny cause she used to sit for the General's mama in the olden days—back when you could always find good help. Cause today you can't git none of these good-fo-nutin, aimless, shit-talking Negroes to give you one honest day's work to save their natural-born life. Specially them young ones. All they wanna do is listen to that loud-ass talking music. Thank they call it rap or some shit like that! Even my god son was listening to that shit the other night at my house. I told him and his mamma, can't listen to that kind of music in my house, and wish you didn't listen to it no time. But you know how these kids is today", Billy Wayne said with his voice trailing off, revealing his profound lamentations and frustrations over the direction of today's white kids, especially young white boys.

*

Seizing a rare opportunity to say something that would please Billy Wayne, Clifford Morgan, the town's only white undertaker offered support for Billy Wayne's frustration over the choice of music among today's young white kids. Clifford Morgan was a slow-talking, rotund man with a patch over his right eye, the result of having a cancerous eyeball removed twenty years ago. Cliff, as his close friends call him, is a long-time member of the Governor's Political Roundtable, a group of conservative business owners who routinely provide advice and feedback for the governor. He became a member of that prestigious caucus after donating more than two point one million dollars to the governor's re-election campaign. In addition to providing advice and counsel to the governor, the Roundtable develops policies on an array of issues, including the most recent issues of climate change, public education, higher education, and Medicaid. The Roundtable's policy views regarding those four areas are, in order: it is a hoax; they need competition from the private sector; too many colleges—merge or eliminate the black colleges; and too many free-loaders living off the teats of the state. As the senior member of the Roundtable, Cliff exerted a great deal of influence, and thus, on public policy in the state of Mississippi. His views of the aforementioned policies prevailed and were eagerly forwarded to governor for his presentation to the public during the State of the State address. As expected, the governor expressed his unqualified support for the positions the members of the Roundtable took on those four critical issues. He singled out Cliff Morgan for his leadership in crafting those policies.

Clifford Morgan and Billy Wayne Sharp were the only two among the group who did not attend college. Clifford followed in the footsteps of his father, Bailey Morgan, owner of Morgan's Mortuary, Burial, and Crematorium. After Bailey Morgan's retirement from the funeral services business, Clifford became sole proprietor of a flourishing funeral services business that had several financial tentacles attached to it, including seven other highly lucrative funeral homes and hospices around the state. One of those tentacles included ownership of Foster's Funeral and Burial Services, the black funeral home that has served the entire black population of Henderson County for more than five decades. Winston Foster gave up the funeral business and supposedly left town, never to be heard from again after Clifford made an offer to buy him out for a quarter of its fair market value and net worth. A close friend of Winston Foster told Clifford that Foster had incurred some heavy losses at casinos in Biloxi, New Orleans, Atlantic City, and Las Vegas and might be willing to make a deal for his funeral business. Although Foster wanted to maintain the family business, he was more interested in maintaining his physical well-being and what remained of his shaky financial well-being. He understood that his life was in profound peril as long as his gambling debts remained outstanding. Thus, he desperately wanted to avoid the nastiness and ruthlessness of gambling debt collectors, who unlike those who seek debt resolution through normal and legitimate means, had their own methods of collecting outstanding gambling debts. He knew full well that those methods involved the infliction of insufferable pain by well-schooled professionals who maintained a high efficiency quotient and a low remorseful quotient when collecting debts owed to their bosses. As a result, he found few solutions for covering those debts other than grudgingly accepting Cliff's offer. Foster knew he was losing money on the deal, but given his enormous gambling debts and no cash on hand to pay them, he had no other choice but to accept Cliff's offer of twenty-five percent of the funeral home's net worth and fair market value. To ensure that Foster would not renege on the deal, Cliff had a short but pointed discussion with him at Foster's home. Cliff brought to the meeting two burly white men, clad in black overcoats that concealed the bulges at their sides. The men made it clear by their silence and lack of affect that they were there as enforcers, not as negotiators.

"Now, Foster, I know you got a real bad gambling problem, and because of your lack of self-control and just downright stupidity, you have dug yourself a great big ole hole. And whether you know it or not, I'm the only one who can pull you out of that hole or make sure you stay in it," said Cliff.

"I know, Mr. Morgan, suh, but I don't really want to sell the funeral home. I done told you that, I don't know how many times. This is my family's business. My daddy started this business fifty years ago, and since that time, it's been in my family. It's been right here in the same place all them years to provide for the funeral needs of the colored people in the community, and now you just asking me to just give it to you, Mr. Morgan. I can't do that to my sisters. They trusted me to manage this business and keep it in the family, and now you tryin' to paint me into a corner," said Foster in a pleading voice.

Foster stood up from his couch and began to nervously pace in the narrow space between the glass-top coffee table and the couch. He placed his laced fingers and hands atop his head, took in a deep breath, and emptied his lungs in a long, slow exhale. As he continued to amble back and forth along the length of the brown faux leather couch, he swung both arms to his side, made two fists and used each of them to pound his thighs in rapid succession. He was starting to shed huge crocodile tears, hoping that such a sight would earn him sympathy from Cliff and his associates. But he viscerally knew that crying was futile and would have about as much impact on Cliff as a about as useful as. At the moment he hit his thighs for the fifteenth time, the realization finally hit him that crying nor pleading was going to save him from the fate that Cliff had already sealed for him. He sat back down onto the couch with a heavy plop and thought that this must be what purgatory is like.

"Just a goddamn minute, boy. Don't blame me for puttin' your ass in a corner. You did that your damn self 'cause you ain't got the sense to know when to fold, when to hold, and when to cut your losses and wait to play another day. You just like a junkie. You might as well be hooked on crack or somethin', boy. Just like crack eventually gets the best of a junkie, gamblin' done got the best of you, boy. And now look at you... strung out, out of control, and makin' stupid decisions. Naw, boy, I didn't make you no gamblin' junkie. You did that all by yourself, boy. Now, if you thankin' 'bout Welchin' on this deal, I will make you wish them enforcers from Vegas was havin' this conversation with you instead of me. And you know what those sons of bitches would do to you. What you need to know is that I got the same kind of enforcement powers that them boys from Vegas got. You understand what I'm tellin' you boy," said Clifford as he nodded at the two burly men.

"Naw, suh. What you mean," asked Foster.

"Well, let me put it this way. You have a choice. You can have your remains found so that Foster Funeral Home can lay you to rest with a proper Christian burial. Or you can have your remains go missin' for as long as the earth is still spinning 'round the sun. One way or another, Foster, I'm gonna have this funeral home. So, just make it easy on yourself and your sisters, and sign the damn papers, boy 'cause, to be honest, I'm getting tired of havin' this conversation with you. Here. Take this pen and put your goddamn name on the line that says seller," said Cliff.

Despite alerts sent out to police departments all over the country, Foster was never found. After a few years, his family gave up the search, believing that he either did not want to be found or was dead.

To maintain the appearance of a solely black owned business, Cliff hired a management company from Jackson to create the impression that Foster's Funeral Services retained its image of being a black owned business, although most black people in Henderson County knew that Foster no longer lived in Sharpville. However, most did not know why he left. As the only funeral homes that provided funeral and burial services for the black communities and families of Henderson County, Foster's Funeral and Burial Services remained a profitable enterprise for Clifford Morgan.

*

"Yep. Can't tell 'em shit, Billy Wayne. If I was you, though, Billy Wayne, I would nip that shit in the bud right now. Do like I done my grandbaby when I heard her listening to that wild monkey music. That's what I call it, you know. Anyhow, I told her that if she kept on listening to that kinda music, she was gone turn black as ashes, all her hair was gonna fall out, and both her ears was gonna fall clean off her head. I told her that I had a couple of white kids at the mortuary turned out just like that from listening to that mess. Couldn't show 'em at the funeral cause they was so hideous-looking. Course I made it all up, but she believed her old grandpa. And she ain't listened to that monkey music no mo neither," said Clifford Morgan.

"Hell, Cliff, that's pretty goddamn clever of you, boy. I almost forgot how conniving you could be at times, boy. Just like when you had that nigger Foster whacked when he acted like he didn't want to sell you that funeral home. I liked yo' balls on that deal and you did it just like I told you. They got 'bout as much chance of findin' that son-of-a-bitch as they have in findin' Jimmy Hoffa, 'cause, Cliff, you pulled it off the way it was spose to be, and you listened to Ole Billy Wayne on how to git rid of a problem, once and for all. You done just like I told you, didn't you, Cliff," said Billy Wayne.

"Yep, Billy Wayne. Just like you told me. And having them two boys from Slidell there to take care of Foster was a stroke of genius, Billy Wayne. Like you told me, I stayed away from the details until after it was all done. It was you Billy Wayne that told me how they took that ole boy down to Lake Ponchartrain, out by the Tchefuncte River like you said they was gonna do," said Cliff.

"You damn skippy that's what they done to that ole boy. They plugged his black ass full of lead, wrapped him in a waterproof tarp, tied a bunch of twenty-five pound anchor weights around him and dropped in the deepest part of the lake. Been so long ago, what? About five or six years, I believe. Ole boy ain't never been found. I had almost forgot about that, Cliff," said Billy Wayne.

Cliff was like a kid in a candy store. Pleasing Billy Wayne

with cleverness and a display of cojones in carrying out a murder was like having a lollypop, licorice, and bubble gum all at the same time. He was pleased that he and Billy Wayne had arranged to have Mr. Foster killed after Mr. Foster signed over the funeral business to him.

*

"Anyhow, just yestiddy, one of my foremen had to fire a nigger cause he got into the habit of doing mo talkin' than workin'. Some of 'em just wanna sit round and stand round like they the damn bosses. I tell you. These young jigaboos today, all they want do is make babies, drank that forty-ounce, and listen to that monkey music, as you call it, Cliff. Now the forty-ounce I don't mind 'cause that's my biggest selling drink at the stores," said Billy Wayne as he walked over to a wall and straightened one of the oil paintings of Colonel Barramore Sharp that was hanging unevenly.

Billy Wayne never gave any attention to how some of his products affected the lives of his customers. He never saw a contradiction between being a pillar of the community and a professed Christian and the level of alcoholism and chemical dependence he perpetrated within the black community. He never gave a second thought to the ubiquitous billboards in the black community promoting alcoholic beverages. And he never lost a minute of sleep over the horrific automobile accident that took the life of a promising black high school student that took place in his own backyard. She was killed in a head-on collision by one of Billy Wayne's drunken customers, who was obviously intoxicated when he made the purchase of two forty-ounce bottles of Schlitz Malt Liquor Bull. Billy Wayne instructed all of his convenience store managers to ignore customer intoxication. He told them they were no experts in identifying who had too much to drink. And as such, their only concern was ensuring that the customer paid for what he ordered. His written, unequivocal instruction to all convenience store employees was: *Money trumps everything.* His verbal missive was: *If a son-of-a-bitch don't know he done had too much to drank, it ain't yo fuckin' business to tell 'em. You got two jobs here. One, sell as much product as you can, especially the liquid kind. Two, keep niggers from walkin' off with shit they didn't pay for. If somethin' can't be accounted for because some ass-hole took it without payin' for it, then it comes outta yo paycheck.*

Billy Wayne tightly laced his enormous fingers, turned his arms and hands outward, and cracked his over-sized knuckles. After flexing the fingers on both hands, he reached for his half-empty glass of gin and tonic and drained it.

*

Billy Wayne then picked up with his story about General Sumrall's treatment of a black employee who egregiously violated the Jim Crow law forbidding physical contact or the utterance of any remark deemed to be of a suggestive nature by a black man directed toward a white woman.

"But anyhow, the General, out of the pure goodness of his heart, put this boy to work doing little odd jobs for him like shining his shoes, cuttin' the grass, and washin' the car. Of course, with that kinda mind, the boy didn't have sense enough to do nothin' else. Any how, one day the General spied the boy from his kitchen window talking to his teenage daughter—Fannie Mae—and trying to teach her to do some of them wild monkey dances. You know when they dance they like a bunch of wild monkeys, with a hot poker stuck up they asses… kinda like that wild monkey music, Cliff. But hell, him trying to teach her them wild ass monkey moves, that wudn't bad enough. O' hell nah! The nigger then went and put his filthy, black hands on that sweet little gal's waist, telling her she needed to loosen up her hips and that her ass was too tight. Boy, when the General seent and heard this abomination, he rushed out the house with a long black leather strap and commenced to whupping that boy from head to toe. Ole boy couldn't stand up he was whupped so. But somehow, he found enough strength to drag his black ass on away from there when he seent the General run back inside and come out with a shotgun this time. Never saw the nigger again. That's what that school needs now. And by God, that's what we finally got now. And by the way, Cliff, remind me that we need to talk more about that situation later on," said Billy Wayne.

"That's a big ten-four, Big Billy," said Cliff as he readjusted himself in his seat and tapped out a short rhythmic cadence on the top of the conference table.

"Anyhow, we got somebody running thangs out there now who gonna put them damn uppity ass niggers back in their places and put some fear and respect in them whiny candy ass faggot teachers. You know what um sayin'? Just look at what they been doing ever since that let them jigaboos start coming to school out there. And lettin' they asses even go to school out there shoulda been enough. But, naw they started making trouble and made that fine marching band stop playing *Dixie* at the ball games and even made 'em stop using old General Nat as the school's mascot. Said it was an insult to 'em. Hell, what about the insult to all the white people who been enjoyin' listenin' to dear old *Dixie* all them years and then to be told we can't listen to 'em play it no more? What bout my rights as a white man? It seems to me like white people is the only ones that losing they civil rights in this country. Ain't I got the right to have my heritage respected? This is the South, goddamit. That is our song *and* our mascot. And I say if they don't like it, tough shit. It ain't never bothered nobody 'til they started that race-mixing out at the school," said Billy Wayne.

Feeling his blood pressure and anger slowly rising, Billy Wayne slowed his rant but not the volume. Using a laconic, staccato cadence with his voice, he continued.

"Yep! They just flat-ass made 'em stop playing it cause it

insulted 'em. Hell, it's an insult to me to even have them black sambos out there anyways," said Billy Wayne.

Billy Wayne stood, stretched, and retrieved his chain-tethered trucker's wallet from his left rear pocket. Thumbing through papers stuffed inside a pocket in the oversized wallet, he pulled out a folded newspaper clipping. Holding up a copy of the headline of the *Sharpville Register* that read: *Voters Say Don't Change The Flag*, Billy Wayne let out an ear drum-piercing rebel yell, followed by a fist pound to the tabletop.

"That's what um talkin' 'bout. We just flat out kicked the asses of them liberal pinheads who was hell bent on changing the flag. Don't you see that's why we had to make damn good and sho we won that vote last April, fellas? This is the best head-line that paper ever published. And if weeda let them bleedin hearts, rebel-hatin', pinheads win that one, well, we was gonna be set back for a long time to come. Winning that election was a great victory for our way of life here in Mississippi. Make no mistake about it. And what made it such a sweet victory was that it wudn't even close. We won by a damn near two-one mar-gin," exclaimed Billy Wayne.

Billy Wayne paused a long moment to gloat for the ump-teenth time and to let the profundity of the margin of victory soak in. Winning by such a wide margin, in Billy Wayne's world, was affirmation of the natural and numerical supremacy of the white race in Mississippi.

Hell, puttin' it to a vote to let the voters decide if we wanted to keep the rebel battle flag as the state flag or that ugly-ass pizza-looking flag that them liberal ass holes got put on the bal-lot, was a stroke of genius. Them boys in the governor's office and the legislature, hell, they knowed how the election was gonna come out any damn way. We told them that that's the way to do it. That-a-way, they had the political cover and wiggle room to say, well the voters done spoke, so they didn't have to take no heat from the liberal media and them other dick heads. Spoke? Damn skippy we spoke. It showed the right thanking white people in Mississippi that if we just stick together, we can take back our culture and our way of life, and maintain our heritage. Southern white people, specially us white men, gotta stop being little pussies and being so fucking timid when it comes to standin' up for our heritage. Goddamit, this is our state, our culture, our way of life, and if we ain't got the balls to protect 'em, well, we deserve all this fucked-up race-mixin' we been tryin' to stop," said Billy Wayne with an extreme elevation in the volume of his voice.

Billy Wayne was in rare form as he immersed himself even deeper into his heart-breaking lament and anger about the direction society is going. Like a befuddled debater, however, he interrupted his rant in mid-sentence. After a long minute, he inexplicably rose from his chair so fast he looked like a pilot being ejected in an emergency from a cockpit. In fact, he moved so quickly that he had to pause for another long minute to catch his balance after he started feeling faint. Gaining his balance and retaking his seat, he continued.

"Don't know if I ever told ya bout this sign I seent the other day in the back window of this ole boy's pick up truck that was stopped at a traffic light. I was sittin' there in my pickup right behind him and looked up and saw these funny but true blue words plastered across the back window of that boy's pickup, for God and the whole world to see. Now picture this, boys. A bright red, white and blue picture of the battle flag, and right underneath it in big old white letters, *It's a White thang, you wouldn't understand!* I tooted my horn and gave the ole boy two thumbs up to let him know that I was with him all the way, cause them words sum it all up, far as 'um concerned. If you ain't white, you just don't understand how important that flag is to us and to our heritage, and you don't know how important winning that election was to our race... cause we was able to unite and stand as free, right thankin' white people for the rights of all right-thankin' white people and for *our* way of life," said Billy Wayne in a more sedate and solemn tone.

CHAPTER 12

FURTHER REFLECTING ON the way things have changed and continue to change in race relations, Judge Jethro Milliken picked up on the flow of the conversation and offered his own but similar assessment of the evils of integration.

"As we all know, integration is a stain on the memory of our brave ancestors, who gallantly fought and honorably died to uphold our way of life in the war of northern aggression. May those many brave souls continue to rest in peace, nestled in the bosom of our risen savior. They gave their lives and their treasures to uphold the Southern way of life. It was the way of life that everybody in the Confederate States of America accepted and lived by, in which coloreds and whites knew their place, just the way the good Lord intended it to be. Of course, after the war, we all know how the shit hit the fan, don't we? Those goddam pinhead, nigger-loving reconstructionists, carpetbaggers and scalawags started imposing that equal-rights-for-all bullshit on the white citizens of the South, including our ancestors, right here in Sharpville, Mississippi," said Jethro.

As if they were listening to a stump speech by Theodore Bilbo, the patron saint of white supremacy, the others broke into spontaneous applause and let loose several impressive rebel yells. Such a raucous reaction was further prompted by the state of inebriation in which each man was steeped.

After quieting down a bit, they permitted Jethro to continue.

"They say that the spoils of war go to the victor, but what those damn Yankees did was downright evil. They knew the way of life here was sacred to us, but in order to pour salt into the wound, they just kept pushing that God-forbidden talk about Negroes are citizens just like white people are. The feds went so far as to pass the Thirteenth Amendment, making it legal for slaves to be free, who were actually property, bought and paid for, just like any other item you owned. And to add salt to an already painful wound, there was no monetary compensation for the loss of said property. There was no opportunity to seek legal redress of their grievances because the courts were all run by Yankees, and they were not inclined to do any favors for their enemies. But once again, that was the federal government imposing its liberal values on conservative, confederate states like ours. But the good thing is that to this date, Mississippi has never ratified that amendment. So, technically, we didn't vote to end slavery. In reality, as far as Mississippi is concerned, slavery is still the law of the land since we never made owning slaves an illegal activity. But the feds are not going to let us go back to those good, old days, even though it wouldn't work today like it did back then, mainly because niggers today don't have the same kind of reverence for their intellectual superiors as niggers had during the slave days," said Jethro as he lifted his left hand to check the time, a habit he developed when he was a judge in an effort to keep courtroom proceedings moving at a brisk pace.

"Ain't that the truth, Jethro. Once they got a taste of freedom, you couldn't tell 'em shit after that. They forgot just how good they had it on the plantation as slaves. But then, they started thinking that somehow slavery was an inconvenience to them and they wanted to live and work like they were equal to a white man. Legally, they were property, just like cows, goats, and horses. But they were treated better than cows, goats, and horses 'til they started all that 'I want my freedom bullshit'," said Dickey Carter.

Billy Wayne and his friends lived in the proverbial echo chamber when it came to race. They recycled and renewed the same toxic racial animus that has been passed from generation to generation since the arrival of the first slave in Jamestown, Virginia in 1619. Their views about slavery and black people did not differ appreciably from those of the early slave traders, slave owners, and the complicit politicians who legalized the sale and purchase of human beings. As did their early ancestors, Billy Wayne and his friends believed that black people were innately inferior to white people and undeserving of basic human rights, such as life, liberty, dignity, safety, and the pursuit of happiness. They ascribed to the notion that black people were not fully human, but only three-fifths so. They adhered to the belief that black people were no different than cattle, commodities that can be sold, bought and traded. And they certainly did not accept the idea that the framers of the Declaration of Independence and the United States Constitution intended to extend to black people the promise of the blessings and rights so eloquently expressed in those documents. In their world, the more things changed, the more they stayed the same.

"Those are my thoughts, exactly, DC. Why the hell would slaves want to be free any damn way? On the plantation, they were cared for, fed, and didn't have to worry about where they were going to lay their heads. They had steady work. The master took care of them, kept their bellies full, bred them, and made sure they were cared for in the most humane way possible. But, what they failed to appreciate is that if they hadn't been brought to this country, hell, their assess would have still been running around the jungle chasing lions and making whoopee with their cousins—monkeys and baboons and apes. Equal to a white man! That's bullshit. They are not like white people, never have been and never will be. And that's what the Good Book says, not what Jethro says," said Jethro as he pounded the table with his fist, which prompted others to express their agreement by tapping their knuckles on the table.

Billy Wayne lit up another cigar, finished off his third glass of gin and tonic, and announced a lull in the proceedings so that he could go to the bathroom. Like *Pavlov's* dogs, the others automatically replicated Billy Wayne's actions, except for lighting up a cigar. Smoking in the conference room was a privilege that belonged only to Billy Wayne, primarily because Billy Wayne disallowed it. That rule, of course, applied to everyone except him. He claimed that exception because, as he told the group one day, he was the owner of the building, the conference room, and every inch of concrete from the foundation to the rooftop. And he could do what the hell he wanted to do in his own building. If others don't like the rule they have two options. They can stay the hell out of B.W. Sharp Office Complex, or go out and buy their own building, and then they can make whatever rules about anything they wanted to.

Jethro stood and gazed out the window. With his head bowed he blew out hot air, both literally and symbolically. Then he returned to his seat at the table and continued his

invective on the evils of racial integration.

"But like other right thinking white citizens all across the South, our forefathers here in Sharpville responded to that integration-blaspheming talk by putting the fear of God back into those shiftless, no-count, pea-brain Negroes. Yep. That's when all those northern agitators and race-mixing ass holes realized that even the surrender at Appomattox or the so-called Emancipation Proclamation was not going to change the way of life that God intended for both coloreds and white people here in the South. After the Klan organized and started putting the fear of God back into them so-called "freed slaves" all that talk about integration and race-mixing came to a screeching halt. It's amazing what a rope and a tree could do to convince a nigger that it ain't in his best interest to act like he was equal to nothing but a monkey. And we all know that they are not even close to being the equal to even the poorest of white trash you'd find in the hills of Kentucky or West Virginia, let alone being equal to decent and cultured folks," said Jethro with the seriousness and tone of judge lecturing a wayward lawyer.

"You tellin' the truth right there, Jethro. I done seen a lot of hillbillies and I done seen a heap of niggers in my lifetime. As dumb as them backward ass white boys from the hills of Kentucky are, niggers are ten times dumber. One day this nigger that was on KP duty, which was all they were good for during the war, couldn't read the instructions and recipes to fix collard greens. Can you believe that shit? And when was the last time you ever heard of nigger that can't cook collard greens? The problem was Uncle Sam had written instructions on how to cook every damn thang from boiling potatoes to baking an apple pie. And this ole boy couldn't read cat in block letters on the side of a box car, if you spotted him the c and the t. That's the main reason they never should've let niggers into the regular armed forces. If they don't have the intelligence to understand a simple godddamn recipe for cooking collard greens, how the hell they gonna read and understand complicated and complex manuals and maps," asked Dickey Carter as he shifted his weight in his seat and rapidly and loudly exhaled.

With a wink, Dickey indicated to Jethro that he should continue.

"You are so right, DC. And with the way these government schools are run these days, I expect niggers gonna continue to be dumber than hillbillies. But anyway, for decades, the torch of segregation and its enforcement were passed from one generation to the next. The Klan did its job. Supporters and sympathizers of our side including preachers, politicians, lawyers, judges, teachers, the press, and police all did their job as well. Everybody was on the same page back in those days. We were singing from the same hymn book, sending the same message, and stood as one in the face of race mixers from outside the South. If a nigger needed to be made example of by the law, we could count on the prosecutor, judge, and jury doing what they needed to do. If laws needed to be passed by the state legislature to keep 'em in their place, they did it. And if an editorial needed to be written about the evils of integration, we could count on the newspaper doing just that. Now, y'all might remember this, back in the sixties, when some of the local coloreds started having meetings, talking about integration. When those integrationists and outside agitators were meeting one night at the colored Masonic Hall right here in Sharpville over on Mobile Street one night, the fire department did its part. They showed up at the meeting, and told everybody they had to leave due to fire code violations... too many niggers in one place at the same time! So they shut down the meetin' and that was an example of how even the fire chief knew what he was supposed to do in keep those niggers in their places," said Jethro with a tone of self-satisfaction.

"You damn skippy they shut down that meetin'. That was part of the plannin' strategy that had already been agreed on long befo that meetin' even took place. That wudn't no spur of the moment action by the fire department. Oh, hell naw. There was a whole lotta thangs the police and fire department had up their sleeves to make life for them agitatin', race-mixin' pinheads as uncomfortable as possible," added Billy Wayne who nodded to Jethro to continue.

"And you will also recall the time the Sharpville City Commissioners passed a city ordinance that made it illegal for anyone under the age of eighteen to be involved in a march, picket line, demonstration, or any other form of public protest. Well they did that to checkmate those integrationists who adopted an ill-conceived strategy of putting children on picket lines, thinking that the police and firemen would not whup up on their assess like they did the grown-ups when they went against the laws of the state of Mississippi. So, one day after the new ordinance was passed, three little colored boys showed up at the courthouse with signs tied 'round their necks, commencing to marching right along with the grown-ups. It was a Saturday morning, and the little nappy-headed rascals should have been home watching Deputy Dog or Dudley Do Right. Instead, the little urchins chose to intentionally violate a valid city ordinance that clearly forbade them from being out there on that picket line. So, the officers, doing their job in trying to keep niggers in their place and making sure they had proper respect for the rule of law, took the little juvenile delinquents to the jailhouse. They just wanted to put the fear of God in 'em. They wudn't gonna put up there with the adult prisoners, but that might not have been such a bad idea. Bet that would have scared their little impish asses so that they would have had nightmares for weeks. But they did the next best thing. They made 'em sit on the floor when they got to the jailhouse. The room was as cold as a block of ice and the floor was wet from a leaking ceiling. But they made them sit their little asses right down there on the cold, wet floor. The could have let them sit in the chairs, but the officers, again, knew their part in making the situation as unpleasant as possible so those little scamps would not forget their place," said Jethro as he checked his watch but paid no attention to the time.

"I wonder where their mammies was when all of this marchin' and protestin' shit was takin' place. I thank somebody should have called the welfare office, or whatever office that looks after neglected young-uns, and reported their sorry asses. But, what the hell. If that hadda happened, that was just gonna be one mo expense, taking' care of young-uns, that we hard-working taxpayers would have to pay for," added Joe Lee Roberts.

"You ain't off base none at all there, Joe Lee. I say let them suffer the consequences for makin' bad choices. All that welfare, food stamps, and living off the government has just ruined about most niggers in this country. They started gettin' all that free stuff, that ain't free atall, because it's the hardworking taxpayer who's got to pick up the tab. And because of them gettin' all that free stuff, guess what? They done got lazier, fatter, and even more shiftless than before the government started handing out the 'free' stuff. But anyway I want to get back to what I was talkin' about how we got to where we are now. In those days, like I said, everybody was on the same page. We coordinated efforts to make sure there was a strong, unified opposition to all that integration and race-mixin' talk. And that incident with the three little nigger boys being taken to jail, also goes to show you that a nigger ain't never too young to have the fear of God and the white man put into him. Start early enough, they won't forget. All things working together for the common good—that was a blessing from heaven that the good Lord bestowed upon us in abundance in those days," said Jethro.

"Indeed, it was and still is a blessing to know the Lord has favored us so. We have been faithful to his word, and in return, He has rewarded us with such abundance, in so many ways, we can't even begin to count them. I think that is what our meeting is about tonight, men. It's about recounting our blessings, and at the same time sending up a great big old "thank you" to the man upstairs for being so generous to us, Jethro. You may continue," said Cletus Sessum.

"Well, thank you Mr. Sessum for your approval and your permission to do what I was already doing. At any damn rate, eventually, it got so the Klan didn't have to use a rope and a tree too much to send the right message to niggers about staying in their place. Word got around that a heavy price was to be paid by anyone—colored or white—for violating the rules of Southern propriety and the Southern way of life. We used to having a saying back then that went something like this: *Know your place and God will grant you grace. Forget your place and few will be your days.* But starting in the 1960s, when Kennedy became president, things started changing. Y'all know how he tried to convince the rest of the country that colored people in the South were being treated unfairly by white people. That was bullshit, and we all knew it. Coloreds in the South were not complaining, in the slightest. In fact, we know that they were satisfied with the ways things were. In fact, that local colored preacher who was working with the Sovereignty Commission and the White Citizens Council told us many times that the local niggers didn't want have nothing to do with all that talk about integration. They were pleased with life down here. Y'all remember that preacher even told us that he kicked some of them misguided integration-talking church members out the church. The good reverend told them that they were no longer members and that they better not ever show up again for anything at the church. If they did, he was gonna swear out a trespassing charge against them. And like I said before, the law would have done its part and had every one of those troublemakers locked up and taught a lesson about forgetting their place. But that goddam Earl Warren, Thurgood Marshall and the NAACP started stirring up shit and trying to change our way of life with that God-awful *Brown Decision* in 1954 telling us that coloreds and whites had to go to the same school. But we had an answer for that misguided notion. The state legislature simply repealed the compulsory attendance law and started the Mississippi Sovereignty Commission, both of which were like manna from heaven. That froze all that talk about integrating schools for at least decade or more. What those peckerheads up north did not sufficiently comprehend was that after losing a quarter of a million Southern souls in the war of northern aggression, we were not gonna sit by and let a bunch of new northern aggressors come around tinkering and fucking with our way of life. After all, how the hell is a hand full of niggers and nigger-lovers gonna change things if killing a quarter of a million Southern soldiers couldn't do it," said Jethro.

"You damn skippy a bunch of niggers and nigger-lovers ain't gonna never undo what killin' all them brave Johnny Rebs couldn't undo. It's kinda like when you get a mean, ornery, animal cornered and make him feel like he ain't got no way out, you better git ready for the fight of yo life, boys. And that's the situation that them outside agitators and peckerhead, nigger-loving communists found themselves in, coming down her trying to upset our local niggers with all that blaspheming talk about race-mixing. They backed us into a corner, and what they got to see was a bunch of mad white men who decided that we wudn't gonna put up with them liberal communists tryin' to come into our back yard and start tearin' down thangs that's been in place for generations. Nothin' wrong with takin' names and kickin' a little ass, I always say, to make sure they understood that we was just like a wild animal that's gonna fight, bite, scratch, and hurt some people when it feels like it's gonna be harmed in some way. But any way, go on with yo talk, there, Jethro. You talkin' my kinda talk, except you sound like a school teacher giving a lecture to the PTA," said Billy Wayne, triggering uncertain, nervous laughter and a few slaps on the top of the conference table by the others.

"Thank you Billy Wayne. I will take that as a compliment. Anyway, later on, like a white knight riding to the rescue, good old Southern Texas white boy, LBJ, started listening to that

Martin Luther Coon and them other communist pricks and bought, hook line, and sinker, all that bullshit about coloreds being treated unfairly. So, they passed all of them integration laws letting coloreds eat, drink, and take a dump any place a white person did. These laws even said that coloreds didn't even have to show proper respect for the white people on the city buses. Of course, that Parks woman started all that crap about sitting on the front of the bus. What was the big fucking deal anyway about niggers wanting to ride on the front of the bus? The bus took them from Point A to Point B, which is all they should have been concerned with anyhow. But as we all know, our own senators and representatives from Mississippi along with their courageous brethren from other Southern states fought that abominable federal encroachment on the rights of the states. It's spelled out right there in the constitution in the Tenth Amendment, which I have committed to memory and know y'all know it too. In unison they all recited: '*The powers not delegated to the United States by the Constitution, nor prohibited by it to the States, are reserved to the States respectively, or to the people.*' As far as I am concern the only other amendment that is worth a damn, at the end of the day, is the second," said Jethro.

"Boy, the PTA oughta invite you in to give this talk to the young-uns in the schools out there, Jethro. Billy Wayne, don't you think we, I mean you can arrange that with the school board," asked Dickey Carter.

"Damn skippy I can arrange that. If anybody can do it, it's old Billy Wayne. Um gonna call that ole boy, the school board president, Jasper Traylor. That son-of-a-bitch gonna do just what I tell him 'cause these thangs Jethro tellin' us, you ain't gonna find in them liberal textbooks that them kids being forced to read. So, I thank in the interest of fairness, and providin' a balanced view, our view, of how thangs go the way they are, they gonna get the other side of the story, like ole Paul Harvey says," said Billy Wayne, as he motioned with his hand for Jethro to continue.

"But even with those heathen integration laws, which we all know contradicted the wishes of the Almighty, niggers still knew their place. You see, although the laws said that they had equal rights with white people, their minds were still enslaved and in shackles. And that is exactly where our forefathers and we made sure they remained. If you can convince a nigger of his place and he learns to accept it, even if you have to put the fear of God into him, it don't matter what the law says. Back in the day even if a nigger knew that if he, say, was legally allowed to go into the front entrance of a white restaurant, he was not going to do it. And it was because he knew what the consequences were. And the law of consequences would not be repealed, even when those integration laws said he could go through the front entrance of said restaurant. And that's the way it was for a long time, boys. Things were humming along like a well-oiled machine. Everybody, whites and coloreds, knew the rules of the game, they accepted those rules, and everything was just fine and dandy. They knew their place. We knew ours. Another example and y'all know this because you used to see it so many times back in the day, even after the passage of those so-called civil rights laws. Whenever a colored person approached a white person on the sidewalk, hell, the nigger knew his place and knew what he was supposed to do—step aside and yield to the white person. And yielding also required him to lower his head so as to avoid making eye contact with a white person—otherwise the nigger would have thought he was equal to a white man. By yielding the right of way on the sidewalk to the white person, the colored person was not only yielding space on a stretch of concrete, but he was also, more importantly, yielding to the natural superiority and divine authority of the white race," said Jethro.

"It just seems to me that a whole lot of conflict could be avoided between the coloreds and the whites if the coloreds just simply accepted their natural and God-given station in life, as you said, Jethro. Naturally, some of the coloreds here in Sharpville have done well for themselves, like our friend, C.L. Moody and the good Reverend R.W. But we all know that the man upstairs did not intend for everybody to be entitled to the same riches and blessings that he has so abundantly bestowed upon his favorite people—the Caucasoid, and not the Mongoloid and for sure, not the Negroid species. After all, if we were all entitled to and received all of God's blessings and riches, then who the hell would clean our homes, cook our food, nanny our young-uns, and eat our watermelon," proclaimed Cletus Sessum.

"Right again, my learned friend. But if you don't mind, I would like to finish what I started without your pontification," said Jethro.

With a nod and a tsk, tsk sound, Cletus signaled to Jethro that he could proceed with his presentation.

"How the hell, Billy Wayne, am I going to finish what I want to say if these ass holes keep interrupting me," asked Jethro.

"Who the hell are you calling an ass hole, you little fathead, lard ass, midget man," retorted Cletus.

"Ok, boys. Just calm down. We all friends here, and ain't no sense in y'all acting like a couple of young-uns. You both educated men, and you both know a lot shit about a lot of shit. We all know that, and you don't have to show it off to none of us. But you always seem like you gotta show the other one just how smart you are. Sometimes you boys are like two bulls in heat, tryin' to show the other one that he's got bigger balls than the other. Just know neither one of y'all's got balls bigger than Big Billy Bad-Ass Wayne Sharp. Now Jethro, you got the floor again, son," said Billy Wayne.

"Thank you Billy Wayne. I will now proceed... Then we started seeing things change right here in Sharpville and Henderson County. We saw it first in our schools. We know that coloreds and whites been going to their own schools all those years and everybody accepted it as the way of life around here. But then the feds came up with something called Freedom of Choice as a way of forcing school integration on the coloreds and the whites, which neither group wanted. Coloreds and whites supposedly had the freedom to choose which school they wanted to attend. They could go to school with their own kind or they could go to school with the other race. And guess what? All the white kids, said, oh hell nah! I ain't going to one of them nigger schools. I'm choosing freedom and staying right here with my own kind. And we figured the colored kids would feel the same way and say they wanted to stay with their own kind. But to our shock, five black sambo kids showed up for school at W.E. Thomas Junior High School the first day of class in 1966. Some of y'all remember that time. It was a sad day for most of us. The fear we all had about race-mixing was coming true like a nightmare in the middle of a wet dream. My nephew, Jacob, was going to school at Thomas at the time. He told me that he and his friends were afraid of them. They knew niggers smelled like sheep shit on the hot Rocky Mountains and they have a propensity for absconding with items that rightfully belong to others," said Jethro.

"In other words, they steal shit that don't belong to 'em," chimed in Billy Wayne who was beginning to grow a bit impatient with Jethro's long-winded monologue.

"That's another say of putting it, Billy Wayne. Yes. They like to steal shit, as you say. At any rate, Jacob asked me if there was anything I could do to stop this freedom of choice and race-mixing fiasco, since I was a lawyer. I told him that legally, we couldn't do much. The federal courts were stacked with liberal judges who did not understand the Southern way of life. Lawsuits would take too long, and they would likely get thrown out by pinko liberal judges. But I told him that there were other ways—old but proven ways—that he and his friends could employ to remind them niggers of their place. Once they employed these ways, I told him, things would change in a flash. After I told Jacob what he could do to end this God-forbidden race-mixing, he felt the weight of the world falling off of his shoulders. He thanked me and agreed that it was the perfect plan for restoring W.E. Thomas Junior High place as school for whites only," said Jethro.

"What did you tell the boy, Jethro?" asked Cliff Morgan.

"I hope you told him to just walk up a slap the shit out of one of 'em. If that didn't work I would have told him to just let our boys from Slidell take care of it. Them boys from Slidell loved to utilize their skills in enforcing compliance of the laws of segregation. That's kinda how you would have said, Jethro and all legal like," continued Cliff.

"No, Cliff. That is kind of close to what I told Jacob. I think you would have appreciated my advice. I told him that the general plan was to get the coloreds into a fight at school. How they did it was up to them. But if they got into a fight with one of them, that was sure fire justification for the principal to declare that race-mixing was interrupting the educational process in the school due to fights. As a result, the board could have issued an emergency edict that argued that the safety of the students took precedence over integration. It was that simple. So, I told him, one by one, do something to get one of the coloreds into a fight. After all, it doesn't take much for a nigger to want to fight anyways. 'Cause they have those violent tendencies inbred in them. It's in their DNA. They can't help it. Within a week, at the conclusion of fights with all five coloreds, Thomas Junior High would become an all-white school again, the way it was meant to be. So, Jacob got one of his friends to spit on one of the niggers, knowing that something as disgusting as spitting on you would automatically touch off brouhaha. So, this friend of Jacob spied one of the colored boys walking to class one day and just hauled off and spat on the boy. He was aiming for his face, but his aim was off a bit. So, the spit landed on the boy's pant leg. When the colored boy realized what happened, the white boy and his buddies started surrounding him, egging him on. The boy that did the spitting was reading to whup that nigger's ass. And if the white boy needed back up, there was plenty of it there. But lo and behold, the nigger runs, makes a b-line to bathroom and goes on off to class. What kind of bullshit was that? Some of the Martin Luther Coon passive resistance bullshit is what it was. So, anyhow, they kept trying to get the niggers to fight, but wouldn't none of them oblige. They just kept putting up with whatever the white boys were dishing out. So, after all of that planning, it didn't work out the way we thought it would and niggers kept going to school wherever they damn well pleased. But seeing how screwed up things are in the public schools these days, I say let the coloreds have the damn schools. It's mostly coloreds who go to the government schools anyhow. And to boot, they got a colored superintendent now and most of the school board members are colored too. We had the foresight to build our Christian Schools and Academies so our kids didn't have to deal with colored students or colored teachers. Thank the Lord! Of course, thangs hit another snag and went against us when our dear President Reagan went and signed that Martin Luther King Holiday bill back in '84, permitting the federal government, once again, to usurp the power of the state. But in a more positive move, Mr. Reagan did famously and courageously challenge the IRS when they wanted to take away the tax-exempt status of that fine university up in Greenville, South Carolina, Bob Jones University. Bob Jones is the epitome of Christian values. They adhere to a strict code of conduct. Students can't listen to rock music and have to go to church every Sunday. When they finally admitted their first colored student in, I believe, nineteen and seventy-one, they adopted a very fitting policy that reflected their and, I might add, our biblical and theological philosophy that forbids dating and consorting between coloreds and whites. But lo and behold, that precious policy came under fire when President Reagan challenged the decision by the IRS to cancel Bob Jones' tax-exempt status because of their rightful and correct policy to disallow coloreds and whites to date. Now, that is the type of policy we can all get behind, and Mr. Reagan was behind it one hundred percent," said Jethro.

This was like manna from heaven for Billy Wayne. Two of his favorite topics of all time. Ronald Reagan and banning interracial dating. He could not resist chiming in.

"You damn skippy we can all get behind it. I got behind it one hundred percent, just like my hero and the best damn president this country ever had, Mr. Reagan. I like it when a college president has got the balls to tell niggers, you can go to school here, but don't put your black, filthy hands on our women. They put it right there in the policy. So, if a nigger don't like it and wants him a white woman, he best take his ass to one of them liberal, heathen, communist schools up north where they don't mind that kind of bullshit. In fact, to show them how much I backed that policy against niggers foolin' 'round with white women, I made a very sizeable, six-figures, contribution to that fine university when that story came out. I wanted them to know that they had plenty of support out here amongst true Bible believers that believe the same way they do about all that shit— the way kids should dress, can't listen to that integration music, and thank God, can't date outside your race," said Billy Wayne.

Billy Wayne took a moment to light another cigar, which gave Jethro his opportunity to continue his review of past and recent segregation stories. From experience he knew that if he did not take advantage of Billy Wayne's distraction with his cigar, he might never get to finish. After all, once Billy Wayne gets on a tangent about Ronald Reagan and interracial dating, it might take hours for him to finish and another hour to calm down. So, before Billy Wayne could fully inflame his third Cuban import of the evening, Jethro continued.

"And, that was one of the points Mr. Reagan was trying to make. If South Carolina did not take a stand against a private, Christian college, what business is it of the IRS? President Reagan was for the Bob Jones policy, for sure, or why would he have even bothered to taken on the IRS? Hell, there were other cases he and his team could have selected to make their point with the IRS. I tell you why. He thought Bob Jones was correct in keeping coloreds and whites apart when it came to social and dating contact. But he also didn't think it was the business of the IRS to dictate to a private, Christian college how it should run its affairs. Anyway, getting back to that King birthday bill back in '84. That should have been the prerogative of each of the fifty states to decide if they wanted to celebrate the birthday of a known communist, and according to FBI Director, Mr. J. Edgar Hoover, one of the most dangerous men in America. And we know what Mississippi would have done with such a bill, if it would have come up in our legislature. It would have gone down faster than a cheap hooker," said Jethro.

The final remark was out of character for Jethro. It caught everyone by surprise and prompted raucous, knee-slapping laughter from his shocked friends and a response from Billy Wayne.

"Now, Jethro, that's funny shit you just said. That part about that bill would have went down faster than a cheap hooker. I don't care what nobody says, that was funny as hell, Jethro. Didn't know you knew 'bout hookers, boy, other than the ones that work for us down in New Orleans. And as far as I know, you ain't been with one of 'em. 'Cause you know that we all agreed that you don't mess 'round with the help. But it was funny anyway. Go down faster than a cheap hooker! Boy um gonna have to remember that and borrow it from you, Jethro. I like that one. Now go on with your speech. And speed it up, 'cause some of this is puttin' me to sleep, but I know you tellin' the truth, specially that part about Mr. Reagan. I'm waitin' to hear mo 'bout one of my all-time heroes," said Billy Wayne.

"Thanks, Billy. Don't know where that remark about the cheap hooker came from. Guess you can say that since Samantha left, I do daydream a lot and engage in fits of fancy from time to time about such matters. But I would never allow something like that to happen with one of our employees. Anyway, glad I could add some levity to the discussion. So anyway the bill was actually a huge blessing in disguise for us, fellas. Because with the passage of that King Holiday bill, which called for schools and public offices to close, our legislature took advantage of that abomination and passed a state bill that gave equal time off to celebrate our hero, Jefferson Davis. But we all know President Reagan had no choice but to sign the bill and make it law. He didn't really want to. We all knew where his heart was," said Jethro.

"You damn skippy we knew where his heart was. There ain't never been a president that's been friendlier to the South that President Reagan. He stood up against that race-mixing in South Carolina and he championed the conservative values that we follow down here in the South. He stood for the rights of states to make their own decisions. And boy, when he fired them union air traffic controllers, he sent the right message to them communist trade unions and to us conservatives, especially us in the South," said Billy Wayne.

"Thanks Billy Wayne for bringing up that topic. That leads me to my next point. Look what President Reagan did when he kicked off his re-election campaign in 1984. He came right here to Mississippi, at the Neshoba County Fair to announce his re-election campaign. He could have done that damn near anywhere in the country he wanted to. But he chose to come to the land of Dixie. And remember, and know y'all do, Neshoba County had a lot of symbolic relevance. After all, that is where those three so-called civil rights agitators met their, how should I say it, rather timely and fitting demise. His being at the Fair to announce his re-election campaign sent a powerful message to the entire world that he was running for a second term as president of these United States of America as a proud white man with strong support from white Southerners. Now the liberal pin heads thought it was throwing salt on a wound, but I say, so be it. After all, salt toughens up a wound. Hurts a little bit, but it does what it is supposed to do. Deal with it. So, when I and some other members of the RNC—that's the Republican National Convention, in case y'all didn't know that—from Alabama, Tennessee, and Georgia met with his campaign manager, we talked them into seeing the benefits of a Southern strategy that was guaranteed to win him a second term. As we all know this is how the Southern strategy worked. It was actually called the Southern White Strategy, but for public relations reasons, we just named it the Southern Strategy. And it went like this, and it was a stroke of genius on our part and grand example of how when you are given a bunch of lemons that you think you don't want and you think they are worthless, you just turn around and make some sweet-tasting lemonade out of them. You see, when they passed the Civil Rights Act in 1964 and the Voting Rights Act in 1965, the federal government was starting to piss off a lot of us Southern white folks. We were getting tired of having integration imposed on us and the feds trying to make us abandon our way of life in favor that God-forbidden race-mixing. With those liberal laws, liberal judges, and liberal executive orders, they made it so a colored person, on paper at least, could consider himself equal to a white person by dining, drinking, and even pissing wherever a white could. But even though they changed the law, they didn't necessarily change any hearts. Coloreds continued to stay in their place and eat, drink, and piss with their own kind because we still controlled the way they think through fear of the wrath of the Klan in those early days," said Jethro.

"Amen, brother Jethro! The Klan was the best weapon we ever had to keep coloreds in their places. Even though they are not as active as they used to be, the fear that they can bring about is still substantial. But we can't leave it all to the Klan. We still have tools at our disposals that we should be willing to use, when needed. For example, if a colored person is not acting as he should and wants a bank loan, well, there is something the loan manager can do to convince the person that he should change his attitude, if not his behavior. That's what you were saying earlier, Jethro, that we used to be on the same page. All segments of the community worked in harmony with one another to promote the way of life that has been part of our heritage since the beginning. But if this passive approach does not convince the nigger to change his ways, I say kick 'em in the ass, huh, Billy," asked Cletus Sessum.

Billy Wayne had actually dozed and did not hear the question. With a nudge from Jethro to roust him from his nap and Jethro's re-asking the question, Billy Wayne chimed in usual Billy Wayne fashion.

"You damn skippy, you gotta kick that ass. When a nigger just won't listen to reason and starts thanking all of this is just for laughs and we ain't serious, you gotta do him like that man did the mule. Hit in the head with that two by four, then you got his attention, and he will do any damn thang you tell 'em from then on. And if still don't catch my drift, well, we got ways to permanently fix that asshole," said Billy Wayne.

Not wanting to spend too much time on the violent solutions to what he saw as race problems that have gotten out of hand, Jethro returned to his discussion of the more subtle forms of maintaining the superiority of the white race in America. Billy Wayne seemed to assent to that wish by waving his hand to let Jethro know that he was finished and he could proceed.

"But anyway, it was the Voting Rights Act of 1965 that sealed the deal for the design and implementation of the Southern White Strategy. We convinced the RNC that because of the Voting Rights Act, more and more coloreds would become registered voters and join the Democrat Party. And at the same time, because it was Democrats that instigated these laws, white voters in the South would turn away from the Democrats in droves and come on over to our side. And they did. Although our congressional delegation was all Democrat, none of them ever sided with northern Democrats on issues like that. So, it was the beginning of the end of the strangle hold Democrats had in the South, which went back to the days following the War of Northern Aggression, when the Republican Party was the liberal party and the Democrats were the conservatives. Democrats controlled the South and the Republicans controlled the north. Now, thanks to the Civil Rights Act and the Voting Rights Act, it is just the opposite. Democrats are liberal and control the north and Republicans are conservative and control the South. And I think we can all agree that is the way it ought to be. Look at the fact that we just elected the first Republican governor in Mississippi since the War of Northern Aggression ended. The Southern White Strategy was not to try to keep coloreds from

having the right to vote. In fact, we encouraged coloreds to register and vote because, like I said, they just fell in line behind
the Democrats because the Democrats promised them jobs, integration, and equality with the white man. No self-respecting
white person is going to be part of an organization that included
niggers and was promoting something that was not in the best
interest of white people in the South, that is race-mixing. And
the arithmetic tells you that it is nearly twice as many whites
as coloreds in Mississippi. So, it didn't matter that coloreds
were flocking to the Democrat Party. Even though when you
go to Jackson, sometimes you think the coloreds have taken
over our capital city. Anyhow, just look at what the Democrats
did at their national convention in 1964. They had a mess on
their hands when that so-called Mississippi Freedom or Loyal
Democrat Party went to the Democrat National Convention up
in New Jersey and tried to challenge the credentials of the regular Mississippi Democrat Party because it was all white. That
colored woman, Fannie Lou Hamer, was there in front of that
liberal press justa stirrin' up trouble for old LBJ and that motor
mouth, pinko Vice President, Hubert Horatio Humphrey. All
that publicity and national television coverage was working out
in our favor because the white Southern democrat was able to
see right there on national TV how the Democrat party was on
the path to abandoning the Southern white man in favor of coloreds. And you see, Ole LBJ knew he was not going to win the
South without the Southern white vote, because there were not
nearly enough coloreds registered here in the South to make a
difference without the white Southern democrats. So, in order
to placate the coloreds and hold on to his white Southern democrats, LBJ gave the colored Democrat Party a platform to speak
and to make their points about how bad the poor down trodden
Negroes in Mississippi were being treated. Now that generated
some sympathy for them amongst the northern whites, but as far

as Southern whites were concerned, it was a kiss of death for the Democrat Party in Miss-sippi. Like I said, the thinking amongst Southern whites and those of us who came up with the White Southern Strategy was to just go ahead and let the coloreds vote. Like I said and like we predicted, when they got the right to vote and joined the Democrat Party, it would drive Southern whites right over to our side—the Republican Party, not the party of Lincoln, but the party of Reagan—big damn difference. So, the Southern strategy worked, and thanks to Mr. Reagan, it's been working ever since and will continue to work long after all of us are dead and gone," mused Jethro.

"Damn good strategy, Jethro. You and them other RNC boys are some sneaky, conniving, but effective sons-of-bitches. But when it came to them nigger kids going to W. E. Thomas, we still shoulda called on them boys out of Slidell. They would have made sure them nigger scamps and their mamas and daddies got the message, loud and clear. And I guaran-damn-tee you, that race-mixing would have ended once and for all," volunteered Cliff Morgan.

CHAPTER 13

COMING BACK TO his previous ranting about the growing presence of black students on State's campus, and realizing that maybe he was losing control of the discussion, maybe generalizing too much about the contributions of black students at State, and maybe getting too far afield with his chasing of the flag vote "rabbit", Billy Wayne slammed his hand down on the table, scratched his head, and let out a loud chuckle as though he had just gotten the punch line to a joke.

"Now, course the only exception I can see is them coloreds playing ball. 'Cause them boys can flat ass run and shoot that ball. That's all most of 'em good for anyhow. Believe it was Jimmy "The Greek" that hit the nail just right when he pissed off them liberals and that civil rights bunch when he spoke the truth on TV that niggers was bred to be fast strong running young bucks. They got them big thighs, make 'em run strong and work hard in the fields. The good Lord knew what he was doin' when he made up for their lack of brains with an extra helping of brawn. And shit, the way I see it, if we didn't need' em to play ball, I say what the hell we need em for anyway. They got them colored schools for 'em to go to if they just wanna education. Hell that's why they was started in the first place—to make sho none of 'em would ever have a reason to thank about comin' to our white schools. But, hey. I gotta tell you this. God is my witness. Got this from a ole boy over in

Tuscaloosa. He told me that it was Coach Bear Bryant over at Alabama that started bringing in colored boys to play ball at these Southern white schools. Y'all remember back in the late sixties, Alabama got they asses whupped good by Nebraska with a bunch of them greased lightenin', fast-ass colored boys. Them niggers was runnin' so fast, up and down that field, that them po, slow-as-molasses white boys from Alabama just wudn't no match, atall. So, Ole Bear said one day after reflectin' on such a thorough ass-kickin', I got to git me a few of dem big fast runnin' niggers myself. And he did just that. And since that time, Alabama ain't put up with too many ass-whuppin' for sho. And yep, boys, over the years we done got our share of 'em too out at State. And thanks to ole Brock here, we keep 'em comin' cause we keep 'em happy. Hey, Brock. Thata make a nice little jingle for yo next TV commercial. *Shop at Generous Motors, where we keep 'em comin' cause we keep 'em happy.*

"Hey Billy Wayne, that's a mighty fine jingle. I think I will use it next time we cut a commercial. Maybe you oughta have been a jingle writer for one of them ad-writing outfits on Madison Avenue in New York City," said Brock.

"New York City, my ass. Can you see ole Billy Wayne livin' in a sin-sick place like that, with all that race-mixin', and pin-head liberal media? Ah hell naw. I will keep my big fat, Fox news-, Ronald Reagan-loving white ass right here amongst my people. No thank you. Now, let me git back to what I was sayin' there, Brock. You tryin' to git me sidetracked with some good stuff there, but I need to say what I thank about what's goin' on out there at that fine college, that, in my opinion is get-tin' way too black. But anyhow, it done got damn near out of hand. 'Cause every time you look around they got a picture in the paper of some grinnin', big-lip, shiny face jigaboo boy and a white girl posin' together for the whole goddamn world to see. It ain't natural, I tell ya, havin' a colored boy and white girl posin' like that. I can just imagine what goes through the minds of white and colored people when they see somethin' like that. Hell, I don't want to even thank about her screwin' around with somethin' like that. If she is, she can't be nothin' but trailer-park trash anyhow. And, I tell you boys, homecomin' makes me so damn mad I just wanna kick any body's ass. You seen 'em out there in the middle of the football field. King *and* Queen, black as the ace of spades. Make 'em think they own the damn place. Goddamn niggers! But it's just as well. If they put in a jigaboo king, they sure as hell better put in a jigaboo queen. Or vese versa. Then it's all in the newspaper all across the state and in the alumni paper all over the damn country. I tell you the God-honest truth, fellas, if we don't do somethin' 'bout this kind of bullshit, our friends gonna get the idea, we done turned soft. Yep. A fine man he was," said Billy Wayne.

A long pause followed Billy Wayne's intense tirade about his take on the horrors of racial integration and his solemn tribute to the former president of State who epitomized the old Southern way of life in the way he treated subordinates and in his way of dealing with black folk, particularly those who forgot their place.

Speaking of someone who forgot his place, Billy Wayne just stopped talking as if he had all of a sudden forgotten how to talk. After realizing that Billy Wayne seemed both confused and confusing, the others started clearing their throats and fretfully looking at each other and squirming in their seats. Yet they dared not interrupt Billy Wayne's rambling soliloquy or his hopefully momentary state of confusion. They checked the obvious signs of life coming from Billy Wayne—his eyes were wide open, his face was still deep crimson, and he maintained a steady and increasingly hard tapping on the table with the fingers of his right hand. After what seemed like minutes, an angry and embarrassed Billy Wayne rediscovered his focus.

"Joe Lee, what the hell was I talkin' 'bout? I guess I had a brain fart or what they call, one of them senior moments or else I got old timers," asked Billy Wayne.

He loosened everybody again with a booming, vigorous laugh that momentarily belied the fact that such memory lapses had been occurring more frequently in the last year.

"You was talkin' 'bout that coon that tried to enroll at State, and General Sumrall showed his black ass to the curb," responded Joe Lee as he tapped the top of the table in an irregular cadence.

"That's right, boy. Well as I recall, we had to bring in the boys from the Commission to help us out on that one. And them boys wid the Sovereignty Commission knew how to find out some shit on them local trouble-makin' niggers and them outside agitators from the north, and best of all they knew how to spread that shit around just right to make it stank even more. But, personally, I always preferred the direct approach myself, if you know what I mean. Got better results that way and you got 'em a lot sooner. Now y'all remember we all had a meetin' with the General at his office one day to try to figure out howda stave off to this God-forbid race-mixin' that the gubment was tryin' to force down our throat. At least we was tryin' to do our part here in Sharpville. And our friends in other towns all over the South was doin' the same. Anyhow, a fellow by the name of Jack Hudson, who was the field agent for the Commission, met with us over in the General's office. You know I didn't like that fella Hudson a-tall. He was a wussy when it came to handlin' these local trouble-makin' niggers here in Sharpville. He always wanted to do some silly ass undercover shit, like a damn spy in a cold war movie. Doin' surveillance for weeks on end, tamperin' with credit reports, and spreadin' rumors 'bout who was doin' what with who was all fine and good. But, hell this is our frickin' country. Why the hell we got to act like we on the *de*fense, hidin' in bushes, keepin' tabs on who is doin' what, when, and with who and tryin' to sneak up on 'em and catch doin' shit they wudn't supposed to be doin? I say kick 'em in the ass and be proud to let 'em know you done the kickin'. And you know, when you kick 'em hard enough and long enough and other niggers see the results of a good ass-kickin', then all of them damn darkies start rembling' in they boots, and then you won't have no mo trouble out'n 'em. That's like the time, back in my younger days, I was drivin' down Bouie Street goin' home one day. I got to the corner of Seventh and Bouie and seent a coupla colored boys sellin' newspapers. So, I pulled up to where they was standin', rolled down my window, and told the biggest nigger to brang me a goddamn paper. I guess I was tired, or as the missus tells me sometimes, I musta had my habits on. Anyhow, this lazy, slow-walkin' son-of-a-bitch takes his own goddam time to brang me the paper. Ain't never told y'all bout this, have I," asked Billy Wayne.

"Don't believe you have, Billy Wayne. But I'm sure you didn't put up with no disrespect from that boy," added Cletus Sessum, attempting to gain favor with Billy Wayne after losing some earlier when he tried to correct him on the dates of Jeremiah Simpson's attempts to enroll at Henderson State College.

Even though they had all heard the story many times about how Billy Wayne assaulted a young black man for no apparent reason, they never tired of hearing it. Billy Wayne was going to re-tell it anyway, regardless of how many times he had already done so.

"You damn skippy I didn't put up with it. Never have. Never will. So, I jumped out my car and walked up to this big mother fucker and told him the next time a white man tells you to do somethin', you better do it right then and now, goddamit. I said, some of you niggers seem to forgot your places round here and don't' know to move when you been told to do somthin'. The boy said, *sorry boss* and just dropped his head cause he knowed what was comin' next. So, I turned him round by his shoulders and commenced to puttin' all my size elevens up his ass. I musta kicked his big ass fifteen or twenty times. Wore me out! And if he'da tried to do somethin' stupid, like try to hit me back, I had my .22 tucked in my back pocket, and I woulda blowed his frickin' brains out, right there on the spot. But you know what was mo' important that me whuppin' this nigger's ass, was that other niggers passin' by saw what I was doin' and I betcha that put the fear of God back in 'em. At least it did for *that* boy. That royal ass-kickin' taught him a valuable lesson 'bout how to properly respond to a white man. I told him next time a meaner son-of-a-bitch than me might do somethin' a lot worse than put a foot in his ass. So, when I got back in my car, I told both of them boys they better put a little mo pep in they step next time a white man tell 'em to do somethin'. Next time I stopped there to get a paper, guess what? Both of them big ass nigga-boos damn near knocked one another down tryin' to get to me with my damn paper. See what a good ass-kickin' will do for a nigger," asked Billy Wayne with a chuckle.

Billy Wayne reveled in his bigotry, especially when that bigotry turned violent. When verbally assaulting someone was not enough, he did not think twice about resorting to physical violence to further humiliate that person. And given his massive size, he generally dominated physical confrontations, even as he got older, and especially when his opponent was a frightened black man.

"One more thang kinda related to that situation. Just last week I was at the liquor store to check on things there and check the receipts for the week, and there was a drunk nigger standin' outside, just havin' a loud-ass one-way conversation with some invisible person standin' next to him. The nigger was elling' bout some shit that I couldn't even make out at first. When I got closer to 'em, and he spied me and I spied him, he started elling' at me instead of that invisible son-of-a-bitch he was elling' at. Said I fucked him out of his money and took his brand new shoes, his car, and his switchblade knife. And lookin' at this ass hole, you could tell he ain't had n'an one of 'em in a long damn time. Sho as hell didn't have no money, shoes, or a car. Now he mighta had a switchblade 'cause niggers do believe in carryin' them a switchblade so that cut up another nigger real nice like. But anyway, at first I thought the nigger was just drunk and out his goddamn mind and I was just gonna ignore his crazy ass and go on in the store like I came there for. But whenever that son-of-a-bitch got up in my face, elling' in my face, talkin' all that crazy bullshit 'bout his car and shit, I said, look you drunk motherfucker, you better git the hell out of my goddamn face. He said, 'Cap'n, you don't scare me, and I can fuck you up befo' you can say Yancy Motherfucker Derringer.' Yep. Yancy Derringer. That's what the boy said. Y'all remember ole Yancy Derringer TV show. He was a Johnny Reb who that worked for the police in New Orleans. When he needed to get the jump on the bad guy, he'd activate this gizmo that would make his derringer go down his sleeve and into his hand. Cool shit, I thought. Damn good show, but didn't stay on the air but a year. Any damn way when he said that, I took that as a threat. Since he said he could fuck me up befo' I could say Yancy Derringer, and since I didn't know if the nigger had a switch-blade on him or not, and I didn't know if he was high on liquor, crack, or some other shit that might account for him actin' like a crazy man that had some kinda death wish, I took precautions the only way I knew how. I slapped that nigger up side his nappy head so hard, he went down like a sack of potatoes. Then when he tried to git up, I put my foot upside his head. He fell back one 'mo time, but whatever that shit he had in his head made him think he could still whup my ass. So, he got up again, and I kicked him in the balls. And the nigger squealed like a pig at slaughter time. I said, 'Nigger, don't git up again. If you do, um gonna have to fuck you up again.' But the nigger got up any way. Damn fool. Said, 'Enough, boss man. You a bad white boy. Don't hit me no 'mo. 'Um gonna go home now and soak my balls so they don't swell up on me. You Billy Wayne Sharp, ain't ya? You the one they call Billy Bad-ass, ain't ya'. They told me that you don't take shit from nobody, specially niggers. So, good bye, Mr. Sharp, suh.' So, off that nigger ran like he was being chased by a pack of blood hounds," said Billy Wayne.

"Some niggers never learn," added Cliff Morgan.

"Right as two plus two equal four, Cliff. And it's *easy* as two plus two when you use the right approach to teach the right lesson, fellas. I been sayin' ever since we got started with our organization. I been sayin' how a good ass-whuppin' will make a nigger do just what he spose to do, when he spose to do it, and how he spose to do it. That ass-whuppin' not only made him remember that I'm a kick-ass bad-ass, but it brought him back to his senses. I guess you can say I slapped that asshole back to reality, so to speak. 'Cause he stopped all that yellin' and talkin' to invisible people you can't see. But most important he knows next time not to think he can whup *my* ass. And he learned a valuable lesson about disrespectin' white folks. The hard way. And the only damn thang that boy said that made sense was him callin' me Billy Bad-Ass. I kinda like that name. Billy Bad-Ass. Got a nice ring to it. Billy Bad-Ass," said Billy Wayne.

Billy Wayne rose slowly to his feet and ambled over to a coat closet. He dug into a front pant pocket and retrieved a gold-colored key, which he inserted into the lock on the closet door. He flicked on an inside light and began rummaging around inside the closet for about five minutes. As he exited the closet, he closed the door, but did not lock it, which did not escape the watchful gaze of everyone at the table. Then he moved back to the table and announced that his shotgun was just where he left it. He had a habit of checking several times a day to make sure the .410 gauge shotgun, a gift from Senator Lawson, was still where he left it. Everyone at the table was relieved that Billy Wayne did not bring the gun out to show it off, as he had done on one occasion after drinking a few too many straight gins. On that occasion a few months earlier, he retrieved it from the closet and playfully pointed it at each of his friends and made a "POW" sound. Each of the other six men, he said, was a prized twelve-point bucks, and that he was practicing for the real kill. His friends failed to see the humor in the stunt, despite the gun being unloaded.

"Yep. Billy Bad-ass. I like that. Anyhow. I better get back to where I was, fo I forget where I was. Yeah. Yeah. I remember what I was saying, Joe Lee. Thought I forgot again, didn't ya? But if y'all had to try to keep up with as much shit as I have to, y'all be forgettin' what the hell you saying sometimes. So, y'all be a little understandin' with Big Billy Wayne, when he forget what the hell he been sayin' sometime. So, any way, Jack Hudson was into all this undercover covert shit, spying on niggers. That's bullshit. You can't try to out fox one of them tricky jigaboos anyhow. You got to do 'em like you do that stubborn ass mule. Hit it upside the head with that two by four and get his attention. Then he'll do just what the hell you want him to do," said Billy Wayne.

"Yeah. Like you done that boy at the newspaper stand, huh, Billy Wayne?" asked Jethro Milliken, a former circuit court judge and life-long resident of Sharpville. He won five uncontested elections for the county's only criminal trial judge, and prior to his service on the bench, he served one four-year term as mayor. He was married to Samantha Peterson, his mayoral predecessor's twin sister, who was twelve years younger than

Jethro and also a life-long resident of Sharpville. Not long after they were married, Samantha decided she wanted a career of her own, as her twin brother had, and not just be known as Mrs. Jethro Milliken, wife of a successful judge and former mayor. She vowed that she would not be a facsimile of her mother. Her mother lived the life of a traditional wife and was miserable to the point of becoming psychologically damaged and eventually addicted to painkillers and alcohol. The pressure of being the perfect wife, perfect mother, and perfect everything else her wannabe high society husband demanded or expected of her was like a lodestone around her neck. Whenever she tried to assert herself and insist on having a life outside of motherhood and wife, she was summarily physically and verbally abused. Feeling no escape from her torment as a mother and wife, she found escape in daily ingestion of oxycodone and Bourbon. As a young teenager, Samantha watched her mother's spirit and self-esteem plunge like a slow flushing toilet. Mrs. Peterson died of an overdose cocktail of Bourbon and oxycodone at the age of thirty-seven.

Samantha decided to enroll at Henderson State University and pursue a degree in teaching. After graduation, she was hired to teach at Sharpville Elementary School. Judge Milliken initially opposed her plans for pursuing a separate career and identity of her own. He told her he married her so that she would not have to work. Her only job was to be the dutiful, devoted, docile wife, of whom he had dreamed for many years. Her insistence on being Samantha Milliken and having her own career eventually wore down Jethro's insistence that she accede to his ideas of what a dutiful wife should think, be, and do. Over time, he felt her love for him waning, something he feared would happen if she started college. After all, exposure to new ideas and new people is very dangerous and can lead to someone having the gall to actually think for themselves, believe in themselves, and to want a life and career that is not based on compliance, obedience, and subservience. In Jethro's world, such independence of thought and behavior was the antithesis of what a true Southern, servile, genteel woman was put on the planet for in the first place. After seven years of an emotionally empty marriage, Samantha filed for divorce and received a six-figure cash settlement, a Mercedes Benz CL-Class, and most importantly, her freedom. With enough money to last her for the rest of her life, but still in love with teaching, she searched for the ideal place to relocate, which had to have great distance from Sharpville, Mississippi. After watching a rerun of the old black and white television series, *Law Man*, she decided to move to Laramie, Wyoming, where she resumed her teaching career.

Although Jethro experienced hurt and disappointment over his failed marriage, he realized that Samantha could have never been the wife he wanted. He longed for the traditional subservient Southern woman who would cater to her man's whims, wants, and idiosyncrasies without question or complaint. It was clear to Samantha and Jethro that she was not cut out to play the part. So, after a couple of months of immersing himself in a boatload of self-pity, good riddance became his mantra.

Jethro lived and breathed politics. At various times in his life, he served in an impressive array of politically important positions from local precinct captain to delegate to the 1968 and 1972 Republican National Conventions. His vast political network was enhanced significantly after marrying Samantha Peterson, whose twin brother Richard served three terms as President of the Mississippi Municipal League. Before his divorce from Samantha, Jethro took full advantage of his ties to Richard and by proxy, to Richard's network of politically connected elected and appointed state leaders. Those ties served him and the rest of Billy Wayne's cohort quite well. Jethro, with Richard's assistance, arranged a meeting of Billy Wayne and his friends with United States Vice President, Spiro Agnew. The meeting produced excellent publicity for Billy Wayne and his friends. Group pictures along with flattering praise for them by the Vice President were priceless, and boosted their bona fides as major political players who were solidly connected to politicians at the highest level of government. On another occasion, Jethro was able to arrange a meeting between his group of Sharpville's power elite and the Secretary of Commerce, who was more than pleased to expedite the funding of a grant to pay for the expansion of several business interests that Billy Wayne and his friends controlled.

The tentacles of Billy Wayne's clan were potent and extensive, in large part because of the friendships and political relationships that Jethro had created and nurtured during his thirty plus years as a highly skilled political insider. As significant as his role as a political operative, Jethro's primary claim to fame was in his role as Circuit Court Judge, an elected position that he held for thirty-five years before retiring thirty-six months ago. It was in that role that Jethro presided over the most celebrated and controversial court case in the history of Sharpville.

CHAPTER 14

THE FAMOUS CASE involved a white father, Elvin Newhouse, who was prostituting his three daughters at every truck stop and rest area within a 100-mile radius. What was so disturbing and tragic about the case and what gave it even more notoriety was the fact that the girls were fourteen, sixteen, and seventeen, and Newhouse was a preacher at a small holiness church on the outskirts of town. A dirt-poor man with limited income, limited formal education, and mounting medical and household bills, he turned to his daughters for help. He was ashamed to seek financial help from his congregants or from relatives. His shame stemmed from a fundamental belief that being poor is a sin and that God's plan is for him and other believers is to have an abundance of wealth. According to his interpretation of scripture, believers who do not possess wealth, abundantly or otherwise, are clearly lacking in faith—a sin that would doom them to the lake of fire. He considered himself a hypocrite for preaching the importance of wealth acquisition and failing so miserably in acquiring any for himself.

The medical bills were the result of injuries sustained by his wife, who was severely injured in a head-on collision with a drunk driver who was driving the wrong way on an iced-over two-lane highway. She has been on life support since the accident three years ago. The family had no health insurance or savings to cover the enormous cost of her hospitalization. Although doctors have recommended removing her from life support, Elvin Newhouse has steadfastly refused. He believes that only God can end her life, not him or the doctors. As a result her medical bills have exceeded one million dollars, and demands for payments from the hospital are constant.

Initially, each of the daughters was reluctant to be a part of their father's diabolical scheme to earn money to help pay for mom's mounting medical bills. The idea of sacrificing their virginity while fornicating with grown men they didn't know was outright repulsive to them. More importantly, they could not reconcile the Biblical teachings about fornication that they learned from their father *and* the request from him to engage in sexual activities with men to whom they were not married. He convinced them that they would not be truly sinning because they were doing it for the right reasons and because the Bible demands that children obey the wishes of their parents.

After a one-day trial, Newhouse was convicted of pandering and contributing to the delinquency of minors. Judge Milliken sentenced him to twenty-five years at Parchman Penitentiary. But he never made it to Parchman. Reverend Newhouse's transgressions were not only the unholy soiling of his young daughters, but among Billy Wayne and his associates, an equally egregious transgression was that the good reverend was cutting into their own lucrative flesh-peddling business.

Feeling affirmed and self-important that someone appreciated the wisdom of his ways, Billy Wayne continued.

"Absolutely, Jethro. Can't pussyfoot round with a nigger when you tryin' to teach 'em a lesson about how to show proper respect to a white man. But anyhow, we had this meeting and y'all remember how Hudson wanted to spread some talk 'round town bout Simpson messin' with a white woman. He thought that might scare his ass bad enough that he would hop on the next thang leaving Sharpville. But I told 'em, hell no!

That ain't gonna work. 'Cause this nigger got to *feel* something fo he believe we mean bidness. So, I told Hudson that I had been doing some thanking and had come up with a plan that would do just that," said Billy Wayne.

"I told 'em I thought we could put some moonshine in the boy's car the next time he come to campus. 'Cause you know, back then, Sharpville was a dry town and possession of liquor was a misdemeanor, and it called for jail time, depending on who you wuz, of course. But that by itself couldn't take you out of circulation for long, but it could send yo ass to the big house if you git caught with that shine along with some other shit you can't account for. So, as y'all recall. Y'all do recall don't ya," asked Billy Wayne.

With rapid back and forth shakes of their heads and the customary two knocks on the table, they agreed with Billy Wayne that indeed that they did recall. But none of them knew exactly *what* they were supposed to recall. They remembered the story of Jeremiah Simpson as well as Billy Wayne did, but they didn't know whether he was about to go off on another rabbit chase or was going to add something new. They knew that Billy Wayne had arranged with one of the local white boys who ran moonshine for his brother-in-law, to plant a couple of mason jars full of moonshine in Simpson's car and that the Sovereignty Commission knew all about it. But where was Billy Wayne going next with this story, this time?

"Good. 'Cause I don't want to be the only one to have to remember every damn thing all the time. So, as I was saying, I told them the best way to get rid of this nigger for good, short of hanging his black ass, which some of our boys out of Slidell wanted to do. You know, them the same boys that took care of that nigger Mack Parker down in Poplarville, believe it was in nineteen and fifty-nine. Remember him," asked Billy Wayne.

In unison, two knocks of the knuckles on the table.

"He was the coon that had the nerves to force his dirty, nasty filthy black ass on that poor white woman, Missus Waller. Ruined her for life. I don't think I could keep my woman if she been with a nigger, even if she *was* raped. Sad. Sad. Sad. Anyway, y'all remember what happened to Parker's sorry ass, don't ya? Took his no count ass to the jailhouse, which at that time was upstairs on the second floor at the courthouse in Poplarville. After they took him to the jailhouse, the highway patrolman who picked him up gave his gun to Mr. Waller and told him to shoot the nigger on the spot. Hell, nobody would have blamed him, and sure as sin, no jury was gone ever convict a white man for killing a nigger that raped his wife. But that ole boy, bless his heart, said he just didn't have the nerves. Said he wudn't for sure it was Parker. Hell, that didn't make no difference. Some nigger had to pay, and Parker became the unlucky bastard who had to pay. Anyhow, if it was me and that patrolman hadda gave me a gun and said shoot the son-of-a-bitch, I'da blowed all his brain out... clean out through his ass hole and wouldn't uv give it a second thought," said Billy Wayne, pausing to let the graphics of such a scene sink in with his buddies.

"So, anyhow, round bout midnight, the boys went on up to the square and waited round the corner from the jailhouse in their pickup 'til it was time for them to move in. Ole Rowdy Johnson, the County Sheriff, left the keys to Parker's jail cell on his desk befo he left for the evenin', makin' certain the door to the jailhouse was unlocked. Soon as the boys seent old Rowdy pull off in his pickup, they hauled ass on up them stairs and walked right on in, just like Rowdy had set it up. One of the boys took the keys, and as he unlocked the jail door, old Parker commenced to prayin' and a-cryin'. He musta knowed this wudn't no goddamn rescue party comin' to free his black ass. But cryin' and prayin' wudn't gone save his ass that night. In fact, one of them boys got so fed up with Parker cryin' like a titty baby that he whopped Parker hard cross his mouth with one of Rowdy's black jacks, knocked all his damn teeth outta his head. And least that put an end to the prayin', but naturally the boy just kept on cryin'. Fo long they had done dragged Parker's black ass down that long flight of cinder block stairs by his feet. I heard the boy was just a-screamin' and a-carryin' on like a bitch in heat. His head was bouncing like a goddamn basketball on them concrete steps. Plop! Plop! Plop!, with blood gushin' everywhere. Anyhow, after they loaded 'em into the back of the truck, they took him out to the usual spot out at the Pearl River. Course, he was more' an half dead by then, but for good measure, they blowed a hole in him that went clean through his chest, clear out to the other side. Just bout tore the whole upper part of his body clean off. Then the boys did what they always did after a job like that. Hell them boys had so much experience in pullin' off one of these jobs, they coulda done it with they eyes closed, in the dark. They tied a twenty-pound cinder block to boy's feet and chunked him into the river. Didn't want the boy to be fount too soon, you know. And next day I remember tellin' ole Lonnie Dixon what had happened, how we, oh I meant they, had done dumped another dead nigger into the Pearl, and that we needed to get word out to our boys who might be going fishin' out at the Pearl. Lonnie said he knew how to get the word out. So, that same night on his TV singin' show, with a smile and little wink at the camera, he told people not to go fishin' in the Pearl River for a while, 'cause they might find somethin' beside fish. That Lonnie Dixon was a sneaky and subtle little son-of-a-bitch. But we could always count on him," said Billy Wayne.

*

"Anyhow, y'all remember I told Jack Hudson that we could work with the campus security and the boys I had lined up with the shine and have one of 'em put a bottle or two in Simpson's car. And when he comes out of the General's office and tries to drive off. Bam! Y'all catch him with the shit in his car, then take him on off to jail. Just like that. I told 'em I would make sure he gets some big time for this and while at it, I would dry up his feed store credit so he'd be ready for the other trap we got laid for him. So, Simpson shows up one day like he always did, parked his car right there in front of the administration building, and as luck would have it, the boy left his car unlocked. And, just like I was hopin', the General held him in his office a little extra time. You see, we made sure the General didn't know what we was plannin'. If he hadda known, he probably would have tried to talk us out of it. Plus, if questions were ever asked about all this shit, I wanted to make sure the General would have what they call "plausible deniability", which meant he could say he didn't know shit and he'd be tellin' the truth. The General knowed we was up to somethin', but he didn't know what, said Billy Wayne.

"The General told Simpson that befo he could be admitted to State, he had to have a letter of reference from five State alumni who could vouch for his character and fitness to be a student at State. Now, boys, that was one of the General's finest moments. How the hell was this nigger gonna find five white folks to write a letter vouching for his sorry ass character? The General didn't come right out and say you can't come to school here, but making that boy get them letters was a stroke of genius. That way he could have cover if he needed it by sayin' the boy had to meet the same requirements everybody had to meet befo he could be admitted. Now that's the kind of thinkin' that made the General a frickin' general. Wish I coulda seent ole Simpson's face when the General told him 'bout them letters. Wudn't nothin' for his sorry ass to do but to get the hell out of the General's office and come outside, where we had somethin' special plan for his ass. Plus, the General had a Plan C working, just in case Plan A and Plan B didn't work like we planned 'em. Plan C was he had a couple of them glad-handing nigger preachers and teachers and principals, who swore to Hudson that they would do everything they could to keep Simpson outta our school. As a matter of fact, the President of Mississippi Valley State College, that nigger school up in the Delta, and a couple of local colored school principals met with Simpson and told him he was just stirrin' up trouble for all the coloreds in Henderson County. He should just let sleepin' dogs lay. If he didn't stop all that integration talk, somebody for sho was gonna git killed, and he wouldn't want that on his conscience. To get him to go along with what they was tellin' him, they were prepared to offer Simpson a full-ride scholarship to Valley State and a guaranteed job makin' a hell of lot more than a chicken farmer. But the boy declined that very generous offer. But them tricky damn teachers had somethin' else up they sleeves. Clever fuckers! What they wanted was to strike a deal with the governor. Can you believe the nerves of them sons-of-bitches? How the hell you gonna strike a deal with somebody that's way out of your league—who is smarter than you, who is mo clever than you, and who got mo of everything than you got," asked Billy Wayne.

"Anyhow, in exchange for workin' to persuade Simpson to keep his black ass outta State, they wanted the Governor to build a colored college right here in Henderson County. Can you believe them sons-of-bitches? I have to give it to them, though. They had some major league balls to try to pull off a stunt like that. Their idea was that, okay, if you don't want Simpson or any other coloreds to go to school at State, then build us a colored school right here, and none of 'em will ever think about goin' to a white school. But the Governor saw straight through that shit. 'Cause he knew them colored teachers and principals didn't have no leverage since Simpson wudn't gonna get in at State any damn way. So, why the hell would the Governor want to be pushed into a corner to do somethin' he didn't have to do and really didn't want to do? He had all the chips in that game, and them nigger teachers didn't have nothin' to bargain with. You see, as far as we was concerned, and speakin' for the taxpayers in this town, we didn't need no mo' colored schools then—and even today we got too many. I say put all three of the ones we got now together, save some money for our overtaxed taxpayers, and if we are lucky, maybe you will get one decent college outta the mix. One of the colored college presidents thought of that idea last year or the year before. But once word got out, he turned ass and left the state," said Billy Wayne.

"Anyway, the Governor kept 'em on the line long enough til he got tired of toyin' wid 'em. Finally, he told 'em hell no. Missippi can't afford no mo colleges. By then, Plan A was workin' just fine. Didn't need them glad-handin', grinnin' nigger preachers and teachers no damn mo, at least on that mission. We needed them for other missions, but they had overplayed their hands on that one. So we sent them to time out 'til we needed them again. Anyhow, when Simpson left the General's office, the campus security boys was sittin' in they car outta sight from Simpson. And soon as Simpson gets into his car, like a pack of hongry bull dogs on a piece of poke chop, them boys was on Simpson's ass so fast he didn't know what hit him. They pulled him outta the car, cuffed him, and made him sit down on the curb. Cap'n Newly was just waitin' for Simpson to put up a fuss. He was gone snatch a knot in his ass and then add resisting arrest to the charges. But Simpson wudn't sayin' shit. Just sittin' there wid his head down. Wudn't so goddam brave now that his ass was busted. Then one of the security boys looked under the front seat and pulled out two mason jars full of shine. That was all she wrote. The security boys had already called the Sharpville Police and they was already there waiting. So them city boys took over and went ahead and put Simpson in the squad car and they rode him on down to the police station. Anyhow, somebody bailed the boy outta jail, which we wanted. Cause we had mo in sto for this boy that was gonna be the icing on the cake," said Billy Wayne as he leaned back in his chair and clasped his huge calloused hands around the back of his huge head.

"On his way home, Simpson stopped by the Co-Op to buy some feed for his chickens, which we expected since he told one of the boys locked up wid him that his chickens had to be fed that day. I had planned to handle this part of the plan a couple of days later, but him needing the feed that same day made thangs work out even better. Anyhows, I knew he wudn't gonna buy the feed with no cash money on account he had a line of credit at the Co-Op to buy all of his supplies and such. But anyway, I had already made a call to JJ down at the feed store and told him to shut off Simpson's credit, which was part of the plan to finally git rid of this ole boy. So, when Simpson goes by the Co-Op to get his feed on his way home from the jailhouse, he ordered twelve sacks of feed. JJ told him that would be twenty-four dollars and he needed to pay cash. Of course, the ole boy got pissed off and tried to argue with JJ. But JJ told him that he ain't got no mo credit and from now on, he had to pay cash for whatever he needed. So to make sho Simpson knew what was going on, JJ told him he could get his credit back if he stopped agitatin' and stopped tryin' to make trouble out at the college. Simpson was so fired up mad, he told JJ to kiss his black ass, slammed the door, jumped into his truck, and hauled ass back to Nigger Town. Now, boys, here's where we set the snare that finally got him a one-way ticket to Parchman," said Billy Wayne with a big smile.

"Long after it got dark, Police Chief "Trashwagon" Landers got some of his colored trusties to load up twelve sacks of feed and take 'em out to Simpson's mama's house, where Simpson was living at the time. JJ loaned the feed to Trashwagon 'cause, well, he's a good ole boy and cause he knew he'd be gettin' 'em back in a few hours. Anyhow, them colored trusties commenced to chunking all twelve of them bags of feed over that Amco fence into Simpson's mamma's front yard. Course, Trashwagon and his deputies was waiting in the bushes cross the street for Simpson to come out and pick up the feed. Sho 'nuf, out comes Simpson onto the front porch and seent these colored boys tossing the feed right there in plain sight. Simpson musta thought he hit the jackpot. 'Cause he went to runnin' out to where the bags was layin', retched down and picked one of 'em up and started grinnin' like a sissy at a rasslin' match. Them colored boys of Trashwagon knowed what was goin' on. So, they just took off and ran and jumped in Trashwagon's truck and hid under the tarp. That was okay. We didn't need them coons no mo' anyway. Let they asses run cause we wudn't worried bout 'em talkin' none neither. Cause Trashwagon had his niggers under tight control. They knew what would happened if they talked. Y'all remember Trashwagon had this mean ass nigger name Nigger Charley, who would whup any nigger's ass Trashwagon told him to. So, Trashwagon wudn't worried atall bout his boys talkin'. Anyhow as soon as Simpson retch down and touched one o them bags of feed, Trashwagon and his deputies was all over him. Took him on off to the jailhouse, locked him up, charged him with possession of stolen goods, and a few weeks later, he had an all expense paid trip to Parchman. The son of a bitch shoulda stayed there for the rest of his natural life. But some bleedin' heart let his ass out just cause he got sick. Just as well cause he died after he left here and moved to Chicago. Shit, if he'da died here, the state would have had to bury the bastard. So, I said good riddance and let them nigger – loving commies up north bury his ass," said Billy Wayne.

"But we got our message across, boys. That's the thang we can't forget. Not another nigger tried to come out there to that school 'til years later. And you know, boys, that's really when shit started changin'. All that damn race-mixin'. I tell you race-mixin' ain't natural, and for the life of me I can't see why them coloreds and them misguided white liberals can't see that the good Lord didn't intend for coloreds and whites to mix. You see, them boys up at Oxford shoulda took a lesson from us down here when that coon Meredith tried to go to Ole Miss. They just pussyfoot around them feds and the other commies and next thang you know, the nigger is going to class," said Billy Wayne as he stood and stretched and announced that he wanted to talk about something else.

CHAPTER 15

"NOW Y'ALL DO recall too, that this Jew-boy, Gil Berman that was runnin' the newspaper here in town at the time start writin' some editorials complainin' bout the so-called mistreatment of the local coloreds. He kept writin' bout how the civil rights of these po' down trodden Negroes was bein' trampled on by the evil and misguided segregationists," said Billy Wayne before taking his seat.

Gil Berman was a life-long resident of Sharpville. His father and mother immigrated to Sharpville, by way of Ellis Island, Savannah, Georgia, and New Iberia, Louisiana, having fled Poland during the Polish-Soviet War in 1921. The elder Berman owned a printing press company in his hometown of Krakow, Poland where he published a thriving weekly newspaper. As a means of completely dominating the Polish people, the invading Bolsheviks shut down all universities, newspapers, and radio stations. The elder Berman decided to flee his motherland when the Bolsheviks initiated a clandestine program of kidnapping and executing intellectuals, artists, and newspaper writers. Along with their only child, born ten years to the date of their arrival at Ellis Island, he and his wife finally settled in Sharpville. They followed a circuitous route to Sharpville, following several Underground Railroad type relocations sponsored by the Konrad Żegota Committee, which was more famous for its rescue of Jews fleeing Poland during the Nazi occupation prior to

World War II. In order to remove evidence of his Polish but not his Jewish heritage, he officially modified his first and last name from Dawid Bermanski to David Berman.

After settling in Sharpville, David established the *Sharpville Register,* which initially marketed largely to the town's fledgling but growing Jewish community. After another established community-wide newspaper, *The Sharpville Democrat,* folded, the *Register* became the only viable newspaper in Henderson County and the city of Sharpville. The success of the *Sharpville Register* was evidenced by its circulation numbers, which consistently registered in the three thousand to four thousand range. With increased demand, reduced competition, and consistent advertisers, the *Register* went from a weekly publication to a daily.

As a young boy, Gil learned to operate the printing presses and helped out by delivering papers to subscribers and hawking them at the Greyhound Bus Station after school and on weekends. His interest in the newspaper business blossomed even more after he volunteered to fill the position of editorial writer for Sharpville High's student newspaper *The Barramore.* Like a salmon swimming upstream, Gil's editorials and opinion pieces about race relations in Sharpville and in society, in general, went against the prevailing white Southern ethos regarding how black and white people should regard one another. For example, in his weekly column in the school newspaper, *Berman's Musings,* he routinely penned hard-hitting editorials expressing his support for integration of public schools, armed forces, and interstate bus lines. The bus lines were singled out for special focus for many of his well-written and well-research editorials. His focus on segregated bus lines stemmed from his exposure to the segregated waiting rooms at the local Greyhound Bus Station, where he sold copies of the *Register* to bus riders. In one of his more controversial and attention-getting editorials, Gil Berman had this to say: *The unadulterated evil of racial segregation is a cancer that needs to be removed before it further metastasizes and finally destroys the delicate fabric of our beloved country. How can a government—local, state, or federal—with its vast and nearly limitless powers, ensure economic and social progress, when it uses those powers to restrict the freedom, justice, and equality for a segment of our society? How long must that segment of our citizenry be denied the basic human and civil rights that are granted to every citizen of our great nation and guaranteed in that marvelous document called the United States Constitution? How long should our Negro citizens be forced to drink from separate water fountains? How long should they be told that because of their skin color, they are not allowed to dine in certain areas of a public restaurant? How long should our society continue to force those same citizens to ride in the back of city and interstate buses—buses operating with support from taxpayers, including black taxpayers? Ever hear of the phrase, no taxation without representation? In case you missed that American History lesson, that phrased did not come from some communist or socialist. It came from the fathers of our nation as they fought to be liberated from the tyranny of the British government. I think Negro citizens here in Sharpville and throughout the segregated South have every right to appropriate that phrase from our founding fathers and demand the same of a tyrannical government, whether in Jackson or Washington, D.C. How long must we, as privileged, white citizens of Sharpville, Mississippi sit by and accept the Jim Crow practices of forcing Negroes to sit on the back of taxpayer-subsidized buses, to be denied service at a public eating establishment, to be told that they cannot register to vote, or to be told that because of the color of their skin, they cannot take lodging at a public hotel? I call upon our governor, our congressional delegation, our state legislature, and our local city leaders to put an end to the horrible of denying our Negro citizens their constitutional rights. If we fail to do that, I predict that our dear state of Mississippi will forever be destined to be the object of ire from the rest of our nation—and such ire will continue retard the economy growth of our state, thereby permanently making Mississippi the poorest state in the country.*

The principal considered censoring Gil's editorials, especially the aforementioned treatise on the evils of racial segregation, but was convinced by the newspaper faculty sponsor that most of Gil's editorials were harmless enough and are normally ignored by most students. Gil, like his father and mother, was deeply committed to Judaism and took to heart the belief that discrimination, in any form, is contrary to the teachings of God. As a teen, he was active in B'Nai B'rith youth camps, where he was inculcated in the absolute belief of human equality. After graduating from high school, Gil studied journalism at Northwestern University. After graduation, he returned to Sharpville and took over ownership and editorship of the *Register* after his father, David, retired. As he had done as editorial writer at the *Barramore* half a decade earlier, Gil continued to write stinging condemnations of racial segregation. However, unlike his editorials in the *Barramore*, those in the *Register* reached a wider audience, which did not set will with many readers of the paper. However, threats of boycotts of advertisers from individuals who supported racial segregation never materialized, principally because there was no other publication for merchants to advertise their goods and services. But Billy Wayne and his clan were not willing to ignore Gil's constant rant about the evils of racial segregation.

"What Gil Berman meant to say was that he was in favor of that God-forbidden race mixin'. Anyhow, it bothered me and some of the rest of ya bout how he was tryin' to stir up thangs amongst our local niggers, with all that nonsense bout "Negroes got the same rights as white people." But we decided to let it ride since his daddy, David, was still one of our upstandin' citizens and chairman of the Chamber of Commerce. David was a good old boy. Never minded being round that Jew-boy cause he was all about makin' money and as everybody knows, that's what um all about too! But as long as that nigger-loving Berman was just writin' that shit just for local consumption, we just let it slide, even though David tried to talk the boy outta writin' some of that crap. Problem with David was that he was mo concerned about his boy's safety than bout tryin' to preserve our way of life round here," accurately pointed out by Billy Wayne.

"But all of that changed when them commies and nigger-loving, outside agitators up north started readin' that shit Berman was writin' in that good-for-nothin' rag that was good for just lining the bird cage. Don't know how the hell some motherfucker in New York City gonna read somethin' printed in a fuckin' newspaper way down here in Mississippi. But anyhow, some white Jew rabbi from New York sent in a letter to the editor, and of course old Berman just had to print the damn thang. As I recall, the Jew rabbi said he was representin' some liberal pinko outfit called the National Council on Churches or somethin' like that. Any church that's got Jews in it ain't much of church, as far as um concerned... tell you that right now. Anyhow, this Jew rabbi said this group was plannin' on comin' down to Mississippi to work to put an end to segregation in Sharpville. Can you believe the gonads this old boy had? Gonna try to put an end to a way of life down here that done worked for generations the way the good Lord intended it to— niggers in they place and white folks in ours. Oh! Hell naw! To me, all that integration talk was like somebody declarin' war on our sacred heritage. We had no other choice but to start prepping for battle with the enemy. Hell, we couldn't just roll over and let somethin' like that happen, specially in our own back yard," lamented Billy Wayne as he slammed his hand down on the table three times to further emphasized his final words, *own back yard.*

"So, that's when we had to draw the line on what Berman

was doin'. Like I said, long as his editorials and rantin' and ravin' bout the "evil of segregation" was kept local, we didn't have too much concern. Remember, we had thangs under control here with our local niggers anyhow. We had a coupla them broke down glad-handin' nigger preachers keepin' on top of what was goin' on. These preachers was plenty respected amongst the rest of them niggers and whatever they said, the rest of 'em just went long with it. Plus we was payin' em enough to make sure that the locals stayed in they place and ignored all that talk bout integration. The Sovereignty Commission and the Citizens Council had one of them preachers on the hook for more than ten years. Same one that told Simpson to stop tryin' to go to school at State and to forget 'bout all that integration mess. He was one of them high and mighty, Holy Roller, Cadillac-driving Negroes. But he knew his place. Never tried to act like he was equal to a white man. That's what I liked about that boy. Even though he had the biggest colored church in town and owned a couple of outside enterprises, he never got uppity and never tried to act like he was more than what he was. As a matter of fact, the boy tried his damnest to show other niggers the right way to be, how to stay in their damn place. For a long time, he was like the plantation house nigger who kept the rest of the darkies in line. Whenever the Citizens Council needed to know 'bout what the NAACP was up to, the good Reverend was more than glad to keep us in the know. One night he called me on the telephone to tell me some thangs he wanted me to pass on to the Citizens Council. Since I was his main point of contact with the Council, it was only natural the boy would rang me up. Plus, he knowed I was bound to give him a few extra dollars, dependin' on how good the information was," said Billy Wayne as he began to recall one of his many conversations with the pastor.

CHAPTER 16

"HELLO, THIS IS Billy Wayne. What can I do you for," asked Billy Wayne.

"Howdy, Mr. Billy, suh. This is R.W. I just called to give you some information 'bout some kin folks of one of my church members," stated the Reverend Rolando Washington, R.W. for short.

"Oh, R.W. I hope you got some good stuff again. Course, you ain't never give us nothin' but good stuff, boy. You done mo by yoself to keep them niggers, oh, I mean coloreds in line than almost anyone I can thank of," said Billy Wayne as he tried in vain to avoid using the N word.

"You better believe I got some good stuff. I sometimes have to wait til I git all my ducks lined up befo I calls you. It just ain't right of me to give you information that ain't quite as good as it could be. And by the way, you can call 'em niggers all you want, Mr. Billy. Don't bother me none. I thank if a nigger is acting like a nigger, then he ought to be called a nigger. I call some of 'em niggers all the time, if they actin' like a nigger. All us colored people right now need to understand that when they go 'round actin' like dumb, ungrateful, ignorant niggers, they just puttin' all us colored peoples in the same boat. In other words, when one of us is acting like a nigger, then we all should be called a nigger til they just stop acting like a nigger. That way, if you don't want to be called a nigger, then stop them dumb, ungrateful, ignorant niggers from actin that a-way. Um' tryin' to do my part, Mr. Billy. Um tryin' to get niggers to stop acting like they so ungrateful and stupid. But til I do, I be puttin' myself right in that category with the rest of 'em," said Pastor Washington.

"Boy, if we had more niggers in Sharpville like you, we wouldn't have to worry none about all that integration talk. You know how to see thangs the way they should be seen, boy. And I know you gonna keep on doin' what you can do to git others in your flock to see thangs your way," said Billy Wayne as he smiled to himself.

That Reverend Washington would so willingly sell out the black community was not surprising to many black citizens in Sharpville. He made it clear through his church sermons that he believed that black people were better off staying in their "places", as determined by the white majority. He made that point countless times, repeating the same theme in so many of his sermons: *Until black people learn more, earn more, own more, save more, and showed less interest in being equal to white people, the better off they will be.* As the long-serving pastor of the largest black church in Sharpville, he held sway of a sizeable portion of the black community, although he was frequently the target of ridicule from another sizeable portion that referred to him as Reverend Rolando "CUT" Washington. CUT was an acronym for Chief Uncle Tom.

Nevertheless, Reverend Washington was able to exert considerable influence on his flock at New Zion Missionary Baptist Church. He did so through the sheer force of his personality, excellent oratorical skills, personal wealth, and remarkable command of Biblical scriptures, especially those that supported his theological and political slants. Those slants were easily supported also by large sums of money paid to him by his handlers, the primary of whom was Billy Wayne.

"Yassa. Now here is what I done run across, Mr. Billy Wayne.

The uncle of one of my church members is starting to hand out papers in the neighborhood to people," said Pastor Washington.

"What kinda papers you talkin' bout, boy? You gotta a copy," asked Billy Wayne.

"It's from the NAACP. The papers bout the size of a piece of typing paper. I got my hand on one of em, and here's what it says. I got right here in front of me. Um gonna read it to you, if that's what you want me to do. Or I can just brang it by your office first thang in the morning," said Pastor Washington.

"Naw, boy. Read it to me, and then you can still brang it to me tomorrow," said Billy Wayne.

"Here it goes, suh.

Dear Fellow Citizen: Are you tired of being mistreated by the Jim Crow laws of Mississippi? Are you tired of being told you have to order your food from a side window or from a separate dining area? Are you tired of trying to explain to your children why they can't swim at the local public swimming pool? Are you tired of being told that because of the color of your skin, you are a second class citizen in your own country? Are you tired of being told that because of the color of your skin, you cannot exercise your right to vote? And aren't you just sick and tired of being sick and tired? If you answered yes to any of these questions, come to a meeting at the Greater Friendship United Methodist Church in Kelly Settlement, September 11th, 7:00 p.m. Speakers from the National and State NAACP offices will be on hand along with lawyers from the U.S. Justice Department to tell you how to fight for your rights," read Pastor Washington.

"That's a bunch donkey dookey, R.W. Now you know and I know that can't nothin' good atall come outta stirrin' up the nigger community with that kinda talk. We gotta put an end to that kind of outside agitation, once and for all. And we need yo help to make that happen, one way or the other. Let me ask you somethin', R.W. and you thank about it careful befo you answer me," Billy said in a harsh tone.

"Yassa, Mr. Billy Wayne. You just tell me what you needs for me to do, and you know I will take care of it like it ought to be taken care of," said Pastor Washington.

"I know I can count on you, boy. You and I been workin' together for some years now, which of course, will remain our little secret. Now, you gotta a nigger you can send to that meetin' R.W.? We need somebody on the inside at that meetin' at that church who can let us know everythang them communist heathens trying to sell to our niggers," said Billy Wayne.

"Sho do, Mr. Billy, suh. The chairman of my deacon board thanks the way you and I thanks. He don't like all that integration talk neither. He helped me to get word out to the congregation that any talk about race-mixing or integration within our church membership would result in them being immediately terminated from membership in the True Way Missionary Baptist Church. So, I will git him to take care of it. He might not go hisself cause some of the coloreds over at Greater Friendship don't trust too many of our church members. But I will make sho that he makes sho that we will have somebody sittin' on the front row, takin' it all in. And when he makes a report back to me 'bout what they was talkin' about, I call you and tell you everythang," said Pastor Washington

"Sounds like a plan, R.W. Stop by the office in the morning and leave me a copy of that paper. Since that is some really good information, R.W., I thank you should expect a couple of C notes when you drop off the paper. And when yo boy gives you a report on the meetin', you expect another two hundred," said Billy Wayne as he hung of the telephone.

"Next day, the ole boy came by, left the paper and picked up his payment. The night after that, he called me with all the details on the meeting them communist heathens had with them niggers out in Kelly Settlement. Turns out, we was able to pass along to the Sovereignty Commission the names of every last nigger at the meetin'. The Commission was grateful for the information I sent 'em, and they was able to start files on every last one of them communist heathens from out of state and the local niggers that didn't already have a file," said Billy Wayne.

CHAPTER 17

BILLY WAYNE, IN his customary disjointed, story-telling manner, led the listener down one path, and with little or no warning, veered down a different but somewhat related path. Before he related the conversation he had with Reverend Washington, he was reminiscing about Gil Berman, the liberal-leaning local newspaper editor. Both stories showed how he utilized both the carrot and the stick approach to get what he wanted. And what he wanted was to win the war against racial equality. In fighting that war, he used the carrot approach, i.e. bribery to get Reverend Washington to serve as one of his lieutenants in that war. And in the case of Gil Berman, he employed the stick approach to eliminate one of his enemies in that war. He was comfortable in using the carrot approach, but generally, he preferred the stick approach.

His conversation about Berman picked where it left off.

"But when Berman started stirrin' up them outside agitators and invitin' 'em to come down here to try to stir up mo mess and try to get these local niggers to act like they been mistreated, we had to have a serious come to Jesus meetin' wid that boy, even though him and his kind don't even much believe in Jesus. As y'all know, cause y'all was there with me, we went to Berman's office and told him that if he didn't put an end to all this God-forbidden talk bout integration and stirrin' up the local niggers, and encouraging them outside agitators to come down here try to fuck up our way of life, he would suffer the consequences. Now, all the boy had to do at that point was just say okay and everybody woulda been happy. But he got all huffy and self-righteous talkin' bout he was gonna expose us in his next editorial as examples of stubborn white resistance to racial harmony, or some political correctness bullshit like that," said Billy Wayne as he stood up from the table and stretched his arms straight up in the air, revealing his huge, hairy stomach that was punctuated with an equally hairy "insy" navel.

Prompted by his customary excited state when he is about to hear details of blood and gore, Cliff Morgan interrupted with a look of pure ecstasy plastered across his narrow, wrinkled face.

"Billy, I remember what you told that son-of-a-bitch when he threatened to write about us in the paper. You told him, *look you little good for nothing kike, I will fuck you up, if you don't listen to me and do what the hell I'm telling you. You ain't gonna write a goddam thang about me or my friends and furthermore, you best better go back to writin' bout fish fries and church socials in that rag you runnin'. I'll do you like Hitler done yo granddaddy, boy. I'll take you out somewhere where nobody gonna ever find your sorry ass,*" said Cliff Morgan.

"And I remember how much detail you gave him, Billy, to try to get him to do the right thang by us. You said, *I'll stuff your still-kicking, still breathing, blood still-pumping, naked Jew ass into an airtight steel drum just small enough to fit your little puny ass. Then while you packed into that steel drum, folded up like your mamma's wash, I'll pour a whole gallon of gas right there on top of ya. That's right, boy. But I'll make it supreme grade gas since you seem to thank so much of yourself. Then while you squirmin' round with gas in your eyes, ears, mouth, and on your pecker, I will put you out of your misery and throw a match in and watch you sizzle like a roasted pig. Then I'll chunk the drum and your barbecued remains into the Leaf River and let the fish finish you off. And believe me, Jew-boy, you won't never, ever be found,"* said Cliff Morgan.

"Yep, and that's exactly what I had to have done to that boy that same night cause I couldn't be sure he wudn't gonna write what he said he was gonna write. Just couldn't take no chances. Plus, we just had to put an end to all that integration talk. Couldn't have nobody, especially a local white boy, stirrin' up the local niggers and gettin' em to thank they was just as good as the rest of us. So, I called in a coupla boys from Slidell who knew how to take care of shit like that. They got here the same day. They hadn't had much action up to that time, and they was just chomping at the bit. And sho nuf, they took care of that job just exactly like I told Berman we was gonna do it. Fifty-five gallon steel drum, supreme grade gasoline, sizzling pig, and fish meat. Just the way I ordered it. Damn, I'm good! The good thang of course, no more race-mixing editorials and no more Jew boy at the newspaper. Matter of fact, the paper got sold to a bunch of boys outta Atlanta who was mo sympathetic to our cause," said Billy Wayne as he tapped his fingers on the conference table.

"But, goddamit them ass hole preachers came down here from New York any fuckin' way. And fellows, that's when our jobs got a lot harder, trying to uphold our way of life. Society started changing the way they thought about the way niggers was livin in the South. The liberal media started showing that Martin Luther "Coon" on TV, marching and stirrin' up shit all over the damn place. Too bad we didn't have ole Rush, Sean, Alex, and Fox back in them days. They'da showed them liberal media pinheads up north. Thank God we got 'em now. They gonna be real handy in the comin' years. Mark my word. They gonna be the strong and steady voice of us on the right side, and I mean that the way it sounds, of the political spectrum. Liberals got their media pinheads and from Murrow to Rather, they been bendin' the news in their direction. After all, it was them liberal

TV networks that start showin' how we been keepin' niggers in their places all these years. When that started showin' that shit on the TV, thangs started changin'. Now, we on the right got our own TV and radio boys now who gonna tell God's truth the way it was meant to be told," said Billy Wayne.

"Anyhow befo long, King Coon and that civil rights bunch started gettin' more and more sympathy from all of them misguided white folks up north who just didn't understand that the federal gubment can't force states to do shit they don't wanna do. They didn't understand that the gubment can't just force integration on a state if that state don't want it. It's right there in the U.S. Constitution that states have a right to run their affairs the way they see fit. If they want to mix the races and have all them half-breeds runnin' around, that's their damn business. But besides being illegal and unconstitutional, race-mixing is downright immoral and unnatural, contrary to the divine will and wisdom of the Lord. That's what Governor Ross Barnett was standin up for and tryin' to tell them pricks back in the sixties, but they wudn't gonna listen. So, we had to hang tough cause this was a contest. No. More like a holy war betwixt the sacred values that our forefathers passed down to us through the generations, which have upheld our way of life and kept everybody in their God-given places, and them unholy Lucifer-inspired race-mixin' values that come outta them northern, liberal, atheists, communists who wanted to destroy the natural way of life," said Billy Wayne.

"So, you see, it all got to the point where we didn't have no choice but to take care of Berman. Even though the news of Berman's disappearance got them northern preachers and rabbis all riled up and made 'em wanna come down here any damn ways, we was still obligated to take care of Berman, and it was the right thang to do at the time. I'm sho that after hearin' that Berman was missin' and ain't never been found, some of 'em even thought twice bout comin down here, and I'm also sho that some of 'em decided not to come atall cause of what we did with Berman. And boy, when them boys from up 'round Lauderdale County took care of them so-called three civil rights workers, that sho as sin put the fear in some of them candy assess from up north and made 'em stay the hell out of Miss-ippi. This is a war, gentlemen. And like a war, we win some battles and we lose some battles. And winnin' just ain't as easy as it used to be and losing still ain't a bit of damn fun neither. But as far as um concerned, the war ain't over as long as right-thankin', freedom-lovin' Southern white men like us sittin' 'round this table is still standin'. And as for me, it ain't over til they put old Big Billy Wayne Sharp six feet under. In fact, I kinda like what that famous basketball coach from Indiana said 'bout how he wanted to be buried ass up so all of his critics could kiss his ass. And when they bury me, I want 'em to bury me ass up too, so all of them race-mixing, left-wing communist pricks can just pucker up and kiss my big, fat, wrinkle, hairy, Southern, white, rebel ass," said Billy Wayne.

*

Everyone in the room broke into wild laughter, slapping their knees and banging on the table. The humor, however, did not overshadow the fact that Billy Wayne's last remark so perfectly captured, for each of them, their individual and collective views of themselves, the South, and the rest of the country.

After a few minutes, the wild laughter slowly morphed into quiet somberness as they all became silent again, fully appreciating the depth and magnitude of the challenges to their way of life that they have faced over the years and would continue to face in the years to come. However, at least for the moment they each felt emboldened and inspired by Billy Wayne's explosive fervor and his enduring commitment to maintaining the Southern way of life—their way of life. To each of them, the challenges have always been and will always be daunting. Unexpectedly though, the somberness of the moment made them more seriously appreciate the depth and breadth of those challenges, along with their resolve to face them. The more they talked, the more acutely aware they became of the challenges that exist in maintaining racial segregation and the responsibilities required in meeting those challenges. Oh, how happy and humbled they all were that Billy Wayne had decided that they would spend the evening reminiscing.

By now, Billy Wayne was simultaneously energized and tired.

"Boys, I'm tired. But we got a few mo thangs to talk about. So, let's take a break. Jabbo gonna serve some refreshments. Go take a leak or somethin', but don't stay gone too long. I don't want to be fartin' round here too much longer. Margaret spectin' me home fo the sun come up," said Billy Wayne.

They all stopped in their tracks for a long moment, and realized that his remark about flatulence could have been literal or figurative.

"Jabbo! Come on out here boy. We thirsty," yelled Billy Wayne.

CHAPTER 18

JABBO WAS NOT his real name. Jabbo was the name of Billy Wayne's prize hunting dog that died ten years ago. But Billy Wayne needed to show his superiority over this once-proud black man whose given name was Charles Bickford by referring to him by a dead dog's name. Just another demented and intentionally demeaning antic by Billy Wayne to diminish the humanity and humanness of a man he considered unworthy of dignity and respect for no reason other than the color of that man's skin. That he would attempt to so insultingly debase Mr. Bickford was no surprise. After all, he was not above demeaning his own white friends—Cletus, Joe Lee, Charles, Jethro, Brock, and Dickey to whom he afforded a higher degree of humanness and dignity. So, for Billy Wayne to show ignominy toward Charles Bickford in such a cruel manner was as easy and natural as blinking an eye or putting one foot before the other when walking.

Charles Bickford was a native of Sharpville. His ancestors settled in Henderson County after leaving Alabama following the end of the Civil War. His great-great grandfather, Jonas Bickford, was a blacksmith and slave on a thousand-acre cotton plantation in Eutaw, Alabama. Jonas Bickford took pride in his reputation as the best at his craft for miles around, including the adjacent towns of Aliceville, Hueytown, York, Demopolis, Boligee, and Epes. He passed his knowledge and skills of the blacksmith profession to his sons, who in turn, passed them on to their sons. By the time blacksmithing skills reached Charles, technological advances had made blacksmithing relatively obsolete. Nonetheless, using his hands to earn a living was Charles' passion and interest, handed down to him through multiple generations of skillful black men who endeavored to continue the Bickford practice of earning a living with their hands. Doing so was further instilled in Charles by his teachers, most of whom subscribed to Booker T. Washington's belief that black people are better off when they improve their vocational skills rather than their intellectual and academic skills. So, he became a carpenter after serving as an apprentice and journeyman during his last two years of high school at Royal Street High School. After working a few well-paying construction jobs on the Gulf Coast, mainly at the ship yard, the VA Medical Center, and a few strip shopping centers that were popping up like mushrooms along Highway 90, he had earned enough money to ask the love of his life, Dorothea Johnson to be his wife.

Charles was a deeply ebony-hued, slender man with narrow shoulders and a long neck. He normally stood a few inches shy of six feet, however, in the presence of Billy Wayne and his buddies, he physically cowered, which appeared to reduce his height by additional few inches. Also, when he was around Billy Wayne and his entourage, he stirred about nervously and spoke in short sentences, frequently in a soft, subservient, passive voice. Nearly every complete and incomplete sentence he spoke in their presence ended with the word, "suh,"... *yes suh, no suh, be there directly, suh, or I don't know, suh.* In the presence of friends and family, however, he spoke more confidently and enunciated his words with proper diction and clarity. His normal speaking voice was pleasant, clear and a natural baritone. He wore a perpetual smile, no matter in whose presence he was—but the smile, depending on the setting and who was present, suggested either genuine warmth or an unconscious nervous habit. When with family and friends, the smile conveyed genuine warmth. With Billy Wayne and others of his ilk, the smile was an annoying nervous habit. He cropped his hair in a short natural style that perfectly complemented his evenly fashioned mustache and goatee. He dressed neatly, often in a heavily starched and ironed matching shirt and khaki slacks. He wore either black or brown, glowingly polished Stacy Adams wing-tips shoes, depending on the color of his slacks.

Dorothea Johnson moved to Sharpville from the much smaller town of Hermanville, Mississippi with her grandmother and two siblings when she was five years old. Her mother and father died two months apart, both from kidney failure. Each of them had become needlessly dehydrated from working eighteen-hour days picking cotton and not being allowed more than fifteen minutes to rest and take water. Not wanting to lose the only job that paid enough to feed their family, neither of them complained of the fatigue, blood in their stool, or the extreme vomiting and diarrhea. Instead, they literally worked themselves to death, leaving Dorothea and her two younger sisters, age one and two to be cared for by Dorothea's grandmother. Not wanting to live the life of a cotton picker and have that "vocation" passed on to her grandchildren, Grandmother Johnson, relocated to Sharpville with her three granddaughters and moved in with her brother and his wife. Not long after moving to Sharpville, she was able to find work as a maid cleaning the homes of white families in the exclusive, gated community of Hillendale; as a part-time radio dispatcher for the Liberty Cab Company, one of Sharpville's two black-owned taxi cab companies; and as a short-order cook at the Green Door Café, an iconic eating establishment in the heart of black Sharpville. Over time, Grandmother Johnson was able to save enough money to purchase a small shotgun house in a section of Sharpville known as Gomo Alley. With the money she earned from working three part-time jobs, she was able to provide for the basic needs for herself and her granddaughters.

Dorothea graduated from high school with a scholarship offer to attend Campbell College in Jackson, Mississippi. She attended for two full semesters, then decided that being a college student was not to her liking. She achingly missed her sisters, grandmother, and her boyfriend, Charles. Letters, phone calls, and occasional visits were not enough to stave off severe homesickness. She exhibited the classic symptoms of homesickness—sleeping late, missing classes, daydreaming while in class, eating too much, and isolation from other students. The symptoms of homesickness became so acute that she decided that she would rather spend her life in the familiar surroundings of Sharpville without a college degree than try to fit in with people in the big city of Jackson, struggling every day to earn a college diploma. Two months after officially withdrawing from Campbell College and permanently ending her career as a college co-ed, she married her high school sweetheart, Charles Bickford at Star Light Missionary Baptist Church. Star Light was where they first met as members of Mrs. Sims' Sunday School Class when they were both just five years old. From that point on, they became lifelong friends and devoted church members under the spiritual care and the tutelage of Mrs. Sims, the Reverend J.J. Jones and the rest of the Star Light church family. The wedding brought everything full circle for them. They felt blessed and honored to be married in the church where they first laid eyes on each other and embarked on their faith journey.

Dorothea was a short, brown-skinned, petite woman, whose heaviest weight was 125 pounds—and that was during each of her three pregnancies. Her speaking voice was soft yet authoritative, a must when one is barely five-feet tall and tasked with the responsibility of helping raise three teenage daughters.

Her smile was like a magnet. She beamed with an aura that most people found captivating and irresistible. With her warm, angelic, face and smile, she had a way of making people feel at ease, even when they were feeling anything but at ease. It was not only her smile that quieted them, but it was also her soothing voice. She spoke slowly without the customary filler words such as, "uh", "er", and "you know." Her words were soft, reassuring, and steady. She enunciated clearly and easily held the listener's undivided attention from beginning to end with a laser-like focus. She was physically and emotionally present with whomever she was in conversation. At the end of the conversation, if the person began with tears, it generally ended with a smile.

Such was the case with her oldest daughter, Angela, who came to her in tears.

"Mamma, they told me I can't come to the party," said a sobbing Angela.

"You mean the sleep-over party you have been talking about for the past week," asked Dorothea as she placed her large aluminum cooking bowl on the kitchen counter.

"Yes, ma'am. Veronica told me last month that I was invited, and you talked to her mamma and made sure it was okay for me to come. And now Veronica says I can't come now," added Angela.

"Well, did she give you a reason you can't come? Did y'all have a falling out or something? I know how girls your age can be sometimes. You are mad at each other one minute and the next minute you're walking around like Siamese twins, joined at the hip," said Dorothea as she tried to add perspective to the conversation.

She led Angela to the living room where they would have more room to sit.

"No, mamma. We've been getting along fine. At least that's

what I thought, til today at lunch period. She told me that there was going to be some rich girls from out of town at the party, and that they wouldn't—and here is what she said, mamma—feel too comfortable around somebody like me. Like me! What she mean, like me. She was acting like I got two heads or I'm some kinda freak from the circus that's gonna upset her little rich friends," said Angela as she blew her nose on the tissue that her mother handed to her.

"Were you the only girl that was told she can't come," asked Dorothea.

"Yes, ma'am. And that's what I don't get, mamma. I'm no different than the rest of those girls. We all make good grades. We are on the cheerleading squad together and we all took dance together since we were in elementary school. Oh. Except they are white and I ain't. Maybe that's it mamma. Maybe Veronica and her friends don't like me because I'm black," Angela concluded as more tears gushed from her eyes.

Hearing this heart-breaking story from her daughter, Dorothea knew intuitively that the rest of her words needed to be both comforting and empowering. She understood that this was a moment that could either break or bolster Angela's emerging self-esteem and self-worth. She drew her sobbing daughter into her embrace, wiped the tears from her eyes, and sat her down on the sofa.

"Sweetie, what that girl said to you is just plain awful. And you have every right to be mad at her. You thought she cared about you as a friend. But you had no idea she only thought of you as that little poor girl from the other side of the tracks who was not good enough to be in the company of her rich girlfriends. But here is what I want you to keep in mind, and don't ever forget it. First of all, she and her other friends are the real losers here, not you. You see, you are such a fine human being, with so much class and so much love in your heart. You treat people

with respect and you don't judge people based on what side of
the track they live in or how much money their parents have in
the bank. I have seen how you share with your sisters and with
your church friends and the other kids in the neighborhood. Me
and the good Lord brought you into this world and we both fell
in love with you even before then. You were a blessing then and
you have been a blessing to me every single day since then, and
you will be a blessing to me till I draw my last breath and go
home to be with the Lord. And sweetie, I want you to understand something that my granny told me one day when I was
all upset and feeling sorry for myself. She said, Dorothea, you
come from a long line of strong black women, who put up with
a lot more than you what puttin' up with right now. Don't you
dishonor their legacy and their sacrifices and go 'round thinking
that the world is always gonna treat you fair. And what I'm saying to you sweetie is that you also come from a long line of very
strong black women who put up with things far worse that what
you are puttin' up with from this girl who you thought was your
friend. You see, my people and your daddy's people toiled in
the hot sun, picked cotton, and took beatings from mean, evil
men that thought the color of their skin made them better than
the rest of us and more favored by the good Lord. They put up
with all of that mess so that I, you, your sisters, and your future
children won't have to. They put up with a lot more sorrow and
a lot more painful things than who didn't invite them to a slumber party. Now, don't get me wrong. It's okay to be mad and
upset about what you mad and upset about. You just go right
ahead and cry as much as you want to, sweetie. You are hurt,
and I don't want you to think that your hurt ain't important.
I just want you to keep in mind these things I'm about to tell
you," said Dorothea as she repositioned herself on the sofa.

"Okay, mamma," said Angela.

"Alright, here is what I want you to keep in mind. Just like I just told you. You come from a long line of strong black women who put up with a lot of heart ache and heart break, and God knows what all they had to put up with back in the day so that we don't have to suffer what they had to suffer. You see, those women blazed a trail for me, for you, for your sisters, and for other black women. As they blazed that trail, other younger black women and young girls took notice and were taught that they were gonna have to be strong and uphold the right morals and values they had been taught while they continue down that path that their ancestors started out on. And they were gonna have to learn from the examples set before them by their ancestors. They learned how to handle pain, anger, and disappointment from their elders. They learned how take on all the world threw at them. They had no choice, you see. They came from a long line of black women, who, like I said, also put up with much more than they were putting up with, as bad as that was. And now you're getting to that age where it is now your turn to continue on down that path and show others what you learned from your elders and that you are prepared to show to the younger generation what you done learned. And as you go down that path, sweetie, your sisters and other younger girls will be watching you to see just what you done learned and just how you will handle your disappointments, pain, and anger. You see, sweetie, as long as you are female and black, you gonna always have troubles. Ain't no way around it. You old enough to understand that, sweetie. But I also want you to understand that those troubles come into your life for a purpose," said Dorothea

"What purpose, mamma? How can something that makes you cry and mad have a purpose," asked Angela.

"Believe it or not, that purpose is to make you stronger. Now, that don't mean that you don't cry and get mad when something like this or something worse happens to you. It just means that once the crying is over and the mad goes away, you are gonna be stronger for having gone through it and you just move on. I saw a sign one day outside of a church, and I've been carrying the words on that sign with me ever since. It said, *The Lord puts us through these things to prepare us for something bigger.* When I saw those words, it was like the Lord was speaking to my heart because at the time I was going through some tough times when He led me to that sign. I didn't know why I was going through what I was going through, and I can't even remember what it was I was going through at the time. But the point is this: He was telling me that whatever it was I was going through, it was meant to prepare me for something bigger. And every day, when I am faced with a burden or a problem, I just tell myself that it's only gonna make me stronger. And besides, the good book says that the Lord don't put more on you than you can handle anyway. So, sweetie, by going through this upset with these girls, look at it as the Lord is preparing you for something bigger and making you stronger in the process. You don't know what it is, but it is gonna make you stronger. So, what those girls are missing out on at that slumber party is the friendship of a strong, unique, beautiful, fun-loving, gentle, loving human being who brings nothing but joy and happiness into the lives of others," said Dorothea.

"Thank you, mama. I feel much better now. I love you," said Angela as she rose from the sofa and gave Dorothea a big bear hug.

*

Dorothea and Charles doted on one another and effortlessly, yet intentionally, embraced and embodied their favorite scripture, which was read at their wedding—1 Corinthians, 13:4—*Love is patient, love is kind. It does not envy, it does not boast, it is not proud.* They rarely raised their voices at one another. She was his Nubian Queen. He bought her a box of candy and a red rose on their monthly anniversaries, and she baked him his favorite cake, pineapple upside down. They were each other's sword and shield. They protected and supported one another. Except for their love of God, no other love compared to the depth of feelings they had for one another. They were each other's confidant, which came natural to both of them, as they were each shy and not given to gossip. They kept no secrets from one another. Whatever was on their minds, they shared it without having to censor themselves or fear that it would be shared with others. They were poor in material possessions, yet wealthy in love, kindness, and humility.

Dorothea and Charles managed to eke out a decent life for their family of six, until the economy worsened. Due to the downturn in construction, Charles was unable to find steady work. Dorothea, who worked as a presser at a dry cleaners was also laid off. In her second job as a house cleaner, her hours were cut back to five hours a week. At two dollars an hour, she was unable to put much of a dent in their bills and other living expenses. Charles found odd jobs mowing lawns, doing handyman jobs, and selling items at the local recycling plant. But money earned from such jobs was not enough to keep the creditors and bill collectors from calling him demanding payments on appliances, utilities, and credit card bills. Despite their financial hardship, Charles and Dorothea Bickford maintained their tithing at Star Light Missionary Baptist Church. They saved, sacrificed, and exercised extreme frugality in order to make sure that basic family needs were taken care of, even if some creditors went wanting.

*

Another of Charles' creditors was Billy Wayne Sharp. Charles owed money to Billy Wayne for light fixtures, appliances, and other materials and supplies that he purchased on credit from Billy Wayne's hardware superstore to fix up his house. Charles' indebtedness spanned several years, before and during his period of unemployment. He kept going back to the Billy Wayne for more and more supplies on credit, though he did not have the money to pay for what he needed or for what he owed. So, Billy Wayne let him work his debt off by serving parties at his house and serving drinks and refreshments at the power elite's monthly meetings. Charles really never knew how much he owed Billy Wayne, and whenever he asked, Billy Wayne would repeat, almost verbatim, the same response each time.

"Everything will work out for old Jabbo. Don't you worry none, now you hear? Billy Wayne's gonna take care of his boy. Right, Jabbo," asked Billy Wayne

"Yassa, Mr. Sharp, suh. You's been good to me and I don't know what I would do if wudn't for all your kindness and generosity, Mr. Sharp, suh," answered Charles in his normal, soft, and subservient voice.

Those were the exact words in this long-running, seemingly scripted dialogue between callous creditor and dispirited debtor. It seemed like a game—but a game rigged so that only Billy Wayne was guaranteed to win. Like a man caught in the clutches of quicksand, the more Charles struggled to free himself from his seemingly hopeless situation, the deeper he sank. Billy Wayne enjoyed being the overlord of all who were in his sphere of influence, which was quite substantial. He especially enjoyed the role of overlord and overseer when it came to his treatment of and regard for Charles Bickford. He knew that Charles was powerless, helpless, and hapless. He knew that it was because of his manipulation of Charles that a once proud and confident human being had become utterly powerless, helpless, and hapless. Billy Wayne had reaped the benefits of eating the *fruits of a disgraced legacy* for most of his adult life. But also for most of his life, he either ignored or showed contempt for the fact that life strives for balance and symmetry, and without fail it is a reliable, powerful and fair teacher. And one of the lessons that life teaches is that consuming a steady diet of the contaminated fruits of a disgraced legacy leads to pain, self-destruction, and ultimately to a self-correcting force that counters the effects of consuming contaminated fruit. Billy Wayne also chose to ignore or show contempt for two time-tested lessons that he simply thought never applied to him: *What goes around comes around* and *God don't like ugly.*

There was a particularly inane and insulting sophomoric game that Billy Wayne and his buddies played with Charles that was designed strictly for their own entertainment and for the utter humiliation of Charles. The game was to stack a serving tray with empty ten-ounce glasses of liquor, sometimes as many as twenty. Charles would then be told to circle the conference table with the serving tray lifted over his head with one hand. He was to make as many trips around the table in whatever time period one of them demanded, without losing a glass. If one of the glasses fell and broke, Charles was told to clean it up and start over. All the while the pranksters would cackle like brooding hens and laugh as though they had front row seats at a vaudeville show. Charles cringed and cried from the physical pain of holding the tray over his head and from the emotional pain of being the source of his tormentors' sick ideas of fun. If he completed the revolutions around the table in the allotted time without breaking a glass, he was allowed to go home early, in that particular denomination of time. If he were not successful, that amount of time was added to the total time he was required to stay. He would earn or lose time on the job at the whims of Billy Wayne and his buddies who cruelly engaged in a sick form of levity at his expense. More often than not, he ended up spending extended time at Billy Wayne's office and far less time with his family when that impromptu game was played.

CHAPTER 19

ON ANOTHER OCCASION several years ago, Billy Wayne was sitting alone at the conference table, and Charles was sitting alone in the kitchen, awaiting the arrival of the others for the resumption of one of their monthly meetings. While the others had scattered to make phone calls and use the restroom, Billy Wayne was having his usual gin and tonic, more gin than tonic. Charles decided he would take advantage of the opportunity to have a one-on-one conversation with Billy Wayne without the distractions and influences of Billy's buddies. He walked into the conference room, and the bird alarm went off, rousting Billy Wayne from a power nap.

"Mista, Sharp, suh. Can I have a word with you, please, suh," asked Charles.

"Sho can, Jabbo. I'll come out to the kitchen and sit a spell with you, till the boys get back. They'll be along directly. What's on your mind, boy," asked Billy Wayne.

Taking seats in two folding metal chairs about three feet apart and facing each other, Charles and Billy Wayne began a heart-rending conversation.

"Mr. Sharp, you know I been comin' here workin' and servin' you and your friends for now goin' on five years. I 'preciate you lettin' me come here to work off the money I owes you instead of you repossessin' my thangs that me and my girls and Dorothea needs so that we can just have a nice place to live in.

We ain't got nothin' fancy. Just the basic thangs, you know, beds, sofa, eatin' table, dishes, stove, Frigidaire, color TV, and a couple of window air conditioners that give us comfort and make us feel like we got somethin'. And you helped me get most of them thangs I got out at the house—the Frigidaire, TV, stove, air conditioners, and sheet rock and paint to fix up the place to make it look decent. It was important to me to get them thangs done, 'cause I didn't want my girls to be shame to invite their friends over to the house. The place was in pretty bad shape there for a while. Wall paper was peelin', floors were bucklin', and the outside was in bad need of some paint and a new roof. We just had one old black and white television with rabbit ears that we used all sit 'round and watch. But the girls are gettin' older now and they don't always like to watch TV and do stuff with their mama and daddy. They don't say so, but I know how young peoples is. They likes to do what young peoples like to do, not what us old heads like to do. Anyhow, I was shamed of it myself, so I know them gals of mine was feelin' the same way, but, blessed their hearts, they never said a mumblin' word and never complained, not once. And thanks to your generosity, you made all that possible, Mr. Sharp, suh. What I need to ask you, Mr. Sharp, suh is this," said Charles.

Charles slowly lowered his head and steadied his gaze on a two-inch square section of the parquet kitchen floor. After a long minute, he took a deep breath and slowly raised his gaze to the point where he was looking at Billy Wayne directly in his eyes.

"Well, boy, spit it out. I ain't got time to sit here and listen to no goddamn sob story. I got *Fried Green Tomatoes* for that. What the hell you tryin' to say Jabbo. And it better be damn important, like you got the TB or some other catching shit that can make me and the rest of us sick. If it ain't life and death, I can't say um in the mood to hear nothin' else. And if it's 'bout borrowin' mo money for some mo shit for you and them gals of yours, well, you can just forget the hell about that. 'Cause with everything you owe me now, you gonna be the rest of your unlucky ass payin' it off. And fo sho, you better not be askin' me how much you owe me. Like I done told you time and time again, Jabbo, you is finish when I say you is finish. And you a long goddamn way from bein' finished. Why the hell can't you and mo of these coloreds round here be mo like my boy, C.L.? Now that's a nigger who ain't never borrowed a penny from me or nobody else. He worked hard, day and night, his whole entire life to build a decent house and to have lot of nice things. The boy, he didn't beg, borrow, or steal to get where he is today. He worked his black ass off in the hot sun, in the rain, and in the cold, never complained or ask anybody to feel sorry for him or give him nothin'. You see, that's what's wrong with so many of you coloreds today. You wants free shit from the gubment. Welfare, food stamps, Section 8 Houses. Shit you ought to pay for with the sweat of your brow. Instead, y'all 'round here not lookin' for some goddamn handout from the gubment and already overtaxed taxpayers. Hell that boy, C.L. Moody, is livin' better than some white folks 'round here. Now there's lazy ass bunch for you, Jabbo. You take some of that po white trash that live out at the trailer park, they just as lazy and good for nothin' as some of yo people, Jabbo. Tell you boy, you and your people sucking at the teats of the gubment gonna come to an end one of these days. And it's gonna be coloreds like C.L. that's gonna come out okay, and the ones like you and the rest of them that's lookin' for some handouts and free shit, well. Y'all gonna be in such bad shape that y'all gonna be wishin' for the good old days of slavery. At least then, you had a roof over your head and the master gave you three square meals a day. Now look at you. Can't afford to put a roof over your head unless you borrowin' money. Can't have a square meal without going to the Welfare office. But you and yo kind don't' know no better. If you could just a few lessons from my boy, C.L. But I heard how yo people don't care much for C.L. cause he ain't no beggin', glad-handin', shiftless nigger like the rest of y'all. You need to know somethin' 'bout C.L. that you might not know. He don't give a shit 'bout none of y'all good for nuthin leeches, and he don't give a damn if y'all don't never speak to him ever again. He knows it is the good white folks 'round here that's he mo like than yo kind. But anyway, tell me, Jabbo, what the hell you want? It's almost time for the boys to get here and for you to get the dranks together," said Billy Wayne.

"Nothin, suh. I don't guess I wants nothing, Mr. Sharp. Been nice talkin' to you. Um gonna go get everything ready for you and your friends," said a defeated and deflated Charles.

That was several years ago. Reality of the present moment in Billy Wayne's conference room provided further evidence that little had changed in those years. Except, Charles Bickford, on this night, had every reason to believe that in short time, things would indeed change, for better or for worse.

CHAPTER 20

T HE GONGS ON the grandfather clock had sounded eleven times and served as a reminder to Billy Wayne to bring everyone back to the table. He had already tossed down his usual two shots of double gin and tonic that seemed to invigorate him to the point that he began to whistle *Dixie* as it was being sounded out by the grandfather clock. He also tried to march in place to the uneven cadence of his slurred whistling, which was about three stanzas behind the muzak version. Meanwhile, Charles began putting away the drinking glasses as he always did after Billy Wayne and his buddies had finished their drinks. Except this time, his hands were shaking like a leaf in the wind as he took extra care in moving each glass from the serving cart to the dishwasher in the kitchen, which was located adjacent to the conference room separated by a swinging wooden door that emitted a cuckoo bird sound each time it opened.

The bird alarm was added by Billy Wayne as a signal that someone was entering the conference room from the kitchen. Not long after the office complex opened, Charles walked into the conference room while Billy Wayne and his buddies were on a conference call with one of their associates from Slidell. They were discussing a contract hit job on the manager of their chain of adult video stores in New Orleans, who was skimming thousands of dollars a week from the stores' revenues. After reviewing the stores' revenues and expenditures for a four-month period, Joe Lee discovered that the manager was actually maintaining two sets of books—one that he shared with the owners and one that he maintained separately and secretly. The books he shared with the owner showed that business was declining due to a steady but slow reduction in the demand and sale of adult oriented items industry-wide. However, after checking with colleagues who operated adult oriented businesses, Joe Lee discovered that there was no reduction in demand for their products and that they were all making huge profits. So, after suspecting that something nefarious was afoot at the video stores, Billy Wayne and Joe Lee made an unannounced visit to one of the top selling stores in New Orleans. While the manager was on his lunch break, Billy Wayne and Joe Lee located both sets of financial records. Indeed, the secret books showed a huge profit for the previous four months. The official books showed just the opposite. That meant that Billy Wayne and his buddies were being cheated out of thousands of dollars each week by a conniving, embezzling manager, who had worked for them for four years and was trusted to manage five of the eight stores in the New Orleans area. After waiting for three hours for the manager to return from lunch, Billy Wayne and Joe Lee concluded that the thieving manager was not coming back. The clerk who was assisting customers shared with Billy Wayne and Joe Lee that the manager took several thousands of dollars from the office safe and left with a woman in a car. She was carrying luggage as though she and at least one other person were taking a road trip. It did not take a rocket scientist to figure out that the manager had no intentions of returning to the store after lunch or any other time. He and his female companion were on their way to some unknown destination with hundreds of thousands of Billy Wayne's and his buddies' money that he had embezzled for at least four months, maybe longer. Billy Wayne asked the clerk to immediately take on the job of store manager, to which the young college student eagerly answered yes, especially with a pay increase that tripled his current salary. Billy Wayne and Joe Lee drove back to Sharpville filled with so much rage that Billy Wayne sped the entire trip, exceeding the seventy mile-per-hour speed limit by between fifteen and twenty miles. When they reached his office, Billy Wayne immediately called an emergency meeting of his associates. The enforcers from Slidell promptly carried out Billy Wayne's wishes in less than twenty-four hours after receiving the seventy-five thousand dollar contract. The embezzling manager and his blond companion were each shot once in the forehead while sleeping in their car at a roadside park between Southaven, Mississippi and Memphis, Tennessee.

Billy Wayne and his friends abruptly halted the phone conversation with the enforcers just as Charles entered the room with drinks. From that time forward, Billy Wayne decided he had better take extra precautions when he was discussing such sensitive matters, although he was sure Charles would never tell anyone what he heard, if he heard anything at all.

CHAPTER 21

DESPITE CHARLES'S EFFORTS to control his trembling hands, the shaking became so intense that one of the faux-crystal tumblers dropped from his hand, exploded into hundreds of pieces, and careened across the polished parquet floor, provoking a humorous but pointed retort from Billy Wayne.

"Jabbo, you break my wife's mama's cousin's daughter's sister's niece's fancy drankin' glasses, one of 'em gone kick yo black ass. And I'm gonna help 'em. Now make sure you clean that shit up good, so I don't have to clean up after yo ass. Or you can come in here to play the game with us and see how many of them glasses you can really break," yelled a half-joking Billy Wayne.

"Yassa, Mr. Sharp. I'm sorry for dropping that glass. Don't know how that happened. But Jabbo gone git it all cleaned up. Don't you worry none bout that now, suh," said an overly apologetic Charles.

Then in a markedly different tone and volume that only he could hear, Charles said to himself as tears flooded his eyes and cascaded down the sides of his face, *That ignorant bastard. This the last night he gone disrespect this black man. Ain't I a man just like him? What makes him thank that I'm less of a man than he is just cause he gots money and his skin is white. God didn't make him no better. Just made him white. And the good book don't mention nowhere that cause they's white they better than the rest of us. The way he and the rest of 'em done blasphemed the Lord's name, they gonna bust hell wide open, even though it ain't my place to say for sho. The way he and them others done mistreated, killed, and beat up my people. It just ain't right. They messed over they own people like they done for all them years, so it ain't no surprise atall what they done to black folks. Lord, have mercy! I been waiting for so long for this night to come. I done prayed to you Lord and you knows my heart. I know this is what you led me to do. And I know if I hadna done what I done, I sho nuf wudn't be no man. Like the song say, It's been a long time coming, but a change is gonna come.*

Charles's hands continued shaking as he hurriedly swept up the pieces of broken glass and discarded them into the metal receptacle underneath the sink. The shaking was not from fear or nervousness. Instead, it was from the release of years of pinned up anger that he had accumulated while working for and listening to Billy Wayne and his buddies brag about their mischievous and illegal activities. It was from the shame he felt for keeping silent for so many years. And it was from the pain and humiliation of having to endure personal insults and attacks on his humanity from a group of people who, in their own minds, had long ago decided that because of their money, race, and skin color they were naturally more of a human being than he was.

After a few deep breaths, Charles walked outside into the hallway and into the adjacent stairwell where he managed to compose himself well enough to speed-dial a special number on his mobile phone. After hearing the familiar voice on the other end say, 'Speak to me!' he said, "They just finished drinking and they back inside the big room. It's still working? Good. When y'all gone come git these son-of-a-bitches? Okay. Yep, they gone be there for a while longer and they is really liquored up. So, y'all should git some good stuff now," said Charles with a balanced blend of relief and anxiety.

*

After everyone had settled once again in their seats, Billy Wayne chose to reconvene the group with a touchy and controversial topic.

"Okay boys, now that we done all wet our whiskers, and while we can still keep our eyes open, let's talk about that so-called Reverend Elvin "The Wannabe Pimp" Newhouse. Along with that Simpson deal and the Berman deal, this was my other favorite deal to work on because we needed to make an example out of this ole boy so nobody else would even thank about fuckin with us like that again. Now, y'all do recall what that sorry son-of-a-bitch did don't y'all," asked Billy Wayne.

In a perfect and classical *Pavlovian* response, the diminutive Judge Milliken whirled around in his chair, and despite severe arthritis in both knees, effortlessly stood up. After assuming a fully erect and upright position and remaining nearly motionless for several moments with his hands to his side like a raw marine recruit facing a drill sergeant, he ambled slowly over to the large bay window that looked out over the parking lot. The parking lot was empty at that time of the night except for a white van parked behind a row of fledgling magnolia trees. The name Newhouse seemed to have triggered an automatic trance state in Judge Milliken and caused to him to give little notice to the parking lot or the van. He stood there for several minutes with his back to the group, swaying back and forth, heel-to-toe, with hands now planted deeply into the back pockets of his suspendered, blue seersucker trousers. After pin-drop silence had completely replaced the alcohol-induced ruckus of a few minutes ago, Judge Milliken slowly turned around with a grin as big as a Cheshire cat. He savored the attention that was now focused on him, as he knew that no one in the room, except

Billy Wayne Sharp, was more familiar with the Newhouse case than he was. Clearing his throat and slowly wiping his deeply furrowed brow with a red bandana that he pulled from the inside pocket of his blue seer-sucker jacket, he began to pace the shiny wooden floor with heavy footsteps that set off echoes that resounded throughout the conference room. His pacing began to pick up as he circled the egg-shaped conference table for the second time, with his thumbs tugging on his blue suspenders. He could not help but notice that the more he paced, the more his buddies noticed him; and the more aware he became of their steely gaze upon him, the more excited he became. He cherished the feeling of being in an excited state because after his divorce from Samantha fifteen years ago, not much could excite Jethro, except a couple of glasses of Rum and Coke and being amongst his buddies at their monthly get-togethers. Finally, after keeping uncharacteristically silent while someone else had the spotlight, and watching the aimless pacing of Judge Milliken for several agonizing minutes, Billy Wayne had enough.

"Goddammit, Jethro, you need to sit yo ass down or I'm gonna shove one of these pills of mine down your fricking throat. You makin' me dizzy walkin' in circles. Now if you got somethin' to say, let's hear it," said Billy Wayne.

And with a chuckle that signaled an abrupt change in his mood, Billy Wayne continued, "And don't forget I was in on that deal even before you was. So, make damn sho you tell it like it is."

Judge Milliken took a deep sigh, wiped his sweaty brow again, this time taking a few extra moments to blow his nose before stuffing the damp bandana back into his trouser pocket.

He stared for a few long, lingering moments at Billy Wayne and snapped, "Dammit, Billy. I know you were involved, but I'm the one that had to make the

tough decisions."

Then with a laugh so hearty that his dentures nearly popped out of his oversized mouth, Judge Milliken said, "Hell, Billy Wayne, you know I was just funning you, son. Everybody knows that if it weren't for you Newhouse would be still walking around out there somewhere, screwing up things for everybody."

"You damn skippy, boy. And don't you never ever forget it neither. I handled that mess my own damn way and took care of that problem once and for all", replied Billy Wayne who broke into loud laughter as he saw Judge Milliken attempt to realign his dentures. Naturally, everyone, including Judge Milliken, started laughing right along with Billy Wayne until Judge Milliken had successfully put the dentures back into place and had re-taken his seat.

*

Taking a cue from Billy Wayne's cessation of laughter and his nod of the head, Judge Milliken began to recount the much-publicized Reverend Newhouse case.

"Well boys, the first thing the good reverend did wrong was to try to move in on our action. As you all know, we had one of our associates down in Slidell to get word to Newhouse that he was encroaching on someone else's territory and that he should cease and desist post haste or he would be reported to the authorities, or worse, he would be placing himself and his young girls in mortal danger. At first Newhouse denied that he was peddling those young girls, but when our associate showed him pictures of him escorting one of his girls to a motel room, instead of feeling some remorse or shame, he tore up the pictures and told our man that no one would ever believe that a good Christian man of the cloth would ever do something so devilish. As if he hadn't already done enough devilment, he then had the audacity to make an offer of employment to our man. He told our man that he was making enough money to bring him into the action if he would just forget the whole thing and come work for him. Of course, that's the last thing Newhouse should have done. 'Cause one of the things we can all be sure of, is that our people are fiercely loyal to us. We take care of them so as to make sure of that loyalty. Our man told him that he had been thinking about giving him *two* weeks to stop peddling those girls and clear out of town, but since he insulted him by trying to buy him away from his employers, he now had just *one* week to stop. And that if he thought or did otherwise, his employers were going to go straight to the newspaper and to the DA and if it came to it, something quite unpleasant could happen to him or his loved ones. Thinking that he had destroyed the incriminating pictures, Newhouse said that he didn't, quote, give a rat's ass who our man went to. In his way of thinking, nobody would ever believe such a fantastic story and besides, there was no proof. Our man, contrary to our instructions not to lay a hand on Newhouse, then proceeded to slap the shit out of him right across his fat face, and told him that scum like him, parading around so pious with the holy bible in one hand and taking money from peddling his own daughters with the other one did not deserve to walk the earth. And fellows, that is precisely what happened. The good reverend, rest his sin-sick soul, no longer walks the earth. I am certain that at this very moment he is strolling the fiery streets of Hades with none other than Lucifer himself. But, of course, that was his choice. He chose to stoop so low in the first place to peddle his own children. Then he chose to ignore fair warnings that his peddling was interfering with a long-standing and successful operation, and that the owners of that operation were not going to stand for some low-life, especially a jack-leg, blaspheming, dishonest preacher to cut into their business. So, with evidence in hand that included not only copies of the pictures that Newhouse tore up, but also some incriminating video and several eye-witness accounts, the DA did the only thing he could. He filed pandering charges against Newhouse and had Child Protective Services remove the girls from the Newhouse home. Never saw the girls again after the trial. Heard they moved to Houston, turning tricks for a colored pimp. I hear their mama's still laid up in the hospital on a ventilator. Why the hell they don't just unplug that damn ventilator? I will never know. Elvin was just downright selfish and vindictive, keeping that poor thing plugged into that artificial breathing machine. I guess he was hoping that us taxpayers were gonna pick up the tab for her care. And those girls didn't unplug their mama either because they don't want to do us any favors neither. So. What can we do? Anyhow, good riddance. They are in the big city and that's the way things are in the big city, I suppose. Peddling whores in the big city with all that dope being used as currency and all those colored street gangs running things, ain't quite like it is round here, thank God," said Judge Jethro Milliken.

Billy Wayne, knowing Judge Milliken had omitted lots of important and juicy details, chimed in to fill in the blanks.

"Well, you damn skippy he ain't walking this earth no more. I took care of that my damn self. You know that old boy was clearing two to three grand a week, running them girls at every truck stop and rest area between here and Slidell. The money was a big part of why we had to take him out, but it was also the principle of the thang. You know, it's one thang to hire experienced grown-up women for the business, but it's another to use young girls, your own flesh and blood, to make money like that. No fellas, that was so far cross the line of decency that we had to deal with him the way we did. And this ass hole even had the nerves to do business with niggers. I can't even bring myself to imagine how a white man could allow his daughter to lay with a nigger, even if he was making money. So, on the basis of principle and money, and to make sure to send a clear message to other would-be turf invaders, we had no choice but to remove him permanently," said Billy Wayne.

Brock Galloway, who had not said much the whole night, began pounding his fist on the table and muttering softly and incoherently. As his vocal sounds became louder, it was clear that he was having an unpleasant emotional reaction to the Newhouse incident.

"Boys, I don't know. After all, he *was* a preacher, regardless of what else he was doing. And to do harm to a man of God, well it just don't seem like the right thing to have done. Couldn't we have done something else to try to convince him to stop? That's been bothering me for a long time. Sometimes I just can't sleep at night, Billy Wayne, ever since you told me what happened to Reverend Newhouse," said Brock Galloway.

"Well, Brock tell me what the hell you remember me telling you. 'Cause I tell you omething' boy, I sure as hell couldn't sleep none either while this so-called man and daddy of them young-uns, playing like he was a man of the cloth was out there taking money out of our pockets, stealing right from under our noses with no fear of the consequences. Now why the hell can't you see why this couldn't be handled in no other way, Brock? This low down, sorry, son-of-bitch was taking money out of your pocket, my pocket, and every body's pocket sittin' here, and he wudn't gonna give up and leave two to three grand a week on the table without a little convincing," ranted Billy Wayne.

"Yeah, I know Billy. He had his chances and we gave him a fair chance to leave and he wouldn't. And I know that sometimes we have to do some things that are not so tasteful," said Brock.

"Not tasteful! My ass", shouted an angry Billy Wayne.

"The only thang distasteful was this, and let me tell you again and let this be the last time I have to remind any of you. Newhouse was turning tricks with his own daughters. You understand how low you gotta be to do some shit like that? Then he was allowing them girls to lay with niggers. And you all know how low you gotta be to cotton to something like that. And then, the boy was given a fair chance to stop, or as Jethro put it, cease and desist. Instead of him heedin' a fair warnin' that he was fuckin' up, he got all high and mighty, thinkin' that nobody was gonna believe that a Christian man like him would do somethin' so damn... *Distasteful*, Mr.Galloway. You want to talk about distasteful, Brocky Baby?" snorted Billy Wayne whose face was growing redder and the veins in his neck were puffed up like he was having a heart attack, reflecting the intense anger he was feeling over Brock Galloway's description of the disposition of Reverend Newhouse as distasteful.

"Now, think about a young white girl, like somebody like your granddaughter. She's bout fifteen or sixteen years old, ain't she Brocky Baby? Imagine your son was peddlin' her and was also lettin' her lay with niggers, and he done been told to stop. Distasteful as sin, I say, and as unnatural as a dog screwing a cat. And you gonna sit there and tell me that what we done to Newhouse was distasteful. Boy, I tell you somethin'. I find *you* down right distasteful right now Brocky Baby for thinking some shit like that. And I'm sho for the last five years you been thinkin' like this. Hell, if you thank gettin' rid of Newhouse was so damn distasteful, why the hell don't you turn over all the money that that distasteful action made for you. Sure your conscience won't let you keep it. Dammit, give it to me, cause I ain't lost one bit of sleep over takin' care Newhouse," said Billy Wayne with a strong hint of sarcasm.

Without the slightest bit of forewarning Billy Wayne suddenly slammed his hand down on the table, and ejected himself so fast from his seat that it made about fifteen revolutions, spinning like an oversized spinning top. All eyes followed him as he walked over to the bay window and lit up another cigar. He said nothing. In fact, no one said anything. Billy Wayne seemed to be fixated on the view outside the window as the distinct aroma of his illegally imported Cuban cigar began to fill the room, an aroma whose distinctiveness was matched only by the intense silence that had also now consumed the entire room. The innate desire to speak was restrained only by the overwhelming uncertainty of what to say. The silence was not only intense, but it spoke volumes of how touchy the subject of Reverend Newhouse had become and more specifically how sensitive Billy Wayne was about having to justify his actions to anyone.

The silence was finally broken when Billy Wayne queried the group. "Who owns a white van?"

Brock stuttered and stammered out an answer that seemed to satisfy Billy Wayne.

"I saw old Jabbo drive up in it, I think, Billy Wayne. And Billy, don't be too mad at me for sayin'what I said. I know how much you have done for this organization. And if wasn't for you, we wouldn't have been as successful as we are. Because of your background and just the sheer force of your personality, Billy, you have made this organization what it is today— the most influential group of Southern white men this side of Birmingham that is dedicated to making money and keepin' niggers in their place. So, forgive me if I seemed ungrateful and was takin' you for granted," pleaded Brock Galloway.

Now that the silence was replaced with some semblance of conversation, Billy Wayne continued his recollection of the Newhouse story after taking his seat again and continuing to take long drags from his stogie.

"Ah, hell, Brock I ain't mad at you boy. Just keep what you said in mind and what I said, and we gonna be alright. Anyway, Jethro here done a damn good job of handling that case in court. He wouldn't let Newhouse's lawyer get away with trying to convince the jury that Newhouse was just out there trying to get them girls to stop turning tricks. It was a damn good ploy by the lawyer to say that Newhouse went with them girls to them motels and truck stops to pray for 'em and to try to get them to stop selling their bodies. After that, all the lawyer could do it seems was parade a bunch of old church ladies up there and have them talk about how much he visited them in the hospital and at the rest home and what a strong message of love and salvation he brought every Sunday. Truth of the matter is that the only thang that son-of-a-bitch was saving was money from pimping them gals of his. For a while I thought at least one of them jurors was startin' to feel sorry for ole Newhouse. This one ole gal started cryin', not bawlin' but you could see she was wipin' her eyes and wipin' snot from her nose. Didn't take long befo' she dried up, after Jethro gave her that look that told her she better turn off the tears and don't even start feelin' sorry for that bastard. Even with her showin' a little sympathy for Newhouse for a little while, I knew that wudn't gonna be 'nuff to save his ass. Cause ole Jethro and Hopkins, the DA, maneuvered thangs so that when it went to the jury, there wudn't no doubt atall that Newhouse was gone get convicted. They stacked the jury with enough people who see thangs the way we see 'em. All twelve of 'em had clear instructions from Jethro and Hopkins to make good and damn sho that a verdict of guilty was the only one they better come out with. So, when the verdict was read, Newhouse just slumped down in his chair and started prayin' like a repentin' sinner and cryin' like a brand new titty baby. By then, neither one was gonna do him a bit of damn good. When they finally pried his hands from the arms of his chair, he stood and hugged his lawyer, and then the deputies took 'em on back to his cell," said Billy Wayne.

"But he wudn't in the cell for too long, was he Billy Wayne?" asked a chuckling Joe Lee Roberts.

"Nope, he sho wudn't, Joe Lee. After a few meetings with

C.L., trying to come up with the best way to handle this thang, I finally made arrangements with C.L. to make sure that one of the biggest, baddest, meanest white boys up there was in the cell with Newhouse. After gittin' that took care of, I went and made sure that Hopkins was gonna live up to the bargain that I had told C.L. to make with this big old boy. And that wudn't no problem neither cause even though he tries to be a little prick sometimes, Hopkins knows what side his bread is buttered on. Of course, I told C.L. not to let nobody else know how the job was gonna be done. Just make sho that Newhouse never makes it to Parchman Penitentiary. And you all know what C.L. discovered the next morning after the trial. Fo they called the ambulance though, like I told him, C.L. called me to come take a look at Newhouse's remains to see how well that big old boy had done his job. And that big boy must uh put some kinda whuppin' on Newhouse's ass. 'Cause he was all fucked up. Both his eyes was hanging outside the sockets, lips looked liked they had been sliced up with a razor blade, and his nose looked like a twisted noodle. Course, blood was all over the fricking place," said Billy Wayne.

"Tell me, Billy Wayne, how was you able to convince C.L. and that big white boy to go along with your plan? You ain't never told us that part," inquired an excited Clifford Morgan, who seemed to always have orgasmic reactions to tales of blood and gore.

"In the first place, Cliff, you know it don't take much more than a word or two to get ole C.L. to do what I want. That's my nigger, and he knows it. And he wouldn't want it no other way. He wouldn't refuse me to save his own life. Hell, if I told that boy to kiss my boots, he would just ask which one I wanted him to kiss first. If I told him to stand on one leg and holler like a goddamn Indian, he would act like he been livin' on a Indian reservation all his life. So, you see, it wudn't no problem to get

C.L. to take care his part of the deal," said Billy Wayne as he recounted in his mind the conversation he had with C.L. that resulted in the death of Newhouse.

"C.L., I got an important job to be done, and you are just the right one to do it," said Billy Wayne.

"Yassa, Mistah Billy. What you want ole C.L. to do for you," said C.L.

"That ole boy Newhouse, y'all got locked up for pimpin' them gals of his, well I want somethin' done to that ass hole. He screwed up some many ways, C.L. First he pimped his own flesh and blood. Then he let them young gals lay with niggers. Then to top it all off, he was cuttin' into our business. That son-of-a-bitch was clearing two to three grand a week. That was money that belonged to us. So, we got to send a powerful and never-to-be-forgotten-or-ignored message to the next ass hole that thanks he can get away with the shit Newhouse was gittin' away with," said Billy Wayne.

"I understand, boss. You want that ole boy to feel some pain, right," asked C.L.

"Well, C.L. you damn skippy I want that son-of-a-bitch to feel some pain," answered Billy Wayne.

"Well off the top of my head, Mistah Billy, I could arrange for somebody to "accidently" push him down the stairs when they on the way back from chow," said C.L.

"Naw, C.L. That ain't what I got in mind atall. If he fall down some stairs, he might just break a few bones, but I don't want that ass hole to even make it out of the jail in one piece. Breakin' a few bones will just git him out of jail and on to the hospital and then on to Parchman. I don't want this ass hole to leave his jail cell in one piece. The only way I want him to leave Henderson County is in a fuckin' body bag. Understand what 'um sayin', C.L.," asked Billy Wayne.

"Sho nuff, C.L. understands what you sayin', Mistah Billy.

And don't you worry none 'cause I know jest what to do to make sure Newhouse never leaves the jail except in a black body bag without even raisin' no suspicion," said C.L.

"Don't worry 'bout no suspicion, C.L. You a deputy sheriff and ain't nobody have a bit of damn suspicion. It will just be called jailhouse justice," said Billy Wayne.

"Gotcha, boss. Here is what I can do. It's a good plan 'cause we done used it befo on a coupla unsuspectin' niggers who didn't believe fat meat greasy," said C.L. with a loud laugh.

"Now, you and I are on the same page, C.L. When I made it so that you got this job as deputy, I knew a moment like this would come up, and I needed somebody on the inside to take care of such delicate matters," said Billy Wayne with a wink.

"So, I told C.L. that he had to make it happen right there in Newhouse's jail cell. I musta hit the right button that time. Cause old C.L. winked at me, smiled one of them big ole, glow-in-the-dark smiles, and said, 'Boss I knows jest what you wants and you can sho nuff count on Ole C.L. to take care of this very 'potant matter, Mr. Billy, suh.' Then, while we was both sitting there in my car, C.L. laid a couple of jokes on me that just had me rollin'. I won't never forget 'em. I know y'all done heard 'em befo, but I just gotta tell 'em again. Course, I can't tell 'em like Ole C.L. But he said, *One day Jesse James and Frank James stopped a train to rob it. They jumped onto the train and told all the passengers to put they hands up, sit still and nobody would get hurt. Then Frank said, First we gonna rob all the women and then we gonna fuck all the men. Then an old man, shaking in his boots stood and said, Mr. James, don't you mean you gonna fuck all the women and then rob all the men? Then this little sissy boy in the back of the car, said in a high-pitch woman's voice, Now you just let Mr. James rob this train the way he wants to. That was some funny shit. Then C.L. had one mo in him. He said, Boss, how can you tell a nigger been working at the computer? I said how C.L. He said, cause the screen's got white-out on* it. And C.L. has a way of pickin' at and makin' fun of niggers, specially them jet black jigaboos. He told me one day he seen a nigger that was so black, the lightening bugs followed him 'round in the daytime," said Billy Wayne as he and the others laughed like a pack of hungry hyenas pouncing on a wounded impala.

While he had everyone in such a jovial mood, Billy Wayne decided that he shouldn't stop there with the C.L. joke stories. So he continued.

"And one mo like that one. He said he seent an ole colored boy that had on a black turtle neck shirt. C.L. said that nigger was so black you couldn't tell where the shirt ended and the boy's face started. Now that's some funny shit. Hell, that rascal is the funniest damn nigger I done ever seen. I don't know he keeps comin' up with them jokes. I told him one day he oughta write them jokes down 'fo he gits too old and senile to remember any of 'em. Hell that boy could be a joke writer for one of them colored stand-up comedians they show on BET who likes to talk about nigger this and nigger that. If them boys want some good nigger jokes, all they gotta do is pay C.L some cash money, hell, he'll have them rollin' in the aisles and sellin' out the joint," said Billy Wayne.

Everyone continued to laugh, only louder and with much more gusto. What they considered jokes or funny gags caused the tears to stream even faster down their faces. The slaps to the thighs and the pounding on the table became more demonstrable. To Billy Wayne and his buddies, this was just a fun and funny way to show their displeasure with black people and homosexuals. To the rational, objective observer, this was a familiar display of two powerful forms of hatred—homophobia and racism. It was a formula that guaranteed a hearty laugh from individuals who took unabashed pride in being homophobic and racist.

After wiping the tears from his eyes from laughing so hard,

Billy Wayne continued with the details on how he had arranged for the death of Reverend Newhouse.

"So, C.L. told me that they had a big ole country white boy locked up for attempted murder. Ole boy beat the crap out of this other ole boy he caught at the Dew Drop Saloon talkin' to his wife. Damn near killed the boy. The unlucky bastard is still layed up in the hospital, don't even know he in the world, C.L. told me. So, it was easy to see that this ole boy was as mean as a rattlesnake and didn't mind fuckin' somebody up, for the right incentitive, C.L. said. The ole boy had already been locked up for six months, just wait'n for a trial. And it was gonna be another six months befo the DA got around to his case. So, he was chompin' at the bit to git out of stir and get the hell out of Dodge. So, C.L. told me he could git this big boy to take care of Newhouse, if somebody could get him released with time served. I told him that wouldn't be no problem, but I would have to run that by DA Hopkins to take care of the paper work. Like I said, it really didn't take much to make Hopkins see thangs my way. Yeah, he tried to put up a fuss, talkin' 'bout Newhouse's family and church members might git suspicious. I told him that Newhouse had disgraced hisself so bad, you couldn't even git nobody to give him a pot to piss in. He still didn't want to go along, talkin' 'bout his duty to uphold the law and that he didn't want to be involved in somethin' scandalous that might screw up his re-election. Then he said some shit about he would quit befo he did somethin' so shady. I had about 'nuff of that mealy-mouth bullshit. So, I reminded him in no uncertain terms that it wudn't because he was so fuckin' high and mighty that he got elected DA in the first damn place. And it wudn't because he was such a slick ass lawyer, neither. It was because of certain people in the community who put him there and it was because of these same people that he is still there. And then, to end the whole damn conversation, I told him, 'Boy, don't you fuck with me. And don't you ever even act like you don't wanna go long with somethin' I tell you to do. 'Cause if I have to have this conversation with you again, you gonna find yourself out on your ass, chasing ambulances for a livin'. Boy, we made you, and goddamit, we can sure as hell break yo ass. So, just do what the hell you been told, and save that self-righteous, pious bullshit for the voters at election time. 'Cause I don't want to hear it. Do I make myself clear, Mr. Hopkins?' Course, by that time, he was sweatin' and shakin' so and sayin' how sorry he was for speakin' the way he did. I told him that I don't like to speak to him the way I done, but he's gotta learn about how thangs run round here and who runs 'em. This ain't no game of tiddly winks or marbles, where you can stop playin' when you damn well please or because you don't like the way thangs are going. So, he did up the paper work, all legal and legit. And a week or so after they buried Newhouse, that big boy was sent on his way... with thanks from all of us, of course," said Billy Wayne.

Silence once again ensued. But not for long as Billy Wayne reminded everyone again of how important it was to maintain discipline in order to keep the operation productive. He turned in his body in the chair so that he had direct eye contact with Brock Galloway, who was sitting to his left.

"Now Brock, you do understand the difference between penny ante poker and` high stakes poker, don't you boy," asked Billy Wayne.

"Yep," responded a surly Brock Galloway, who was now standing with his arms folded across his chest and looking out the bay window at the empty parking lot. "But what's your point, Billy? I done apologized already."

"My point? Hell my point is that if you just playing penny ante poker, boy, all you gonna win is fuckin' pennies. But when the stakes is high, like two to three grand a week, like what Newhouse was raking in, hell, that's different. A helluva lot different, and I thank you would agree, Brocky Baby, that stakes like that are little bit higher, don't you know? So, quite naturally, that calls for some high stakes responses. Now if Newhouse had been runnin' just a little small-time penny ante operation, just to get off on some kinky, perverted bullshit, and not out to make a whole lotta money, his ass would probably still be walkin' 'round preachin' the word, savin' souls, and visitin' the sick and the shut-in. But naw! This ole boy was playin' with high stakes, which naturally made the stakes high for us too. And when a son-of-a-bitch won't listen to reason and won't stop pimpin' his own flesh and blood, well all I can say is that he got just what the hell he deserved," said Billy Wayne.

Billy Wayne paused again, and glared at his fat, hairy, ring-less fingers, perhaps searching again for some timely and fit-ting jewels of wisdom that could further bolster his arguments to Brock and the others that killing Reverend Newhouse was completely justified. By then, Brock had offered a heart-felt mea culpa and sought forgiveness from Billy Wayne for questioning the decision to have Newhouse killed. But Billy Wayne had a penchant for maintain grudges. And that is what scared Brock and had him wondering how long before Billy Wayne would explode again and go after him for expressing reservations about killing another human being.

CHAPTER 22

A S QUIETNESS FELL over the group, everyone knew that with Billy Wayne maintaining such a long gaze at his hands accompanied by deafening silence meant only one thing. After what seemed like several long minutes, Billy Wayne set off that piercing sound of flesh colliding with wood, causing everyone to jump in their seats as he slammed both hands down loudly onto the table and let out a loud pig-like snort from his huge nostrils that produced a line of snot that reached the bottom of one of his chins. After wiping the clear mucus with the back of his hand and then wiping the hand on his pant leg, he now confirmed what everyone suspected. He was about to embark on another one of his tortuous chases of the proverbial rabbit.

"When I was in the Army, boys, fightin' them Gerries over in Africa, we all had our orders. We had to have discipline in order for stuff to run right. Lotta times my sergeant would send me out on reconnaissance to look for where some of them Gerry soldiers might be hid out. I ain't lying when I tell ya I was scared as cat in a room full of rocking chairs cause, hell, that was some dangerous shit. One of them sneaky ass Gerries catch yo ass, it was lights out and good night Irene," said Billy Wayne as his eyes started glazing over as though he was in a self-induced trance.

"Anyhow, I was out on patrol one evening just as it was 'bout to turn dark. Sarge had asked me if I would volunteer to lead a recon group up a hill that overlooked this village where some Gerries had been seen earlier that day. Of course, I always thought how funny it was that Old Sarge and them other officers would ask if you wanted to volunteer, like you had some choice in the matter. Anyhow, I led this unit up this hill that was lined with dead bodies, mainly women and old folks, but a couple of Gerry soldiers was sprawled out there amongst 'em. There was this other boy in the unit, big old cock strong country ass boy from Louisiana who wudn't feared of nothing or nobody. When we got to the top of the hill, we spied a couple of Gerries sittin' on top of a concrete wall, with they backs to us. This big boy, we called him Louisiana Red, picked up his rifle, aimed, and clicked the trigger. But it jammed. I ran over to him and said who the hell told you to do that? He said, Billy, I had a clear shot. I ain't shot no Gerry since I been here, goddamit and that was my chance. I said boy, you don't go shootin' til you know where all of the rest of them Gerries is hid. We just see two from here. Sarge thanks its probably a dozen or more of 'em up in that house. You go shootin on yo own like you at some kinda carnival shootin' gallery, we all gonna git shot to hell. See, this boy, Louisiana Red, was lackin' in discipline. He failed to realize that in order for thangs to work, he had to play his part and not go off half-cocked. And when you been told that you fuckin' up, then you oughta have 'nuff sense to stop, like Louisiana Red done. See, that's where Newhouse went wrong. He didn't have sense God promise the billygoat, no sense atall to stop when he been told to. But old Louisiana Red at least listened and done what he was told. Later on he ended up transferring to a unit that went to Italy. Heard he got shot in the ass and sent back to Louisiana with a medal pinned to his chest. He apologized after he knowed how close he came to gittin' everybody's ass shot to kingdom come. Still, I had to write him up, cause the law of consequences ain't repealed cause you young and green. But after that, never had no mo trouble outta him cause he understood how thangs worked and he had to follow orders and not act like he was the Lone Ranger. But anyhow, I took a coupla boys with me round the other side of this house where we knowed now for sure that some mo of them Gerries was holed up," said Billy Wayne.

Like a schoolboy mesmerized by a spell-binding mystery/thriller, Cletus Sessum asked, "Billy, did you take old Louisiana Red with you? Sounds to me like a big old boy like that coulda been a big help if you were gonna have to have hand-to-hand combat with them Gerries."

"Naw, Cletus. I wudn't gonna take that boy up in there. First, cause I wudn't plannin' on doin' no hand-to-hand combat. I was plannin' on usin' my M1 to blow the hell outta of 'em, or if I needed to, I had my bayonet ready to carve up some Ayrian meat. Naw! Louisiana Red was just too green and was too anxious to kill somebody. That kinda attitude will get you in a whole heap of trouble when you out there in the middle of combat. You gotta use yo wits and not your brawn, so much. Ah, hell what the hell am I telling y'all about the rules of combat. 'Cept for me and DC, the only uniform any of you pussies ever wore was a Boy Scout uniform. Anyhow, I created a diversion by making some racket, knowing that them two that was sittin on that wall was gonna come lookin' for what was making the racket. But them boys shoulda known that the cat ain't the only one to get fucked up by being too damn curious. They probably thought it was one of them local hookers tryin' to get they attention, cause they came a strolling round the corner whistlin' and smilin' like they was 'bout to get them some Tunisian snatch. Soon as they come round the corner of the house, me and another fellow—can't recollect his name—grabbed 'em round the neck and jammed our bayonet right underneath the ribs and thrust straight up, puncture the lungs and they drown in their own blood. Then they dropped like a chopped down tree, 'cept they made a lot less racket. Then we went on inside and took care of the other ones inside," said Billy Wayne

"How did you take care of them, Billy?" inquired Cliff Morgan, who again was becoming aroused by thoughts of blood and gore.

"Hell. The same way we took care of the other two out front. But we had to work a lot faster 'cause it was just two of us and twelve or so of them. See, we was trained how to kill the enemy quiet, so as not to rile up nobody, especially in a situation like we was in. And just like I said, I just shove that bayonet right through the ribs and go straight up. And when you hit it just right with that razor-sharp bayonet you stick a big old hole in the lungs, and when a son-of-a-bitch can't breathe right, he can't say a word, and then that's all she wrote. Hell, they wiggle a lil bit, with blood shootin' out of 'em like water gushing out of a fire plug. But befo long they just laid there, deader than dead," said Billy Wayne.

Billy Wayne stood, stretch, yawned, blew his nose, and dabbed lightly at his eyes. He placed the handkerchief back into his front pocket and walked over to the window. As he stared out the window, his mind went to a deep, dark place, just as it always does whenever he thinks about the killing fields of Northern Africa. He thinks about the slaughtered bodies, both enemy and foe: Comrades in arms. Innocent women and children. Helpless orphans and elderly, disabled hospital patients. Sobbing widows and mothers. As he continued his gaze out the window, he noticed nothing except those haunting images from the war that were being conjured up in his mind. He did not like going to that unpleasant place with the unpleasant images. But in that moment, he wanted to finish his story about his expertise in rendering his enemies permanently incapacitated. He had a point to make. In fact, he had several points to make.

The story contained unambiguous information regarding the rules of engagement and the importance of maintaining discipline while on the battlefield. The main rule he want to highlight was that he was fully capable of inflicting pain on enemies, foreign and domestic and that the combat rules of discipline were non-negotiable and critical to the success of any plan. Failure to understand the rules of engagement or failure to understand the importance of individual and group discipline invariably would result in problems. He took his seat and continued his points about rules of engagement in battle and the importance of maintaining discipline among the troops.

"But my point in tellin' y'all all of this is that when Sarge sent me out to hunt for Gerry soldiers, if I acted like I wudn't gonna go out lookin' for them sons-of-bitches, my ass would have been locked up for disobeying an officer, or worse, someone would have shagged my ass, you know... accidentally, on purpose put a fucking bullet between my eyes. So, what I'm sayin' is that because everybody in the platoon knew his part, even old trigger-happy Louisiana Red, we had discipline. The discipline came about from everybody knowing what to do, when to do it, who to listen to, and most important, knowin' the consequences, if they didn't do it. It's the same thang here with our operation. We have to make sure everybody knows what to do, what their role is, including the Newhouses out there, and what will happen if they forgit or don't want to go along with what they been told to do, or need to be reminded what to do, like Hopkins. Or else, you don't have discipline. You got chaos, and everything is shot to hell. You see. Everybody here has a part. And better than anybody else sittin' round this table, I know *my* part. That's why I had Newhouse took out. That was somethin' that I was supposed to do cause that's *my* part and without *my* part, none of this shit gonna work. It kinda reminds me of a song that colored woman that used to work for the Colonel used to sang when I spent the night at the Colonel's house when I was a little boy. I still remember the words, and it explains what I been tryin' tell y'all 'bout all parts workin' together. Hell, y'all done heard it too. Can't sang it like she could. She could sang like a one of God's little angels. But bein' a nigger, no way she was gonna be an angel of the Lord. Anyhow, here the words:

Your toe bone connected to your foot bone
Your foot bone connected to your ankle bone
Your ankle bone connected to your leg bone
Your leg bone connected to your knee bone
Your knee bone connected to your thigh bone
Your thigh bone connected to your hip bone
Your hip bone connected to your back bone
Your back bone connected to your shoulder bone
Your shoulder bone connected to your neck bone
Your neck bone connected to your head bone
I hear the word of the Lord," said Billy Wayne.

"See what um sayin'? It's all connected and when one part don't work the way it's supposed to work, then don't none of it work. I wouldn't have asked you to do that Brock or any of the rest of you, cause ain't none of y'all got the gonads for that kinda rough stuff. Now I ain't complaining. I kinda likes to be the arranger when it's necessary and even the enforcer when the opportunity presents itself. I know y'all ain't got the stomach for it. But the only thing I say is, don't question me when I take care of shit that y'all too candy ass to mess with. Y'all understand, specially you , Brock, what um telling y'all," asked Billy Wayne.

In unison: "Yes, Billy Wayne. We understand."

"Now fellows, we got just two mo thangs to go over and we can all go home and get some rest. Don't wanna be looking like somethin' the cats drug in when we go to church tomorrow. First, I need to give each of y'all your quarterly pay from the revenues from the Biloxi operation, the whorehouses, and the videos. Y'all know that all three of them is just makin' money hand over fist for us boys. If the money wudn't so damn easy, I think I'd retire," said Billy Wayne as he tried to address an itch inside his ear by sticking an index finger into his ear and vigorously wiggling the finger until he removed the wax-covered digit with a sigh of relief.

"But like I said earlier, we gotta decide about keepin' thangs goin' or callin' it quits. But irregardless of whether we hold or fold, a few outstanding markers need to be called in. I'm thankin' bout, in particular, a couple of county supervisors who still owe us for some money we fronted them for their last two elections. First, they ain't even bothered to offer to repay us, even though we wouldn't of took it cause it wudn't no loan. We just ask for consideration when we needs something. Jackson's been pretty good about doin' what we ask him, but he could be doin' a lot mo. He did give us a heads up on that property just south of town to let us know that that strip mall was comin' to town. He knew we was thanking bout selling it. And if weeda sold it when we was thanking 'bout sellin' it, we would of left a shit load on money on the table. Turns out, we made a killing' on that deal. But he's been slow as Blackstrap molasses in gettin' that road to the airport built. That's gotta be done soon or some of them tenants out there gonna move out and start using trucks and rail to move they cargo. That's makin' a lotta money for us boys, and Jackson gonna have to git his ass in gear and build that road. Goddamit! I hate it when people don't do what the hell they been told to do. Um gone go see that boy first thang tomorrow morning, and DC, I want you to go with me," said Billy Wayne.

The success of the cabal was in direct proportion to the amount of cooperation it received from its clients and partners. Of course, that cooperation was proffered voluntarily or involuntarily, depending on the client or partner and the level of

importance assigned to that cooperation. In the case of the cooperation needed to complete a promised road at the airport, the
client was a county supervisor, who was nothing more or nothing less than a wholly-owned subsidiary of Billy Wayne's cabal.
All of their partners and clients were easily replaceable cogs in
an enormous wheel that was under the complete control of Billy
Wayne and his buddies. And one of the things that irritated them
more than anything else was for one of their subsidiaries or cogs
to pretend it was anything other than a convenience that existed
solely for the pleasure of and at the discretion of the cabal.

"No problem, Billy. I need to be there to kinda make sure he
understands that there's a lot riding on this road deal. My wife's
cousin just started a concrete and paving outfit out of Ellisville
and this would be a good start for him," said Dickey Carter.

Billy Wayne continued with his tirade, "I gave them tenants
my word it was gonna git done, and I'll be damn if um gonna
look like I—I mean we… ain't still running thangs 'round here."

Judge Milliken thought he would remind Billy to remind
them what the other county commissioner owed them before he
got too far into his tirade about Supervisor Vincent Jackson.

"Now Billy, before you go too far down that road, remind us
about Supervisor Tarrant and what he owes us."

"You damn skippy Tarrant owes us. You know that we
made sure his name got on the ballot in the first damn place. He
missed the deadline to file by two weeks and we had to "make
arrangements" with his opponents and the county clerk to make
sho there was no problem with his name gettin' on the bal-
lot. We even went another extra mile for him and "convinced"
one of the candidates in the race to drop out so there would be
only one runnin' against him. And that was just for show cause
Lonnie Carson was in the race just to make it look like a real
election. And Tarrant wins by a frickin' landslide. First time out,
never even run for public office befo. But then when time came

for him to vote on a proposal to exempt one of our tree farms from county taxes, this ass hole voted against it. Dumb fucker. He was the only one to vote against it. His vote didn't hurt us, but it's the principle of the thang and it's the lack of respect and the need for discipline I was talkin' bout earlier, where everybody needs to know they part, go out and do it, or they suffer the consequences. But anyway, we had somethin' special lined up for him and that leads us to the next subject," said Billy Wayne.

"But, Billy, don't you want to take care of the revenue payments before you start on that new subject", asked a nervous Brock Galloway.

"Oh yeah, Brocky Baby. Shit I damn near forgot. Okay hold on a second." Billy Wayne got up from his chair and walked over to a wall safe hidden by a twenty-four by twenty-four beautifully framed portrait of a white-bearded Colonel Tom Sharp immaculately attired in his dress confederate grays. He walked back to the table, sat down, and placed a large nine by eleven inch brown envelope on the table.

CHAPTER 23

"OKAY BOYS, I already divided it up into seven envelopes. You will find, hopefully to your delight, gentlemen, a grand total of two hundred thousand dollars in your envelope, brand new, crisp bills, in various denominations. This is from all three operations. Like I said, boys. This is some high stakes money here, and we gotta be some of the luckiest sons-of-bitches on God's green earth to be able to sit here and receive such "rich" blessings. So, each of you take your envelope, count it if you want to. Ain't shorted you none. My take is the same as yours. Just make sho as usual, and Joe Lee you tell 'em since you the CPA, don't go depositin' all of this cash at one time. Just mix it in with some of yo other transactions so bank inspectors don't git suspicious," said Billy Wayne.

Seizing a chance to speak with some authority and expertise, Joe Lee Roberts chimed in on cue.

"Yep. You're right Billy Wayne. And I feel like even though y'all been hearing this sermon every three months for the last umpteen years, it won't hurt to give it again. Don't want to take nothing for granted. First of all, don't go out and spend it on something outlandish that will attract a lot of attention to yourself. You won't have no problems if you mix it in, like Billy said, with some of your normal transactions. But the main thang is don't go out and buy a yacht or a Rolls Royce and don't go and make a cash deposit of two hundred thousand dollars in your bank account. If them bank auditors, who work for the Federal Reserve, come snoopin' 'round, there ain't much we can do to hold them boys off. And also it's a good idea to spread it around to different banks into different accounts. Set up some dummy accounts in different names. And like we all have been doing, continue to use out of town banks and best of all, sink some of it in the stock market. I can help any of you with that."

Billy Wayne continues.

"Okay boys, we just about done now. But befo we leave and since it'll be another month befo we get together again, I wanna, just for a little while, talk about what y'all thank about throwing in some money to help pay for a lawyer for old "Pops" Pierpont. Y'all know they got that old boy charged with first degree murder. Can you believe that shit? That shit happened more than forty years ago and instead of lettin' sleepin' dogs lie, that goddam ACLU and them liberal pinheads over at the Poverty Law Center over in Montgomery made such a fuss and done got the Attorney General involved in it. Now I tried to put an end to all of this crap when I called the Governor a while back to remind him of some favors he owed to me. I told him that we need them charges drop against "Pops" and he needed to make sure it got done. Well, from what I can tell, he ain't done a damn thang to get them charges drop cause old "Pops", who ain't even got a pot to piss in, is still stuck in jail, and can't afford a decent lawyer, 'cept one of them public defenders. Hell, them ass holes ain't nothing but wannabe lawyers any damn how who couldn't get an old, blind, cripple woman off on a fuckin' jay-walking charge. Any how a couple of days ago, I talked to "Pop's" son-in-law, can't remember the boy's name," said Billy Wayne.

"Bobby Lee is who you talking 'bout, Billy. Y'all know that Bobby Lee married "Pop's" oldest daughter, Ida Mae, who was maid of honor at our wedding," volunteered Brock Galloway.

Pausing for a long moment , clasping his thin hands behind

his balding head while stretching his long legs to their fullest extension, then crossing them and inclining his bony body, followed by a wide smile across his well-worn, wrinkled face, Brock plunged into a yarn about his first serious girlfriend.

"Yep! She and me, we used to have a good thang goin' on befo I fell in love with her best friend, Susanna. Ida Mae was my first... first kiss, first puppy love, and first cherry. Used to spend all of my time, when I wudn't working, with that gal, at my house, her house, the church house, anywhere. I was smitten by Old Cupid real good. I tell you, fellas, no shit, for damn near a year that gal had me eatin' outta her hand and outta anywhere else she wanted me to eat. Ooo-wee. Boy, did that gal teach me some thangs about love-making! Y'all know what I mean? But, hell once Susanna throwed them big baby blue eyes on me, well, I just couldn't resist her. But I felt bad for Ida Mae, cause she was a good gal, did any damn thang I told her to do. And as I said, was damn good in the sack. But when really true love comes into your life, well you just gotta go with your heart. And cause the two of 'em were best friends, Susanna asked her to stand up for her at the wedding. It was the natural thang to do, I suppose. But I sho did feel something mighty awkward standing there befo the preacher, God, family, and friends with two women that I had been with," said Brock Galloway.

Regaining control of the direction and tenor of the discussion, Billy Wayne slammed his huge right hand down onto the table. His massive bespectacled face turned candy apple red, causing everyone, in unison, to gasp and turn to Billy Wayne for a clue as to what could have set him off this time.

"Goddammit, Brock. I didn't ask you all about your frickin' love life and how you managed to git two women you been screwing to show up at the same church, at the same time, to be in the same wedding. Hell, we tryin' to get the fuck outta here, and you go ramblin' on bout some bullshit that ain't got a damn thang to do with what we talkin' bout. I just wanted to know the boy's name. His name is Bobby Lee, and that's all the fuck you needed to tell me. Sometimes, Brock. Jesus Christ," yelled Billy Wayne as he slammed his hand down on top of the table.

Brock simply lowered his head and mumbled, "son-of-a-bitch" under his breath. There was Star Trek's Wrath of Khan, and there was Sharpville's Wrath of Billy Wayne. Offering and giving forgiveness be damned. How long would he have to pay for his bothersome doubts about their role in the death of Reverend Newhouse, he wondered.

"Any goddamn how, Bobby Lee came to me the other day and asked if I could help old "Pops" out. He said what "Pops" needed more than anything else was a lawyer to help git him out of jail and to keep him out. I told him I would do what I could. A fine man like "Pops" Pierpont ain't got no mo business bein' in stir than any one of us. And, of course, we been know-ing "Pops" for damn near all our lives. "Pops" started the local Klan chapter here, chartered the White Citizens Council, and spent half his life trying to stave off all this integration shit by utting' the fear of the Klan in every nigger and nigger-lover that ever lived in this area. Now, y'all do remember what they locked up old "Pops" for, don't ya," asked Billy Wayne.

The customary two knocks of the knuckles let Billy Wayne know that no one had forgotten how the arrest of Cecil last spring had come as a shock to everyone in town. Pierpont was the owner of "As White as They Get", a string of five area dry cleaners, which for decades, since the first one opened in 1953, refused to serve black customers. He maintained his illegal Jim Crow practice until he was bought out in 1977 by a mega clean-ers franchise headquartered in Jackson.

Pierpont had been a suspect in the 1963 killing of Mr. Leondis McPherson, a local black civil rights activist. Mr. Mac, the owner of successful grocery store in the all black community of Sheeplo, made it known to the citizens of Sheeplo and to those in Sharpsville proper, that he was willing to pay the poll taxes of any black citizens who wanted to register to vote but could not afford the three-dollar tax. Further, he offered to drive anyone who needed transportation to the Henderson County Courthouse, to personally escort them to the Circuit Clerk's office, and if necessary, assist them in completing the voter registration application. Using his own resources, Mr. Mac was directly responsible for the registration of nearly one hundred black citizens in a span two months.

Mr. Mac was respected by most black and white citizens of Sharpville, primarily because of the many years of selfless benevolence that he showed to anyone who needed help, for any reason, regardless of race. Whether it was a white family in nearby White's Settlement that lost its fall harvest because of drought and needed food for the winter or an unemployed black father in the neighboring community of Kelly Settlement, who did not have enough money for a family Thanksgiving dinner, he could always be counted on to lend a helping hand. He was even revered by many white business owners primarily because he was not an economic threat to any of them and because he was successful in making the free enterprise system work for himself and his family. Although Mr. Mac was a successful business owner and enjoyed the respect of many white business owners, his decision to become involved in the local efforts to register black citizens, generated deep animus toward him by some white business owners, including Cecil Pierpont. Pierpont, with the assistance of six fellow Klansmen, murdered Mr. Mac, as he drove home late one night after dropping off several recent registrants following a mass meeting in town earlier in the evening. Although, there was ample evidence that Pierpont was involved in the murder, including five spent shells from a semi-automatic handgun found near Mr. Mac's body that matched his registered Glock 21C. But owing to the intervention of Jethro Milliken and Billy Wayne Sharp, no state murder charges were ever filed, although Cecil Pierpont was briefly held for questioning.

A few days after Pierpont's arrest, Jethro convened a meeting in his chambers with prosecutor and defense counsel to discuss the disposition of the case before it went any further. Defense counsel proposed that all charges be dropped due to insufficient evidence, reluctant witnesses, and the strong possibility that it was blacks that did the killing.

As a fait accompli, District Attorney Hopkins said, "Okay. That sounds like a plan. I will go along with that, but for the public consumption, I will have to openly express my strong disappointment over having to drop the charges. After all, the mood in the community was that something should be done about McPherson's murder. But I am more than willing to refuse prosecution on the grounds that a murder conviction would be hard to win in this community. I only prosecute cases that are winnable. And this ain't one of them. Not by a long shot. So, to pursue prosecution of this case would just be a huge waste of taxpayers' money. And in tight budget times, we need to scrimp and save every dime we can. And my office should take the lead in setting the example for austerity. Plus, in my considered opinion, a trial like this would create too much racial tension, invite the presence of outside agitators, and the liberal press would—like they always do—paint towns like ours as backwards and all that other nonsense. And all of that could very well lead to race riots. As the chief law enforcement officer of this county, I am bound by my oath to protect the lives and reputation of our fair citizens. And I would be violating my oath of office if I subjected the good citizens of Henderson County to unnecessary ridicule and unnecessary publicity, not to mention the unnecessary cost. So, this is not a problem for me. I mean defense counsel's recommendation and your plans for how you will move forward," said Mr. Hopkins.

"The arguments you make are very convincing, Mr. Hopkins. If you hadn't made them, I certainly would have. But I can tell we both have been talking to our dear friend Billy Wayne," replied Judge Milliken.

"Yep. We had a heart-to-heart over the Newhouse matter. And I think we are on the same page now. And that's all I want to say about that," said Mr. Hopkins.

All three laughed like hyenas, slapped each other's back, left the meeting, and had drinks together at the country club. The next day, in a written statement to the press, DA Hopkins informed the public about his decision about the McPherson murder case.

Dear Citizens of Henderson County: It is with deep regret that I must inform the good and fair-minded citizens of Henderson County that my office will not proceed with the prosecution of Mr. Cecil Pierpont in the allegation that he murdered Mr. Leondis McPherson. As a result of our investigation, I have concluded that, given the paucity of evidence and the lack of credible witnesses, to pursue prosecution at this time would be fruitless and a waste of precious resources that could be put to better use in maintaining law and order in our community. In other words, I cannot prove beyond a reasonable doubt to a jury of his peers that Mr. Pierpont murdered Mr. McPherson.

I speak for everyone in our fair county, when I express my deepest sympathy to the family of Mr. McPherson, which has endured considerable heartache following the loss of their loved one. I say to the McPherson family and to all of our good citizens, my office will not rest until we have brought the killers of Mr. McPherson to justice. You can trust me on that. You have returned me to office each time I have asked you to do so because of that sacred trust, and I know that you will continue to maintain your trust in me as we move forward from this tragic incident. May God bless you. Sincerely, Hank Hopkins, District Attorney for Henderson County.

For decades, everyone thought that press statement would put an end to any effort to bring to justice the person or persons responsibility for murdering McPherson. However, last spring, at the instigation of the Mississippi ACLU, state charges of first degree murder were filed against Cecil Pierpont and the other suspected accomplices.

*

Despite the lateness of the hour and the fact that everyone in the room had more than a casual familiarity with the problems that had recently befallen Mr. Pierpont, it was clear when Billy Wayne reared back in his chair, took another hit from his gin and tonic, and lit up another cigar that everyone was about to hear it again.

"Well, you know, being a Klansman back in them days meant somethin'. It ain't like today when some of these pencil heads just wanna walk around dressed up in the robe with the MIOAK (Mystic Insignia Of A Klansman), but ain't willin' to do a damn thang but light the cross and have a march. Hell, they can git the women and children to do that. These new uns, they don't know shit bout important stuff like remindin' a nigger of his proper place in Southern society and how to put the fear of God in 'em if he ever thanks about losing his place. I tell you what. Old "Pops" knew how to put a nigger in his place and then how to make good and sho his black ass don't never forget his fuckin' place ever again. Like I said befo, sometimes you gots to put the fear of God in a nigger befo he'll do what you tell him. You see, I learned how to deal with niggers from "Pops" and other proud, strong white men who wudn't afraid to stand up for the white race. Just like the rest of you' ens, I put on the robe, went to rallies, listened to speeches, and lit the cross, but it was men like "Pops" Pierpont that took me under their wings and

254

showed me how to prepare for the way the battle was gonna have to really be waged. Talkin' is fine as long as niggers is listen'. But when them motherfuckers stop listenin' you gotta go beyond talk and git down to some serious ass-kickin'" said Billy Wayne

"How did Bobby Lee say old "Pops" is getting along, Billy, and why do we need to get that po fella a lawyer?" inquired Cletus, trying to lead Billy Wayne back to idea of helping "Pops" hire an attorney and hopefully helping him to find a quick end to the evening's meeting.

"He's scared shitless, Cletus. How the hell would you feel if you was charged with first degree murder for some shit that happened more than forty fuckin' years ago, and you damn near eighty something years old, and ain't got a penny to your name? And why ain't he got a copper penny? He got hard up for money, and instead of coming to one of his friends for help, he sold all of his dry cleanin' stores. He was always a proud man and didn't want too many people to know how bad his bank account was. I got on the phone one mornin' and tried to tell "Pops" not to sell out to them tightfisted Jews out of Jackson. They had the ole boy over a fuckin' barrel, and befo he knowed any damn thang, they had done Jewed him outta all five of his stores. Yep. Lock, stock and barrel, they got them stores for a quarter on the dollar. But "Pops" never was good when it came to takin' care of his money the right way. And within six months, "Pops" was on my dole, where he's gonna stay as long as he needs to. You see, fellas, I knowed all about that shit him and them boys from Laurel was planning. I kinda liked old Mac, but when he went to stirring them niggers up over that voter registration shit, well, I had to tell "Pops" he had my blessin' to take care of Mac. And "Pops" knowed I was gonna give my blessin' cause that's how he taught me. Kinda funny, ain't it? I learned how to handle niggers from old "Pops", and he come to me for my blessin' to do what he done taught me to do. But he come to me out of respect and because he didn't want me to hear bout it from nobody else. Plus, he knowed that if somethin' went wrong, Jethro and me was gonna have to find a way to git his ass out of trouble. And sho as sin, we had to do just that, didn't we Jethro," asked Billy Wayne.

"Yep, Billy we sho did. But like you said, "Pops" was an icon amongst the right thinking people and the right acting people and the righteous people of this town. When old "Pops" was first arrested back in '65, when the matter first occurred, Billy called me to tell me to git down to the jail house. I had been on the bench for about a year at the time and had pretty much learned how things worked around the courthouse, and more importantly, I learned that when they didn't work the way you wanted them to, just how to make 'em so. Anyhow, when I went to the jail house, I told the boy from the DA's office, not to even consider bringing charges against "Pops", cause they wudn't gonna stick. And if he thought differently, well he just oughta take it up with the District Attorney, Mr. Hopkins. I probably didn't need to tell him cause the DA wudn't gonna file charges any how because I had already arranged a meeting in my chambers with the defense counsel and the DA, and we came to a meeting of the minds about how to dispose of this touchy situation. So, the same day, "Pops" was let go, and since then ain't made much a fuss atall with the Klan. Like you said, Billy, these young ones today who have taken over couldn't hold a candle to men like "Pops" Pierpont. At their strongest, these young ones ain't in the same class with "Pops" when he is at his weakest," said Jethro.

"You damn skippy they ain't no where near to bein' in the class with "Pops" Pierpont. Hell, that's true of most white men in this town. Any how, "Pops" talked with me bout how he was gonna take care of Mac. He said that him and the boys had been following Mac around town for a couple of days, checking out his routine and his moves. In the army, we called that recon. They noticed that round sun down, he would be hauling a carload of niggers back to Sheeplo and after he dropped the last one off, he'd take his time driving back to his house, stopping here and there visitin' with folks on the way. Usually, it was pretty damn late when he finally drove up to his house for the evening. So, "Pops" said that he would arrange for a fella to look like he was broke down on the side of the road with a flat tire, broke fan belt, or any damn thang that would make Mac stop. 'Cause being the Good Samaritan he was, Mac was sho to stop and ask the boy if he needed help. So, that Thursday night round bout 10:00, the fella parked his car bout two or three miles from Mac's house and pulled off on the shoulder with the hood up. "Pops" had it timed down to the second. He studied Mac's driving habits, his speed, and how long it took him to git from one place to another. So, once the boy was in place with his car, it was just a matter of a few minutes befo Mac shows up. And just like they figured, Mac pulls over behind the boy's car. He gits out and asked him if he needed somethin'. Just bout that time, "Pops" and his boys jumped from behind some bushes, liked to scared the shit out of old Mac. They grabbed him by the arms and legs and dragged him back further up into the woods into a little clearing. Once they got him there, they made him git on his knees. This is the part I told "Pops" he should do. While on his knees, they told Mac to say that he was sorry for stirring up all them local niggers with all that talk bout votin' and shit. "Pops" said Mac told him to go to hell. And boy, when "Pops" heard that nigger tellin' a white man to go to hell, he just went postal on that boy. He pulled out his pistol and commenced to taking target practice on Mac's head and chest, and then rolled him over and shot him in the ass. Them other boys was damn disappointed cause befo any of them could git their first rounds off, hell Mac was deader than a bantam rooster on the losing end of a cock fight," said Billy Wayne as he thumped ashes from his half-smoked cigar into a pile of cigar butts in the ashtray setting in front of him at the table.

"Well anyhow, I say we give Bobby Lee at least a hundred grand to hire one of them lawyers out of Bogalusa who got experience in defending men like "Pops". And shit, if it takes more than that, we give him that too. And hearing no objections, it is so ordered. I'll take care of it first thing in the morning," said Billy Wayne, hitting the table as though he was striking it with a gavel.

CHAPTER 24

"OH! ONE MORE thang before we leave. I put a lotta damn work into this project, and I just wanna take a few minutes to show it to y'all. I'll explain it, and then you can take your asses home. I made a chart of all the major actions that have taken place just here in Mississippi during the early days when a nigger knew his place and if he didn't it was easy to remind his ass. I been workin' on this for a few weeks, and now um ready to debut it for you knuckle heads. I ain't showed it to nobody else cause y'all the only ones who could 'preciate the pride and achievements that's reflected in this chart. To me and know to you too, these are a lot more than just words, names, and dates on a piece of card board, fellas. When you thank about it, it is a written history of our accomplishments as protectors of our way of life," said Billy Wayne as his voice trailed off to a barely audible whisper.

"Now I want y'all to keep in mind that this don't count the actions that ain't never been discovered and those that took place outside of Miss-ippi. When you see it, y'alla be able to see just how effective we were in carryin' out our responsibilities to uphold our sacred heritage, handed down to us through the blood shed by nearly one hundred thousand brave soldiers who fought in the War of Northern Aggression. They did their part. We did our part. As I read this list to you, let us all be proud of that fact," said Billy Wayne as he again lowered his booming bass voice as it cracked like a friend delivering a eulogy or a proud parent bragging on a child. His countenance and mood were noticeably subdued.

Billy Wayne stood to retrieve his chart from a closet and placed the ten foot by ten foot trifold poster on a giant easel. He used a wooden black tip pointer to direct his audience's attention to the first item on the chart.

"Let me just read the names of niggers that had to learn the hard way what their place was. And when I read 'em, I will tell you which ones we or our boys had a hand in. Looka here. See, I got the names and the dates the shit went down. Goes all the way back to the '50s," said Billy Wayne.

With pointer in hand, Billy Wayne directed everyone's attention to the first of sixteen names—names of fathers, sons, uncles, and brothers who lost their lives for no reason other than the color of their skin and the hatred directed at them because of their race. Their names were spelled with large block letters that reflected the work of a professional chart designer and maker. The date and reason for being killed were listed by each name.

"Start with this nigger Lamar Smith from Brookhaven—1955 for stirrin' up niggers 'bout votin'.

"Emmett Till—1955 for wolf whistlin' at a white woman over in Money.

"Mack Parker—1959 for raping a white woman down in Poplarville. Our boys took care of that one.

"Herbert Lee and Louis Allen—1961 for stirrin' up niggers 'bout votin' up in Liberty.

"Roman Duckworth—1962 for just bein' in the wrong damn place at the wrong damn time. We was involved in that one too. Felt bad for a quick minute when I found out he was a soldier boy.

"The big fish—Medgar Evers, 1963 in Jackson for just bein'

an agitatin' nigger runnin' all over the state, stirrin' up niggers 'bout votin' and that other so-called equal rights shit. Beckwith damn near got away. I met that boy down in Slidell. He done jobs for us a few times. But he just got unlucky when he took out Evers.

"Charles Moore and Henry Dee—1964 over in Meadville to send a message to them northern agitators 'bout what would happen to them if they came down here stirrin' up our local niggers.

"They had to do the same thang with them so-called civil rights workers in Philadelphia in 1964—Chaney, the nigger, and Goodman and Schwerner, the Jew boys.

"Vernon Dahmer—1966. Well don't need to say no mo bout that situation.

"Ben White—1966 over in Natchez, for the same damn reason—know your place, nigger and if you forget, somebody gonna show you.

"Had to do the same thang in Natchez the next year—1967 with Wharlest Jackson 'cause that nigger took a job promotion that shoulda went to a white man. Nigger was getting' uppity thanking he was just as qualified as a white man for that job.

"Benjamin Brown—1967 up in Jackson. He was just damn unlucky 'cause police start shootin' at niggers for distrubin' the peace with them marches and picket lines. Wasn't personal. The boy just got in the way of a bullet from one of Jackson's finest. Should not oughta had his ass out there in the midst of all that shit in the first place," said Billy Wayne.

Billy Wayne stood, stretched, and exhaled, blowing air across his fluttering lips, which emitted sounds that mimicked a motorboat. After taking a couple of swigs from his drink, he lowered the glass back to the table, re-took his seat and continued regaling in navel gazing.

"Again, let's take pride in our accomplishments over the

past forty somethin' years, fellas. Not just because of this list I just gave you, but for all our efforts, successful and not so successful, to honor the sacrifices of our dead ancestors and brave soldiers who did their part and who in turn, expected us to carry on the tradition of protecting our way of life. Plus, we all know and believe in our heart that we had the grace and divine guidance of the good Lord on our side throughout it all because the good Book tells us how thangs were set up and how they were supposed to remain. Ain't no way to get 'round that, fellas. When the Lord gives us the plan and the vision to keep thangs the way he set 'em up we gotta respond. And um convinced that we have done what He wanted us to do. If some got inconvenienced or disadvantaged so to speak in the process, well that is just the consequences of people not heedin' the word of the Lord. And when he meets us at the Pearly Gates, um sure he's gonna say, job well done, my true and faithful servants," said a somber but not quite completely sober Billy Wayne.

"Now, let's have a prayer before we adjourn. Bow your heads and lift your hearts to our risen savior. *Dear Lord, we come to you as your humbled and obedient servants who have dedicated our lives to your Word. You know our hearts. You know that we held up the blood stained banner just like you told us to. We have not been perfect. We have sinned. But like you told us, in Romans 3:23— For everyone has sinned; we all fall short of God's glorious standard. But because of the blood you shed on Calvary, you cleansed us and made a new covenant with your chosen people and granted forgiveness for their transgressions. So, Lord where we have fallen short of your glorious standard, we ask your forgiveness. Where we have met those standards, we ask that you continue to give us the strength and the wisdom to keep your mighty word. I ask that you continue to bless those assembled here this evening. Bless our families and keep all of us safe. This we ask in the name of the one true savior, Jesus Christ. Amen,"* said Billy Wayne.

"Now, let's do some serious drankin', boys fo I start cryin' like I been watchin' *Fried Green Tomatoes again,"* said Billy Wayne.

CHAPTER 25

DICKEY CARTER GOT up from his seat, walked over to the bay window and noticed that the white van was now moving. Remembering that Brock Galloway had noted earlier that he thought Charles had arrived in the van, Dickey Carter gruffly announced to the group, "Dammit! I did want to get another drink before Jabbo left. But I guess I waited too late. Looks like his sorry ass done already left. I see the boy drivin' off," said Dickey Carter.

Actually, Charles was still in the kitchen, dressed in his street clothes, which consisted of a sky blue turtleneck sweater, navy blue khaki Dockers, and black wing tip shoes. He hated wearing that server's uniform he was made to wear when serving drinks to Billy Wayne and his buddies. Wearing the white waiter's jacket, black tuxedo pants, starched white tuxedo shirt, black bowtie, white cotton gloves and black patent leather shoes made him seem more like a house slave than like a free man. Shedding those servant's clothes was the closest he could ever get, until tonight, to shedding the loathsome burden of being Billy Wayne Sharp's long-suffering servant.

"Well if that boy done left without tellin' me, um gonna have to take his black ass out to the woodshed. I don't like for him to leave till he done checked with me to see if we want somethin' else to drank. If I done told him once, I done told him a hundred million times. Don't leave befo you check with me. Now DC, looks like you gonna have to go in the kitchen and serve your-self, and hell you might as well serve the rest of us while you at it. Anybody else want somethin' to drank? Last call for alcohol," shouted Billy Wayne.

After everyone else gave a negative reply in unison, Billy Wayne said, "I guess it's just you and me DC. These pussies here done wimped out. Fix me my gin and tonic and make it a dou-ble. Mo gin than tonic, no ice. Should be some clean glasses in there somewhere, if Jabbo didn't go and break all of 'em."

Hearing Billy Wayne's instructions to Dickey Carter to go into the kitchen to get the drinks, Charles quickly exited the kitchen through a side door that opened into the hallway. Tiptoeing to the end of the ebony and ivory checkerboard tiled hallway, trying to avoid making any sounds with his usually noisy heavy wing-tipped shoes, he slowly moved to the exit door. Once there, he pressed the silver crash bar with his left hip and slowly opened the huge shiny olive green metal door. From behind the door came five men, three African American and two white, each dressed in navy blue windbreakers and tan khaki slacks. Each man, slowly and soundlessly, moved pass Charles, pausing long enough to shake his hand and embrace him with a couple of soft taps to the back. Charles then followed closely behind the stealthy quintet down the hallway toward the area that sequestered their cloistered and unsuspecting targets. Once there, Charles took up a position just outside and to the right of the bolted wooden double doors that opened into what he came to regard as a cesspool of evil and what Billy Wayne and his associates regarded as their man cave, free of snoops and spies. Charles could hear the customary sounds of merriment and hilarity emanating from behind the doors. There were the same voices, same laughter, and same mischief which he had wit-nessed for more years than he cared to remember. The clinging of alcohol-filled glasses. The distinctive but indistinguishable twangy Southern drawls. The slurred speech. The boisterousness of their individual and collective voices. The effusive profanity. The unabashed utterances of vile racial epithets. The cacophony of disgusting sounds coming from that cesspool was nauseatingly familiar to Charles and delightfully pleasing to Billy Wayne and his buddies. But with God's help, tonight, he thought, would be the last night that Billy Wayne and his sinister cabal would heap their filthy feculence upon him. He stood with his back pressed against the matted white wall that separated him from Billy Wayne and his buddies. He stared straight ahead with rapid, intermittent back and forth glances at the leader of the group and his cohorts. His knees felt like jelly, and his breathing had become shallow from the adrenalin racing through his body. Unsettling thoughts entered his mind: What have I gotten myself into? What will happen if something goes wrong? What if...? Interrupting Charles' foray into a cloud of self-doubt, the tall, bald, muscular black man in charge of the group signaled to Charles with his left gloved hand to remain where he was and to not make any noise.

Sensing the surreal nature of something special unfolding before his very eyes, Charles was beginning to allow himself to imagine the unimaginable, to believe in the impossible, and to embrace the inevitable. By extension, his visceral reaction was to invoke the legacy and memory of the scores of black people who have suffered and continue to suffer at the hands of bigots and haters. In doing so, he contemplated how much times have changed, although Billy Wayne Sharp and his buddies seemed to be the exceptions. He especially noted, with justifiable pride that a black man was in charge of this unfolding operation. There was a time when such an occurrence was unfathomable. The contrast between yesteryear and now caused him to relax a bit and even bolstered his resolve to see this operation to the end, no matter the outcome.

Charles, a man whose biological age was fifty-nine but appeared ten years older, found his thoughts retreating back in time as he recalled how his own father was beaten by police because he did not say, "Yes, sir!" when asked if he lived in Sharpville. A simple and polite, "Yeah!" was enough to justify an unprovoked slap to both sides of his head, a knee to the groin, and several brutal and sadistic kicks to the ribs. He also recalled the Scottsboro Boys, nine black teenagers who had been unfairly convicted of raping a white woman in Scottsboro, Alabama. He recalled the hideously disfigured face of Emmett Till that appeared on the front page of the *Pittsburg Courier*. He also remembered Mack Parker, Leondis McPherson, Vernon Dahmer, Jimmie Lee Jackson, and the many other brave and martyred warriors who sacrificed their lives so that he and others of his race could realize the promise of justice, equality and freedom.

He also conjured up fond memories of his childhood when he and his friends would pick black berries and sell them to the white owner of the black neighborhood's only grocery store—Preacher's Grocery Store—for a nickel a bushel basket. Although they were paid far below fair market price, he and his friends considered a nickel a basket plenty enough to buy several bags of two-for-a-penny cookies at Preacher's Grocery Store or a bag of parched peanuts from Mr. Blue. Or, if they exercised enough patience, they would wait until just before dusk when the ice cream truck signaled its daily arrival with the familiar musical jingle that made everyone stop whatever they were doing and line up for a cone or two of ultra-sweet, soft-serve vanilla ice cream.

Warmhearted memories continued as he remembered how he and his friends would make pop guns, which were not intended to be nor capable of inflicting harm. He and his friends would spend hours fashioning pop guns from hollowed-out, round, thick, dry tree twigs and a shaven-down stick with a moistened, frayed tip. The hollowed-out tree twig was the barrel and the stick served as a piston. Once they finished both items, they would test their efficiency and if necessary, make adjustments to either the barrel or piston or both. Testing involved inserting the piston/stick into one end of the hollowed out tree twig/barrel with enough force to cause the ammunition, which was typically a green, pea-size China Berry, to exit the twig/barrel with enough pressure to create a popping sound. Armed with weapons born of imagination and creativity, Charles and his friends pretended to be Hopalong Cassidy or Roy Rogers fighting the bad guys. It was fun, he remembered, when life was simpler, or at least it seemed so. His biggest decisions as a fun-loving child was how many black berries to pick in one afternoon to buy enough cookies, ice cream cones, or peanuts; or whether he could avoid getting caught climbing Mr. Griffin's China Berry tree to retrieve enough ammo for him and his buddies to make their afternoon of fighting bad guys last until the street lights on, which signaled the end of play time for the day.

Other random thoughts easily drifted back to his teenage years. A smile formed across his mouth as he recalled the many nights he and his friends would stand underneath the corner street light engaging in their favorite pastimes—singing songs a cappella in three-part harmony and singing along with and listening to radio music. He recalled that for hours on end, he and his friends would sing and harmonize the soulful tunes from their favorite singing groups, The Drifters and The Dells. They would spend an equal amount of time listening to R&B songs that were broadcast on Charles' black leather-encased AM transistor radio over the airwaves of WLAC in Nashville, Tennessee or WDIA in Memphis, Tennessee. Only on overcast nights, however, was the signal strong enough to fully hear and feel the rhythm and blues tunes that were the only genre of music played on those two iconic radio stations.

The local radio stations in Sharpville played only rock and roll and country and western music, neither of which appealed to teenage Charles and his friends. One R&B song in particular, he recalled, frequently prompted a contest among the four or five friends gathered on the corner of Fredna Avenue and Charles Street. The contest was to see who could come closest to matching the length of the extended note sang by Marvin Junior, lead singer of The Dells, as he belted out his solo in the classic soulful ballad, *Stay in My Corner*. Owing to strong lungs and plenty of practice, Charles more often than not, won bragging rights by matching the fifteen-second note, second for second. Yes, those were simpler times. Where did they go and how did they go so quickly, he thought?

CHAPTER 26

CHARLES NOTICED MELANCHOLY intruding on his joy as he thought about his wife and three daughters. He wondered whether they were disappointed in him as a husband and father because he had not been able to provide much in the way of material things or the latest in women's and girl's fashion. They never complained, but he wished he could have afforded to buy his girls new shoes and dresses for school, instead of the used ones he purchased at the thrift store. He wished he could have bought his wife a new hat, shoes, and a fancy new print dress for Easter, instead of the hand-me-down ones she purchased at the salvage store in Palmers Crossing. But he hoped, despite not being able to buy them new shoes, hats, and dresses, that they would know that his love for them was boundless, unconditional, and never-ending. As often as he could, he told them that he likes them for always and loves them forever. Nothing, absolutely nothing, could ever make him stop loving them, he told them frequently. He wasn't sure how tonight's unforgettable episode was going to turn out—a major success or a miserable failure. Either way, he hoped that his family would be proud of him for at least trying to do the right thing. Of course, none of them knew what was about to happen at the B.W. Sharp Office Complex. They would likely find out from reading the newspaper the next day or depending on the outcome, they just might hear it directly from him that same evening.

He hated keeping secrets from his wife. They had always been open and honest with each other, no matter what. They were each other's confidant, having never kept a single secret between them—until now. He wanted so many times to tell Dorothea what he had done, but he knew she would only worry and be frightened. In turn, she might have even tried to talk him out of what he had already done and what he was about to do in the next few moments. The idea of not doing what he knew was the right thing to do— then and now—was simply not an option he would consider, not even for her sake. And it was for her sake that he willingly and gladly took on the burdens of worry, fear, and anxiety all by himself. He regarded those as burdens that he alone should bear. It would have been terribly unfair for him to place upon her the fear, worry, and anxiety that accompany every decision and action from the beginning to the present time. He just hoped that she would forgive him for keeping tonight's events a secret and not trusting her with the truth. But given the choice between burdening her with the knowledge of tonight's events or taking on the burden all by himself, the choice that he made was easy and not at all one that he regretted.

He also started thinking about other dear friends from his childhood. Some had passed away. Others were still around, and like him, all stuck in Sharpville with few viable life and employment options. He thought of the ubiquitous sights of out-of-work black men, of all ages, standing in the rain, the cold, and the heat at the Drake stands desperately hoping someone would come along and offer them a job of any kind that would help put food on the table. He thought about opportunities missed, like moving to California with an uncle right after high school. He often wondered, in the long run, whether he would have been better off in California or staying in Mississippi. His

Uncle Percy tried to persuade him to join him, his wife and four kids for the 2,500-mile journey to what they believed would be akin to the Underground Railroad—a pathway to freedom. Percy Bickford told his nephew that a black man could make it out there in California, working in the airplane factories, construction, or loading docks. A black man, Uncle Percy told him, could be a man and take care of his family and not have to work for slave wages. Job prospects were plentiful, he told Charles, and a hiring boom meant that anyone who was willing to put in long, hard hours could carve a decent middle-class existence for himself and his family. That was a convincing argument, then and now, he thought. Nothing was more important to Charles than being a man and taking care of his family. God knows he tried his best to be a man. But the self-pride and dignity that usually accompany a fulfilling and self-affirming manhood, for so long, had gone wanting within his makeup and constitution, especially when he worked for Billy Wayne. How could he call himself a man when he subjugated himself to the whims of those evil men? How could he call himself a man when he was not able to stand up to the relentless bullying from Billy Wayne and his associates? How could he call himself a man after he had internalized so much of what the Billy Waynes of the world had decided about his worth as a man? He often wondered whether he would forever remain *Jabbo*, the beaten down black man who played the role of servant to his masters for too long, or if *Charles* would one day claim his rightful place as a proud black man with God-given dignity and self-respect. Regrets, self-doubt, and loss of manhood and dignity haunted him daily. Such pessimism and negative self-impressions, over time, accounted for the stress-induced rapid gait and poor posture that characterized his physicality.

Yet, all the stress, anxiety, and self-doubt, born out of his life in Sharpville, Mississippi, were mitigated by his growing self-confidence—confidence that was ignited by a series of courageous decisions and actions on his part that has led to the present moment. His self-doubt was further assuaged by recalling the famous quote from Edmund Burke that he learned in high school: *The only thing necessary for the triumph of evil is for good men to do nothing.* He knew he was a good man and that evil had triumphed long enough.

Owing to a deeply-held desire to be more courageous and to rid himself of his growing weariness of being sick and tired of being sick and tired, Charles began to reframe self-respect, self-pride, and by extension, his manhood, not by how Billy Wayne and his buddies treated him. Instead, those elusive qualities would be defined by a brand new set of more important metrics: the number of times he saw his wife and daughters laughing, the number of excellent grades his daughters received in school, the number of conversations he had with God, and the number of spontaneous hugs and simple *I love yous* from his wife. His focus was now on the new joy the he was becoming acquainted with, joy that had eluded him for so long. Through the fog of self-imposed and other-imposed diminution of his personhood, he was finally re-discovering the self-affirming joy that he derived from his wife and daughters and God Almighty.

He found joy in the fact that he and Dorothea had created a home, not defined by what they *did not* have but by what they *did* have. That was real, indestructible joy because, no matter his financial situation, no matter the number and types of burdens he bored, no matter the transitory hassles of life, he knew he had something at home that was worth more than money and all the material things he could have ever dreamed of owning.

With so many thoughts and emotions running through his mind and heart, he felt the need calm himself again. He reminded himself—stay in the moment. What's done is done. Can't have regrets now, he thought. But for sure, if he had moved to California, he would not have known the joy of being married to Dorothea Bickford for twenty-five years. Nor would he have known the treble joy of bringing three healthy bouncing baby girls home from the hospital every other year, starting eighteen years ago. Except for God, nothing or no one meant more to him that those four fabulous females, as he affectionately called them. Although his life equation contained more negatives than positives, he was beginning to feel, for the first time, a measure of courage mounting inside of him that had eluded him for so many years under the servitude of Billy Wayne Sharp and his buddies.

Moreover, the stress, anxiety, and self-doubt were further mollified by his growing reliance on his flourishing faith journey to guide his path to be more Christ-like. Despite the many challenges he has faced throughout his lifetime, including tonight's, Charles recently began finding strength and answers to those challenges and conundrums by going to the Bible, which he had studied in great depth, in preparation for his service as a deacon at Star Light Missionary Baptist Church. As an antidote for the fear and trepidation he was presently experiencing, he remembered Joshua's admonition to the Israelites: *Have I not commanded you? Be strong and courageous. Do not be terrified; do not be discouraged, for the Lord your God will be with you wherever you go.* He also recalled Paul's message to believers in Galatia: *Do not get tired of doing what is right. Don't get discouraged and give up, for we will reap a harvest of blessing at the appropriate time.* Thus, for the first time that entire day and maybe in his entire live, Charles realized that the appropriate time to reap a harvest had come.

As calm and contentment commanded his body, soul, and spirit, he noticed that the jelly-like sensation in his legs had been transformed into rock-solid sturdiness, and that the adrenalin-induced shallow breathing was returning to its normal rate and pace. A deep breath, a slow exhale, and a barely audible whisper, *Thank you, Jesus!*, and he knew he was going to be okay. And there he was. A humble yet self-assured man. An ordinary yet blessed man. A frightened but courageous man. An uneducated but wise man. A man poor in material things but rich in the blessings of love, faith, and hope. A testament, he thought, to God's penchant for using the oppressed, the marginalized, and the unpopular to bring about change and to manifest the goodness of His word. God had used the lowly shepherd boy, the prostitute, and the tax collectors to do just that, he recalled from lessons in Mrs. Sims Sunday School Class and from sermons by Reverend J.J. Jones and Reverend Sanders at Star Light. He knew that God was directing his path and using his lowliness to lift up his word. He knew that he was about to be part of something that would unequivocally ensure that the beating that his fathered received at the hands of bigoted Sharpville police officers and the murders of the many martyrs of the Civil Rights Movement would not be in vain.

CHAPTER 27

*K*NOCK… *KNOCK… KNOCK… Knock… Knock…*
The five knuckled knocks on the two-inch thick, solid oak conference room door were loud and came in rapid succession. The loudness of the knocks prompted Charles to refocus, take another deep breath, and send up one more silent prayer.

Billy Wayne yelled at the door, "Jabbo, what the hell you doin' at that door, boy? Thought you was gone any damn way. Don't know 'bout you sometimes boy."

"This is the FBI. Open the door and slowly move away from the door. Now!" yelled the commanding baritone voice on the other side of the doors.

"What the hell's goin' on," Billy Wayne asked.

"Sounds like somebody said FBI. Must be old Jabbo playin' a trick on you, Billy," answered Jethro Milliken.

Billy Wayne walked over to the door, and as he yanked it open, shouted, "Jabbo, goddamit, boy!"

The five men walked in with weapons drawn and unsmilingly instructed everyone to place his hands high above his head. The leader announced again that they were agents of the FBI, flashing his gold plated FBI badge so that each of the thoroughly perplexed perps could plainly see that they were legitimate FBI agents.

"Are any of you armed, and are there weapons anywhere

in this room," the leader asked in an unmistakably serious and authoritative voice.

"What the hell you mean, boy? You damn skippy I got a weapon. I got a four hundred and ten pump action shotgun in my closet. I use it for huntin'... huntin' coons. Get it, boy... coons. I hunt coons, the four-legged ones, not the two-legged ones like you, boy," said Billy Wayne as he faked a laugh that quickly disappeared when he realized that no one, including his buddies, laughed at his misguided attempt at levity at the expense of the black leader of the FBI team.

The agents continued to point their weapons at the stunned men. They moved cautiously and soundlessly, surrounding the men just as a trained sheep dog herds his frightened but compliant flock. Frightened and compliant were apt descriptors for the state of mind of each of Sharpville's soon-to-be former king makers and king breakers, except for Billy Wayne Sharp.

"And you need to know somethin' else, boy. And I ain't tryin' to be funny this time. 'Cause you see, boy, and this is damn important, so pay attention. I am a life-time, card-carrying member of the NRA—that's the National Rifle Association to be exact, in case you ain't never heard of the most important organization in the whole country. And 'um a veteran of DUBYA DUBYA Two on top of that. And I done earned the right under the *second* goddamn amendment of the *goddamn* constitution of the *goddamn* United States of America to have a *goddamn* gun. And guess what? Ain't nobody gonna take it from me. The goddamn Supreme Court made it plain as the black on your face, boy, that I got a right to have a gun for my protection and for huntin' coons. So, you can't do a damn thang about me having no goddamn gun in my possession, at least in my closet in my possession. Hell, you know I mean. And if you can't understand my understandin', just remember what my president, Charlton Heston said. Want me to tell you what that patriotic American hero said, boy? And when he said it, he was speakin' for me and all the rest of the patriotic Americans who spilt blood for this country. He said the only way you gonna take my guns away from me is from my cold dead hands," said Billy Wayne as he attempted to sit atop the conference table, the effects of his highly inebriated state, but stopped when he heard the sound of splitting wood coming from underneath the table.

The leader went to the closet, retrieved the weapon and handed it to one of his colleagues.

"Mister Billy Sharp, Mr. Jethro Milliken, Mr. Cletus Sessum, Mr. Joe Lee Roberts, Mr. Brock Galloway, Mr. Richard Carter, and Mr. Clifford Morgan. You are all under arrest. You have the right to remain silent...", said the FBI team leader.

A defiant Billy Wayne Sharp snapped, "What the hell y'all doin' breakin' into a private meetin' and tellin' us we under arrest for? And you can't take my shotgun, neither. I bought and paid for that gun. So, when you done had your say, get the hell outta my goddam office, and put my gun back where you fount it. And ain't a damn thang wrong with grown-up men drinkin' legal sealed whiskey. And if you was a real G-man, you would know that, ass hole. And them cigars um smokin was a gift to me from U.S. Senator Tim Lawson. Go ask 'em, if you don't believe me. Go on over there and use my phone. His number is 202-224-3121. That's the switchboard number. Just ask for Senator Timothy Lawson. I'll spell it for you if you can't spell, boy. L-a-w-s-o-n. He the only one there with that last night, I mean last name. So, shouldn't have no trouble reachin' him. I got his direct number, but that's for his closest friends, not for some black ass bureaucrat, wannabe bad-ass like you. Hell, we ain't broke no damn laws. What the hell y'all charging us with," said Billy Wayne, in a tone that clearly reflected his inability to be rational and coherent, two states of mind that became casualties of his advanced state of inebriation.

"Anything you say can and will be used against you in a court of law," said the leader of the FBI team.

An even redder-faced Billy Wayne continued his rant in an even louder tone.

"Goddamit boy, um talkin' to you. You must don't know who the fuck you messin' with here. I'll have yo *goddam* job and all of the rest of you ass holes, if y'all don't get the hell out of my *goddam* office and put my *goddamn* gun back in the *goddamn* closet," shouted Billy Wayne.

"You have a right to speak to an attorney and to have an attorney present during any questioning. If you cannot afford a lawyer, one will be provided for you at government expense. Do you understand each of these rights I have explained to you," asked the leader of the FBI team.

Billy Wayne took his hands down and started walking toward the FBI team leader. Actually, it was more like a stupor-induced stagger, another casualty of too much gin and tonic, more gin than tonic.

"Sir! Do not take another step. You are under arrest. Turn around and place your hands behind your head. NOW," warned the FBI team leader in a tone of voice that left no doubt that he had just about enough of Billy Wayne's lip.

For the first time in his life, Billy Wayne Sharp was being faced down by not just any man, but a black man, which induced a never-before-seen bizarre and befuddled look on his face. Billy Wayne possessed a boatload of looks that matched his wide range of emotions. But the present look plastered across his candy apple-red face was new, even to him and his associates, all of whom were closely studying the novelty of the look, try-ing to discern it. The opinion of an objective person would have been that the look on Billy Wayne's face seemed to be an unusual blend of fear, anger, confusion, and sadness. Nevertheless, he stopped in his tracks when he saw the agent cock his revolver and take aim at his chest.

The FBI team leader placed restraints on Billy Wayne, tightening the nylon zip tie restraints to their fullest extension. Billy Wayne winced and gasped from the pain caused by the tautness of the restraints. The FBI team leader led a compliant but still slightly defiant Billy Wayne to the conference table where envelopes stuffed full of brand new crisp hundred dollar bills still lay.

Standing toe-to-toe with Billy Wayne, less than an inch from his face, the agent who was an inch taller stared him straight in the eyes and continued to address Billy Wayne.

"Sir, you *will* sit down. *Now!* And I warn you again that you have the right to remain silent and that anything you say can and will be used against you in a court of law," shouted the FBI team leader.

Billy Wayne complied with the order to sit, but not with the suggestion to keep silent.

"I gotta right to say any goddam thang I wanna say and I don't need no fuckin' lawyer to tell me when I can talk and what I can say. I'm free, white, and over twenty-one, goddamit! Shit, ain't none of us done nothing but have a meetin' like we been doin' for forty fuckin' years. Ain't nobody said nothing befo now. So, tell me, Home Boy, Kunte Kinte, Leeroy, Jamal, Tyrone, Hakeem, Willie or whatever yo tar baby mama named you, what the hell you say we done to be treated like a bunch of common criminals? We are law abidin' citizens and you can't go 'round treatin' law abidin' citizens like they criminals," Billy Wayne said in his normal liquor-induced slurred manner.

"Billy Wayne, shut your goddamn mouth for once in your sorry ass life! You are making things worse every time you open that drunken, filthy mouth of yours," yelled a red-faced and trembling Jethro Milliken.

"But Jethro. They ain't tellin' us what they arrestin' us for," said Billy Wayne.

"If you would shut your goddamn mouth long enough and let the man do his job, we will all find out why," snapped Jethro.

"Sir, I am a retired officer of the court. Would you please tell me the charges that are being alleged against my friends and me," asked Jethro.

"Each of you is being arrested for suspicion of money laundering, racketeering and conspiracy to commit murder. That is all I can tell you for now. The United States Attorney and the State Attorney General could possibly file additional charges at a later date, sir. Do you understand your rights as I have explained them," asked the FBI team leader.

In a remarkably subdued and submissive fashion that sharply contrasted the arrogance and crudeness that typified them for most of their lives, each responded with a submissive and barely audible, *yes sir*. That is, each of them, except Billy Wayne Sharp, who in typical defiant fashion, and no doubt still feeling the effects of his five double-gin-and tonics, yelled, "Hell fuckin' yeah! I heard every damn word you said, boy. Now what you gonna do, Mr. G-man? I know what you better damn well do. And that's to git the hell outta my office befo' you really piss me off."

The other agents patted down and placed nylon zip tie restraints on each of the other six men, and the leader calmly but sternly gave further instructions.

"You will be taken downstairs where a police van will take you to the Henderson County jail where you will be fingerprinted and have your mug shot taken. Following that, you will be placed in a holding cell. At the proper time, you will be allowed to contact your attorney or anyone else you choose to call. After your attorney has arrived, a judge will officially inform you of the charges, and if bail is granted, you will be allowed to post bail at that time. We will now proceed in single file to the elevator and go to the van that is waiting at the front entrance of this building," announced the FBI team leader.

As each of the securely restrained men staggered from the conference room under the firm grasp and control of an FBI agent, they glanced to their right where they saw Charles Bickford standing. Tears streamed down his face, tears that quietly masked the overwhelming joy that he was feeling inside. He mustered up the courage to defiantly look each them square in their eyes as they passed his location. The look in Charles Bickford's eyes delivered an unmistakable message that mirrored the theme of the 1968 Memphis Sanitation Workers Strike: I AM A MAN. All of his life, Charles had been so thoroughly inculcated in Jim Crowism that he had become conditioned to internalize the notion that he was not only a second class citizen but also a second class human being. The evil of racism and white supremacy had so infected his mind, soul, and body that he could barely remember a time in his life when he was not aware of the fact that being black in Sharpville meant that he was different and because he was different, he would be treated differently. Of course, the only difference was something simple, natural, and nothing he could change—the color of his skin.

As part of that inculcation, Charles was taught to never defiantly look into a white man's eyes, for fear that doing so would result in him being considered uppity. There was ample evidence in and around Henderson County, Sharpville, and indeed throughout the South, that served as a lugubrious reminder of what happened to a black man who dared cross the Jim Crow line by staring into the eyes of a white man.

But without blinking, Charles Bickford stared unblinkingly at each one of Billy Wayne's associates as they made their way to the elevator. While staring down each of them, he thought to himself, Jim Crow be damned and you right along with him!

Ironically, it was they, the former pillars of the community and the embodiment of white supremacy in Sharpville, Mississippi who broke the stare and lowered their heads, the exact behavior expected of any black person who encountered a white person in Jim Crow society.

Billy Wayne was the last of the restrained perps to stagger from the now empty man cave. The FBI group leader held a tight grip on Billy Wayne's arm—and as they approached Charles' location, he instinctively tightened his grip. The FBI leader ceded to Billy Wayne's request to pause a moment in front of Charles.

Billy Wayne looked at Charles with the same amalgam of facial expressions— fear, anger, confusion, and sadness—that he displayed when the FBI leader pointed his weapon at him and told him to stop walking toward him. The only difference was the thick mucus exiting Billy Wayne's flaring nostrils and equally thick, white, foamy spittle streaming from the corners of his mouth. With arms handcuffed behind him and unable to wipe away the disgusting body fluids from his face, he could have been easily mistaken for a destitute man instead of the millionaire that he was. And despite warnings from Judge Milliken to not say anything else, Billy Wayne Sharp could not resist.

"Jabbo, what the hell you know 'bout all of this? You in on this somehow, ain't you boy? I tell you what. You know what's good for yo black ass, you'll keep yo trap shut," said Billy Wayne, swaying from toe to heel searching for a more stable equilibrium that was quickly fading from his control.

"Mr. Sharp. No. No 'mo Mr. Sharp. I'm gonna call you Billy Wayne, cause you don't scare me no mo. And I ain't your damn flunky no mo neither. I done had 'nuff yo evil and wicked ways. You gonna finally get what's comin' to you, suh. All of you is. You see, I been knowin' for years all of the crooked stuff y'all been doin' round here, and just a-braggin' and a-boastin' bout how y'all run this town and run people's lives. And all of the illegal stuff y'all been doin', while the good people in this town goin' 'round thankin' y'all all high and mighty and better than the rest of us. And I ain't been too proud of myself none atall in not reportin' what I know to the police. But I knowed I couldn't tell these local police 'round here cause you got 'em all sewed up in yo back pockets and yo front pockets. So, I went and contacted the FBI down in New Orleans and told 'em everythang I know about what y'all done done over the years. Yep. You thought I was just some po, dumb ass nigger who didn't have sense to know about all that devilment y'all been doin' 'round here. But I been listenin' and keepin' my mouth shut for years. But finally I had to be a man and stand up and help put a stop to what y'all been doin and to make sho y'all pay for all that dirt y'all done done all these years," said Charles Bickford in a loud, full-throated defense of his manhood and his role in the night's drama.

"Hell, Jabbo, it's just gonna be yo word gainst mine. And who the hell gonna believe a ignorant ass nigger's word over the word of an upstanding citizen of Sharpville. You overplayed yo hand boy and you gonna pay plenty for this," yelled Billy Wayne, spewing more spittle from his mouth.

"You might thank it's yo word against mine, Billy Wayne Sharp. But what you gonna say when all your words get played in a court of law for everybody to hear 'em? You see, Billy Wayne Sharp, not only was this ignorant ass nigger sittin' outside listenin', but with the help of them FBI boys we put a eavesdroppin' bug right there in the middle of all y'all. Everythang y'all been discussin' for the past nine months been recorded on video and on tape. So, it don't matter if yo white friends believe me or not. When they hear in yo own words how evil you and the rest of 'em is, well all I can say is Lord Have mercy on your sin-sick soul. 'Cause you gonna need it," countered Charles Bickford.

"After all I done for you, Jabbo, and you gonna turn on

me like that. Why, Jabbo? Why? You ungrateful black son-of-a-bitch," screamed Billy Wayne.

"Billy Wayne Sharp, you ain't done a damn thang for me but keep me in debt to you and tried to make feel like you was better than me cause of your money and your skin color. And, suh, you needs to know that slavery was over a *long* time ago and as of tonight, and it's been a long time comin', but praise the Lord, I am finally a free man the way good Lord intended me to be. And one mo thang fo they lock you up. Somethin' I been wantin' to say to you for years, Billy Wayne Sharp. And I'm gonna ask for the Lord's forgiveness even befo I say it 'cause it ain't necessarily the most Christian thang to say. You see, Mr. Sharp, I seen this movie one night that had Della Reese in it, and she told this fellow somethin' that I been wantin' to say to you for a long time, Billy Wayne Sharp, *suh*," replied Charles Bickford.

"Yeah? Ain't nothin' you can tell me but you done lost your fuckin mind, boy,"

Billy Wayne retorted.

"No, Billy Wayne Sharp, my mind is as sound as it can be, and my heart is light as a feather. But what I wanna say to you now gonna make me feel a whole lot better. And I can't say it like Della Reese, but here it goes. Billy Wayne Sharp, or Billy Bad-Ass, like you like to call yoself, kiss my entire ass," announced Charles Bickford with the pleasure of a man who just felt a heavy load dropped from his shoulders like a boulder falling off the side of a cliff.

With a tug on his arm by the FBI leader, Billy Wayne turned and walked away with his head bowed like the defeated man he was. He kept mumbling a phrase that the FBI leader found bizarre and puzzling. In a slightly muted voice, Billy Wayne repeatedly uttered, *that goddamn gypsy man was full of shit. He can kiss my entire ass.*

EPILOGUE

IN SHARP AND fitting contrast, Charles walked away with his head high and back straight for the first time in decades. Unspeakable joy and peace consumed him, aided by a prayer he uttered to himself. *Thank you, Lord. Thank you for keepin' me safe and keepin' me strong here tonight. I didn't know if I could do it, but I knew that as long as I had faith in you, Lord, you would be right there with me. You wudn't gonna leave me. Just like you was there with the three Hebrew boys when you brought 'em outta the fiery furnace, you was with me tonight. And just like you was there with little David when slew that big 'ole boy Goliath, you was with me tonight, Lord. And Lord, bless them FBI boys for bein' there too. Everythang that happened here tonight was yo way of remindin' me and the rest of us that in the end, yo goodness is bigger than anything the devil tries to throw our way. You reminded all of us, who believe in you, that good always wins out over evil. Always. And there was plenty evil goin' on 'round this place, but yo goodness is mo powerful than all that evil. Thank you, Lord. Thank you for being my salvation, my rock, and my shield. And finally, Lord, may these men that were arrested here tonight one day find out about yo savin' grace and let you come back into their lives. Help them git rid of all that hate and meanness that's been eatin' at 'em all these years. Touch their hearts and make 'em realize that you love all your children, no matter their skin color or how much money they got in their bank accounts or if they got a bank account atall. As the Good Book says: God shows no partiality, but in every nation anyone who fears him and does what is right is acceptable to him. Nuff said. Amen.*

He had done what was right and acceptable, he concluded, in contacting the FBI. He had also done the right thing, he concluded, in not allowing his fear to displace his sense of duty. And finally he concluded that he had done the right thing in not letting Dorothea know about his part in the night's drama. His nerves were beaten down like a hammer striking a nail. Only God knows what Dorothea's nerves would have been like had she known what was taking place that night and if she had known all those months, what he and the FBI had planned. As he strolled toward the elevator, Charles Bickford's pace was swift and bouncy. His posture was erect, the tears were gone, and ironically, yet with acerbic and unflinching intentionality, he found himself whistling *Dixie* as he walked pass each of Sharpville's soon-to-be former power brokers.

*

Before getting into his car, Charles Bickford paused to shoot a glaring glance at the B.W. Sharp Office Complex. He noticed that, except for the lights left on in Billy Wayne's conference room, the entire building was dark and bleak, apt metaphors for the heart and soul of the building's owner, he noted. The parking lot was empty except for the shiny, luxury vehicles that belonged to Billy and his friends… as empty as the lives of the men whose cars now occupied it, he thought. As he paused and unhurriedly took in the entirety of the Office Complex, he also allowed himself to take in the magnitude of what had just happened inside that enormous edifice constructed to pay homage to Billy Wayne's enormous ego. The preceding thirty minutes were unlike any he had ever experienced in his entire life. Although the Hollywood-like drama was only thirty minutes long, it was actually more than thirty years in the making. A better script could not have been crafted by the creative minds of movie studio moguls than the real, unscripted, unrehearsed drama that had just been played out in Billy Wayne's conference room. There was a smile on Charles' face, as he stood there in his existential aloneness, and realized that he nearly single-handedly brought down a group of dangerous, ruthless, and arrogant men who had spent their entire lives building an empire they thought would outlive each of them. In the end, he thought, Billy Wayne and his friends craved and consumed too much of the dying and decaying fruits produced by the trees of segregation, racism, and bigotry. Their legacy, like the fruits and the trees that produced them, is rotten to the core and poisonous to anyone who dares celebrate it.

Like Charles, Billy Wayne Sharp and his buddies had just witnessed an improbable, surreal scenario. A man whom they all considered their intellectual, moral, and social inferior had just brought down Billy Bad-Ass and his presumably Teflon-coated cabal. Perhaps, they should have paid attention to the words of fellow Mississippian, William Faulkner who opined, *to live anywhere in the world today and be against equality because of race or color is like living in Alaska and being against snow.*

Climbing behind the wheels of his old, beat-up, charcoal-gray Monte Carlo, Charles could not wait to get home to his four, fabulous females to share the good news with them. He knew they would be proud of him. He also knew he had to do make a special appeal to Dorothea to ask her forgiveness for keeping secrets from her, although he thought the odds were pretty good that she would forgive him.

The headlines of the next day's newspaper summed up the essence of the event: *Local Secret Corrupt Cabal Exposed.* The newspaper reporter penned a thorough and detailed account of the allegations and charges against Billy Wayne Sharp and his buddies. The story also included an extensive interview with Charles Bickford that highlighted his involvement with the entire operation from beginning to end. Over the ensuing days, the story was picked up by the Associated Press, CNN, and the other major television networks. As a result of the national publicity and a guest appearance on the Oprah Winfrey Show and the Larry King Show, hundreds of letters, messages, and telephone calls, many of which included job offers for Charles, flooded into the Bickfords' home from all over the country.

After giving due consideration to all serious job offers, Charles decided to accept the offer from Henderson State University to serve as Lead Foreman for Carpentry and Masonry in the Physical Plant Department. He could have accepted any number of more lucrative job offers in other states, but he and Dorothea wanted to remain in Sharpville among friends and family. That was not a difficult decision at all for either of them. Each had deep roots in Sharpville and did not want to start over someplace else. The idea of moving to another part of the country to start anew reminded Charles of the offer from his Uncle Percy decades earlier to move with him and his family to California following his high school graduation. Although the times and circumstances were different, he had no doubt that he made the correct decision both times.

*

Each defendant, except Billy Wayne Sharp, pled guilty to federal charges, including income tax evasion, racketeering, violation of the RICO Act, operating an illegal betting operation, interstate trafficking of women for purposes of prostitution, and money laundering. State charges of murder and conspiracy to commit murder were also lodged against all seven, to which each entered a plea of guilty, except Billy Wayne, whose arrogance and pride would not allow him to do so. Despite advice from his attorneys to the contrary, Billy Wayne honestly thought that he would be exonerated on all charges. That seriously misguided thought was born of his stubborn belief in his previously dependable "Teflon" protection and his mistaken belief that no one in Sharpville would dare go against him.

Six of the former power brokers and king makers began serving fifteen-twenty years for the federal convictions and will begin serving life sentences for the state convictions of murder and conspiracy to commit murder after their federal sentences have been completed. Given their advanced years and the heavy racial overtones of their crimes, it is likely they will die in prison, either from natural causes or from retribution at the hands of fellow inmates.

Billy Wayne's trials in federal and state court each ended with convictions, which were aided by compelling testimony from Charles Bickford, who recounted all of the first-hand information he possessed regarding Billy Wayne's and his co-conspirators' well-documented track record of law-breaking. The prosecution was aided by Jethro Milliken and C.L. Moody, both of whom, in exchange for reduced sentences, reluctantly testified against Billy Wayne. C.L. was convicted of conspiracy to commit murder in the death of Elvin Newhouse. His and Jethro's testimony netted each of them sentences of twenty-five years at Parchman Penitentiary instead of the life sentences handed down to the other defendants. The video and audio tapes, also used as convincing evidence to help the all-white juries render unanimous verdicts of guilty, incredibly chronicled the gruesome and ghastly details of the many years of illegal and mischievous conduct of Billy Wayne and his buddies. The tapes and the testimony left no doubt, reasonable or otherwise, that Billy Wayne Sharp and his buddies were indeed the powerful, ruthless, arrogant, and stealthy kingpins they endeavored so mightily to become.

Billy Wayne's convictions cost him lifetime accommodations at federal and state penitentiaries and forfeiture of all his cash and personal and business possessions, not to mention his cherished status as one of Sharpville's leading citizens. Henderson State University removed all artifacts, plaques, and signage from the buildings that bore his now sullied name. Business owners in downtown Sharpville removed plaques from their establishments that honored Billy Wayne and his contribution to their success. Each of the elected and appointed officials and leaders who had been contaminated by and benefited from the corruption and mischief of Billy Wayne saw their tenure in those positions come to an abrupt end. Some resigned. Others were voted out of office in special recall elections. Further, the broadcast of the video tapes on *Court TV* resulted in profound embarrassment for the families and friends of Billy Wayne and his callous cabal.

*

Imogene Parsons Roberts gave up her positions as Lay Leader and Chair of the Board of Trustees at the Sharpville Presbyterian Church, which she did from the pulpit in front of the entire congregation on Communion Sunday. She came to that decision after a good deal of praying and a particularly heart-to-heart with her brother and pastor, the Reverend Lonnie Parsons, Jr.

"Lonnie, Jr., I've come to a decision, and I want you to be the first to know about it," said a red-eyed, sniffling Imogene as she sat in one of the lavender, high-back, crushed velvet visitor's chair, across from her younger sibling's desk in the pastor's study.

"What is it, Imogene? What are you talking about? What in the world are you planning to do? Nothing drastic, I hope. I know things are not looking too bright right now, sis, but don't you go and do nothing crazy," replied a genuinely concerned and bordering on frenetic Lonnie, Jr. as he quickly rose from his seat behind his large L-shaped mahogany desk and escorted Imogene to the white leather couch located on the opposite wall, underneath an enormous oil painting of the Reverend Lonnie Parson, Sr.

"No. Nothing crazy, at all, Lonnie, Jr. Well, I don't think it's crazy, but some might consider me certifiable for doing what I'm planning to do," replied Imogene as she slowly lowered herself onto the couch next to Lonnie, Jr., while deeply exhaling and dabbing her nose and eyes with her embroidered, bone-colored, IPR-initialed handkerchief.

"You see, Lonnie, I know the congregation is wondering how all of this terrible and embarrassing mess about Joe Lee is gonna affect my status and position in the leadership of the church. And quite honestly, how it's gonna affect the church overall because Joe Lee has been a part of this church for many, many years. His presence in this church has been substantial, both monetarily and spiritually. Everybody knew him and he knew everybody. His tithing was solid, although it hurts me to no end to know that some of his ill-gotten gains went toward his tithing obligations. So, we can't go 'round pretending that none of this is not gonna affect me, you, and the church," said Imogene, adjusting her glasses with an upward thrust with an index finger.

"Well, you got a point, there Imogene. I've been praying over this whole mess for some time now. I've been praying for Joe Lee's poor ole tortured soul, for your own heartbreak, and for guidance on how to bring healing and understanding to our church family. People in the church are talking amongst themselves about Joe Lee, oftentimes huddled in small groups around the water fountain or in the hallway, some in a fashion more akin to gossip and backstabbing than in a Christian fashion where we should be building up and sending up prayers to help our poor brother or sister. More than ever, we need to go to the Lord and ask for his deliverance, grace, and mercy," said Lonnie, Jr.

"I've been praying, too, Lonnie, Jr. every day and night, asking the Lord what I need to do, as Joe Lee's wife and as Lay Leader and Chair of the Trustees Board. And here is what the Lord put on my heart and told me I need to do, Lonnie, Jr. Now, hear me out before you say anything, Lonnie, Jr. I have given this a lot of thought and prayer, and I will not be persuaded to change my mind. You see, I have been torn in some many directions. At one point I thought the Lord wanted me to just be quiet and let it all blow over. Then again, I thought he was telling me to rid myself of Joe Lee, to just unburden myself from him altogether. But I have come to believe in my heart that neither of things is what He wants me to do. So, this is exactly what the Lord has told me to do. He told me to go and stand before the congregation next Sunday, Communion Sunday, and ask for the congregation's forgiveness for the sins of both me and Joe Lee. The Lord told me that this was the only way for me to cleanse my soul and to once and for all, put this whole sordid mess behind me. This church is my family. The members are my dear brothers and sisters in Christ, and I owe that much to them. I owe them an explanation of what happened, what drove Joe Lee down that road of sin and immorality, and why some of it, maybe all of it, was my fault. Maybe that way, there won't be all that water fountain gossip going on, which is not healthy for anybody. The Lord don't like it when we gossip, say hurtful things toward one another, and use our tongues and ears to tear somebody down. I owe them my confession about how much of the blame for Joe Lee's wrongdoings rest on my shoulders. But most important, I owe each of them fine, God-fearing people the chance to hear my plea from my own mouth. By doing that, they can cleanse their own hearts and souls of any ill-feelings they got toward me by granting me their unconditional pardon. You see the Lord made me see things that way, Lonnie, Jr. This way, I can cleanse by own sin-sick soul by confessing my sins and asking for the congregation's forgiveness, and they, at least the ones that are still harboring bad feelings toward me, can do their Christian duty by forgiving me," said Imogene after blowing her nose and dabbing at the trickle of mascara trailing down her cheeks.

"Sis, is there anything I can do to help you do that? Do you want me to tell the congregation for you just how sorry you are? Or if you prefer, you can write a letter to the congregation in the next newsletter asking for their forgiveness. It all works the same—in person or in writing, as far as I'm concerned. That's important, sis, and I agree with you that asking for the church's forgiveness is the first step in your and the church's spiritual healing," said Lonnie, Jr.

"No, Lonnie, Jr. I don't want you fighting my battles for me like you did when we were kids," said Imogene with a slight chuckle and a reflexive twist of her wedding band.

"Is that what I'm doing? I guess in a way I am. But I also guess that I just can't help myself. You are my sister, and you know I just love you to death. I will do anything, I mean anything to spare you of the hurt you must be feeling now. Like Daddy always used to tell us, when one member of the family is hurting, we all hurt," said Lonnie, Jr. as he smiled a planted a brotherly kiss on Imogene's jaw.

"But that's like you, Lonnie, Jr., to want to bear everybody's burden. That's why the Lord called you into the ministry, I suppose. I remember once when Mama and Daddy came home from revival meeting one night and the sink was full of dishes, the floor hadn't been swept and mopped, and the trash was just running over the sides of the trash can. Mama and Daddy had told me before they left going to McComb for the revival, that they wanted me to take care of doing the dishes and mopping the floor because that was a woman's job, not a man's. But putting out the trash was a man's job, and it was yours all by yourself.

At any rate, when they walked into that house, I thought Daddy was gonna lose all the religion he had just put inside of himself from that revival meeting. He started yelling and hollering to the top of his lungs about how we had ignored his very clear, unambiguous instructions for us. After ranting and raving for more than ten minutes, he finally calmed down and wanted to know why I had disobeyed him and Mama. As he was saying that, he was also taking off his big black belt. And we knew what he was planning to do with that big thing. And just as he was about to lay into me with a whupping that I know I wasn't gonna ever forget, you came to my rescue," said Imogene with a smile that was congruent with the gleam in her dry, but still heavily mascara-smeared eyes.

"Yep. I remember that. I told Daddy it wasn't your fault that the dishes hadn't been washed and the floor hadn't been swept and mopped. I told him that it was all my fault, and that I deserved the whupping," said Lonnie, Jr. as he removed his glasses and cleaned the lenses with the underside of his necktie.

The telephone rang, and caused both of their bodies to judder at the loud sound of an unexpected and unwelcomed audible intruder. He walked over to his desk, turned off the telephone's ringer, and rejoined Imogene on the sofa, offering an apology for the interruption.

"I will never forget how quickly you came up with that story to cover for me, Lonnie, Jr. You said that you had agreed to do my chores in exchange for me helping you with your English homework. What a whopper you told, and Daddy seemed to believe your little white lie. I did agree to help you with your homework, but it was not in exchange for you doing my chores, though," said Imogene with a smile and a light tap on Lonnie, Jr.'s leg.

"Yep. I think Daddy must have known I was covering for you, because you will recall, he decided not to whup me. I remember he just stared and me for a minute or two, smiled, and without warning, recited the text he used for his sermon that night at the revival," said Lonnie, Jr.

"He said the text of his message that evening came from Saint Peter, I believe," said Imogene.

"I will always remember that scripture, which from that moment to the present, became my most favorite passage in the Bible. It comes from First Peter, verses four through eight: *And above all things have fervent charity among yourselves: for charity shall cover the multitude of sins.* Daddy knew I was being charitable when I decided to cover for you and to take your punishment. You know, Imogene, I will always believe that it was actually in that very moment as Daddy was staring at me for what seemed like an eternity, but was just for a minute or two, when I first heard the Lord calling me. As you know, I kept running from Him for a long time, until I just couldn't run no more. I finally gave up running and told the Lord to just have His way with me," said Lonnie, Jr.

"God has blessed you with some mighty powerful and special gifts, Lonnie, Jr. I know the Lord is proud of the way you have served Him and helped build up His kingdom. The church membership has more than doubled under your leadership. Our ministries are thriving, and we keep responding to the needs of the congregation and the community by adding new ministries all the time that help bring more and more people to the Lord. And it's been your leadership that's done it. It couldn't have been easy for you, Lonnie, Jr. Following in the footsteps of a beloved icon like Daddy is never easy. Despite that, I know Daddy is especially pleased that you stopped running from the Lord and let God just have His way with you," said Imogene as she patted Lonnie, Jr.'s shoulder.

"Sis, you sure you want to stand there in front of the whole congregation and bare your soul and dredge up something that painful," asked Lonnie, Jr., gently clutching Imogene's hand.

"Yep. I have never been more sure of anything in my entire life before. As I said before, the Lord put this on my heart. So, I ain't really got no choice in the matter, now do I? When the Lord tells you to do something, you'd better do it. You know that better than I do, Lonnie, Jr. When He told you to start preaching the Word, you found out that you had better do exactly as He told you. Well, it's the same with me. I have to do what He has told me to do, just as any of His obedient children must do," said Imogene.

"That's gonna be really hard on you, hard on them, and hard on me too, but as long as you are doing what the Lord wants you to do, He's gonna be there with you every step of the way, with every word you utter, and with every tear you shed," said Lonnie, Jr.

"You are absolutely right, Lonnie, Jr. It's gonna be hard, and it's gonna be painful, for me, you, and the congregation. And I know that I will need a big ole box of Kleenex tissues by my side. But spiritually, I know I'm ready, and the Lord keeps telling me that the congregation is ready too," said Imogene.

"I don't know what you're planning to say, Sis. And maybe you don't either at this very moment. But I hope you don't be too hard on yourself. Joe Lee is a grown man. He is not a child. And now we know he had some powerful demons living inside of him that you, me, and nobody else, except for Billy Wayne and the rest of them heathens knew about. He did what he did, and the law is gonna take care of its part, and when the time comes the good Lord is gonna take care of His part. Remember, you can spare yourself a lot of grief and tears, if you would just let me do this for you or you can just take some time and write something in the church newsletter," said Lonnie, Jr.

"I know all of that, Lonnie, Jr. I know that the Lord is gonna take his revenge on Joe Lee, just like He will all unrepentant sinners. And the law's got to do what its gotta do. And what I have to do is what I have to do. I've been accused of being a lot of things over the years. I have been called vindictive, bossy, mean, moody, self-righteous and everything but a child of God. And if I'm honest with myself, most of that is true about me. I can be bossy. I can be vindictive, and I'm so full of self-righteousness and piety that I can't even stand myself sometimes. But one thing I have never been accused of. And that's being a coward," said Imogene.

The day arrived for her to do her mea culpa before the congregation. The first Sunday, Communion Sunday, was the date she selected. The symbolism of that event was evident to her. She was speaking on a special day in which believers receive the elements of wine and bread as symbols of the blood that Jesus shed and the sacrificing of his life. In taking those elements, believers would be reminded of the gift of forgiveness that is made manifest through Jesus' suffering and sacrifices. For Imogene, such a setting could not have been more apt. She was there to seek forgiveness from her church family, while at the same time, she was confident that because of Jesus' living, death, and resurrection, her transgressions were already forgiven.

Near the end of the service, Lonnie called his sister to the pulpit. They warmly embraced each other and smiled. After breaking the embrace, she slowly turned to face the congregation, and walked over to a microphone attached to a lectern. The congregants had no idea what was about to come. Any one of them could have naturally guessed that she was there in her role as Chair of the Board of Trustees or as Lay Leader to present a report on one or both of those important leadership positions. She stood erect as she had so many times at the Debutante Balls. But unlike the Debutante Balls, there would be no spotlight in which to revel or standing ovation to affirm her supreme worthiness as the alpha female of Sharpville's high society. She took a deep breath, slowly exhaled, and looked out over the crowd that numbered more than a thousand. No more delays, she thought. The moment of truth has arrived.

"My brothers and sisters in Christ, I stand before you in both sin and shame. My heart is burdened, and it's broken into a million little pieces. My life is in ruin, and my marriage is in shambles. My reputation, honor, and good name have been ripped to shreds by the willful and hurtful actions of a very disturbed man. Despite those hardships, my faith in our Risen Savior remains strong," said Imogene, pausing for a long moment as her voice cracked, and she cleared her throat.

"That's okay, Sister Lee," shouted one congregant seated in a front pew.

"Just let the Lord have His way, Sister Lee," shouted another congregant from the rear of the sanctuary.

"Thank you. And God bless you. You see. That's what makes this so hard *and* so easy at the same time. It is hard because of the fact that I even have to stand here before you and bare my soul to you like this. Believe me, I don't like having to humiliate myself standing here before you like this. But on the other hand, I believe in the redemptive powers of suffering, confession and atonement. And let me also say from the bottom of my heart, which makes this easy, you are my church family, my brothers and sisters in Christ. Like family, we are always there for one another. And from the bottom of my heart, I want to say how grateful I am that, despite the ugliness of the situation, and the embarrassment, and the shame that I feel, I, nevertheless, feel uplifted by your prayers, your many words of encouragement, and the many acts of support that you have expressed to me. Those acts of Christian love mean more to me than any of you will ever know. I have prayed many a night, asking the Lord to show me what to do next. Not what to do next week or next month. But what to do in the next moment. Because the present moment is all any of us has got anyway. Just getting through one moment at a time is all I can ask of the Lord. And the Lord told me that I, as a believer and a sinner, was to come before this congregation of fellow believers and sinners and tell you what's on my heart. At a time like this I like to go to God's words and let those words just shower over me and just let Him put a big ole bear hug around me and hear His sweet words of forgiveness and love. And if you would indulge me for just a few more moments, I want to share those words with you in the hope that you, too, will find solace and comfort in the Lord's words. In First John, chapter one, verse number nine, it says: *If we confess our sins, he is faithful and just to forgive us our sins and to cleanse us from all unrighteousness,*" read a now steady Imogene.

"In the fifth chapter of Romans, verses three, four and five, it says, *Not only that, but we rejoice in our sufferings, knowing that suffering produces endurance, and endurance produces character, and character produces hope, and hope does not put us to shame, because God's love has been poured into our hearts through the Holy Spirit who has been given to us,*" Imogene announced with a strong elocution.

"And finally, by brothers and sisters, in First Peter, fifth chapter, verse number ten, it says, *And after you have suffered a little while, the God of all grace, who has called you to his eternal glory in Christ, will himself restore, confirm, strengthen, and establish you,*" said Imogene with a noticeable crack in her voice.

"You see, my brothers and sisters, we love to confess about the Lord's goodness when something good happens in our lives. We want to stand on the rooftop and let the world know just how good the Lord has been to us. And I think we are right to do that. When we get a pay raise, when we get a new job, or when something else good happens to us, we will quickly give thanks to the Lord, which, again, is the right and proper thing to do.

But I believe that we have to also confess and acknowledge that same goodness when things get downright messy in our lives. And believe me, my life is downright messy right now. The Lord who looks over us when things are going well in our lives is the same Lord who looks over us when things get a little messy. But I am not here begging for your sympathy because of the mess I find myself in. Instead, I am here begging for your forgiveness, face-to-face, for the mess I'm in. I'm here asking, right here and now in front of you, for your forgiveness for my transgressions that have brought disgrace and shame on our community and our church. So, that is why I rejected a suggestion from a dear family member, who thought it would be easier on me and on the congregation if I simply wrote all of this in the church newsletter. But I know that person was only looking out for my welfare and the welfare of the entire church family because of that dear person's love for me and you. But because you are my church family, and I believe that my sins have already been forgiven by the blood of my dear savior, Jesus Christ, that makes it easy to stand here. No matter how messy my life is, no matter had sullied my name is, no matter how shattered my marriage is, I know that you love me and most important, I know the Lord loves me," said a sobbing Imogene.

"We love you Sister Lee," shouted a member of the Chancel Choir.

"I love y'all, too," replied Imogene

"My heart is broken and shattered into so many pieces by what Joe Lee Roberts did. But I refuse to become bitter or spiteful. The Bible says, vengeance is mine. So, I'm not going to go down that road of vengeance and bitterness. That is a lonely road to travel, and I have traveled it many times, I'm embarrassed to say. I'm here to tell you that it is paved with the black, sticky tar of bitterness, hatred, and retribution. And I know that some of you here today have traveled that road too, and maybe you are still on that dark, desolate road to nowhere, with its many dangerous curves, blind spots, and drop-offs that can only end up leading to a whole lot of harm to yourself and to others. But I want to admit something to each and every one of you here my brothers and sisters in Christ. And I prayed and prayed over this thing for many a night and day, asking the Lord to tell me what he wanted me to do about the devilment that Joe Lee got himself into. And the Lord told me to do just what I'm here doing right now. He told me to come and stand before you on Communion Sunday and confess my sins out in the open so every single one of you can hear directly from me and not have to hear it from somebody else. So, that's what I'm fixing to do, my brothers and sisters in Christ," said a dry-eyed, animated, and energetic Imogene, sounding more like an evangelical preacher at a tent revival than the normally composed and stoic Imogene Parsons Lee.

"Joe Lee Roberts had some very powerful and diabolical demons inside of him. Those demons and Joe Lee had gotten so used to each other to the point that they would not let go of one another. To be honest with you, they would not let go of him because he didn't want to let go of them. You know a demon will stay with you as long as you want him to. He is present every moment, just raring to jump into your relationships, into your family, into your work, into your bank account, and into your soul, if you let him. But Joe Lee, at the end of the day, was a grown man, not some wild teenager who didn't know right from wrong. For what he did, he's gonna have to answer to the man's law and to God's law. Man's law has already dealt with him, and when judgment day comes, the Lord will deal with him according to His will. And now that leaves you and me. How are we going to deal with Joe Lee Roberts, what he did, and the fact that his despicable and downright evil doings have brought shame on our fair city and on our church? I can't tell none of y'all how to answer any of these questions. That's between you and God. And something you gonna have to work out in your own heart. And while you are doing that, I would encourage you to have conversations with your family and to be honest in those conversations about all of this. As you talk and listen to one another, ask yourselves how something like this could have happened in our town? What could I (you) have done to keep that kind of evil out of our community? I'm not suggesting that anyone sitting out there in these pews bears any responsibility for what Joe Lee Roberts and the others did. I just think that we should turn the focus of our thoughts to ourselves and be absolutely honest about this, I think. And I want to tell you something that might surprise and shock some of you. And this is it. After posing those troubling questions to myself and being brutally honest with myself with some answers, I now feel partly responsible for Joe Lee's demons and for what he got himself into," said Imogene as she stepped from behind the pulpit with the hand-held microphone in her hand.

"Now, I know some of you are just sitting there wondering and saying to yourself, what is this woman talking about? Has she lost her ever-loving mind? She wasn't on none of those awful tapes, using such awful language, and blaspheming like someone who never in his life encountered our Lord and savior. How and why is she taking any of the responsibility for her husband's transgressions? Well here is how and why I'm acknowledging my role and fault in my husband's wrongdoings. You see, I have spent so much of my time over the past decades being in charge and running things here in Sharpville and here at the church. Now, y'all know all the things I have been running all these years. I've been running the Christmas parade, the Debutante Ball, the Board of Trustees, and the list goes on and on. And I put in a lot of time, energy, and effort in being successful in running those things, foolishly thinking that those things were the most important things in my life. But in the midst of running all those things, what I seemed to have forgotten is that a wife's first duty is to her home, to her husband and to her family. I firmly believe that if I had been a better wife that paid attention to her proper, God-given role as a wife, Joe Lee would not have done any of those terrible things he was charged and convicted of doing. And here is why I say that and why I own up to my part in bringing shame on my family, my town, and my church. You see, the Bible says that a wife is supposed to be obedient to her husband. Being an obedient wife means that I am supposed to honor my husband, who is the head of the house. Just as Christ is head of the Church, the husband is the head of the household. And it says in First Timothy, second chapter, verses eleven and twelve these words: *Let a woman learn quietly with all submissiveness. I do not permit a woman to teach or to exercise authority over a man; rather, she is to remain quiet.* And in the fifth chapter of Ephesians, Saint Paul says this: *Wives, submit to your own husbands, as to the Lord. For the husband is the head of the wife even as Christ is the head of the church, his body, and is himself its Savior. Now as the church submits to Christ, so also wives should submit in everything to their husbands.* Some people don't like to hear these words, but these words came from the Lord through his saintly disciples. And I say, and the Word also says, that if you gonna be a full-time and not a part-time Christian, you can't go around picking and choosing which parts of the Bible you are going to obey. And this is where I went wrong because somewhere along the way, I became a part-time Christian and elected to obey the parts of the Bible that suited me and my lifestyles and ignored the parts that didn't. Contrary to the teachings of Christ, I started taking on more and more of the leadership role in my family and even ignored my husband's wishes for me to spend more time at home cooking and keeping the house clean, rather than hiring help to do what I should have been doing myself. Although Joe

Lee was supportive of my work in the community, I know deep inside his heart, it cut him deeply to have me out gallivanting around town, running this and running that, instead of running what I should have been running. And what I should have been running was the kind of house and home that would make my husband happy and content enough that he would not have any reason at all to stray into the alluring den of iniquity. You see, when I started stepping outside of my role as the obedient wife and doing things that took me away from that role and responsibility, the Lord wasn't pleased with that at all. He gave me many signs and spoke to me many times about what I was and was *not* doing that went against His wishes and teachings. But I was too busy to heed those signs and messages. I arrogantly and foolishly thought that city of Sharpville and First Presbyterian Church could not function without Imogene Roberts. So what did the Lord do to show me the errors of my ways? What He did was He took my family away from me," said Imogene, choking back tears.

Taking a moment to compose herself and to wipe away a stream of tears flowing from both eyes, she cleared her throat and said, "Whew! This is hard". Regaining her composure, she continued.

"You see, family is a gift from God, and God tells us that if we don't use our gifts to glorify and honor Him, he will take away those gifts and give them to someone else. So, because of my failings as a wife, God has taken away a precious gift that, quite honestly, I had taken for granted and treated every way but precious. He could have taken away that gift of family through divorce, through death, through disease, or through any other way He wanted to. But He chose this awful mess that Joe Lee got himself and me into and the mess that I could have prevented had I been a more obedient and subservient wife. I believe that He chose this as a way to remind me, and quite honestly to remind everyone sitting here today, of His awesomeness and His insistence that we obey his word, or else be ready to pay the consequences. So, in closing, let my suffering and shame be a warning to each of you. Listen to what the Lord is telling you. When the choices in life are serving man or serving the Lord, just know which choice the Lord wants you to make and which choice man wants you to make. The flesh is here but for a moment, but the Lord's grace, mercy, and salvation are eternal. In order to earn my salvation and be worthy of God's grace, I am announcing, effective immediately, I will be stepping down as Lay Leader and as Chair of the Board of Trustees of this church. I need to spend time resurrecting my life and that of my husband. And I am also relinquishing my position and my membership in the Ladies Auxiliary. Please pray with me. *Dear Lord, I come before you as a sinner and believer. I am a sinner because of the flesh and a believer because of the blood you spilled for me on Calvary. I know that I have been disobedient. I have failed to heed your calling and messages you sent to me about what I was doing wrong in my life. And as a result, you have once again, shown me and the other members of your flock, that you are an omnipotent father, who finds it necessary to chastise and punish his children when they have gone astray. And we know that you do that out of love for us and we humble ourselves before you in your awesomeness, asking your forgiveness. We also ask for the powers of discernment so that we can recognize the work of the devil, especially when devil and his evilness come wrapped in nice, little pretty packages, tempting us to open and partake of them. Give us the strength and the wisdom to turn away from such evil and turn, instead, to your goodness. Bless this congregation, its leadership, and the Sharpville community as we struggle to pick up the pieces and put them back together again. And please Lord, bless Joe Lee Roberts. Help him to see the errors of his ways and bring him back to the reassuring light of your goodness. You told us that you are the truth, the way, and the light. And, dear Lord, if we just keep that in our minds and hearts and not allow the flesh to become the truth, the way and the light as we too often do, you will continue to bless and keep us. This we ask in the name of the risen Savior, Jesus Christ, your Son and our redeemer. Amen,"* said Imogene as she placed the hand-held microphone back into its stand, moved toward the open arms of her dear brother, Lonnie, Jr. and sobbed, using nearly half a box of Kleenex. Church was over. And an important part of Imogene's and Joe Lee Roberts' legacy was also over. The congregation sat incredulous and stunned. No movement or chatter was made or uttered for nearly thirty seconds. After a long moment, pew mates turned to face one another, and soon a din of chatter replaced the stunned silence. A rare occurrence had just been witnessed by members of the First Presbyterian Church and would surely be part of the folklore of Sharpville for generations to come. The undisputed Alpha female of Sharpville high society and the *de facto* head of the largest congregation in Henderson County had just join the ranks of the rest of the mere mortals of Sharpville.

The most heart-rending decision Imogene made, however, was to relinquish her role as President of the Ladies Auxiliary and all that went with it, principally, the Debutante Ball. She vowed, however, that she would remain married to her husband and help him through this dark period of his life. This act of con-trition by one of the most powerful women in Sharpville was stunning to most who witnessed or heard about her announce-ment that she was stepping down from her three most treasured positions. Those prize positions gave birth to her essence, gave her life meaning and purpose, and solidified her alpha female status in Sharpville, Mississippi. With the loss of those posi-tions and the power that went with them, Imogene fought val-iantly to find purpose to her life. As she so heart-wrenchingly expressed to her church family, she decided that rehabilitating her husband's tattered life and her own disoriented one would become her raison d'etre.

Imogene decided to remain in Sharpville, despite her diminished social status and blotted reputation. She travels to Atlanta monthly to visit Joe Lee Roberts at the Atlanta Federal Corrections Facility. The two of them will never again have a normal marriage. They will never again enjoy an embrace, share a loving touch, or have a romantic meal at their favorite restaurant. And neither would Mack Charles Parker, Elvin Newhouse and Leondis McPherson.

Nevertheless, she has concluded that some marriages exist on paper and some exist in the heart. There are couples who live under the same roof and are as distant as the sun is from the earth. As far as she was concerned, her marriage was still an unbreakable bond and a holy, blessed union of two hearts. She decided to take a tip from Tammy Wynette to stand by her man. If the shoe were on the other foot, no doubt Joe Lee would stand by his woman. Besides, her monthly trips to Atlanta—for her—are a form of self-flagellation and penitence for the shame and embarrassment that she feels for her role in not being there for Joe Lee. If she were allowed to visit Joe Lee every day, she would. The more she is with him, the more she feels that she vicariously takes on the burden of incarceration and punishment. Although she gave up her leadership role in her father's church, she still occasionally attends church services.

*

Sara Mae Carter had a much different response to the news of her husband's arrest and conviction. She did not attend any of the trials, and she never visited Dickey Carter in jail. She refused to answer reporters' questions about her husband—and to help ensure her privacy and seclusion, she discontinued her mail, newspaper, cable, and telephone service. She holed up in her home for weeks, daring not venture out for fear that someone would ask her about DC or the "mess" that he had created for her. In her view of things, DC's wrong-doings were a direct reflection on her as a wife and as a member of Sharpville's gentry class. Those two statuses—being Mrs. Dickey Carter and being an original and revered member of Sharpville's nobility—were what gave meaning and substance to her life. Now that neither was any longer part of her well-crafted and well-manicured public persona and raison d'etre, she was at an existential loss.

Sara Mae's lament was not that DC had committed such egregious crimes against the people of the United States of America, Sharpville, Henderson County and the state of Mississippi. Instead, her regret was that he let himself get caught, and that in the process of getting caught and convicted, he had created embarrassment and hardship for *her*. The extent to which those crimes affected DC or his victims was irrelevant and inconsequential to her. Self-absorption over her own misery combined with a suffocating sense of betrayal and aloneness contributed to extended pity-parties for Sara Mae. She severed ties with all her friends and fellow members of Sharpville's nobility, except for Imogene Parsons Lee. The two became kindred spirits, spawned by a common calamity foisted upon them by low-down dirty snakes in the grass, masquerading as husbands, as they came to describe their wayward spouses. They regularly turned to one another for consolation, generally during the nightly walks at midnight they shared in order to avoid the prying eyes of neighbors and news reporters. She shared with Imogene, during one of their walks, that she regrets turning down the modeling contract from the Ford Modeling Agency when she was in high school. At least, she confessed, she could have retired from the modeling business and settled into Sharpville with her dignity, if not her looks, intact. Instead, Sharpville was like being interred in her final earthly resting place. She would not allow Sharpville to become her real or symbolic place of entombment.

So, without money, a home, work skills, or prospects for maintaining the lifestyle to which had grown accustomed, Sara Mae filed for divorce from Dickey Carter and moved to Memphis to live with an ailing aunt. Her aunt's only income is her social security check of one thousand five hundred fifty dollars a month. To supplement that income, Sara Mae took a job at Wal-Mart as a greeter.

*

Other spouses of the Billy Wayne clan also left Sharpville. Billy Wayne's wife, Margaret, moved to Anniston, Alabama and remained married to Billy Wayne. She was forever devoted to Billy Wayne and took to heart her wedding vow to remain married to him, for better or for worse. Now that things had become worse, she was as devoted to her husband as she was when things were better. She chose to move to Anniston because of its relatively close proximity to the Talladega Federal Corrections Institution where Billy Wayne was in residence. She treasured her privacy and unfussy, low-key way of life. Maintaining such a low-key life style was very easy for Margaret, whether she would have chosen to remain in Sharpville or taken up residence in some other city. Her parents were deceased. She had no children, siblings, or other relatives. So, there was no compelling reason for her to remain in Sharpville. She cashed in her IRA, tapped into an inheritance from her father, and sold some antiques to help reestablish her new life and home.

As a hobby, she has taken up gardening at her Anniston duplex, located just off Interstate 20. She volunteers at the public library, shelving books and working in the juvenile section. She also volunteers at the local senior citizens home, where she reads to residents and helps them draft letters to send to loved ones. On occasions, she tutors her neighbor's fifth grade child and has helped him to learn to write cursively. She does not regularly attend church but is still faithful.

Doreen Sessum moved to Natchez, Mississippi, where she opened a bed and breakfast that caters to tourists during the annual Natchez Pilgrimage Tours. While married to Cletus, she managed to create a rather hefty cache of "clean" money that she surreptitiously deposited, over a ten-year period, in her own name in a bank in Florida. With her largesse, she invested in a growing industry that will keep her financially sound for the remainder of her life. She decided that she would divorce her third husband and declare herself terminally single and perpetually unavailable for romance. She took her maiden name of Mulberry and cleansed her mind and heart of anything remotely remindful of Sharpville, Mississippi or Cletus Sessum.

The otherwise good citizens of Sharpville were left with picking up the pieces of a broken community that grudgingly and gradually confronted its decades-old and outdated racial attitudes and behaviors. They also had to confront the value system that led them to turn a blind eye and deaf ear to what was going on right under their noses. They had become complacent and comfortable with the privileges of being white. They enjoyed the many privileges they had accrued but had not earned, as simply being white was the only criterion for accruing those privileges. It had never occurred to them that their community had become a pigmentocracy, not a democracy, or a meritocracy. Pigmentocracy—one's skin color being the sole determinant of social status and privileges—dominated life in Sharpville. The practice of pigmentocracy more than delineated the haves and have-nots. It more than separated the powerful from the weak. It went much further. Pigmentocracy affirmed the centrality and supremacy of being white. And it conveyed the very powerful message that characterized and dictated life in the South for generations: *If you are white, you are alright. If you are brown, stick around. If you are black, get back.*

Eventually, however, the resilience, love, and humbleness of the entire community forced it to face the daunting task of restoring its image and figuring out how to make sure that Sharpville has indeed purged itself of its pigmentocracy. Moreover, they had to figure out how to make sure that no attempt to spread evil and racial discontent would ever go unchallenged by the good citizens, black and white, of Sharpville, Mississippi. Thanks to the courageous actions of Charles Bickford, white citizens of Sharpville were forced to come face-to-face with the embodiment of evil in their beloved community. Many were forced to look into the mirror and ponder their own roles in creating and enabling the Billy Wayne Sharps, Jethro Millikens, Dicky Carters, Joe Lee Roberts, Cletus Sessums, Brock Galloways, and Clifford Morgans of Sharpville. In doing so, many ordinary citizens and leaders of the business, faith, and educational communities had to take a long-hard look at their own culpability in, at least, contributing to the atmosphere that that allowed Billy Wayne and his buddies to get away with their misdeeds for so long.

For starters, unexpectedly, voters elected a black mayor whose enthusiasm, energy, and positive nature have sparked a renewed sense of hope and optimism in the city. His election came as a surprise to many who believed that Sharpville was not ready to break its uninterrupted string of electing only white mayors. In fact, the white candidate, who was an adherent to the philosophy that black citizens, while deserving of the right to vote and to rights on par with white citizens, believed that then was not the time to elect a black mayor. Maybe at some point in the distant future, he claimed, a black person might come to possess the requisite qualities and attributes to serve as mayor, but now was not the right time. In speeches before white-only crowds he expressed the view that the black candidate in particular, and black people in general, did not, as yet, possess the level of education, intelligence, and temperament to serve in a position of leadership in the city of Sharpville or any other Mississippi town.

The white candidate nearly won by appealing to voters of like sentiment, who also believed that the black candidate lacked the necessary intellectual, educational, and temperamental qualities to serve as mayor. He also nearly won by employing a strategy recommended to him by consultants from his state political party. The strategy became known in the black community as the catfish-fried-chicken-watermelon-pick-five strategy. In an effort to siphon off potential black votes from the black candidate, the white candidate's consultants and campaign advisors arranged for cookouts and gatherings in black sections of Sharpville that included all you can eat fried catfish, fried chicken, and watermelon. Staying with the belief that one of the sure ways to a black person's vote and support is through food, they employed another strategy that involved giving some black voters something called Pick five coupons. Pick five coupons could be redeemed for a mix or match olio of up to five food items for only nineteen dollars and ninety-nine cents at participating grocery stores. In exchange for the food, groceries, and the money, cooperating black voters were required to sign a pledge that they would vote for the white candidate, urge their neighbors, friends, and family to do likewise, and display a campaign sign in their yards. It worked in the late 1960s, why would it not work in the late 1990s, thought the candidate's brain trust. Sticking with the nostalgia of the past, the campaign utilized the crudest form of co-option. They paid certain black individuals in the community to take very public and vitriolic stances against the black candidate. A week before the election, with television cameras rolling and reporters' pens in hand, a black minister proudly announced at a press conference his support for the white candidate. In response to a reporter's question regarding his decision to publicly endorse the candidate, the minister empathically and unapologetically stated that his primary reason for supporting the white candidate was the fact that the candidate brought his family to his local church for Sunday worship service. The minister said that was all the proof anyone needed that the white candidate genuinely cared for the black community and that by taking the time to worship at the black church he and his family had earned his unqualified support. The truth of the matter was that the minister was only tangentially local. Years ago, he pastored a church in Sharpville, but was asked to leave by the congregation. He relocated to Racine, Wisconsin and had actually been flown to Mississippi from Wisconsin by the white candidate's campaign. He was paid a fee to be a party to a shameless charade that was designed to give the impression to the community-at-large that there was legitimate black grassroots support for the candidate. The strategy failed, but it came close to succeeding as significant numbers of black voters were willing to trade their votes for money and food. There remained a significant number of white voters who believed that a black man was not ready, at least for the present, to lead the city of Sharpville. Nevertheless, whether motivated by guilt, shame, anger, remorse, or resolve, the majority of voters expressed a desire to deviate from the patterns of the past and to seek atonement and redemption for the evil that they had allowed to infect their community.

By helping elect a black man to lead the city out its embarrassing morass, white citizens of Sharpville were beginning to accept their role as enablers of those seven faux community stalwarts, thereby beginning the process of seeking atonement, forgiveness, and healing from black Sharpville. In the words of the new mayor, "The overall goal of my administration is that, going forward, there will be no black Sharpville or white Sharpville, only Sharpville, home of loving and forgiving people." Nevertheless, the sting of the negative publicity created by

Billy Wayne and his buddies remains raw. Undoubtedly, only the healing salve of time will expunge the hurt and embarrassment caused by the saga of Billy Wayne.

The hope for the future in Sharpville also lies in the collective awareness that the convictions and guilty pleas marked the end of an unpleasant era in Sharpville's glorious history and made the misdeeds of the Director of Public Utilities seem like petty shoplifting.

Hope also lies in an unexpected but welcome spiritual revival whereby, black churches and white churches regularly hold joint worship services, for the first time in the history of Sharpville. Black and white pastors are conducting services at other race churches, although church memberships continue to be separated by race. Church leaders of both races have planned community improvement projects in which both groups will participate as equal partners.

The membership of the Ladies Auxiliary has taken three bold and unprecedented actions, which have drastically altered the group's mission, programs, and purpose. One, they have actively recruited black women to join. Dorothea Bickford accepted the first invitation sent to a black woman to join, and she has recruited two other black women to become members. Currently, nearly half of the membership is black. Two, the Ladies Auxiliary has begun to include black communities and neighborhoods in its monthly awards for outstanding and most beautiful neighborhoods and houses. Three, they have openly reached out to black families to invite black teenage girls to participate in the annual Sharpville Debutante Ball. The Annual Debutante Ball has been drastically transformed into a community gathering that is welcoming to all of its citizens. The Ladies Auxiliary has adopted a motto that appears in all of their correspondence: *All girls and their families, regardless of race, are invited to experience the joy and excitement of publically debuting their beauty, confidence, poise, and grace.*

While much work remains to fully resuscitate and renew Sharpville's spirit and image, there is a discernible and qualitatively different attitude permeating Sharpville and Henderson County. People of different races greet one another at grocery stores, department stores, and on sidewalks with warm smiles and friendly hellos. The prevailing sentiment is that Sharpville has been given a second chance at expiation and redemption, and all of its citizens consider it a blessing to be granted that chance. As a result, the racial divide that dominated the community for decades is slowly starting to narrow.

For sure, there remain many among Sharpville's denizens who will never accept the changes that have taken place since the arrests and convictions of Billy Wayne and his buddies. In their own stubborn ways, they reject the notion of racial equality. They are members of the clergy, law enforcement officers, elected and appointed government officials, educators, members of the media, and low information voters who hang on to every word of radio talk show hosts who feed their insecurities, bigotry, and ignorance. They will forever believe that being white has unique privileges that should be exploited for their own selfish purposes, and that white exceptionalism grants them certain privileges and rights that do not apply to people of other races. They have failed to accept the reality that the disgraced legacy that they believed made them exceptional, ultimately, produced only bitter fruits that corrupted all who partook of them. Many of the Jim Crow, die-hard holdovers still have faith in the nonsensical notion that God endorses white supremacy and that white people are His *only* true people. They reject reconciliation and atonement as signs of weakness among the white majority in Sharpville and as a conspiracy among non-whites to diminish Euro-centric values and alter the traditional Southern way of life. They remain unalterably married to the idea that there is a perpetual war of will, philosophy, ideas, tactics, and strategies between their twisted, delusional world of white supremacy and the real world in which the majority are a diverse and rational thinking people, who desire to live in peace and harmony with their neighbors. They believe that, eventually, they will win because in their world, losing is not an option. In their way of thinking, life is a zero sum game. If they win, the other side loses, and if the other side wins, they lose. In reality, however, just the opposite is true. Authentic reconciliation and atonement are signs of strength, not of weakness. They reflect an unmistakable desire to heal rather than hurt—to become whole rather than remain fragmented parts.

Furthermore, there is a nascent belief among the majority of citizens of Sharpville, Mississippi that Saint Timothy (6:10) was right when he proclaimed: *The love of money is the root of all evil*; that Job (34:22) was right when he declared: *There is no gloom or deep darkness where evildoers may hide themselves*; that St. Matthew (3:10) warned that, *even now the axe is laid to the root of the trees. Every tree therefore that does not bear good fruit is cut down and thrown into the fire*; that Mahatma Gandhi was right when he asserted: *When I despair, I remember that all through history the way of truth and love have always won. There have been tyrants and murderers, and for a time, they can seem invincible, but in the end, they always fall. Think of it—always*; that Albert Einstein was right when he avowed: *The world is a dangerous place to live; not because of the people who are evil, but because of the people who don't do anything about it*; and that Dr. Martin Luther King, Jr. was right when he imparted: *I believe that unarmed truth and unconditional love will have the final word in reality. This is why right, temporarily defeated, is stronger than evil triumphant.*

ABOUT THE AUTHOR

Anthony J. Harris was born in Hattiesburg, Mississippi. He was an active participant in the local Civil Rights Movement and and has been a champion for ethical leadership for the greater part of his life. Though Dr. Harris has published other books and scholarly articles, Fruits of a Disgraced Legacy is his debut novel. In his previous two books, *Gifts of Moments: Being Somebody to Somebody* and *Ain't Gonna Let Nobody Turn Me 'Round*, he reflects upon life lessons learned through love, injustice, leadership, and power. He has been featured on PBS and conducts keynote addresses on topics pertaining to the Civil Rights Movement, the educational success of young black males, and leadership. Since 2008, Dr. Harris has served as Professor of Education at Mercer University in Atlanta, Georgia. He and his wife, Smithenia, have two adult children, Ashley and Michael.

CONNECT ONLINE

www.facebook.com/FruitsofaDisgracedLegacy
To arrange a speaking engagement with Anthony J. Harris, please contact the Tandem Light Press Speakers Bureau at speakersbureau@tandemlightpress.com.

www.ingramcontent.com/pod-product-compliance
Lightning Source LLC
Chambersburg PA
CBHW021458110726
47899CB00001BA/207